Praise for *The Midnight Bargain*

"A sparkling, incisive, and razor-sharp fantasy of manners. A must-read."
—Tasha Suri

"Seamlessly blends Regency class issues, subversive intrigue, and fantasy together in a heart-racing seaside romance where everything hangs in the balance. Polk's magical elements are so integral to the romantic plot that the two are inextricable, much as all of the characters, from the leads to the seamstresses, now have a firm place in my heart. I loved every intricate inch of *The Midnight Bargain* and am hoping for many more tales set in this world."
—Fran Wilde

"I was utterly charmed. . . . The perfect blend of fantasy and romance."
—Kat Howard

"An absolute dream—at once sparkling and romantic, delightfully magical, and deeply thought-provoking. This book is a fantastical homage not only to the balls and matchmaking and strong-minded heroines of Regency romances, but the questions of gender, class, family obligation and personal ambition that lie at their beating heart."
—H. G. Parry

"A lush, intensely romantic and intensely political book about love, friendship, freedom and magic."
—Aliette de Bodard

"A delicious mix of forbidden magic and social ritual, with dangerous secrets, impossible choices, coded grimoires, and stolen kisses dressed up in a sensory feast of fancy carriages and corset stays. *Pride and Prejudice* meets *Jonathan Strange & Mr. Norrell*, with two brilliant clandestine sorceresses up against the patriarchy!"

—Melissa Caruso

"[Polk] delivers sharp social commentary in this excellent Regency-flavored fantasy. . . . Expertly balances propulsive pacing, a rich multicultural world, and a vivid and subversive cast of characters."

—*Publishers Weekly* (starred review)

"The author's penetrating social critique and deeply felt depiction of one woman's struggle for self-determination are balanced by her charming take on classic Regency romance. . . . An expertly concocted mélange of sweet romance and sharp social commentary."

—*Kirkus* (starred review)

"A subversive tale of magic and manners. I stayed up all night to finish this one."

—Ellen Klages

"Polk's foray into a society of magic and politics places the woman in the secondary role, but neither Beatrice nor Ysbeta will stay in place. Fans of romantic fantasy set in a multicultural world will find this a fascinating read."

—*Library Journal* (starred review)

The MIDNIGHT BARGAIN

Books by C. L. Polk

The Midnight Bargain

The Kingston Cycle

Witchmark

Stormsong

Soulstar

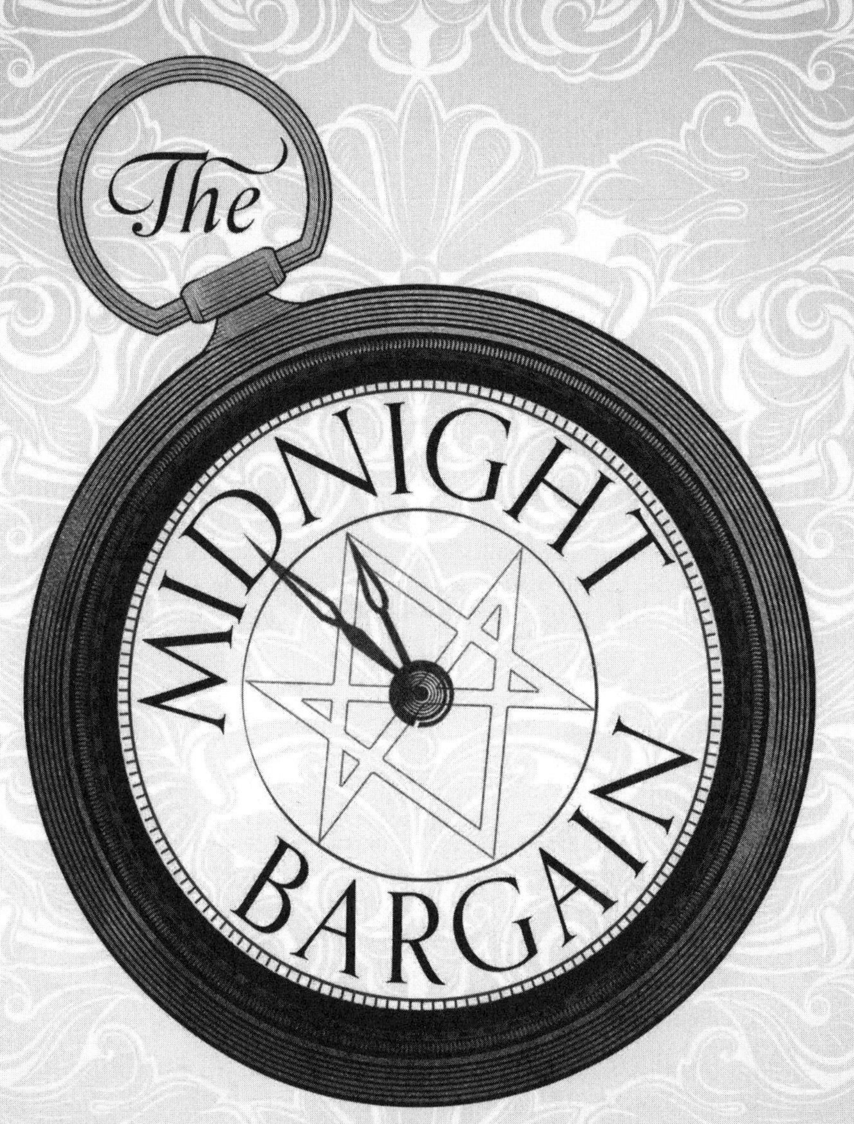

C. L. POLK

EREWHON

This is a work of fiction. All of the characters, organizations, and events portrayed in this novel are either products of the author's imagination or are used fictitiously.

THE MIDNIGHT BARGAIN

Edited by Sarah T. Guan

Erewhon Books
2 W. 29th Street, Suite 3S
New York, NY 10001
www.erewhonbooks.com

Erewhon books are available at special discounts when purchased in bulk for premiums and sales promotions as well as for fund-raising or educational use. Special editions or book excerpts can also be created to specification. For details, send an email to specialmarkets@workman.com.

The Library of Congress Cataloging-in-Publication Data is available upon request.

ISBN 978-1-64566-029-3 (paperback)
ISBN 978-1-64566-014-9 (ebook)

Cover design and interior elements by Micaela Alciano
Cover images by Shutterstock
Author photograph by Mike Tan

Printed in Canada

First US Paperback Edition: November 2021
10 9 8 7 6 5 4 3 2 1

To Alexis, Kim, and Sarah
you know what you did

CHAPTER I

The carriage drew closer to Booksellers' Row, and Beatrice Clayborn drew in a hopeful breath before she cast her spell. Head high, spine straight, she hid her hands in her pockets and curled her fingers into mystic signs as the fiacre jostled over green cobblestones. She had been in Bendleton three days, and while its elegant buildings and clean streets were the prettiest trap anyone could step into, Beatrice would have given anything to be somewhere else—anywhere but here, at the beginning of bargaining season.

She breathed out the seeking tendrils of her spell, touching each of the shop fronts. If a miracle rushed over her skin and prickled at her ears—

But there was nothing. Not a glimmer; not even an itch. They passed The Rook's Tower Books, P. T. Williams and Sons, and the celebrated House of Verdeu, which filled a full third of a block with all its volumes.

Beatrice let out a sigh. No miracle. No freedom. No hope. But when they rounded the corner from Booksellers' Row to a narrow gray lane with no name, Beatrice's spell bloomed in response. There. A grimoire! There was no way to know what it contained, but she smiled up at the sky as she pulled on the bell next to her seat.

"Driver, stop." She slid forward on the fiacre's padded seat, ready to jump into the street by herself. "Clara, can you complete the fitting for me?"

"Miss Beatrice, you mustn't." Clara clutched at Beatrice's

wrist. "It should be you."

"You're exactly my size. It won't matter," Beatrice said. "Besides, you're better at the color and trimmings and such. I'll just be a few minutes, I promise."

Her maid-companion shook her head. "You mustn't miss your appointment at the chapterhouse. I cannot stand in for you when you meet Danton Maisonette the way I can at the dressmakers."

Beatrice was not going to let that book slip out of her grasp. She patted Clara's hand and wriggled loose. "I'll be there in time, Clara. I promise I won't miss it. I just need to buy a book."

Clara tilted her head. "Why this place?"

"I wrote to them," Beatrice lied. "Finding it is a stroke of luck. I won't be ten minutes."

Clara sighed and loosed her grip on Beatrice's wrist. "Very well."

The driver moved to assist, but Beatrice vaulted to the street, tight-laced stays and all, and waved them off. "Thank you. Go!"

She pivoted on one delicate pillar-heeled shoe and regarded the storefront. Harriman's was precisely the kind of bookstore Beatrice sought every time she was in a new town: the ones run by people who couldn't bear to throw books away no matter what was inside the covers, so long as they could be stacked and shelved and housed. Beatrice peered through the windows, reveling at the pang within her senses that set her ears alert and tingling, her spell signaling that a grimoire awaited amid the clutter. She hadn't found a new one in months.

The doorbell jingled as Beatrice crossed into the bookkeeper's domain. Harriman's! O dust and ink and leather binding, O map-scrolls and star-prints and poetry chapbooks —and the grimoire, somewhere within! She directed hersmile at the clerk in shirtsleeves and weskit waiting at the front counter.

"Just having a browse," she said, and moved past without inviting further conversation. Beatrice followed her prickling thumbs between stacks of books and laden shelves. She breathed in old paper and the thin rain-on-green-stones scent of magic, looking not for respectable novels or seemly poetry, but for the authors certain young women never even dared whisper to each other in the powder rooms and parlors of society—the writers of the secret grimoires.

It was here! But it wouldn't do to be too hasty, to follow the pull of her senses toward the stack where the volume rested, its spine bearing an author name like John Estlin Churchman, or J. C. Everworth, or perhaps E. James Curtfield. The authors always bore those initials on all of the books in her modest collection, stored away from curious eyes. The clerk might wonder at how she knew exactly where to find the book she wanted in all this jumble. She browsed through literature, in history, and even in the occult sections where other patrons would eye her with disapproval, because the realm of magic was not suitable territory for a woman of a certain youth.

Just thinking of her exclusion made Beatrice's scalp heat. For women, magic was the solitary pursuit of widows and crones, not for the woman whose most noble usefulness was still intact. The inner doors of the chapterhouse were barred to her, while a man with the right connections could elevate himself through admittance and education among his fellow magicians. Anyone with the talent could see the aura of sorcery shining from Beatrice's head, all the better to produce more magicians for the next generation.

Oh, how she hated it! To be reduced to such a common capability, her magic untrained until some year in her twilight, finally allowed to pursue the only path she cared for? She would not! And so, she sought out the works of J. E. C., who was not a man at all, but a sorceress just like her, who had published a multitude of volumes critics dismissed as incomprehensible.

And they were, to anyone who didn't know the key. But Beatrice had it by heart. When she lifted a dusty edition of *Remembrance of the Jyish Coast of Llanandras* from the shelf, she opened the cover and whispered the spell that filtered away anything that wasn't the truth hidden amid the typesetting, and read:

> *To Summon a Greater Spirit and Propose the Pact of the Great Bargain*

She snapped the book shut and fought the joyful squeak that threatened to escape her. She stood very still and let her heart soar in silence with the book pressed to her chest, breathing in its ink and magic.

This was the grimoire she had needed, after years of searching and secret study. If she summoned the spirit and made an alliance, she would have done what every male initiate from the chapterhouses of sorcery aspired to do. She would be a fully initiated magician.

This was everything she needed. No man would have a woman with such an alliance. Her father would see the benefit of keeping her secret, to use her greater spirit to aid him in his business speculations. She would be free. A Mage. This was her miracle.

She'd never leave her family home, but that didn't matter. She could be the son Father never had, while her younger sister Harriet could have the bargaining season Beatrice didn't want. Harriet would have the husband she daydreamed about, while Beatrice would continue her studies uninterrupted by marriage.

She stepped back and pivoted away from the shelf, and nearly collided with another customer of Harriman's. They jumped back from each other, exclaiming in surprise, then stared at each other in consternation.

Beatrice beheld a Llanandari woman who stood tall and slim in a saffron satin-woven cotton mantua, the under-gown scattered all over with vibrant tropical flowers, the elbow-length sleeves erupting in delicate, hand-hooked lace. Hooked lace, on a day gown! She was beautiful, surpassing even the famous reputation of the women of Llanandras. She was blessed with wide brown eyes and deep brown skin, a cloud of tight black curls studded with golden beads, matching a fortune in gold piercing the young woman's ears and even the side of her nose. But what was she doing here? She couldn't be in this affluent seaside retreat away from the capital to hunt a husband just as Beatrice was supposed to be doing. Could she?

She stared at Beatrice with an ever-growing perplexity. Beatrice knew what the young lady found so arresting—the crown of sorcery around Beatrice's head, even brighter than the veil of shimmering light around the woman's. Another sorceress attracted to the call of the grimoire Beatrice clutched to her chest.

"Ysbeta? What has your back like a rod?"

He spoke Llanandari, of course, and Beatrice's tongue stuck to the roof of her mouth. She knew the language, but she had never spoken it to an actual Llanandari. Her accent would be atrocious; her grammar, clumsy. But she plastered a smile on her face and turned to face the newcomer.

Beatrice beheld the same features as the lady, but in a man's face, and—oh, his eyes were so dark, his hair a tightly curled crown below the radiant aura of a sorcerer, his flawless skin darker than the girl's—Ysbeta, her name was Ysbeta. He was clad in the same gleaming saffron Llanandari cotton, the needlework on his weskit a tribute to spring, a froth of matching lace at his throat. Now both these wealthy, glamorous Llanandari stared at her with the same puzzlement, until the young man's brow cleared and he slapped the woman on the back with a laugh like a chuckling stream.

"Relax, Ysy," he said. "She's in the ingenue's gallery at the chapterhouse. Miss . . ."

"Beatrice Clayborn. I am pleased to make your acquaintance," Beatrice said, and hardly stumbled at all. This young man, achingly beautiful as he was, had seen her portrait hanging in the ingenue's gallery at the Bendleton chapterhouse. Had studied it long enough to recognize her. He had looked at it long enough to know the angle of her nose, the shape and color of her eyes, the peculiar, perpetually autumn-red tint of her frowzy, unruly hair.

Ysbeta eyed the book in Beatrice's grip, her stare as intense as a shout. "I'm Ysbeta Lavan. This is my brother, Ianthe. I see you admire the travelogues of J. E. Churchman." She spoke carefully, a little slowly for the sake of Beatrice's home-taught Llanandari.

"His telling of faraway places enchants me," Beatrice said. "I am sorry for my Llanandari."

"You're doing fine. I'm homesick for Llanandras," Ysbeta said. "That's a rare account of Churchman's, talking about the magical coast where Ianthe and I spent a happy childhood. It would do my understanding of your language some good to read books in your tongue."

"You speak Chasand."

She tilted her head. "A little. You are better at my language than I am at yours."

Flattery, from a woman who knew exactly what Churchman's book was. Beatrice's middle trembled. Ysbeta and her brother walked in the highest circles in the world, accustomed to wealth and power. And Ysbeta's simple statement betraying a feeling of loneliness or nostalgia confessed to an assumed peer were the opening steps of a courteous dance. The next step, the proper, graceful step would be for Beatrice to offer the book to soothe that longing.

Ysbeta expected Beatrice to hand over her salvation. The book carried her chance at freedom from the bargaining of fathers to bind her into matrimony and warding. To hand it over was giving her chance away. To keep it—

To keep it would be to cross one of the most powerful families in the trading world. If Beatrice's father did not have the acquaintance of the Lavans, he surely wanted it. If she made an enemy of a powerful daughter of Llanandras, it would reflect on every association and partnership the Clayborn fortunes relied on. Weigh on them. Sever them. And without the good opinion of the families that mattered, the Clayborn name would tumble to the earth.

Beatrice couldn't do that to her family. But the book! Her fingers squeezed down on the cover. She breathed its scent of good paper and old glue and the mossy stone note of magic hidden inside it. How could she just give it away?

"It hurts me to hear of your longing for your home. I have never seen the coast of Jy, but I have heard that it is a wonderful place. You are lucky to live in such a place as your childhood's world. I wish I knew more about it."

Her own desires presented as simple sentiment. A counterstep in the dance—proper, polite, passively resisting. She had found the book first. Let Ysbeta try to charm her way past that! Frustration shone in her rival's night-dark eyes, but whatever she would say in reply was cut off by the intrusion of a shop clerk.

He bowed to Ysbeta and Ianthe, touching his forehead as he cast his gaze down. "Welcome to Harriman's. May I be of assistance?"

His Llanandari was very good, probably supported by reading untranslated novels. He smiled at the important couple gracing his shop, then flicked a glance at Beatrice, his lips thin and his nostrils flared.

"Yes," Ysbeta said. "I would like—"

"Thank you for your offer," Ianthe cut in, smiling at the clerk. "Everyone here is so helpful. We are browsing, for the moment."

The clerk clasped his hands in front of him. "Harriman's is committed to quality service, sir. We do not wish you to be troubled by this—person, if she is causing you any discomfort."

"Thank you for your offer," Ianthe said, a little more firmly. "We are quite well, and the lady is not disturbing us."

Ysbeta scowled at Ianthe, but she kept her silence. The clerk gave Beatrice one more forbidding look before moving away.

"I'm sorry about that," Ianthe said, and his smile should not make her heart stutter. "It's clear you both want this book. I propose a solution."

"There is only one copy." Ysbeta raised her delicately pointed chin. "What solution could there be?"

"You could read it together," Ianthe said, clapping his hands together. "Ysbeta can tell you all about the tea-gardens on the mountains and the pearl bay."

Beatrice fought the relieved drop of her shoulders. People would notice Beatrice's friendship with such a powerful family. And to make friends with another sorceress, another woman like her? Beatrice smiled, grateful for Ianthe's suggestion. "I would love to hear about that. Is it true that Jy is home to some of the most beautiful animals in the world?"

"It is true. Have you been away from Chasland, Miss Clayborn?" Ysbeta asked. "Or do you simply dream of travel?"

"I dream to—I dream of travel, but I haven't left my country," Beatrice said. "There are so many wonders—who would not long to float through the water city of Orbos for themselves, to stroll the ivory city of Masillia, or contemplate the garden city of An?"

"An is beautiful," Ianthe said. "Sanchi is a long way from here. You must call on my sister. She was born in the middle of the sea. The horizon has captured her soul. You should be friends. Nothing else will do."

On a ship, he meant, and that last bit made her blink before she realized it was poetic. Beatrice gazed at Ysbeta, who didn't look like she wanted to be Beatrice's friend. "I would like that."

Ysbeta's lips thinned, but her nod set her curls bouncing. "I would too."

"Tomorrow!" Ianthe exclaimed. "Midday repast, and then an afternoon—it's the ideal time for correspondence. Bring your copy book, Miss Clayborn, and we shall have the pleasure of your company."

Access to the book. Friendship with the Lavans. All she had to do was extend her hands to let Ysbeta take the volume from her grasp and watch her grimoire walk away, tucked into the crook of a stranger's elbow, taken from this unordered heap of insignificant novels, saccharine verse, and outdated texts.

She glanced from Ysbeta's dark gaze to Ianthe's merry-eyed humor—he meant for his compromise to be fulfilled. Beatrice sorted through a mental selection of her day gowns. Would they suffice for such company?

This was no time to worry about gowns. She had to tread this situation carefully. She offered the volume to Ysbeta. Once in her hands, Ysbeta offered her only smile, betraying slightly crooked lower front teeth.

"Thank you," she said. "Excuse me for a moment."

They left her standing in the stacks. Ianthe left for the carriage as Ysbeta signed a chit guaranteeing payment on billing, then marched straight for the exit. The bell rang behind her.

Ysbeta had no intention of giving Beatrice an invitation card.

Beatrice had been robbed.

Off in the distance a turquoise enameled landau turned a corner, and as it vanished from sight, the rippling sense of the grimoire faded.

Lost. Stolen! Oh, she would never trust the word of a gentleman again! She had found her chance to be free—drat politeness! She should have refused. She should have said no!

A pair of women stepped around her with clucking tongues. Beatrice hastily moved to the edge of the promenade. She couldn't have said no. That would have gone badly for her family. She was already planning to tarnish the respectable name of the Clayborns with her plans to remain unmarried. That was trouble enough. She couldn't bring more—there was Harriet to think of, after all.

Beatrice's younger sister drew pictures of herself in the green gowns of wedding ceremonies. She read all the novels of women navigating the bargaining season, set in a world that was positively overrun by ministers and earls who fell in love with merchants' daughters—Harriet wanted her fate. Beatrice couldn't destroy her sister's chances.

But the book! How would she find another?

She waited at a street corner for the signal-boy to stop carriage traffic and joined the throng of pedestrians crossing to Silk Row. Large shopwindows featured gowns mounted on dress dummies, wigs on painted wooden heads. Heeled slippers suspended on wires mimicked dancing. She walked past displays and stopped at Tarden and Wallace Modiste.

Tarden and Wallace was the most fashionable modiste in Bendleton, led by its Llanandari proprietress. Its design magazines were printed, bound, and sold to young women who sighed over illustrations of gowns that maximized the beauty of the wearer, with nipped-in waists, low, curving necklines, and luxurious imported fabrics. This shop was the most expensive, and Father had paid for her wardrobe without a murmur.

Beatrice caught herself chewing on her lip. Father would have chosen another modiste if he couldn't pay for this one. He would have.

She pushed open the door and stepped inside.

Everyone turned their attention to her entrance, took in her windblown hair, her dusty hems, and her gloveless hands. Two women, sisters by their identical floral-printed cotton gowns, glanced at each other and covered their mouths, giggling.

Beatrice's face went hot. She hadn't stayed in the carriage, and now she showed the signs of walking along the common promenades. The weight of *A Lady's Book of Manners and Style* balanced invisibly on her head, correcting her posture. She fought the urge to bat dust off her plain tea-dyed skirts.

Clara emerged from a dressing room and smiled. "You'll love everything, Miss Beatrice. Tonight's gown is ready, and I have ordered four more—"

An assistant followed Clara out of the dressing room, carrying a half-finished green gown in her arms, and Beatrice swallowed. That was meant to be her wedding dress. She was supposed to wear it to a temple and be bound in marriage to a moneyed young sorcerer, losing her magic for decades. She averted her gaze and caught Miss Tarden herself staring at the same garment with a sour pinch to her full mouth.

"Miss Beatrice? Did you want to try on your gown?" Miss Tarden asked, her accent rich with cultured Llanandari.

Beatrice stared at the wedding gown with her heart in her throat. "I have another engagement, I'm afraid."

Clara gestured toward the fitting room. "We'll be cutting it close, but we can take a few minutes to—"

"No, that's all right," Beatrice said. "Tell me all about the new gowns on the way to the chapterhouse tearoom."

The sisters glanced at each other in surprise. Beatrice ignored them.

Clara bobbed her knees, hoisting the case in one hand. "It wouldn't do to be late."

Beatrice led the way out of the shop. Clara swung the case as she boarded the fiacre Father had hired for Beatrice. "You didn't buy any books."

Beatrice watched a herd of gentlemen on leggy, long-maned horses ride past, laughing and shouting at one another. They wore embroidery and fine leather riding boots, but no aura shone from their heads. Just young men, then, and not magicians. "The volume I wished to purchase was taken by someone else."

"Oh, Miss Beatrice. I am sorry. I know how you love old books," Clara touched Beatrice's arm, a delicate gesture of comfort. "It'll turn up again. We can write to all the booksellers asking after it, if you like."

Clara didn't understand, of course. Beatrice couldn't tell her maid the truth, no matter how much she liked the slightly older woman. She couldn't tell anyone the truth. Drat Ysbeta Lavan! Couldn't she have turned up just five minutes later?

She had to get that book back in her hands. She had to!

"But now you have tea with your father to look forward to," Clara offered, "and meeting your first young man. Do you suppose Danton Maisonette is handsome?"

Beatrice shrugged. "With a title and the controlling interest in Valserre's biggest capital investment firm, he doesn't have to be."

"Oh, Miss Beatrice. I know you're not concerned with the weight of his pockets! Leave that to Mr. Clayborn. It's his worry, after all. Now, what do you hope? That he's handsome? That he's intelligent?"

"That he's honest."

Clara considered this with a thoughtful frown. "Sometimes honesty is a knife, Miss Beatrice. But here we are!"

Beatrice had been trying to ignore their approach to the chapterhouse. The carriage stopped in front of the building that dominated the south end of the square it presided over, its shadow cast over the street.

The Bendleton chapterhouse was the newest one built in Chasland, with a soaring bell tower and matching spires. Its face was polished gray stone. The windows sparkled with colored glass. Beatrice stood on the promenade, glaring at the building as if it were her nemesis.

She glared at the heart of social life and education for mages all over the world, the exclusive center of men's power and men's influence denied to women like her. Even when she was finally permitted to practice magic in her advanced years, the chapterhouse had no place for her. She was permitted—when escorted by a man who was a member—to enter the gallery and the teahouse, and no farther.

Boys aged ten to eighteen sheltered within, learning mathematics and history alongside ritual procedure and sorcerous technique. Full members shared trade secrets with their brothers, decided laws before they even reached the Ministry, and improved their lot through their magical skill and fraternal vows.

The chapterhouse held facilities for crafting and artificing, suitably appointed ritual rooms, even apartments where brothers of the chapter could claim hospitality. Thousands of books of magic rested in the scriptorium, written in Mizunh, the secret language of spirits. Centuries of tradition, of restriction, of exclusion were built into the very stones of this building—Beatrice stared at her nemesis, indeed.

"Don't scowl so, Miss Beatrice. You can't ruin this with every feeling that flits across your face," Clara urged. "Smile."

Beatrice stretched her lips and made her cheeks plump.

"With feeling. Think of something pleasant. Imagine doing something wonderful."

Beatrice imagined that she had a right to every inch of the chapterhouse, that she and her greater spirit would be known scholars of the mysteries. That gentlemen smiled at her not because she was beautiful, but because she was respected, and girls hurried from one lecture hall to another, openly studying the art and science of high magic. She thought of the world she wanted and remembered her posture.

She smiled as if the chapterhouse were her friend.

"That's much better!" Clara praised. "I'll take these gowns home, as you will be returning with your father. Good luck!"

"Thank you," Beatrice said, and set her path for the tall double doors.

Cool and dim, the arched ceiling of the grand foyer picked up her footsteps and flung the sound across the room purposed as the display of the ingenue's gallery. Vases of costly flowers stood next to fourteen painted canvases, their scents mingling with the clean, cool stone of the hall. Beatrice walked toward the portrait of Ysbeta Lavan, stunning and vibrant in a gown of deep turquoise, her hand outstretched to catch a topaz blue butterfly attracted to the lush, drooping blooms of the perfume tree in the background. A jeweled diadem held back her light-as-air crown of tightly curled hair. She dominated the room with her splendor and beauty; her portrait hung in the principal position in the center of the room. Empty spaces flanked her image as if nothing and no one could compare.

Beatrice's own painting was in a dim corner next to a couple of girls who were plain-faced, but still obviously wealthy. She had sat in velvet, and the painter had captured both the soft glow of the fabric and the unfashionable puffed sleeves on her gown. She held her violon across her lap.

She barely remembered the smell of linseed oil and the cursed dust in the air making her want to sneeze. Or the incredible boredom of having to sit very still with nothing to occupy her mind but the desperate desire to scratch an itch. But most of all Beatrice remembered the peculiar feeling of being so thoroughly examined while the truth of her remained invisible as the artist from Gravesford painted her.

It could have been interesting. He had been on fire to paint Beatrice with a rifle after he met her carrying one tucked in the crook of her elbow after a morning ride through the wood. Beatrice tried to explain she only had the rifle due to the dangers of encountering wild boar, forest manxes, and even the occasional bear, but the painter was too enamored with his vision. Father ended the painter's inspiration by threatening to send him home without pay.

If only he'd gotten his way. The canvas Beatrice was exactly what a viewer would expect. She ought to have carried a rifle under her arm—or a pistol, dangled from one hand while she slouched in her seat like a gentleman at ease. Something to show that she was a person, anything to show that she was something more than what people expected of a woman: ornament, and trained silence.

"Starborn gods, what an aura. You must be Beatrice," a voice in accented Llanandari said.

She turned and regarded a young man who must have been—"Danton Maisonette. Good afternoon. Have you seen the new chapterhouse?"

"They're all new, in Chasland," Danton said with a dismissive little sniff. "Valserre's been part of the brotherhood for seven hundred years. Chasland is running itself to tatters, trying to keep up with the better nations."

Beatrice pressed her lips together at the string of slights and insults. "It's not to your standard, then?"

He glanced up to the stone, laid with all the skill of Chasland's masons, and dismissed it with a shrug. "It's the latest style. Chaslanders are all gold and no taste."

Beatrice had to search for a hold on her temper and the right words. "Then what would you have done? Valserrans are known for their—knowledge of beauty."

"Aesthetics," Danton corrected. "Building in an earlier style would have been pretending to a legacy that doesn't exist here, come to think of it. But chapterhouses ought to have gravity. They should be timeless, rather than fashionable."

Beatrice searched for the right words, but Danton filled the silence for her. "Though the quality of the sound in the working rooms is startlingly good."

"That would be thanks to the builders," Beatrice said. "The designer was a Hadfield, the family who build holy sanctums for generations."

"Built," Danton corrected her Llanandari once more. "You all sing to the gods for worship. It must sound impressive at Long Night. Can you sing, then?"

"I have trained," Beatrice began, "like any Chaslander lady."

Danton's mouth turned impatient. "But are you any good?"

This rude . . . oaf! The arrogance! Beatrice lifted her chin. "Yes."

"You're rather sure of yourself." He contemplated her for a moment. "But I believe you."

He turned his head, taking in the sight of Ysbeta Lavan's portrait, then back to her.

Danton Maisonette was scarcely taller than her, but his brown coat and buff-colored weskit were satin-woven Llanandras cotton, well made and embroidered in tasteful geometric patterns. He was handsome enough, but his thin little mouth clamped up so tight Beatrice couldn't imagine a kind word escaping it. He stood with an upright, chest-forward posture, his bearing reminding Beatrice of a soldier—which made sense. As a Valserran heir to a marquessate, he was expected to take a high position in that nation's army. His hooded eyes were a watery blue, and he had a direct, pointed stare.

Or perhaps it was just that he was staring at her. He examined her so completely it made Beatrice's stomach shiver. When he turned his chin to compare what he'd seen to the portrait Beatrice on the wall, Beatrice seethed behind a smile that matched the demure curve depicted on the canvas.

"You really are pretty," he said. "Too many redheads look like they're made of spotty chalk."

"Thank you." That wasn't what she wanted to say at all, but she promised Father she'd be kind. If only someone had made Danton promise the same. Her wish for honesty had been answered. She hadn't expected to be treated like a clockwork figurine, incapable of being insulted by whatever thought flitted from Danton Maisonette's mind to his lips.

"This meeting's going to be boring talk. Trade and investment. Did you bring handwork to amuse yourself?"

If only she could widen her eyes. If only she could drop her jaw. But she smiled, smiled, smiled at this rude, demanding man. "I'm afraid I don't have anything with me."

One side of his mouth turned down as he said, "I had an interest in joining the conversation."

Instead of the labor of keeping her amused, since she hadn't brought a lace hook. Beatrice kept her smile up and asked, "Have you seen the chapterhouse gallery?"

"The only thing that's new is the ingenues," he said, leaving the hint to escort her through the gallery gasping on the floor. "Only fourteen of you this year. Private negotiations are becoming too popular."

Beatrice blinked and cocked her head, and Danton knew an opportunity to explain when he saw one. "People are arranging marriages outside of bargaining season. Ha! Chasland's number one export, since you all have children by the bushel. Most of the best-bred ladies are already bound. Where are you from, that you don't know this?"

Ladies do not strike people. Even rude, insufferable churls. "Mayhurst."

His eyebrows went up. "The north country," he said in titillated horror. "That's practically the hinterlands. Have you ever been to Gravesford?"

No. Not this man. It didn't matter that he was heir to a marquis. She would not marry him and travel to distant Valserre, far from her family, to become his wife—indeed, she would not spend an unnecessary minute in his presence. "We traveled there before coming to Bendleton."

"For your wardrobe, I imagine." He took in her walking suit and shrugged. "I don't think you have much need for fine-woven Llanandras cotton when you're outrunning boars."

"Oh, we have rifles." Beatrice realized what she'd said, but too late.

He stared at her, aghast. "You shoot?"

"I am good at it," Beatrice said, and at last her smile had some real feeling in it.

"I see," Danton said. "How perfectly ferocious of you. We should have tea. Do you have tea, in the country?"

Beatrice coated her grin with sugar and arsenic. "When it comes to us. By dogsled, one hundred miles in the snow."

"Really?"

Beatrice's smile widened. "No. There's at least six ports up north."

Now he didn't like her at all. Perfect.

Beatrice glided beside him as he took her to the tearoom. She smiled prettily at the marquis and took her seat, ignoring the hired musician toiling over a piano sonata to pay attention to the talk of trade and investment Danton had promised would bore her. She asked questions and ruined her genteel display of curiosity with remarks of her own. Father bore it well, but he frowned at her once they bid the Marquis and his son farewell and boarded the landau hired to take them back to Triumph Street.

Father settled on the bench across from her and sighed. Beatrice's heart sank as Father, handsome in brown cotton, even if the jacket and weskit bore a minimum of adorning needlework, gave her a look that deepened the worry lines across his forehead, his mouth open as if he were about to say something. But he glanced away, shaking his head sadly.

"Father, I'm sorry."

Beatrice had a decent guess what she was supposed to be sorry for, but Father would fully inform her soon enough. She waited for the inevitable response, and Father gave it with a pained expression. "Beatrice, do you realize how important it is for you to be agreeable to the young men you meet while we're here?"

"Father, he was awful. Snobbish and arrogant. If I had to marry that man we'd square off from morning 'til night."

Father ran a hand over his sandy, silver-shot curls, and they tumbled back in place, framing his fine features, lined by experience and too many burdens, including her willful self. "That perfectly awful young man will be a marquis."

"Marquis de Awful, then. I couldn't be happy with him, not for a minute."

"I had hoped you would be less difficult," Father said. "This meeting was a special arrangement. And you told him you knew how to shoot? What possessed you?"

"It just slipped out. And I apologize. But he laughed at me for being from the country, and assumed me an ignorant fool, as if Chaslanders didn't have an education of any kind."

"I probably should have sent you to a ladies' academy abroad," Father sighed. "Too late now, though perhaps Harriet could enter a finishing school."

Paid for with the financial support of Beatrice's husband. "Harriet would adore that."

"If we can manage it, she will go. But there are only fourteen of you." He brightened at the notion of a brides' market, and the number of young men who would crowd around Beatrice simply because she was one of only a few ingenues left to woo. "But if you'd kept him on your string . . ."

"There are more young men where he came from," Beatrice said. With luck, she'd alienate them all. And then she needed more luck, to get the grimoire in her hands once more—

The thought clanged in her mind like a bell. She could get the book back. She knew exactly how. Excitement surged in her, filling her with the urge to leap from the landau and run faster than the showy black horses could trot. She clasped her hands and fought to appear attentive as Father chided her.

"It's not that I want you to marry a man you can't abide, Beatrice. Just—try, will you? Try not to judge them hastily."

Beatrice nodded, but her mind was already consumed by her plan. "Yes, Father. I will try harder next time."

She watched the tree-lined streets of Bendleton, hazed green with new spring buds and heavy with sweet blooming flowers, and couldn't wait to get home.

CHAPTER II

The air grew sweeter the closer the landau drove to their leased townhouse on Triumph Street, a fashionable address on a gently curving road bordering Lord Harsgrove Park. Cherry petals tumbled through the air, their perfume gently choking Beatrice as her father explained the opportunity he'd lost.

"The marquis's latest venture plans on revitalizing the most miserable, wretched parts of Masillia into respectable neighborhoods. They mean to build in the Canal District. The shares from such a venture would have kept your mother in comfort."

Beatrice sobered. Father had the family to worry about, and his plans depended on the support of Beatrice's new family to shore up his own. "I'm sorry the lead has come to naught, but perhaps that's not such a disaster."

"You're right, my dear. There are still the public shares, after all."

"Actually, I meant something different," Beatrice said, and smiled as Father looked curious. "The trouble with the real estate development is that it will take years before the development is finished and your investments will see fruit."

Father's expression folded into a downturned mouth. "Beatrice—"

She rushed on. "If the marquis is seeking investors here, he's probably also looking for supply partnerships. He will need timber and iron, and a little research will tell you who in Bendleton runs a forestry firm or a mine. If you invest with them—"

"It's a fine idea, my dear, but please don't trouble yourself trying to decipher the world of finance. I have more meetings besides the marquis planned."

Why wouldn't he listen? Valserre wasn't the only country with an eagerness to build major projects. Investing in timber and iron made sense! Beatrice forced herself to smile. "That's a relief. Will you be attending tonight's dance?"

Father's cheeks quivered as he shook his head. "I regret to say that I will not, but happy to report that I have an invitation to Compton's. I have received a letter from Sir Gregory Robicheaux asking me to attend a meeting about a trade expedition to Mion. Cotton, I expect, as the Lavans hold the exclusive rights to their cacao."

Beatrice tried not to grimace at the mention of the cheating, stealing Lavans. "I hope it is successful."

"I'm sure it will be," Father said. "Sir Gregory is a clever man. This is a singular opportunity. If only I could bring the news of this expedition home. It will be sure profits."

Not like the last time. Beatrice fought to keep smiling. "I'm so happy to hear it."

The Westborne Trading Company's orchid expedition had also been a singular opportunity. Father had contributed heavily to the voyage, believing in the international craze for exotic orchid species—a craze that had been abandoned for miniature dogs while the expedition returned home with once fabulously expensive specimens. Plenty of people lost considerable sums, and very few of the investors had bought insurance on their shares, including Father, and all the neighbors in Mayhurst who had listened to his dream-stirring predictions of the fortune investors would make. They had thrown cabbages at him for a week. No one was at home for Mother's calls. They had snuck out of Mayhurst in the dead of night and didn't stop the carriage until they were miles away, and someone in the roadside inn had still heard the story of how Father had ruined the fortunes of his neighbors.

Bad luck plagued Father's investments. He had taken a generous dowry and learned that the way to have a small fortune from speculation and investment was to start with a large one. If Father hadn't risked so much, they could have put off the trip to Bendleton until next year. Beatrice could have had more time to learn what she had to before it was too late. But Father wouldn't tell his family just how badly off they were, and he was sparing no expense to send Beatrice out to Bendleton's social life.

How much money did Father have left? Was it really enough to pay for all the hats and gowns and an address on Triumph Street? Or had he put all his money into one sure thing—Beatrice's appeal as a bride?

It wasn't wise. Beatrice's mother was one of the respected Woodcrofts, but they tended to bear girls rather than boys, often only producing one heir to carry on a legacy. Mother had married for love rather than status, and so the Clayborns were unremarkable members of the middle class. There were ingenues more elevated than her, certainly wealthier—she couldn't reasonably expect to net a duke or a cabinet minister's son, could she? And she didn't have the wealth or connections a foreign mage hunted for, at that.

But she didn't want a duke or a minister's son. She didn't want to marry a man from another land. She wanted to be a magician, and marriage stood squarely in her way. She had to retrieve the grimoire Ysbeta had stolen from her. It was her only chance!

"And starting tonight, you will be pursuing opportunity as well," Father said. "I know I don't need to explain to you how important your social debut is to us. I have every trust in your ability to evaluate the people you meet tonight. But enjoy yourself and make friends. Don't forget to take pleasure in it."

Tonight marked the official beginning of the calendar of parties, outings, performances, and events that would allow Beatrice to rise as far as her charm and skill would allow—or sink, if she embarrassed herself. How was she to manage both social success for her family and romantic failure for herself? "I will do my best, Father."

She didn't need to say more. Father helped her from the carriage. "Good luck will smile on you, I am sure of it."

He was more correct than he knew. "I have to get a tray from Cook and then rest before the dance. I will probably miss dinner with getting ready."

Father let her leave with an indulgent smile. "You will make me proud, my dear."

Once inside, Beatrice went upstairs to allow Clara to undress her and tuck her in bed. When the tray arrived, Beatrice kept it, saying that she would nibble at it while she read.

After Clara had freed her of the fashionably tight corset and left Beatrice to rest in rag curls prepared for tonight's Assembly Dance, she silently counted to one hundred, then sprang out of bed. Tonight's gown was laid out where she could gaze upon it until she dozed off, but she scuttled past it without another glance, leaping for the pull-cord dangling from the ceiling.

Moving the lunch tray to the attic was clumsy work. She had to balance the tray on a step scarcely wide enough to hold it, climb a stair, and rest the tray on a higher rung. She'd nearly dropped it twice as she climbed the narrow trapladder up to her bedroom's attic one-handed. The darkness above smelled like dust and old paper. Beatrice hoisted herself into the space clad only in her shift. After closing the hatch so she wouldn't stumble through it and break her neck, she groped for her striker-box. She whispered a charm to make the spark light a candle stub, and then as she touched the flame to all the others, she whispered, "Give light, and bring no harm to anyone."

The wicks caught and glowed, throwing flickering shadows on the sloped attic roof. Beatrice pulled out a book from her tiny hoard—*Tales of Ijanel and Other Heroes,* by E. James Curtfield, and found the spell encoded among the verses:

To Call a Lesser Spirit of Chance

She set it on a lap table with one uneven leg.

Beatrice reread the instructions. She wondered, once more, if the summoning words would really work without being written in Mizunh—but Chasland had master magicians before adopting the chapterhouse tradition. It had to work. She practiced the signs she needed for the summoning. She checked and double-checked the sequence of sigils, then chalked down the marks in the order described without uttering a word.

Now she wavered, just for a moment. This was more complex magic than she had ever dared—but she had to master it if she was ever going to have the skill to summon a greater spirit of her own. She must perform the ritual, and she could not fail.

She held her palm over each chalked symbol, breathing in the accepted pattern to infuse each mark with her will. She drew in the correct breath, held and vibrated exactly the right way to activate her circle and put her between the realms of flesh and spirit. Every mark had to be charged with the correct breath, the exact vibration, shaped by the positions of her fingers held just so—and as she worked the air shifted, pressing against her skin as the summoning built itself, mark by mark, breath by breath, sign by sign.

The energy flickered and built just at the corner of her eye, bluer than candlelight, shot through with iridescent flashes of gold, rose, green. It made the air fuzzy and alive as her actions unmoored her from the world of the flesh, rubbing against the realm of spirit.

She held down the urge to stare at it, to gasp in wonder like a child. But magic tingled all through her. She touched the aether and held power in her hands, her breath, her body—it was better than the sweetest music, the finest meal. Knowing power, drawing nearer to the mysteries, nothing was its match. Nothing was its equal.

She breathed in magic, shaped it with her need, and charged the circle closed. She was *between*. Her body felt bigger than it was. Her awareness had expanded to the skin of her aetheric form, the body that spirits and magicians could see, glowing softly within the circle spun of her mortal life. But she trembled, her hands shaking as she gathered more power within herself, more and more until she was full as a waterskin, preparing herself for the ritual.

"Nadi, spirit of chance, I name you," she whispered. "I have brought sweet nectar and flesh for you. They are yours if you help me. Nadi, spirit of chance, I know you are near."

She held out a handful of strawberries, shiny and red, and put one in her mouth. She bit and reveled in the sweetness on her tongue.

"Nadi, spirit of chance," she murmured, the taste of strawberry on her lips. "You are hungry, and I have sweets."

A light flickered outside her circle. :Nadi wants that. Give it to me.:

It spoke in her tongue, and Beatrice melted with relief. It had worked, even without knowing Mizunh. "I need your luck, Nadi. I will give it in trade."

Nadi grew and shrank, probing at the tiny dome that kept it out, lured by the only thing spirits delighted in—the allure of the corporeal.

Spirits wanted the world of the flesh. They wanted to eat. They wanted to drink wine. They wanted to run, and dance, and touch everything they could. They wanted the walls of a body, the taste of a berry. But before all, above all, they wanted those things forever, and so the art and science of the higher mysteries were closed to women, to guard against the danger of a spirit getting exactly the thing they craved the most—a home, dwelling within an unborn child.

"There is a book," Beatrice began. "An exact book. I held it in my hands. Circumstance and a clever tongue stole the book from me. I want you to help me get it back."

:Yes,: Nadi said. :I see it in your memories. I feel the leap of your heart as you read it. I know what you want from it. What will you give me, if I tread on Fate to return it to you?:

Beatrice held out the berries. "All of these are yours, and flesh besides—I have the smoked cheeks of a hog, glazed in honey. I have white cheese from the caves of Stillan. And I have Kandish wine."

:But when you have the book, I know what you will do with it,: Nadi said. :You will call an ally spirit. You will make the great bargain. And then Nadi will have no one to bargain with, no nectar, no flesh. Nadi wants more.:

"Another magician will call you, Nadi. Another incanter will need you," Beatrice soothed. "Nadi will always be needed."

:Nadi wants more now.:

"I can't break the circle to bring you more food," Beatrice said. "All I have to offer you is already in its bounds."

She heard what she'd said an instant after she'd said it, and clenched her jaw shut. The luck spirit brightened, lengthened.

:You have more to offer me,: it said. :You can give me a greater gift.:

Oh no, no, she couldn't. This was her first lesser summoning! She had meant for the spirit to instruct her, not to let it ride in her body as she retrieved the grimoire. She had asked for the best offering the kitchen could provide, had barely picked at it, and hadn't allowed Clara to take the tray away. This spirit of chance wasn't a very strong spirit, but all her rich food and Kandish wine wasn't enough.

Nadi wanted her to host it.

She had never hosted a spirit, not even any of the minor spirits she could call without the protection of a summoning circle. She had always asked for small bits of knowledge, paid for with offerings of food. What if she couldn't control it? What if Nadi took command of her limbs, made her say something outrageous, or embarrassed her? What if she lost control to it completely, and the spirit, clad in her flesh, hurt people who crossed it? She could fail completely. She could be condemned to death. She could hurt someone she loved.

No. She knew who she was. She could do this. "An hour," Beatrice said.

:A day,: Nadi said.

"Impossible. To sundown."

:To dawn.:

"No. Midnight," Beatrice said. "I'm going to an Assembly Dance. There will be music—"

:Music?: The spirit brightened, swaying. It let out a happy moan. :Dancing?:

"Yes."

:Cake?:

"Yes."

:Starlight?:

"If the night is clear."

:It will be clear,: Nadi vowed. :And a kiss.:

Beatrice scoffed. "No."

:I can make it happen,: Nadi said. :You can choose who. The book will be yours. But I want a kiss. Pick the handsomest man you desire.:

"That's another bargain," Beatrice objected.

:Not this time. Just a kiss, Beatrice Amara Clayborn. Your first kiss, by midnight. I want it.:

Beatrice bit her lip. If she danced twice with the same young man at an assembly, it was permission to court her interest. To kiss a gentleman meant rather more than permission to court her. She couldn't do it. But then she would have the book. She would have the book and she would gain her greater spirit, and then she would have what she wanted. Wasn't a simple kiss worth that?

"Nadi, you will wear a fine gown. You will dance. You will eat cake. You will see starlight. You will have a kiss by midnight, and then our bargain is done."

:It is struck,: Nadi said. :Chance will favor you. Let me in.:

Beatrice stretched out her hand, touching the barrier that shielded her from the world of Spirit. It resisted her touch as if she were attempting to press two lodestones together.

Beatrice steeled herself for the sake of the book. She pushed through the border of her protection. The spirit seized her fingers. Its touch chilled as it seeped into her flesh. It slid inside her body, filling out the spaces under her skin.

:Yes,: Nadi said. :Carry me to midnight, magician.:

Her hands raised without her will. She touched her own face, her throat. Her lungs filled with a deep breath, and she lunged for the strawberries, popping one red fruit after another into her mouth. Nadi gobbled every last scrap on the tray, tipped the goblet straight up to catch the last droplets of wine, and she smacked her lips, hungry for more.

"Nadi!" she said. "You can't indulge yourself like this. It's unseemly."

:It's so good,: Nadi replied in her mind. :Delicious. Delicious. I want more.:

"We'll get caught," Beatrice said, "and if we get caught,

there will be no music. And no cake. Or starlight. And you won't know your kiss. You must behave."

:Let's go outside,: Nadi said. :I want to feel the sunlight. I want to feel the wind. I want to go outside.:

"There's a terrace outside my room," Beatrice said. "We can go out there, but you must be good."

:Good,: Nadi said. :I can be good. Let's go, let's go.:

The spirit inside her fidgeted as she took the circle down, spinning the power back into herself. She cleaned the chalk marks off the floor, snuffed out every candle, and carefully picked her way down the ladder into her bedroom, where the clock had only a quarter hour left to tick before Clara would come to prepare her for the dance.

The opening dance of the assembly hall of Bendleton was as densely attended as Clara had predicted. Music barely made itself heard above the laughter and conversation of the dance's attendees—so many young people, all squeezed into the gowns and dancing suits that showed off their best qualities. They leaned against the fashionable gilt and seafoam-painted walls, stood in clumps of elegantly gowned friends, glanced at her and let their eyes slide past her face, her hair and ensemble observed, judged, and dismissed.

Clara had chosen every detail of the ensemble Beatrice wore, had draped and laced and pinned Beatrice into a silk gown dyed to the exact shade of a springtime sky embroidered all over with pansies, had pinned every lock of her hair into the high, curled style that was all the fashion, laced her stays tightly enough to nip in her waist, and refused to attach a fichu to the gown's alarmingly low neckline. Beatrice had given up trying to pull the stomacher a little higher. Now she was breathing against the boned restriction of her stays, trying not to let her chest swell.

A young man in ivory silk watched, half a smirk on his face. Beatrice snapped her fan open, shielding herself from his sight.

:Kiss him,: Nadi said. :He likes you.:

:He does not like me,: Beatrice thought back. :He's unsuitable.:

:Hmph.: Nadi lifted her head and turned her gaze to the crowd. Danton Maisonette stood with other young men of fashion. He watched her as he tilted his head toward another gentleman, this one unadorned by the crown of sorcery. He glanced at Danton, surprised, and turned back to stare at her, his lips moving in a comment that made Danton and his company laugh.

Beatrice's stomach clenched. They were laughing at her. Danton had probably twisted the whole story and made her out to be a shrew and a status climber, and the tale would spread all over the dance.

:Why do you think they're talking about you?: Nadi asked, and the memories bloomed in her mind. :Oh. He's mean.:

She had worked out the trick of speaking to Nadi in her mind, and so she thought her words so clearly she could hear her own voice inside her head. :Think nothing of it, Nadi. You said you wanted cake.:

:Cake, yes. I want cake. Give me some.:

:We have to wait in line,: Beatrice scolded. She maneuvered her way to the refreshment line and groaned at her mistake—young men waited for a chance at refreshment, on the errand of bringing some to a lady they favored.

:Men,: Nadi said. :Kiss that one, in the peach.:

:I will not.:

Beatrice took her place at the end of the line. Cake. Starlight. A dance, and then an impossible, brazen kiss. She could do everything but that one thing, not if she was to remain a lady—

"Excuse me, miss. Please go ahead." The young man waiting at the end of the line bowed and invited her to stand ahead of him.

Beatrice shifted her mind, searching for the correct form for speaking politely to a stranger in Llanandari, though the gentleman was almost certainly local. "Thank you, but I am content."

"I must insist, miss. Please take my place."

"What's that?" asked the man ahead of him. "Oh, miss. Please allow me to give way."

"Thank you, but it's really not needed," Beatrice protested. "The line is already moving so fast—"

For it rippled as each gentleman, upon investigating the commotion behind him, stepped politely aside to allow Beatrice to move all the way to the front, much to the amusement of others standing nearby. Beatrice accepted a napkin with a square of cream-yellow cake and tried to escape, cheeks blazing.

:I want to eat it,: Nadi said. :It smells so good. So good.:

:In a minute,: Beatrice replied. :We're going outside to look at the stars. You remember? Starlight.:

:Starlight,: Nadi said. :Yes. Hurry.:

But she could not. She maintained the graceful pace of a lady with nowhere in particular to be, aiming for the open doors leading to the gardens. She could find a place just a little separated from the rest, where she could look at the stars and let Nadi gobble cake like a child. Then she would find a patch of wall and wait out the evening. She would look for a girl who looked kind and understanding, strike up a conversation, and when the evening had passed, she would kiss her cheek.

:No,: said Nadi. :A real kiss. A real kiss. You won't get your book without a real kiss.:

Drat the spirit squirming around inside her! Nadi would expect her to deliver exactly what it wanted. There would be no escape.

Nadi flinched, and the spirit attempted to hide itself behind her pounding heart.

:No, not the noise again.: Nadi shuddered just under her skin. :It's awful. Awful. Make it stop.:

:Hold on, Nadi.: She turned in a circle, straining to hear whatever had Nadi shaking like the sound was horrible. As if it hurt just to listen to it.

A woman and a young girl rounded the corner of the assembly hall, the light from a torch lamp turning their carefully styled hair to blazing copper. Beatrice suppressed a groan as the girl's hand shot up to wave excitedly.

"Beatrice!" Harriet exclaimed.

Beatrice closed her eyes and prayed for strength. "Hello, Harriet."

Harriet Clayborn was the beauty of the family. She'd taken after Father's looks, and at fifteen was blessed with a perfect heart-shaped face, Father's delicate, precise nose, and an expression that always looked like she was about to share a joke. Her hair, bright as a fox's coat, was piled magnificently atop her head, shining as brightly as the blue crystal beads pinned among her curls. Harriet wasn't old enough to be in the ballroom, but she had convinced Mother to peek in so she could sigh at all the young ladies and young men dressed in their best. She dragged Mother along, her chin thrust out as she stared Beatrice down.

"Why aren't you dancing?" she said.

It took a moment for Beatrice to catch up to the words. "Not you, too!"

"You need to practice Llanandari," Harriet said. "You should be dancing. Mother, Beatrice looks like she's about to cry. You can't cry, Beatrice. You'll ruin your maquillage."

"I'm not crying," Beatrice said, surrendering to her sister's insistence. "I wanted some cake."

"Who fetched it for you?" Harriet asked.

"No one," Beatrice said. "I fetched it myself."

Harriet gasped in horror. "You didn't! Mother! She got her own cake!"

Mother patted Harriet's shoulder, her features a mirror of her elder daughter, moved forward in time—the same round, high forehead, the same wide-set eyes, the same gentle dimple in the middle of her chin.

"Harriet, dear," Mother said. "Stop squealing so. You are a young woman now."

"But Mother, she's doing it all wrong!"

"I just wanted some cake."

Harriet threw her hands up with a huff of disbelief.

Beatrice couldn't help smiling. "What should I do, then? I don't know anyone, and everyone already seems acquainted. How do I get to know people?"

"Tell the matrons," Harriet answered. "They'll quiz you a little, and then they will arrange a dance for you, or introduce you to a daughter or a niece. From there, you should ask more questions than you answer, to keep your partner talking."

The matrons were the women who organized the assembly dance society, who issued subscriptions and presided over each event. They had approved her family's membership—of course they would be able to make the appropriate introductions. Harriet might be overly excited at being at the ball she had read about in dozens of novels, but she had learned so much from studying them. "I shall speak to the matrons, then. Thank you, Harriet."

Mother lifted her head and smiled at Beatrice. The sigil-inscribed band of silver locked around her throat glittered in the light from the ballroom. Beatrice breathed through the terrified flutter that unsettled her insides whenever she saw it.

"Don't frown so, my dear. You will be a success; I am certain of it."

Mother had been locked into that collar at her wedding and wouldn't be free of it until her courses had stopped for a full year. Could it be—

:Nadi, is it my mother? Is she making the noise?:

:Her, it's her. What is that?: Nadi hissed in her mind. :I don't like it. I don't like it.:

:It's a warding collar.:

:It stings,: Nadi said. :I hate it. It's too loud. I hate it.:

:I hate it too, Nadi.:

That was the success her family wanted for Beatrice. What did it feel like, to have magic taken away from you? How did Mother bear it? She couldn't ask. She didn't dare ask. If her family suspected her rebellion, it would break their hearts. And then they'd make her marry anyway. They couldn't know until she had triumphed.

So Beatrice smiled back. "Thank you, Mother. I'm so nervous."

"Don't be," Mother said. "You look beautiful. There are all kinds of young men looking for someone like you."

What could she say to that? "I should eat my cake."

"We should return to the ladies' lounge," Mother said.

"But I want to see the dancers," Harriet objected. "We've only just arrived."

"Come along, Harriet." Mother took Harriet's hand and drew her away. Beatrice waited until they were out of sight.

:Nadi wants cake now.:

:Very well.: Beatrice tucked herself into a shadow, where she would be hard to see. :Small bites. Take your time—:

But her hand lifted again, and her jaw stretched wide, and Nadi stuffed half the square in Beatrice's mouth, sighing in bliss at the taste. :Delicious. Delicious.:

:Nadi! Look what you've done. I said small bites!:

:It's so good,: Nadi said. :Get another piece.:

:No.: Beatrice chewed. Did she have icing on her nose?

She tried to swallow and glance about. She groaned as she saw Danton Maisonette and a young woman glide effortlessly out of the ballroom, dressed in the color-matched attire that was the fashion for siblings. They were elegant, dressed in a style that Chaslanders would rush to imitate the moment the latest foreign fashion magazines reached their tailors and dressmakers. Beatrice stepped backward and let the shadows fold around her.

"He was particularly solicitous, was he not?" The young woman snapped open a fan and made it tremble, wafting ocean-tinted air at her face. Beatrice listened, straining to understand the woman's rapid Valserran. "He danced so beautifully and when it was over, he bowed so low. I think I have his interest."

"I trust your judgment in these matters," Danton said. He produced an enameled box and popped the lid open. He set a scented cheroot burning in a blur of motion, and he exhaled a cloud of illusion, shaping an intricately detailed archer with his bow drawn at the moon.

Beatrice watched the smoke archer until the breeze tore it apart. It was a beautiful bit of magic, and illusion mages were more than just entertainers. They could be dangerous. Everyone knew how adroit they were in battle, conjuring the illusion of soldiers so accurate that no commander could gamble that a force charging them was a mere phantasm, or that the empty path off the battlefield wasn't full of invisible cannoneers, ready to ambush.

Danton made another smoke illusion of a man in court dress, but instead of the usual fore-curls and queued hair, this man wore a glorious globe of hair like Ianthe Lavan's. "He asked for your card, unless my eyes deceived me."

"He did!" She clasped her hands together, her ruffled sleeves blocking the view of her stomacher. Everything about the girl's primrose gown was overmuch—ruffles, bows, rosettes, lace, and embroidery? Clara would have tactful things to say if Beatrice ever tried cramming that much ornament on a single gown. "Danton, I cannot contain myself! Ianthe Lavan could call on me tomorrow!"

The Lavans were here! Beatrice's head came up, and she coughed delicately before stepping out of the shadows. Danton glowered, and the young woman eyed her with the bland stare of superiority Beatrice knew from those who lived abroad and would only come to Chasland to seek brides.

"It's a pretty evening, isn't it?" she asked. "It's so warm in the ballroom, but the spring air is so clean. I'm Beatrice Clayborn."

"That accent. Llanandari, spoken through mud." The young woman looked at Beatrice's outstretched hand, and then back at her face. "Is this the country girl you met at tea today?"

"Yes," Danton replied.

The young woman lifted her hand, dabbing at the air just above her mouth. "She has cake frosting on her lip."

Heat climbed up Beatrice's neck and cheeks. Frosting on her mouth, as if she were a small child. She wished she could disappear, her tongue stilled by embarrassment.

The girl laughed. "I thought you had been exaggerating, Danton. My apologies."

The heat coursing through Beatrice made her clench her fists. Ladies did not strike people in anger, but she made a tight stone of her right hand, as if she were to throw a punch and demand satisfaction.

Nadi coiled up inside her. :I'll show you.:

A gust of wind blew a stately-looking urn from its place on the terrace, spilling cut flowers and water all over the woman's gown before landing on the gentleman's toe. They shrieked and collided with each other, their outfits ruined.

"Oh! Are you all right?" Beatrice covered her mouth in feigned shock. :Tell me you didn't. Oh, you did!: She mustn't smile. She mustn't laugh.

But Nadi did. :Serves them right. I want more cake.:

Beatrice stepped back from the wreck of cut flowers and water spreading across the floor. Her anger had fled, and now anxious flutterings filled her stomach. She had repressed her own hand and let Nadi lash out for her. :Should you have done that? You ruined her dress.:

:She laughed at us. I don't care.:

She had to keep Nadi from these outbursts. Spirits were like small children, and Nadi would settle down if she pleased it. She needed time alone, to calm it down and explain that they couldn't run around like wild things, gobbling cake and kissing strangers. Beatrice slipped the cake-napkin into her pocket and walked past the soaked couple without looking back.

The south terrace had the benefit of being deserted, thanks to a chilly breeze that raised the gooseflesh on her skin. Beatrice strolled along the terrace, looking up at the sky.

:So many,: Nadi said, :so far away. How far are the stars, Beatrice?:

:Many millions of miles, the stellarists say.: Beatrice craned her neck, seeking out the star that never shifted, the heart-home. :There you are. You have had starlight, and music, and cake—:

:Now a kiss,: Nadi said. :Your first kiss by midnight.:

How much time did she have? How was she going to please Nadi, fulfill the bargain, and get her book? :What if I can't do it, Nadi? What if I can't?:

:You have to,: Nadi said. :Just kiss one. Kiss that one.:

:Who?:

Beatrice turned away from the stars and spied a figure crossing from ballroom to terrace—tall, in shining cloud-gray silk and fountaining cascades of lace. Crushed pearl powder highlighted his elegant cheeks. Ianthe Lavan from the bookstore stood peering into the night.

:Ohh. Yes. Him. Kiss him,: Nadi said. :How your heart pounds to see him, Beatrice. Kiss him.:

:No.: She shook her head just as Ianthe turned to regard the shadow she stood in.

"Miss Clayborn?" He took a step closer.

"Mr. Lavan," Beatrice said. "What a surprise."

Ianthe smiled, and it wasn't fair that a man could have a smile like that. It wasn't fair that he made her tremble. He stole her book! Helped steal it—oh.

This was Nadi filling its end of the bargain. Beatrice dipped her knees. "I didn't expect to see you again."

"I've been looking for you. Ysbeta forgot to give you her card, and she regrets the oversight. She's looking for you too." Ianthe said in her tongue, his accent clearly taught by a native speaker. He moved closer. "Are you enjoying the dance?"

"You speak Chasand."

"After a fashion." Ianthe paused at the terrace railing. "I fear I'm rusted."

"No, no. You're good at it. To answer your question, I fetched my own cake."

He smiled. "I saw that."

Oh, now she wanted to die. "And I haven't danced yet."

:Kiss him. Kiss him. Kiss him!:

:No!:

:You want to,: Nadi said. :He's beautiful. He's handsome. Oh, and he smells so good.:

Beatrice's weight shifted, and she leaned closer. Nadi sighed over the intriguing scent of cocoa, and roses, a layer of pepper and something warmer under it, warm and sweet and—

She stepped back and Nadi pouted.

"Would you like to? After you get some air. I only just stepped outside myself, to greet the stars."

"I shouldn't disturb you, then."

"Oh no, please do disturb me. You're supposed to share the sight of the stars when you greet them."

Nadi stirred. :Look at the stars with him.:

"Do you suppose that they're all worlds like ours, as the stellarists say?"

"That is the belief," Ianthe said. "Will you watch them with me?"

Beatrice stopped beside him and looked at too many stars to count. A streak of light blazed across the sky, and Beatrice caught her breath.

:Beautiful,: Nadi said.

"A messenger star," Ianthe said. "It's good luck to see them, in Llanandras."

"Here, too," Beatrice said. "They're said to bring good news. I could use some."

"Have you come to misfortune?" Ianthe asked.

"It is nothing," Beatrice said. "Idle words, spoken cruelly."

"That can wound surely as an arrow. How can I help?"

Beatrice smiled at him. "Your kindness is help enough. I shouldn't have brought it up."

"Then we must change the subject. I assume you enjoy books, by the location of our first meeting," Ianthe said. "Do you have opinions on the latest novels?"

"I'm rather behind."

"So far behind that you haven't read *Rodale Park?*"

Beatrice smiled. "Not that far behind. One makes time for the novels published by the House of Verdeu, even if they shock society."

"I'm still upset by Odele's betrayal," Ianthe said. "William loved her."

"But Odele loved music more. She honored that love, I believe," Beatrice said. "Her gift was too precious to waste, simply because she was born a woman."

"That's a daring opinion," Ianthe said, but he smiled at her as if daring opinions were among his favorites. "Do you believe that ladies ought to be allowed to profit off their pursuits?"

"Poor women work all the time," Beatrice said.

"But ladies do not," Ianthe said.

She should demur. But Ianthe's gaze held no superiority or amusement at her notions, and it made her bold. "I believe it is our right."

Ianthe smiled back, and it wasn't fair that he was so handsome. It wasn't fair at all. "I've not been here very long, but I've never met a woman in Chasland who believes in her rights."

"You probably have," Beatrice said. "We just keep it quiet."

"I hadn't thought of that," Ianthe said, and that simple admission stunned Beatrice. "May I tell you a secret?"

"One tells friends secrets."

"And I would like the privilege of your friendship."

He meant that. It was plain in the seriousness of his expression, in the cloak of privacy that encircled them. They stood in plain sight of anyone in the ballroom who happened to look out to the terrace, but they were alone, with only the stars to peek at them.

"I shall protect the honor of your disclosure with my silence," Beatrice said. "What is it?"

Ianthe moved in closer, and the intriguing scent of his expensive perfume tickled her nose again. "I fear for my sister's happiness."

"What do you fear?"

"I'm not here to seek a wife," Ianthe said. "Our mother

brought us to Chasland because she wants a connection to the family of a friend of mine here."

"Ah," Beatrice said. "What sort of friend?"

"His father came to Llanandras years ago to expand upon our trade agreements and he brought his son. Bard and I went to the chapterhouse together," Ianthe confirmed. "Mother senses an opportunity to invest in Chasland's new industrial efforts. But I wish Ysbeta would be allowed to choose someone else."

"Someone she loves already?"

"As far as I know, my sister holds no such affection for anyone. I mean that she should be allowed to choose someone not from here." He shrugged and gave an apology of a smile. "I am sorry, but there are customs among Chaslanders that I find unpleasant."

He didn't laugh at her as Chaslanders would for believing that women should be permitted to pursue profit—his own mother was a force in his family's business, in fact. He agreed with her radical notions. What other beliefs did Ianthe hold?

"I don't care for them all either," Beatrice said. "What will you do about your sister?"

Ianthe shrugged. "What can I do? It's a daughter's duty to obey her mother's wishes. I can't really interfere, even if I hate seeing her handed over like a bauble in exchange for a trade agreement."

Beatrice weighed Ianthe's statement for half a moment before she answered. "Are you truly without recourse, Mr. Lavan?"

"What do you mean?"

"Consider this," Beatrice said. "If your sister had to betray your family's expectations, or else face the diminishing of her spirit the way Odele had to, would you support her in betrayal?"

His eyebrows rose, then settled as Ianthe mulled the

question over. "You ask a precise question. One I can't answer until after some thought."

"Other people's problems are easier to see than your own," Beatrice laughed softly. "I have never enjoyed that particular irony."

Ianthe's gaze went sharp and grave. "Is there something that troubles you?"

There was, but Beatrice shook her head. "It is my trouble to bear."

"I wish to be of use. If it's within my power—"

"It is not something I could ask of you."

:Ask him. Ask him!:

:No!:

"Then wish on a star," Ianthe said. "Wish on Jiret, the heart-home. Don't tell me what it is, but wish."

He took her hand and held it, and a sensation like the prick of nettles without the sting slid up her arm and over her skin: hot, then cold, then soft as fur—

Magic. He cast magic to lift her wish to the sky.

He squeezed her hand. "Wish."

Her mind went blank. "I don't know what to wish for."

"You have more than one desire?"

"And choosing one closes the door on the other."

"Then wish for a clear path," Ianthe said.

Beatrice looked to the sky, finding the brightest star among them. She gathered her power and wove it around Ianthe's, sending her wish to Heaven: Skyborn Gods, tell me how can I be happy when you have sent me this terrible choice? Who do I save: my family, or myself?

An hour ago, the only thing she wanted was magic. An hour ago, she didn't know what it felt like to look at a man and have her heart leap. She'd never dreamed that she would capture the attention of such a highly placed gentleman, or that she would thrill to his attention, his politeness, his respect.

"What did you wish for?" Ianthe asked.

"That's secret."

He smiled. "So it is. Then what can I give you that will help you get it?"

:He'll do it.:

:I know.:

"I can't ask for it," Beatrice said. "It's indelicate."

He moved closer. "Then give me the honor of keeping your secret. I must help you. It is my only wish. Be indelicate, Miss Clayborn. I'll not breathe a word."

:Kiss him.:

Young ladies didn't kiss gentlemen. Not ever. Young ladies did not ask gentlemen to kiss them. They did not invite such intimacies. But everything depended on it.

"It's a kiss," she said.

"A kiss?" Ianthe asked. "That is the answer to your woes?"

"It's a long story."

"Then we should make it a good one. May I?"

He meant to kiss her. Beatrice's breath stopped in her throat. Nadi pushed, and she nodded her head, stepping within the circle of his arms.

Ianthe looped an arm around her waist and pulled her in, kissing her so her senses blurred. He had anise on his tongue, and it blended with the sugar-butter-vanilla on hers, and the kiss flowed through her body like slow, glowing lightning.

Nadi reveled in it, singing in glee. The world spun around them, falling away until there was nothing but Ianthe holding her, kissing her, melding into her senses as she melted into his—and Ianthe's kiss stole everything from her.

She couldn't think of anything that wasn't him. She couldn't breathe without drinking him in. She pushed herself closer, forgetting starlight and dancing and the taste of cake on her lips. She gasped when he pulled his mouth away, half-dazed, her body suffused with feeling.

:Fortune is yours,: Nadi said. :Here she comes.:

Who? Beatrice pulled away just as footsteps sounded on the paving stones and Ysbeta Lavan rounded the corner, head high and gazing down her nose.

"I see you've found my brother."

"Er. Yes." Beatrice freed herself from Ianthe's hold and fought the urge to pat her hair.

Ysbeta smiled for an instant. "I'm glad he found you. We were in such a rush to leave that neither of us remembered about our cards."

That was a lie, but Beatrice smiled her forgiveness. "It's lucky we found each other."

"Indeed. I should like to speak to you tomorrow, if I may pay you a call?"

Ysbeta wanted to speak to her? "Yes. Please do."

Beatrice reached inside her pocket and removed a card holder, producing one of the printed cards bearing her name and an invitation to call at her address.

"I should also like a card," Ianthe said. "If you would welcome a visit."

Beatrice turned her startled gaze to his face. "I—"

"Not tomorrow," Ysbeta said. "I have reserved the first visit."

"I could come with you."

Ysbeta scowled. "I don't want you to."

Ianthe shrugged, the smile still on his lips. "Then I will attend the chapterhouse and make pleasant conversation until you are ready to return home. If I may ride into town with you?"

"I'll allow it," Ysbeta said. "Now let's get out of here before another gentleman asks me to dance."

Ianthe accepted Beatrice's card with a bow, and then they walked away, Ysbeta's words floating in the air behind them. "You shouldn't kiss Chaslander girls, Ianthe. They take it too seriously."

Ianthe's reply drifted out of earshot. Beatrice waited for another count of one hundred and went in search of her mother. If Ysbeta was bringing the book back to her, then she wanted to be at her best.

"Why are we leaving so early?" Harriet thumped sulky heels against the carriage bench. "You couldn't have danced more than once. We hadn't finished visiting with Mother's old friends. We should still be there!"

Nadi whimpered and shrank into a dense little ball in Beatrice's stomach. Beatrice laid a hand on her stomacher and tried to soothe Nadi, but it couldn't be comforted.

"No more Llanandari, please. I'm not feeling well," Beatrice said. "And it's not that early. It took me some time to find you."

"But it's not even midnight!"

"It will be in a few minutes," Mother said. "Beatrice getting sick at the dance would have made an unpleasant impression."

"Exactly," Beatrice said. "Would you want me to cast up my last meal on the shoes of a gentleman?"

Harriet gave her a scornful look. "This is the most important night of the bargaining season. The most important! Did you talk to the matrons?"

:You could have stayed to dance,: Nadi said.

"There wasn't time. I started feeling so strange, I needed fresh air." Beatrice rubbed her upper arms, banishing the shivering tingles racing along her limbs. "I couldn't stay another minute."

She could still taste anise on her tongue. She could still smell marvelous rich cocoa and roses. She touched her lips, still plump from Ianthe's kiss, and dropped her hand back in her lap before Mother noticed. Or worse—before Harriet noticed.

"Harriet, dear." Mother tapped Harriet's knee with her fan. "Beatrice isn't feeling well. She said that. There will be another Assembly Dance in two weeks."

"That's too late!" Harriet wailed. "Your prospects depend on who you meet at the first Spring Assembly Dance. It's the premiere of the season, your chance to meet everyone in town, and you're going home early, without having met anyone."

:We could have danced,: sighed Nadi. :One dance. One more kiss from beautiful Ianthe.:

"It was too much," Beatrice said. "It's so hot in the ballroom. It smelled like a perfume store and sweaty silk, and the elderflower punch made me dizzy."

"That's why you're sick! There's gin in it," Harriet said, as if she were the one aged eighteen and Beatrice the fifteen-year-old child. "You're only supposed to have one, to enhance your humor. Did you have more than one?"

"Yes."

Harriet sighed dramatically. "I didn't know you knew nothing about bargaining season. This is important. I won't let you blunder. We can't afford a second season if you fail."

"Harriet," Mother said, "talk of money is unseemly."

Harriet said nothing, but she turned a meaningful look at Beatrice. Beatrice looked at the carriage curtains and stayed silent. Harriet was right to worry. But she'd fulfilled Nadi's wishes. She would get the grimoire back in time.

The carriage leaned in its springs as the driver took the sedan around a corner. In the distance, the chapterhouse clock tolled midnight.

Nadi faded from her awareness, slipped out from under her skin to return to the ethereal realm. Beatrice felt strangely empty, feeling for Nadi's presence as if it were a lost tooth.

Beside her, Harriet shivered.

"Regardless. It was time to go home," Beatrice said.

"How many cards did you give out?" Harriet twisted in her seat and squirreled her hand into the pocket-slit on Beatrice's gown. "You stole cake napkins?"

"I couldn't find anywhere to put them."

Harriet yanked her hand from Beatrice's pocket and pulled out a card case, inspecting the small stack of address cards nestled inside. "Beatrice! Did you give out a single card?"

"I did," Beatrice said. "I gave out two."

"Only two?"

"Harriet, please don't shout so," Mother said. "To whom did you give your cards, Beatrice?"

"To Ianthe Lavan and his sister."

Mother and sister went dead silent. The carriage wheels crunched and rattled, their vibrations jostling the carriage out of tempo with the horses' clipped two-beat gait. Harriet made a strangled squeak and clapped her hands to her cheeks.

"Ianthe Lavan?" Mother asked. "His prospects are excellent."

"Ianthe Lavan? He's perfect. Beatrice! How could you?" Harriet flicked her wrist and smacked Beatrice's knee with the closed vanes of her fan. "You can't leave the Spring Assembly Dance having given out only one card to a man like Ianthe Lavan! It makes your intentions far too plain! You need him to compete against several suitors for your attention. You can't just lay your heart at his feet and hope he chooses you."

Beatrice snatched the fan out of Harriet's hand. "That's enough. I am tired of you parroting out the plots of all your lace-ruffle novels as if they paint a real picture of bargaining season. I am not a prize for a raft of gentlemen contesting among themselves to win me, and I will not manipulate anyone into competing for my hand."

"That's exactly what you need to do, though," Harriet huffed. "If you think yours is the only card he claimed, you are in for a long fall."

Beatrice flinched at the sting. "I never made that assumption. In fact, I know it was not."

"Ianthe Lavan is heir to a shipping fortune so vast we can't conceive of it. He wears the rose sword of the first mystery of the chapterhouse. He's an expert horseman, a superb dancer, an able sword-fighter, the figure of fashion—he is miles above a banker's family." Harriet's eyebrows pushed worried lines across her forehead. She held Beatrice's arm, shaking it as if it would make her words carry more weight. "His family has more connections than a spiderweb. Their wishes become laws. He claims dukes and princes for friends, speaks four languages—Mother. She'll never land him if she doesn't do this properly, don't you see?"

"Leave Beatrice be," Mother said. "I'm sure she will do very well, even without the wisdom of your bargaining season knowledge. She is so strong in the power, gentlemen will want her even without playing hunt and chase with multiple suitors."

"But it's the best way," Harriet insisted. "Multiple suitors increase Beatrice's appeal. But now she'll look like she set her sights too high, and everyone loves a comeuppance."

"Harriet," Mother said, and her even tone had lost its patience. "I did not raise you to be the kind of girl who indulges in theatrical despair at the slightest disturbance. Did I?"

"No, Mother. But I never had a chance to meet any of the younger set. It's not just Beatrice's chances that were diminished by leaving early. I need to make friends too—and so we should go back."

"We can't go back," Beatrice said. "I told you, I feel ill."

But she wanted to be back on that terrace. She wanted to

kiss him again—wanted it so profoundly it frightened her. No, no. Let him call on Danton's awful sister, the one with the overly busy gown. She needed to keep her distance.

"We are already home," Mother said, and just at that moment, the carriage rolled to a stop before their door.

Harriet gazed at Beatrice, worry etched so deeply on her brow that Beatrice wanted to soothe her. A girl Harriet's age shouldn't have such worries. And she had to make sure that her actions didn't bar Harriet from the debut she wanted when she was of age. When Father saw the benefit of commanding a greater spirit's abilities and knowledge to enhance his business ventures, he would agree to let her go quietly into spinsterhood while they worked together. Thornback sorceresses were rare and considered a bit tragic, but if she were too valuable to Father, he'd never make her marry.

But for now, she had to continue with the plan—social success, romantic failure.

Beatrice twisted to touch Harriet's arm. "The next major event is the cherry blossom ride. Perhaps someone will buy my lunch basket. I'll even let you pick my riding habit, and I will follow all your advice. It's not too late, I swear."

"The violet," Harriet said. "It's your best. But if we don't get out there and meet people, no one will bid on your basket at the charity picnic."

"Done," Beatrice said. "We'll go out and meet people, I promise."

Beatrice climbed out of the carriage. She took a deep breath of salt air and paused to make out the dark spots on the wide stone stairs. Scattered across the steps were the tiny blue-violet heads of springtime's kiss, dark and fragrant in the lamplight from their carriage. Beatrice's heart went still—and then she gasped as Harriet landed on the sidewalk next to her and shrieked, grabbing Beatrice around the waist and jumping for joy.

"He came! He came! He must have flown to get here in time, but you have a suitor!"

"Stop jostling me," Beatrice said, but Harriet was already picking up each blossom, gathering them in one hand. "Maybe it wasn't Ianthe."

"You only gave out one card to a gentleman. Who else could you have met who would leave springtime's kiss on your step?"

Beatrice's face tingled. "No one, I suppose."

"I don't know how you did it, but you're a success. You need to press these in a book. Oh, this is so exciting! You have to wear your best day gown tomorrow, and practice your chamber music, and—"

Ianthe. It had to be him—he had raced from the assembly hall to scatter hastily picked flowers across her step, a gesture that signaled his particular interest. What would Ysbeta have said to that detour? She touched her lips and the memory of that kiss shivered through her, the sensation as powerful as the magic she cast in secret.

Beatrice turned to her mother, who watched her with a proud smile, the warding collar glistening in the lamplight. Beatrice tried to smile back, but she couldn't look away.

CHAPTER III

Beatrice awoke with the echoing pressure of a headache and Clara laying out a dress choice for a day cooped up indoors waiting for callers—a printed cotton stripe trimmed in thirty-point lace, the skirt a soft conical increase to be worn without a fulling cage.

Clara halted with the gown in her arms and smiled. "Good morning, Beatrice. Are you ready for your caller?"

It was time to wake up. It was time to smile, and be unfailingly polite, and find out why Ysbeta Lavan now wanted her acquaintance when she clearly had not wanted it at the bookstore. "Good morning, Clara. The stripe will do."

"Not the peach with the lady-slipper embroidery?"

"My caller is to be Ysbeta Lavan, not Ianthe. She insisted on seeing me first."

"Hm. There could be a dozen reasons for that." Clara laid the gown on the foot of the bed and moved to Beatrice's bedside, dabbling a cloth in a basin of water. She wiped Beatrice's face. "You're frowning."

"Headache."

"You drank too much elderflower punch." Clara swiped down her neck. "I'll have Cook mix you a potion. I'll bring it to you in your bath. Up you come, out of bed."

Clara guided Beatrice to the bathing chamber and unbuttoned her nightgown, leaving Beatrice to descend into the water herself and place a cool cloth over her eyes.

She had these few moments to herself, before she was expected at breakfast, and then she would be pinned and laced into a gown that displayed her like a jewel and sent an artful message —that she, expecting a quiet afternoon at home, had dressed herself simply, but the cut of the gown from neckline to hem was meant to flatter her youth. She was meant to be interrupted at a creative pursuit, designed to reveal her education and skill.

She was expected to display a sense of beauty and the skill to produce it. She played violon, though few women performed for public entertainment. She could draw in colored pastel and paint in oil, though few women's works hung on display in the galleries of Chasland. She was proficient in knitting, hooked lace, and simple embroidery—all skills that would be displayed on her children's clothing. Beatrice's head pounded, and she flipped the washcloth over, trying to sink into its soothing, cooled embrace.

Mercifully, the door opened, and Clara hustled inside. Beatrice lifted the cloth from her eyes and accepted the dose-bottle, tipping it to her lips. Cook had tried to sweeten it, which only made it worse.

"Skyborn Gods, that's awful," Beatrice gasped. "Thank you, Clara. Is there water?"

"I'll get it." Harriet, having just come in, crossed to the jug and poured a cup.

"Oh, I'm going to die, just die," Harriet whispered. "Ianthe Lavan is coming to call on you. He's beyond a Valserran marquis. He's beyond even a minister! Beatrice. It's just like *Crossing Quill Street,* where young Laura Cooper catches the attention of the Margrave of Went, and—"

Oh no. Harriet didn't know the truth. "Harriet. It's not what you imagine."

"But he helps her father catch a hen!" Harriet insisted.

A what? "We do not keep hens."

"Neither did they," Harriet countered. "It was from the market."

Beatrice didn't want to begin untangling her little sister's logic. "As you say."

"Harriet," Mother called. "Come here, please."

Harriet huffed, but she left Beatrice alone.

Once clean, Beatrice donned a dressing gown and went downstairs to breakfast. A copy of the morning's broadsheets sat next to Father's empty place, and Beatrice picked one up, turning the pages to the shipping and finances section. Harriet leaned over to swat at her hands.

"You'll get ink smudged on your fingers."

"Ink comes off." Beatrice leaned away from her sister and read. "Robicheaux Automations is putting on a display of the latest inventions from Vicny. These automatic wonders will delight onlookers as they usher in a new age of productivity and convenience."

"Here in Bendleton?" Mother asked.

"In Meryton. I should like to see them. I understand that they can spin fine thread at astonishing speeds. It would be worth investing in manufactories for cotton, if one acted quickly—"

"Beatrice," Father said. He walked into the breakfast room and plucked the paper from her hands. "What did I say about ladies reading the paper at breakfast?"

"That it leads to squinting and wrinkles. But Father, have you considered what I said about timber and iron yesterday?"

Father gave Beatrice a look of patient disappointment. "You shouldn't be troubling yourself with such thoughts. You should be bursting with news of the Assembly Dance last night, of all the gentlemen you met. How many did you meet?"

Father moved to the head of the table, and servers moved into action, bringing heated plates of breakfast dishes to the family.

"We left before midnight, Father," Harriet said. "Beatrice hardly had a chance to meet anyone."

Father folded the paper so he could peer over it. "I thought the Assembly Dance was important."

"It is!" Harriet exclaimed. "But Beatrice got her own cake. She didn't dance once."

"Beatrice," Father said. "I do wish you would take your duties seriously. Look at Harriet. She needed to be at that ball to make friends her own age. Leaving early cost her opportunities."

"I'm sorry, Father."

"She wasn't feeling well," Harriet said, defending her sister at last. "But for all that, she has a suitor, and he's going to call on her today."

"He's not."

"Which suitor?" Father asked.

"Ianthe Lavan."

Father's smiling, indulgent gaze flicked from Harriet to land on Beatrice. The smile melted into open astonishment. "You spoke to Ianthe Lavan? What did you speak of?"

"Fidelity," Beatrice said. "Honoring one's family. The stars."

"Romantic," Mother said.

"Intellectual," Harriet said, and wrinkled her nose.

Beatrice dropped her gaze to her plate. "We only talked," she lied. No one needed to know the rest. Besides, Chaslander girls took kisses too seriously. It hadn't meant anything. Not from him.

"I hope you weren't too free with your knowledge," Father said. "A man expects to guide his wife in all things. Displaying too much cleverness can make a woman seem less appealing."

"Mother is clever."

Mother smiled, picking up her teacup once more. "Your father is correct, my dear."

"We understand the shrewdness of women," Father said. "Your education is unusual, compared to a woman of higher birth. I stand by my decision to teach you the keeping of accounts and records even though your husband is likely to have a secretary. It's more than you need to manage a house, but you'll know if your suppliers are cheating you. That is where a wife's cleverness shines."

She could do rather more than that. She hated the idea of pretending to be less than she was for the sake of her husband's comfort, and the hundred little ways she was expected to bend and give way. Ianthe had listened to her opinion. He had thanked her for it. He was the kindest man she'd ever met.

But was it enough?

"And he's coming here," Harriet exclaimed. "Today!"

"He's not," Beatrice said, but Father set down his paper and his cup.

"What are you doing, dawdling down here? You must get ready!"

"But he's not coming here today."

Father laughed. "It's noble that you're not getting your hopes up, but you need to get ready for his call. Upstairs with you. Be sure that Clara covers every detail."

"But I know he isn't."

"Go."

Dismissed, Beatrice rose from the table.

Clara waited in Beatrice's room ready to dress her for the day. Beatrice braced herself as Clara laced her stays tight as a noblewoman's. She tilted her head back, sitting patiently through the painstaking application of her maquillage. She held very still, trying not to wince at the heat radiating from Clara's curling tongs. After a hasty breakfast on the terrace, Beatrice retired to the drawing room, where Harriet joined her with a sketchboard and attempted a rendering of the bundle of springtime's kiss gathered from the doorstep.

The windows stood open, and from between the gently billowing sheer curtains, the scent of cherry blossoms wafted into the room. Harriet suppressed a delighted noise when Beatrice picked up her violon case. She plucked the strings to tune them, inspected her bow, ran a handful of arpeggios along the six strings, fine-tuning along the way.

Below them, the front door jingled.

"He's here!" Harriet said. "Play something, play something."

Beatrice played a dashing, nimble-fingered tune, welcoming Ysbeta up the stairs. Harriet clasped her hands in delight, watching the doorway. She leaned forward, as if the action would make the sight of Beatrice's caller come sooner, but it was the curving brim of a lady's hat that came into sight.

Ysbeta Lavan stood in the entry to the conservatory, every pleat and fall perfect. Her saffron cotton gown gleamed, her cream leather gloves held in one hand, her cartwheel hat set at the perfect angle to shadow one eye. The other fixed on Beatrice, her eyebrow arched inquisitively. Ysbeta carried a clothbound book with her.

Beatrice's heart kicked a little faster. Beside her, Harriet deflated.

"Good afternoon," Ysbeta Lavan said.

Ysbeta spoke in Llanandari. Beatrice held her bow in two careful fingers as she dipped her head in greeting. "Miss Lavan. My little sister, Harriet."

"Harriet. What a fetching gown."

"Thank you," Harriet said, Llanandari falling easily from her tongue. "I like yours, too. Is your brother still with the horses?"

"Ianthe has other engagements today," Ysbeta said. "He's at the chapterhouse."

Harriet shot Beatrice a telling look. "Perhaps some other time, then."

"I imagine so," Ysbeta said. "I would like to speak to you, Miss Clayborn. Would you entertain me?"

Now she would know what Ysbeta wanted, at last. She held back a relieved sigh. "I would be happy to, Miss Lavan."

Ysbeta swiveled her glance to Harriet, sitting on the edge of her chair. "Alone."

"Harriet. Go."

Harriet bit down on a protest, kept her expression demure, and even bent her knee in courtesy before she picked herself up and left the conservatory, closing the door behind her.

Ysbeta glanced at the closed door. "Your home is lovely."

"We're renting it for bargaining season," Beatrice said. "I understand you live out of town? Toward Gravesford, or on the Meryton road?"

"Meryton," Ysbeta said. "The house was just finished last autumn."

A new, fashionable home along the Meryton Highway—locals called it Money Road, for all the lavish homes dotted between beachside Bendleton and the port town that handled a third of all shipping for Chasland. It was probably the size of four homes on Triumph Street, with extensive grounds and filled with luxury. It was certainly more impressive than Riverstone Cottage, the Clayborns' home in the north country.

Ysbeta nodded to the humble bunch of springtime's kiss in a slender ivory vase. "I see you kept the flowers."

"Yes. I was touched to have found them."

"My brother is charmed by you. He tried to include himself in my visit today, but I insisted on coming alone."

"I'm happy to receive your visit." Beatrice set her violon in its case. "Would you take fresh air on the terrace with me, Miss Lavan?"

"I would enjoy that. I imagine your view of the sea is quite pleasant."

"Thank you."

The terrace was small enough to press the hems of their skirts together, but the view from beyond the wrought-iron railing was peaceful. Soft gray sand met the jewel-blue water of the sea, its waves cresting white as the sea's breath carried on, unceasing. Bright spots of color dotted the sky as beachgoers flew kites on the ocean breeze. Dotted across the beach were fabric cubicles meant to preserve a lady's modesty as she lay with as much skin exposed as she dared, bathing in the sun's rays to gain a fashionable, healthy glow. Beatrice looked down at those enclosures with a little envy. She couldn't stay out in the sun long, or her skin would turn red, and then peel, and then when the ordeal was over, she would be just as pale as when she began.

Beatrice closed the terrace door firmly shut and stood beside Ysbeta, her hands curled on the railing as Ysbeta's did. Sunlight sparkled on a jeweled wristwatch encircling Ysbeta's wrist, a bauble worth hundreds in gold.

"My sister listens at doors," Beatrice said, "but this will be private."

"Thank you." Ysbeta breathed in the sea air, the breeze playing gently in the plume on her hat. "I've come on business, you see."

Beatrice's heart pounded. "I am curious to hear it."

Ysbeta swallowed. "Yesterday I acquired a grimoire right out of your hands," she said. "I know the spell that alerts me to their existence, but the problem I had before I walked into Harriman's persists."

Beatrice waited, wearing a face of polite curiosity. "And I might be of help?"

"That is my hope. Can you read the grimoires, Miss Clayborn?"

On the distant shore, a child squealed in delight.

"I can," Beatrice said. "The book you took from me is very precious. It—"

"I would like you to prove it, please." Ysbeta reached into the satchel and produced a book. Beatrice's tongue went dry. *Woodland Mammals of the Oxan Flatlands*, by Edward C. Johnson. Not her grimoire. Not one she had ever seen before. She flipped open the cover and called on magic, breathing in the soft green smell of the grimoire's code. She murmured the correct phrases while dragging her smallest finger over the text, her hand curled in the sign of revelation. The words wavered and re-formed into the transcribed spell.

Translating aloud was tricky, but Ysbeta waited for her to speak. "'*A Directorie of Greater Spirits and Their Arena of Might*,'" Beatrice read aloud. "Wandinatilus, Greater Spirit of Fortune. Quentinel, Greater Spirit of Mending. Hilviathras, Greater Spirit of Knowledge—"

Ysbeta's eyes went wide. "That's a treasure. I had no idea this information was available outside a chapterhouse. Are they all greater spirits?"

Beatrice scanned through the magical code. "Yes. There are only twenty listed."

"That's more than enough," Ysbeta said. "And they're not written in Mizunh. So you Chaslanders knew how to summon greater spirits before you petitioned for the opening of a chapterhouse?"

"Yes," Beatrice said. She held the book to her chest and let the relief and elation wash over her. Nadi had done more than simply cross Ysbeta's path with Beatrice's. Her hands trembled as she set the book back on her knees. "This book —it's the other piece of the puzzle. The last piece."

"What do you mean?"

"The book I found yesterday told how to summon a greater spirit to make the great bargain."

Ysbeta took the grimoire from Beatrice's hands. "That's exactly what I need. I couldn't have found this anywhere else in the world." She breathed deeply, Beatrice guessed, of the moss-covered stones smell of the magical code. "I'm saved."

Saved. Ysbeta didn't want to marry. She wanted to be a master magician, like Beatrice. "How did you come to know the finding spell, but not know the spell to read them?"

"I had only one source directing me to the secret grimoires of Chasland. A woman who married a friend of the family who is a director of international commerce."

"Susan de Burgh! I read about her in the papers," Beatrice said. "Chasland was amazed by the match. She was a poor relation to Lady Wilton."

"And here I was trying to keep her confidential."

"Her marriage was everywhere. It was quite the irresistible story," Beatrice shrugged and smiled. "My younger sister was mad for it. She clipped every article she could find about the match. So she's well, in Llanandras?"

"I'm sorry," Ysbeta said. "She didn't survive her first child."

"She didn't? They never reported it. Oh, that's so sad." Beatrice clenched the railing more tightly. "She told you about the books, but nothing else?"

"She told me about the books, but she said decoding them takes years of study," Ysbeta said. "I need you to teach the reading spell to me. In return, I shall encourage Ianthe's pursuit of you."

"Oh," Beatrice said. "I see."

Ysbeta smiled and turned her attention to the shore. "He is, as I am sure you know, an excellent match. You cannot hope to attract the attention of another who stands so high. You will ensure the prosperity and status of your family with his hand in marriage, and your sister will want for nothing when her own bargaining season comes. Will you teach me the spell?"

Any girl would fall over themselves for Ianthe Lavan. They would. Ysbeta's pride in her brother was not arrogant, but earned, and it made sense that the daughter of an actuary would jump at the chance.

He was beyond even Father's dreams for a son-in-law. Ianthe was more than he had hoped for. He was sophisticated, handsome, skilled in the gentlemanly arts, and no one had listened to Beatrice the way he had. If her portrait featured her with a rifle rather than a violon, he would have been intrigued.

An echo of shivering delight ghosted along her skin. She never knew a kiss could feel like that. She didn't know that she had been asleep to such feelings, or how once awakened, they made her crave more. Ianthe was an ideal husband.

And if she chose him, she could never become a mage. She would never hope to gain the alliance of a spirit so powerful she couldn't even imagine what she could do—what could she and a greater spirit of Fortune accomplish?

Could she give all of that up, even for him? Could she give him up, even for power?

"Well?" Ysbeta asked. "The choice should be simple."

"Perhaps," Beatrice said, smiling in apology. "But I must ask—what do you expect to do, once you have a decoded translation of that grimoire?"

Ysbeta turned her head to lay a piercing stare on Beatrice. "Cast the spell," she said. "Bind a great spirit, so I may continue pursuing knowledge."

Beatrice kept her face neutral and attentive through this explanation. "I'm afraid it won't be that simple. Summoning spells are dangerous. You need to be skilled enough to handle complex magic just to handle a lesser spirit, and the greater spirits are a different order of difficulty."

"I'm not afraid."

Children ran up to the shore and shrieked as the waves crashed into them. Beatrice folded her eyebrows into a stern squint. "You should be. If you're going to survive the ritual, you need the practice in summoning."

Ysbeta's pointed chin rose. "Are you a practiced summoner, then?"

Beatrice's pride stole her tongue. "I am."

"Then you will teach me how to do this. I will smooth the path to Ianthe. We must begin immediately."

"It's a generous offer," Beatrice began. "However, I don't think it's that simple."

"What more could you want?"

Beatrice now understood that she could want a great deal. Didn't Ysbeta have her doubts? "How many grimoires have you found, Miss Lavan?"

She gave Beatrice a smug look. "I have found twelve."

Beatrice blinked. "So many? I only have four. Have you been here that long?"

"Two weeks. I have scoured bookstores here and in Meryton," Ysbeta said. "Lavan House is nearly equidistant to both. I found more volumes in Meryton, however—I wonder why?"

"I don't know," Beatrice murmured. "But I wish to bargain with you. I will teach you conjuration, including the spell to bind a greater spirit—after I have copied the books in your collection."

Ysbeta leaned away, scrambling for a response. "That will take several visits."

"So it will."

"We will have to appear to be friends."

"I'm afraid so."

Ysbeta smiled at the joke. "You will have no use for that knowledge once you marry."

"Neither will you."

Ysbeta turned her face to stare at the sea. "I have no wish to marry."

"Miss Lavan. I have spoken with your brother, and he

told me that your family came here to meet a friend of his."

Ysbeta sighed. "What my mother wants and what I want are opposed."

"Then if I may ask, what is your goal in Bendleton?"

Ysbeta tapped the pages of the grimoire. "Chasland is unique. Only the women of Sanchi have any access to the higher magics, and they keep their tradition so secret all I know are tales of what they can do. I met Susan, and she told me of the grimoires. So much knowledge is lost. Chasland has adopted the techniques of the chapterhouse. But Chaslander women have, I suspect, preserved or hidden Chasland's tradition in these volumes. How are they made?"

"I don't know how to make one. I'm sorry. I can only find them and read them."

Ysbeta leaned closer. "I must appeal to you. Help me preserve the knowledge of magic unclaimed by the chapterhouse. Teach me what you know of the magic inside these grimoires."

She had to understand what Beatrice wanted. Ysbeta wanted the touch of magic. She wanted the knowledge. She wanted the same thing Beatrice did. "I am happy to support you in your chase, Miss Lavan. Let us walk together on the path of the Mysteries. Such alliances are rare and precious."

"So they are," Ysbeta said. She slipped her hand inside the folds of her gown and produced her card. "Please consent to visit me tomorrow, where we will discuss this further. Do you play hazards?"

"I have played enough to know the rules."

Ysbeta smirked. "I would believe that of a seven-year-old Chaslander, but not a woman fully grown. We shall play hazards. We shall use the time to negotiate."

"You will not agree to my bargain?"

"If we're bargaining, then I'm interested in far more than simply knowledge of one spell. I wish to learn all the magic you know. I want the contents of whatever grimoires you have. We will be inseparable friends for bargaining season. And Ianthe should turn up before it's time for you to leave tomorrow, so you can see him."

All the magic she knew. All the grimoires she had for all of Ysbeta's. It was fair. "All the magic I know. My word on it," Beatrice said, and offered her hand to Ysbeta. Ysbeta took it and gripped her wrist as mages did when they encountered a brother in the street.

"Be prepared for many questions," Ysbeta said. "I am most impatient to continue my studies."

"I will do my best to bring light."

"Illumination," Ysbeta said.

"Illumination. Thank you."

"You learned conversational Llanandari?"

"I read a little. I should read more."

"I have novels to lend. I look forward to your visit," Ysbeta said. "Good afternoon, Miss Clayborn."

They bent knees to each other in politeness, and Ysbeta Lavan left the conservatory, hardly sparing a glance at Harriet, who lurked just beyond the room.

Beatrice stopped in the doorway. Had Harriet listened? Perhaps she hadn't heard.

Beatrice smiled and extended her hand. "Shall we practice our duets?"

Harriet stared at Beatrice's hand with a scowl. "No. Why did she come instead of Ianthe?"

Careful. She assembled her words into the most plausible explanation for Ysbeta's visit. "Ysbeta wished to discern my intentions. She has invited me to call on her in the coming days."

Harriet's lips thinned. "That's not what you said. I just wanted to see if you would lie."

And she had lied. But Harriet shouldn't know that, unless she had—

Beatrice pitched her voice to a whisper. That Harriet, of all people would do such a thing! "Harriet, did you use a charm to eavesdrop on us? I thought you avoided magic! How could you—"

Harriet jabbed an accusing finger at Beatrice. "Don't. You lied. You're going to play with summoning. If I tell Father—"

"Then I'll lose my connection with the Lavans," Beatrice said. "Since you heard everything with your rhyming charm, you know that."

Harriet stuck her chin out, but she didn't have a ready retort. Beatrice leaned closer, pressing her advantage. "Ysbeta's portrait sits at the apex of the ingenue's gallery in the chapterhouse. She is the most eligible, most influential girl in Bendleton. Llanandari girls don't attend bargaining season in Chasland—have you ever heard of such a thing, outside of novels?"

Harriet grumbled. "No."

"Besides," Beatrice said, reaching for the obvious. "If I'm closer to her, I'm closer to Ianthe. My connection to her is worth anything she asks."

"But this? It will come to no good. You shouldn't even know magic. You shouldn't have those books. This is too dangerous."

"I know what I'm doing."

"You don't." Harriet said. "But I'll keep your secret."

"Thank you."

"For now," Harriet said.

"They're secret! Harriet, if you tell Father about grimoires—"

"No." Harriet flung up her hand, stopping Beatrice's words on an open palm. "If you get too deep, I will tell Father you're dabbling in magic."

"But if he finds out about grimoires . . . Harriet, please. They're secret."

"Everything depends on you, Beatrice. You don't know how to handle yourself in Bendleton. If it had been me—"

"You'd already have a string of suitors," Beatrice said. "Very well. You will teach me what I need to know with all the connections I will gain from Ysbeta Lavan's friendship. You will decide what I wear and advise me. All right?"

"I will handle everything," Harriet said. "Do as I say and you'll be a success. You need a nap, Beatrice. Ask Clara to make a rosewater and kelp powder poultice for your complexion, and to make a cream mask for your hands. You need to look fresh at all times."

CHAPTER IV

"Ysbeta Lavan, in this house," Father said. "My dear. You have done this family proud. Such a friendship must be treasured."

Harriet glowered at her over a fillet of sea bass. Beatrice finished chewing an asparagus tip and nodded. "I feel most fortunate. Ysbeta Lavan is an influential young woman."

"The wealthiest, most beautiful woman of bargaining season. Every gentleman will be vying for her attention, and with you standing by her side, a measure of that regard will naturally fall your way."

Beatrice glanced at her plate. "Yes, Father."

Father picked up his ale cup. "I don't praise her to diminish you, my dear. Simply that her looks and her wealth mean she has the pick of any gentleman she cares for—but she can only choose one. And friendship with her brings you closer to meeting her brother, the highest choice of all."

She'd met him. He'd talked to her, shared her secrets, and stopped the world when he kissed her. But she couldn't tell that last part, so she ate some of her greens and nodded.

Harriet fidgeted in her seat and picked at the bass. "It would have been better if your caller had been Mr. Lavan. He could have been visiting someone else."

"Beatrice will outshine any other choice," Father said, and cut roasted skirrets into bite-sized pieces. "She's a lovely girl, and I've heard more than one comment about the strength of her talent."

Perhaps her suitors would inspect her teeth and withers. "We only talked."

A lie, but she would not reveal the kiss that staggered her even to remember it. Father would make an awful fuss, where the much more liberal Llanandari wouldn't even blink an eye. She exchanged glances with Mother, who kept her opinions to herself.

Father shoved a forkful of sea bass into his mouth and talked around it. "Did you and Miss Lavan have a pleasant visit? Are you friends now?"

Beatrice swallowed a mouthful of bass, nodding. "I'm going to her house tomorrow."

Harriet turned a jaded eye on Beatrice. "What has Ysbeta Lavan invited you to do at her house?"

Oh. Harriet wasn't content to pick her gowns. She meant to hold Beatrice's secret over her head. She could blurt out the secret any moment now. It would all come out. Her room would be searched, the attic found, her grimoires discovered. Father wouldn't hear her explanations—would never understand them, or her, or what she wanted most of all. He would never hear her voice again, no matter how loudly she shouted or how bitterly she wept.

Father had never punished Beatrice with an application of pain to the flesh. Instead, when she had transgressed, he would forget her right before her eyes. She would cease to exist, cast out of the warmth of his love and regard while pain spread over his features, pain she'd caused by being such a grave disappointment. If he knew she had practiced magic stronger than a rhyming charm, if he knew she was going to teach another girl the knowledge inside the grimoires . . . but worst of all, if a man learned the secret of them . . .

Harriet must not tell Beatrice's secret. If she tattled, Father would never look at Beatrice again. She had to be the one to ease Father into the idea of letting her assist him with the business. She nearly had the means in her grasp. And she already had the name she needed: Wandinatilus, greater spirit of Fortune. She would have the means to alter chance to find the gaps that brought surprising profits to the one who invested without trying to chase trends. She would be blessed with good timing, solid hunches, and the means to escape unwise investments. With Wandinatilus bound to her, she could raise the Clayborns to prosperity while Harriet made the match that would make her a happy bride.

But not yet. Not until she had bound the spirit and proven to Father that she was worth more as a thornback than as a wife.

"Beatrice?"

Beatrice held up her hand, asking for a moment to finish chewing. "She invited me to play hazards with her. I didn't know there was a hazards course between here and Meryton."

Father chewed thoughtfully. "Score well early in the game. Watch how she reacts. If she's not a good sport, let her win."

Beatrice reached for her own wine cup, but it didn't still her tongue. "In other words, we must not threaten the powerful any more than women can disrupt a man's need to be the better."

"Beatrice," Father said, sharply. "There is an order to the world. People may rise above their place, given hard work and the blessings of the Skyborn, but you ascend a great distance to join Ysbeta Lavan at her side. Cross her, and you will come tumbling down. Do you understand?"

"You can't ruin this," Harriet said. "Ysbeta Lavan's friendship is a handful of pearls. Don't lose this opportunity."

Harriet was right. Beatrice didn't care. "I would like to have a true friendship, rather than a tiresome dance of manners and obsequiousness."

Father and Harriet turned identical stern expressions on her. Mother set down her empty wine cup and touched Beatrice's arm.

"And you have an opportunity to gain one. They're just asking you to be careful. To think about how your words and actions can ripple out past what you intend. Let your association bloom slowly—you grow a friendship the way you would a prized rosebush."

"You're right, Mother."

"And that is the proper way of a clever wife," Father said. "You will do well, Beatrice. I know you understand your duty, and you will be as clever as your mother."

And she needed all the cleverness she could use to smooth her way. Beatrice leaned back in her chair, and a serving-man took her top plate away. "Perhaps in the morning Harriet and I could take to the track. It's been days since we've taken out Cloudburst and Marian, and the park will be crushed during the Cherry Blossom ride."

Harriet sat up a little straighter. "The whole track?"

"All twelve miles," Beatrice said. "We'll ride it and then I will get ready to call on Ysbeta Lavan."

"That's excellent. We should encounter many gentlemen if we ride the whole track."

Harriet couldn't just skip out to the stables and saddle her horse any time she wanted, the way she could at Riverstone—their riding horses were boarded a mile away in the stables Father had leased along with the townhouse. She was too young to go riding without company in town, and so depended on Mother or Beatrice to take her out.

"I'll have the footman take a note to have them ready at nine o'clock," Beatrice said. "And then we'll ride the whole track."

"Yes," Harriet said. "And you'll wear your blue habit?"

That wasn't really a request. "I will wear my blue habit,

and so will you, to match. May we, Father?"

Father chewed on a mouthful of bass and shooed them with his hand. "You may. It will be a fine morning for riding. And there will inevitably be gentlemen."

She returned Father's pink-cheeked smile and managed to finish her dinner.

Harriet didn't utter a word of Beatrice's dealings with Ysbeta Lavan for the rest of the meal, and even went to bed early to be fresh for the day. In the morning she made a huge fuss over Cloudburst, her dapple, and was in the saddle in a twinkling, arranging her skirts once she had planted her left foot in the stirrup. "Hurry, Beatrice."

Beatrice settled into Marian's saddle, fitting her right leg in the curve of the top pommel, and let Harriet lead the way to Lord Harsgrove Park. Harriet was a better rider than she, more comfortable, more daring, but she kept an easy pace as they rode through the morning streets of Bendleton to a wide swath of green, ducking under the blooming branches stretched across the gate to the park.

The cherry blossom–scented track was empty, and Harriet was silent for three breaths before she finally turned to Beatrice. "I really think you and Ysbeta Lavan shouldn't dabble in magic."

"I know you think we shouldn't, but I have no power to stop Ysbeta from doing as she wishes," Beatrice said. "And I know you could have told Father anyway, but you didn't. Why?"

Harriet sighed as pale pink petals nodded gently overhead. "You honestly don't know why I didn't tell Father?"

"Because you're my sister and you love me?"

"Because it would have destroyed everything," Harriet said. "If Father knew what you were doing, this bargaining season would be over and we'd be ruined."

"If the story got out," Beatrice said. "I understand."

"You don't understand," Harriet said. "You don't understand at all. Do you have any idea how much all of this costs?"

"I do," Beatrice said, lowering her voice so only the blossoms would hear. "I know this habit cost at least twenty crowns, and the riding boots six—"

"You have four riding habits," Harriet said. "You have twenty day dresses and as many dinner and ball gowns. You have two dozen hats, sixteen pairs of gloves, the best cosmetics from all over the world, seven parasols, thirty-two pairs of shoes, and they all cost money."

Beatrice shifted in her saddle. "Well, naturally, but—"

"We have a fashionable address in Bendleton. An ideal address," Harriet said. "It has a view of the sea on one side and the south end of the park on the other. It's on the right street. We have footmen, maids, and a housekeeper. We have memberships to the assembly hall, park privileges, a subscription to the theater—you really haven't thought about it? Not even once?"

"I have," Beatrice said. "I've noticed that Father took himself hunting through winter and cut his annual trip to Gravesford short by two weeks. But he's simply making little economies, isn't he? Father wouldn't be going to all this expense if he couldn't pay for it. I know the orchid expedition hurt our finances, but it couldn't be as badly as I thought, since we're here—"

"Father mortgaged Riverstone to pay for it," Harriet said.

Beatrice's heart flipped over. Father couldn't have lost that much of his principal with the failure of the orchid expedition. Riverstone was more than a snug country cottage and its pastures, more than its trout stream and rambling forest. It was the foundation of the Clayborn fortune. It was their home! Beatrice had been born there. Harriet, too. How could Father have done such a thing? "He couldn't have—how do you know this?"

"I saw the papers. I was looking for him, and he wasn't in his office, but the books were out. I looked at them."

Harriet was a bundle of curls and curiosity. She wouldn't have been able to resist it. Father's accounts, out on his desk instead of securely locked away? Beatrice would have looked too, if it were her. She had to get that grimoire back from Ysbeta. There wasn't any time to lose! "We shouldn't have come, then. We shouldn't be here at all."

"You don't understand this yet? You're our only chance, Beatrice." Harriet stared down the trail, watching for anyone coming. "If he has to pack you away in disgrace, this whole bargaining season will be for nothing, and then the bankers will come to call."

"If I don't marry this season, it's over. There might not be time for me to save us any other way."

Harriet scoffed. "Finally, you understand how serious this is. You have to put away these notions that Father will let you indulge your fancies. You have to get married. If word gets out that you dabble in magic, you'll be seen as difficult. Do you imagine Ianthe Lavan wants a difficult wife?"

"He has a difficult sister," Beatrice said. "Do you imagine she will appreciate me backing out of our bargain?"

Harriet sighed. "You can't. But why? Why couldn't you just leave it alone?"

"Don't judge me. All you know are rhyming charms," Beatrice said. "You've never cast a circle of power. You've never experienced what true magic feels like—"

"And I won't," Harriet said. "You made a terrible mistake the first time you ever cast a working. Magic doesn't belong to us. It can't."

"Why shouldn't it?" Beatrice demanded. "We can raise the power, and the spirits flock around us—"

"And you know why that is. Terrible things happen when women mix with magic. You know that. If you get caught playing with higher magic, you'll bring disgrace to all of us. You'd be warded before your marriage! Everyone would think you a hoyden or worse, a rebel, and many gentlemen would never consider taking a difficult bride into their homes. And if you birthed a spiritborn—they'd make you watch the execution, Beatrice! Your own baby. And then you'd be next."

They would be burned, the ashes banished to the sea; Heaven would deny them entrance. Their families would be forever marked with disgrace. "I don't want to talk about this."

"I know you don't." Harriet let out her reins and urged Cloudburst to speed his pace to a jog, pulling ahead of Beatrice. "It gets in the way of what you want, so why should you?"

"Are you saying I'm selfish?" Beatrice sat up in the saddle and Marian quickened her pace for a few steps. She tightened her thighs around the pommels but didn't interfere. Where Cloudburst went, Marian followed.

"You are selfish," Harriet said, not looking back. "Only a selfish girl would put her family in such jeopardy without a moment's thought. Only a selfish girl would grab for what she can't have!"

"But we should have it!" Beatrice retorted. "We should have the mysteries. They should belong to us! We should—"

"Hush," Harriet said. "Someone's coming."

Hoofbeats and laughter drummed along the path ahead. Harriet sat up straight. Beatrice lifted her chin as three riders on black horses rounded the bend, causing an uproar as they sighted the sisters. The lead rider raised one hand to halt.

Beatrice gasped as she recognized Ianthe Lavan riding with two gentlemen of Chasland.

"Good morning," Harriet said, the wide brim of her hat tilting as she nodded.

"Good morning," the lead man responded. "The Clayborn ladies, I presume."

"I am Harriet. My sister, Beatrice," Harriet said, gesturing to her side. "We are determined to ride the full track this morning. Are you bound for the jumping course?"

"Miss Clayborn." Beatrice beheld Ianthe Lavan, severe and elegant in rose-trimmed gray. He smiled at her, and Beatrice sucked in a little breath before smiling back. If she opened her mouth, all the butterflies in her middle would fly out.

Ianthe bowed at the waist in his saddle. "It is a pleasure to see you, Miss Clayborn. Did you enjoy your visit with my sister?"

"I was happy to have Miss Lavan's company," Beatrice said. "I shall be calling on her to play hazards."

"I hope you enjoy our course," Ianthe said, and Beatrice did not let herself gape. They had their own hazards course? At home?

"I look forward to learning it," Beatrice said. "I love to play hazards."

"Introduce us, Lavan," a young gentleman in a ruby-colored riding suit said. "Oh, never mind. I will do it. Ellis Robicheaux. I humbly request to be of service, Miss Clayborn."

He did something with his knees and his horse, a gleaming black gelding with a white star between the eyes, bent his head and bowed, graceful as a king's knight. Ellis swept off his hat and smiled as he and his mount returned to proper posture.

"How do you do?" Beatrice asked. The Sir Ellis Robicheaux, the son of the exclusive dealer of automatons from the Eastern Protectorate. The Robicheaux family didn't have sorcery in their line—but they could certainly change that, with the right bride. Father would dance in his chair if he knew of this meeting.

"Back up, Ellis," another rider—this one clad in green—said. Shouldering his way forward, he touched his hat. "Bard Sheldon, Lord Powles. I am delighted by the honor of your presence."

Not just heir to a dukedom. Lord Powles's father was the minister of trade, one of the twenty-five men who ruled Chasland.

"You are Mr. Lavan's school friend," Beatrice said.

Mr. Sheldon smiled, and his handsomeness magnified. "You are the lady from the Assembly Dance. I've already heard so much about you."

Ianthe had spoken of her to a duke. The Sheldons owned a shipbuilder's wharf up north and sailed a fleet of a dozen ships about the world gathering riches. There was no higher match than the son of a minister in the country—

This must be Ysbeta's intended match. Any girl would leap at such a union, and Ysbeta didn't want him.

"I hope the talk was pleasant, my lord."

"He sang your praises. He called you singular." Bard extended a stiff card engraved with an invitation. Harriet, being closer, accepted it.

"Please attend our little gathering, Miss Clayborn," Lord Powles said. "I would be desolate if you weren't there."

Harriet began with, "We—"

"I would be glad to," Beatrice said, but beside her, Harriet's back went stiff. She ignored it and went on. "You may count on my presence."

"We will all be there," Ellis declared, "and may the winner of our contest have the honor of partnering you at the tables."

"A contest?" Ianthe laughed. "What do you propose? I shall win, of course."

"Fastest one through the oblong," Ellis said.

"It won't be you, on that fancy prancer. Come along and be beaten," Bard said. "Good morning, Miss Clayborn, Miss Harriet."

"Good morning," Beatrice and Harriet chorused.

The gentlemen rode toward the racing oblong, and Harriet wasted no time in turning furiously in her saddle, a frown reddening her face. "You said yes?"

"Harriet, why are you angry now? That was a minister's son handing me an invitation. Will you never be pleased?"

"Beatrice! You can't go! It's a card party! Why did you say yes?"

"You said I had blundered at the Spring Assembly Dance. You wanted a pack of wealthy gentlemen at my heels, and you got your wish! How was I to know it was a card party? You had the invitation!"

"You never gave me a chance to say! I had the perfect excuse, and you trampled right over it with your unthinking acceptance!" Harriet looked up at the sky, as if to beg one of the Skyborn to descend and save them. "What are you going to do? Father will give you the money, of course, he has no choice, but you can't lose, Beatrice! Oh, what are we going to do?"

Beatrice repressed the urge to shout. Harriet had the card, not her! How was she to know? Oh, she had walked straight into disaster. She knew how to play cards, and she was familiar with the rules, but she lost to Harriet as often as she won. She couldn't depend on her middling skills to win the day.

Father would give her a purse without a murmur, no matter what it cost him. He'd never trouble his family with their uncertain situation—for him, Beatrice's hunt for a well-placed husband was what mattered, and while the Lavan fortune was too vast to really understand, Ellis Robicheaux, while not a magician, commanded healthy sums. Father would be delighted by the potential match.

She couldn't attend a card party, but to fail to attend after promising she would? She didn't need Harriet to tell her that it would be terribly rude. She had to tell Father. She had to attend. There had to be a way out! There had to be a solution—

All at once, calm and relief stole over her, easing her breath and unknotting her hands. There was a way to make all this come out safely.

"Hush," Beatrice said. "It will come out all right. I won't lose Father's money, Harriet. I promise you."

"You can't promise that," Harriet said.

"Yes I can," Beatrice said. "I already have a plan. Let's hurry back, I have to prepare myself to visit Ysbeta."

CHAPTER V

Ysbeta had sent her family's plush turquoise landau to bring Beatrice to Lavan House, and she had never experienced so soft a ride in her life. The spring-steel padded white leather benches were shaped in a way that cradled the body. The dappled gray horses pulling the exquisitely sprung landau were gait-matched and speedy, and people gave way before the turquoise coat of the driver who led them to the Meryton Highway and out of town.

She sat perfectly upright, her cartwheel hat shading her face. She hoped she didn't look too absurd, dressed in pale cream cotton printed with swirling, fanciful flowering vines and long-tailed show-birds. The cloth had come all the way from Kerada, her underskirt a more sedate sister to the extravagance of her mantua. It was her best day gown. She'd have to step down in quality after this.

A shallow bowl full of gin-infused fruit intended as refreshment tempted Beatrice as she rode under a mercilessly cloudless blue sky. The fruit rested on a mound of ice, an expense so astronomical Beatrice had trouble believing Ysbeta would offer it if Beatrice hadn't possessed something she desperately wanted.

She bit into a plump berry as the carriage veered to the north side of the road, continuing down a drive that led to a gate guarded by men in turquoise coats. They rushed to open the way, and the carriage sailed through without pausing.

No one could see her sitting on the landau bench, staring

at the spectacle of Lavan House. Even from this beech-lined distance, the sheer size and symmetry of this modern country house stunned her. Red bricked, black-roofed, perfectly balanced—doors and windows meant for convenience and light that disregarded the additional tax expense calculated each year—it was the finest house Beatrice had ever seen outside of an illustration.

In the center of the house's circular drive, a fountain trickled crystal-clear water from the ewers of burnished bronze statues representing three tall, slender, and distinctly Llanandari women with draping, textured robes and hairstyles she could never imitate.

She stared at the water-bearing women until a footman helped her from the carriage and ushered her inside a cool marble foyer dominated by another bronze woman, pouring trickling water into a basin.

She knew what this one was for. She allowed the maid to peel her out of her gloves so she could ritually wash her hands. What was she doing here? She thought she had understood wealth. Now following the maid through the damask-lined halls to an enormous conservatory, she knew she had no idea how the best families in the world lived.

The maid took her to a sunny terrace, where Ysbeta sat overlooking a garden with a twisting, labyrinthine path in the center. She drank sweet lemonade and sampled tidbits from a small mound of the same gin-laced fruit Beatrice had been served in the landau. Colorful wooden balls and long-handled mallets rested on the table, waiting for their players. A hand fan floated impossibly on threads of magic, wafting air over the table.

"The maid saw that," Beatrice said. "She saw you using magic."

"It's just a charm." Ysbeta shrugged. "We don't frown on women using their gifts in Llanandras. It's a lovely day, though. I'm glad it never really gets hot in Chasland."

Beatrice smiled her way through the sun trying to bake her into the stones. "Thank you for sending your carriage. The ride was pleasant."

"Excellent. I shall send it again the next time I bring you to visit. I have just finished walking the bending path, asking for clarity of action."

She waved at the labyrinth in the garden below.

"That's the road of right action, correct?"

"It is," Ysbeta said. "It clears the mind wonderfully to walk the bending path. If you have a dilemma, you ought to try it."

Perhaps she should, but it seemed disrespectful to use part of Llanandari faith simply because she wanted the benefits for herself. "I think I should stick to asking for guidance through stillness and meditation."

"As you will," Ysbeta said. She pinched her eyebrows together, staring at Beatrice. "You are the strongest sorceress I have ever met. I've never seen an aura so dazzling."

"Thank you," Beatrice said, for want of any other response. "You shine too."

"But not nearly as much. Sit for a moment. I'm not finished with this fruit."

Beatrice gazed at the waving fan. "How are you doing that?"

Ysbeta lifted her hand, all the fingers spread wide. "Fan me," she said, and the fan waved a little faster. "Imagine what you want, wrap your fan in it, and then tell it what to do."

"In Llanandari?"

Ysbeta shook her head. "Your first tongue. It's only a charm. It works because you understand what you want your power to do."

Beatrice imagined the fan floating before her, wafting air on her face. She pushed the vision through her spread fingers, wrapping it around the tines.

"Open."

The fan snapped open, showing her the swallows painted on its silk fabric.

Beatrice licked her lips. She raised her hand, and the fan rose in the air.

"Fan me."

It fluttered, and the soft breeze cooled her face. "But it didn't rhyme."

"Rhyming makes it seem special," Ysbeta said. "Rhymes have more power because we believe that they do."

"That makes sense," Beatrice said. "I believed the rhymes were important. I think we all did."

"Belief matters," Ysbeta said. "I suspect the same thing is true of Mizunh. The chapterhouse uses the tongue to hide their secrets, and all the ceremony and pomp surrounding Mizunh made the language itself magic, not anything inherent to it."

"What a wonderful convenience this charm is." Beatrice turned around to let the charmed fan waft air over the back of her neck. "Do all Llanandari use the lesser magics like this?"

"Why wouldn't they?"

"Well, only children play with lesser magic. Small spells they play in games. Then boys go to the chapterhouse or take on an apprenticeship if they're not gentlemen. Girls stop doing charms when they start their courses."

Ysbeta sniffed. "With all the ways charms are useful? That seems a waste. Shall we play hazards?"

Beatrice took a mallet, and then considered the fan still floating before her seat. She beckoned to it. "Follow me."

The fan darted forward, and the breeze from its flapping cooled her neck.

Ysbeta smiled. "You learn fast. Come on."

Beyond the formal, restrained garden lay a rolling, perfectly groomed lawn where a planned and designed wicket course wound all the way to a controlled bit of wilderness, which was honestly no such thing. Safe from forest manxes, wolves, and boar this far south, it was a pleasant, shady refuge.

Ysbeta was a fierce player. She huffed the first time Beatrice ignored an opportunity to knock her lead ball into a hazards trap. "If you can beat me at this game, then do it. I need a partner for mixed hazards, and I need someone who will cut throats."

She could cut throats. So could Ysbeta. They battled all the way down the course, playing just short of committing fouls.

"Much better," Ysbeta said. "Tell me what you know how to do."

"The most difficult thing?"

"Yes."

"I have bargained with a lesser spirit of fortune."

"I have never seen anything come even close to conjuring a lesser spirit outside of the chapterhouse methods, in all my travel and learning. Did you carry it?"

"Once," Beatrice said. "It's like minding a child who knows how to run toward danger and throw fits when it doesn't get what it wants."

"Like a child," Ysbeta mused. "A dangerous, demanding child. What did you want from it?"

"The chance to meet you again, so I could regain my book."

"My book," Ysbeta corrected.

"I'll be happy to copy what I need from it."

"Not yet. First, tell me how the grimoires work."

"Have you ever broken a language code? *Word Puzzles to Delight and Distract*, by Eliza Charlotte Jenkins?"

"Yes." Ysbeta shrugged. "Children's rainy-day distractions. I preferred to draw. Wait. Did you say Eliza Charlotte Jenkins?"

"Correct," Beatrice said. "I learned to decode from the activity books. My mother bought them for me. She made me learn them."

"She made you?"

Beatrice watched the breeze play in the trees before launching her ball over the course. "When I solved an entire book, she'd give me something special."

"So she wanted you to learn them."

"Yes." It had never occurred to Beatrice to wonder why Mother had wanted her to learn code breaking beyond a girl's usual amusement. Mother had put her on the path to learning about the grimoires—had she done that on purpose?

Ysbeta took a practice swing. She sighted along the course and launched her ball toward the wicket. Or—no. Beatrice's shoulders slumped as Ysbeta's ball collided with hers. "How did you go from word puzzles to a spell?"

"I'm getting to that. The books became more difficult. But the more advanced books had typesetting errors."

Ysbeta set her foot on her wooden ball, and hammered Beatrice's ball into a grass trap. "That must have been irritating."

"It was, until I imagined that the typesetting errors were actually a code within the book."

"A second code?"

"Yes. And those ones taught magic beyond the rhyming charms children learn. Like the spell to seek the secret grimoires, and the spell to read them without decoding by hand."

Beatrice winced as a patch of sod flew after the ball she sent arcing through the air.

Ysbeta nodded. "Susan taught me one, but not the other. I think I know why."

"So you would bring grimoires to her, and you would need her to decode them?"

"Precisely. But now I have you. You can teach me higher magic than charms and small spells. I will call a greater spirit and go through the ordeal. Once I'm safe, you may have the grimoire you wanted as payment."

"It will take too long to teach you summoning," Beatrice said. "You have to start at the beginning and work your way through each difficulty. You have to learn to hold vision, breath, intent, and gesture all at the same time, and it's a feat of such focus to do all four at once. I started learning the higher magics when I was still a child. I'm eighteen now."

"That's the principle of harmonic evocation," Ysbeta said. "How do you synthesize the wave-patterns of each discrete line of casting? How does it interact with the lesser principle of combination?"

Beatrice stared at Ysbeta. "I don't have the least idea what any of that means."

"How do you summon without knowing it?" Ysbeta asked, agog. "I've listened to Ianthe chant out the mnemonics to himself for years. He had to be able to recite them word for word before they let him take the Ordeal of the Rose."

"You just . . . you practice," Beatrice said. "You master all the forms one at a time. Then you practice each pair in combination. Then triads. Then all four at once. You don't need to memorize the principle of harmonic . . . whatever it was you said."

"Harmonic evocation," Ysbeta repeated. "I know a hundred different charms. More. I understand magic better than you think. I certainly know more of the theory."

Maybe she did, but it still put Beatrice's chin up. "Theory isn't practice."

"So I see, from your own example. You spent those years hunting grimoires. You can see any of the books in my collection, so long as you teach me what's in them. And then you may have the book about Jy. Not before. Now, tell me how a conjuring works."

They were far from the house, but Beatrice glanced around for gardeners.

"We're alone," Ysbeta said. "It's safe."

"All right. I'll begin at the beginning. I won't risk a gap in your understanding."

"I understand. How do we begin?"

Ysbeta's eyes sparkled with excitement, and Beatrice found herself smiling back. "You begin by casting a circle," Beatrice said. "The circle marks the piece of the world you are moving from the mortal world into the aetherial world, where the spirits dwell . . ."

". . . That's almost correct," Beatrice said, and hammered her first shot on the last course on the grounds. "The circle is a protection, but you must breach that protection if you decide to accept the bargain you made with a spirit. And if you summon too powerful a spirit, they can break your circle as if it's made from cobwebs."

Ysbeta crouched, considering her best strategy for a winning shot. "So I can't start with a greater spirit right away."

"I'm afraid not. First minor, lesser, then greater. This is why conjuration is so dangerous."

Ysbeta stepped up to the mark, set her ball down in the proper place, and swung. The ball launched into the air, landing well ahead of Beatrice's, but deep in a hazards trap. "Drat."

"You're still ahead."

"We're close to the old sanctum," Ysbeta said. "You could show me how to summon a spirit."

"We don't have any names of the spirits."

"Surely you know the name of one," Ysbeta said.

"You've done this before."

"Only once."

"Did you forget its name?"

Beatrice scanned the carefully trimmed hedges, looking for a reason to demur. "No, but—"

Ysbeta stared at something over Beatrice's shoulder. "Damn. We have a visitor incoming."

They stopped play to watch as Ianthe ambled toward them, smiling. He was in Keradi cotton, the cloth vented by embroidered eyelets sewn all over the jacket, weskit, and breeches. In defiance of the subdued colors favored by Chaslanders, he was brilliant in azure, with a soft green weskit and white, shining lace. "I'm glad I caught you."

"I'm not. Beatrice is about to trounce me in hazards. How fares the *Pelican?*"

"He awaits your consultation with the cargomaster before he sails again," Ianthe said. "I managed that part of my business, at least."

Ysbeta looked him over and put her fists on her hips. "Something happened. Is it to do with my ship?"

"Not a bit of it. There's a commotion in Meryton. It's an unpleasant business. I have to take the news to Bendleton Cathedral. We need a brace of lawyers," Ianthe said. "I shouldn't like to speak of it. I apologize, Miss Clayborn, but I hoped for the pleasure of driving you home."

"Take her anyway," Ysbeta said. "You need a sympathetic ear."

"Then I'd be burdening Miss Clayborn, and the news I take to the chapterhouse is terrible."

He wasn't telling her. That meant something personal, something that could frighten her. "I think we would rather know. What happened in Meryton?"

Ianthe sighed. "Very well. A three-year-old set her minder on fire."

"That's terrible! Was it an accident?"

"Oh, Skyborn. You mean the child did it with magic," Ysbeta said. "She's spiritborn."

Beatrice touched her bare throat, unable to breathe. "No. Oh no, that's too awful."

Spiritborn children were the reason for warding collars. Unprotected, a sorceress with child was too great a temptation for a spirit, whose eternity as a disembodied, yet thinking being was dull and lifeless compared to the tether of a mortal body in the material world. And the child's body growing in the womb, with all its fingers, its toes, but no soul yet in residence was the perfect home for such a spirit. They would slip inside that growing body, ready to be born and have the whole world in their hands.

Spiritborn babies were difficult pregnancies. They kicked and fussed, exhausting the mother. Their births were dangerous, often going footling in labor. They were colicky babies, but quick to crawl, walk, and speak—

And when they were thwarted, objects would fly off the walls. Burning logs would spill out of a hearth. Doors would slam, fly open, slam again. Accidents happened, hurting, sometimes killing the people who angered them. A spiritborn child had all the sorcerous might of the spirit, and none of the morality needed to dissuade them from their destructive rages. And some poor woman in Meryton had fallen pregnant without a warding collar to protect her.

Tears prickled at Beatrice's eyelids. She'd never get to have a child if she succeeded in her pursuit. That was the price of the magic she wanted—never to have a baby of her own, for fear of birthing a monster.

"Could it have been an accident? With a lamp, or a candle?"

"There was a witness. The mother is terrified. And Meryton doesn't have a chapterhouse."

"So they have asked the Bendleton chapterhouse for help. Is the child in custody?"

"I saw her myself," Ianthe confirmed. "I've never beheld such a creature, and I hope to never see one again. How could her mother have been so careless?"

"Hold on," Beatrice said. "How old is she? The mother, I mean."

"I don't know," Ianthe said. "Nineteen? Twenty?"

"Oh! She was a child," Ysbeta said.

"Sixteen is old enough to marry in Chasland, if your parents consent."

Ysbeta turned to stare at Beatrice. "Are you defending him?"

"I'm saying that they may not have known the danger, if her gift was weak," Beatrice said. "What about the father?"

"Denies it was him. They weren't married—" Ianthe looked away. "I shouldn't be telling you all of this. It's not a fit subject for ladies."

"So it could happen to us, but we shouldn't know about it?" Beatrice said, and Ysbeta nodded her agreement.

"It would never happen to you. You are ladies."

"That may not be as much protection as you think," Ysbeta said. "And it shouldn't have happened to that girl. Poor family?"

Ianthe nodded. "She named a prominent business owner as the father. Not a chapterhouse magician, and he doesn't have the talent. He has lawyers, and she does not."

"So he'll escape the pyre," Beatrice said. "It's awful."

"I shouldn't have upset you," Ianthe said. "I'm sorry. We should change the subject."

Ysbeta hefted her hazards mallet. "You were intending to tell me about my ship."

Beatrice picked up the thread dropped by the horrible news. "Yes. I was going to ask earlier. You own a ship?"

Ysbeta scowled at Ianthe. “Only one. But he’s mine by right, and I’m the captain of record.”

“Ysbeta received the *Pelican* for her fifteenth birthday, for her maiden property. She owns Lavan House, here, as well as a tea garden and a seaside home in Jy.”

“Like a—” Beatrice fumbled for the word. “How do you say dowry in Llanandari?”

Ysbeta frowned at the word.

“Bridal gift,” Ianthe said. “We don’t have dowries.”

Ysbeta looked like she was ready to burst into thunder. “The property is mine.”

“Until you marry a Chaslander,” Beatrice said.

“I’m a Llanandari citizen. I have rights that cannot be eliminated by marriage.”

“But you can’t legally decide what to do with your property if you marry in Chasland,” Beatrice said. “Not until your husband dies, and then you’re holding it in trust for your son, who will then be able to decide to do whatever he likes with it when he turns eighteen.”

“And if I don’t have a son?”

“Then the administering of the property goes to the closest male relative, who will hold your possessions in trust.”

Ysbeta wore an angry expression. “That’s vile.”

“I’m sorry, Ysy,” Ianthe said. “Miss Clayborn is telling the truth.”

“I will not have my property stripped from me. I won’t. Beatrice, how can you accept something like that?”

“I’m only one woman,” Beatrice said. “I hate it, but I can’t fight it alone.”

Ysbeta put her hands on her hips, her expression sour. “Do you honestly believe you’re the only woman to object?”

“No,” Beatrice said. “But if we had the power to change it, wouldn’t it already be done?”

Ysbeta shook her head. "I can't do it. I won't be abandoned in this backward country with nothing to my name. I have to tell Mother."

Ianthe stirred, regarding the house thoughtfully. "Mother probably already has some legal agreement she's going to push for, but I don't know how it would hold up in Chasland. I've been against the match from the start. Maybe if we both talk to her, she'll decide it's not worth it."

Ysbeta gave Ianthe a skeptical glare. "Do you think you can give Mother your big-eyed look and she'll abandon her plans to marry me to an uncultured lout in a cravat?"

"Bard's not that bad."

"All the same. I don't want to marry him. I don't want to live here."

"We'll argue for the happiness of her daughter," Ianthe said. "That does matter for something."

"It ought to," Ysbeta grumbled.

"I'm sorry I have to leave you," Ianthe said, "but I have to get to the chapterhouse."

"And you'll take Beatrice back with you?" Ysbeta asked. "It would be simpler. You can talk about something else."

A gleeful little thrill raced under Beatrice's skin. "We've nearly finished our game. Shouldn't we finish it?"

"I've seen enough," Ysbeta said. "We will partner for the charity hazards tournament. No one will beat us. Come again tomorrow and we'll practice."

"I'll see you home swiftly," Ianthe said. "I'm sure the curricle is ready."

Ianthe's curricle was enameled turquoise, the back of the carriage covered by a painting of sailing ships going about their business. Leggy, gleaming chestnuts stood hitched to the tall two-wheeled vehicle, standing still for the grooms who brushed them until their coats gleamed. They were fresh from the stable, so the horses that brought Ianthe back to Lavan House were resting somewhere. How many horses did they own?

"Do you like it?" Ianthe asked, in her tongue.

Beatrice switched back to Chasand with gratitude. "It's a fine curricle. The nicest I've ever seen. And they're gorgeous horses."

"And fast." Ianthe helped her up to the tall seat. "All set?"

She smoothed out her skirts and nodded. "Yes."

Ianthe leapt up to the driver's seat and set the horses to cantering. The well-sprung curricle only jiggled a little as they dashed up the long drive to the Meryton Highway.

"I'm sorry I have to rush," Ianthe said. "The situation in Meryton is deeply unpleasant."

Beatrice didn't want to think about it, but she shivered. It was horrible. That poor girl, who never had a chance —"How had it come to this?"

"You were right. They didn't know she was a sorceress," Ianthe said. "Not until fires tended to start around her child. They explained their own home as lost to a dirty chimney and hoped the child could be taught."

"It's so sad," Beatrice said. "But I understand why they tried to hide it."

Ianthe shook his head and let the horses slow to a trot. "If you do, explain it to me."

"Have you spent much time around babies?"

"Not really."

She hadn't really expected he had, even if Llanandari men were reputed to be indulgent husbands and fathers. "Even when they're not yours, you know they have to be protected. It's a baby. They rely on you for everything—food, cleanliness, comfort—and you love them. You can't help it. How old is the child? Three?"

"Almost four," Ianthe said. "They kept that spiritborn hidden longer than most."

"But by the time the child is two, the family is hopelessly in love."

"Love? But spiritborn are monsters."

"But they begin as babies," Beatrice said. "Helpless, adorable, innocent babies. The family's had time to bond with that baby, and if it seems to be uncanny, that's just their child being precocious."

Ianthe sped past a wagon plodding along the highway. "Because you can't tell until they're old enough to walk and start to talk."

"Exactly. And the family isn't stupid. They know what's happening. They know what must be done, but they're deliberately not facing the truth because that spiritborn is their baby. And if they're careful enough, loving enough, they can stop the inevitable."

"That's awful."

"It's horrible."

Ianthe eased the reins and called a canter. Bendleton grew closer, the spires of the chapterhouse visible from higher ground. Traffic thickened, and he drove around slower-moving carts and wagons, his expression pensive.

"This doesn't happen in Llanandras," Ianthe said. "All non-mageborn children are tested for potential while they're in school—"

"Chasland doesn't have compulsory child education."

"I could rant about that particular backward practice for an hour, and still have wind to start in on another," Ianthe muttered. "And so weak sorceresses wind up in this terrible situation."

"It's rare. Sorceresses are terribly valuable."

Ianthe didn't react to the bitter twist in her voice. "But because no one tested this poor girl, I'm going to the cathedral to fetch a lawyer. And then I'm going to gallop back to Meryton, so we can examine the child and the mother, and then—"

Beatrice looked down at her hands, folded over her stomach. "And then they have to die."

"Chaslander law blames the mother for consorting with forces she's incapable of controlling. By tomorrow they'll be burnt alive. It's monstrous. It's a terrible fate for a sorceress."

"They're all terrible fates," Beatrice muttered.

"I'm sorry?" Ianthe asked. "What do you mean?"

She twisted to face him. "The talent for sorcery in women is a curse, when it ought to be a blessing."

She should have deflected with an innocuous comment, said that it was nothing. She should have lied to him the way she lied to everyone. It was too late. She had spoken the truth, and he would withdraw his interest. That's what she should want. She couldn't marry. But she trembled, anticipating his disapproval, and wished she could take it all back.

"But sorcery is marvelous," Ianthe said. "How can it be a curse?"

"I misspoke. My apologies."

"I don't think you did." Ianthe slowed the horses to a walk and turned to study her. "You've already been eye-opening on the matter of spiritborn. Please tell me why you consider sorcery a curse."

Beatrice searched for words. She needed exactly the right ones, so she could make her point without offense. "It's not sorcery itself that is the problem."

"Then what is it?"

"It's being a woman with sorcery," Beatrice said. "Imagine that you were considered too weak-minded and incapable of learning the higher magics, but even that didn't matter, because your worth as a sorceress lies in your womb."

"But that's not how we do it in Llanandras," Ianthe said.

"Chaslanders and the rest of you northerners just lock women inside a collar for the duration and ignore the ways one can plan for a pregnancy. Llanandari women only wear the warding collar when they're actually pregnant."

They didn't wear them constantly? Ysbeta's casual use of the fan charm made more sense. "That's much more sophisticated," Beatrice said.

"I've tried explaining to Chaslanders, but they won't hear of it. Honestly, I think it's barbaric."

Ianthe was correct—Chasland, with its tall, sturdy timber and its deep veins of precious metal and gems, was long on wealth and short on social progress, but Ianthe's words felt a touch too smug. "Do Llanandari women join the chapterhouse?"

"Women don't do the higher magics the chapterhouse teaches," Ianthe said, and shrugged. "It takes years of study, and you have to start young. What woman knows that she has no wish for the most natural drives in the world at ten?"

Beatrice bridled the urge to snap. "I cannot answer that, as no one makes a habit of asking ten-year-old girls what they want. And even if someone did, there's really only one acceptable answer."

"All right," Ianthe said, and made way for a faster carriage galloping for Bendleton. "When you were ten, what did you want?"

"Magic," Beatrice said. "I wanted to answer the call of High Magic. I wanted to be an initiate in the chapterhouse, painstakingly copying passages from books in my own commonplace book. I wanted a sponsor. I wanted to learn Mizunh and all the signs and sigils to call spirits and—I wanted magic, and everyone told me that I couldn't have it."

Ianthe licked his lips and looked away. "It's not as simple as that."

"Then why?"

Ianthe's shoulders went up. "I'm not really supposed to say."

"More of your brotherhood's secrets. But is there a real reason that women can't learn the higher magics?"

"All right," Ianthe said. "I'll tell you as much as I can, since I have the privilege of your friendship. But this is all skirting very close to things I cannot tell you, because of my oaths of initiation."

"I will not ask you to break your oath," Beatrice said. "I know that you cannot. But what is the reason women cannot do the ordeal?"

"Because the moment you had to put on a warding collar, your connection to your greater spirit would be lost. And you would only be able to bond another if you were still younger than twenty-five."

"Why is that?"

"Honestly, I don't think anyone knows," Ianthe said. "There's a hypothesis that you cross the threshold from growing to aging then, but that's just the prevailing best guess."

"But if you have the means to allow a woman to control her own fertility and plan her family, why couldn't she train, marry, have a child or two, and then bind a greater spirit before she's too old for the ordeal?"

"Because you have to go into the final ordeal with a bound lesser spirit," Ianthe said. "And you must have the pact of a lesser spirit to bear the weapons of the rose. If you lose the bond, the rank is stripped from you."

"Does that happen?"

"It's a severe punishment," Ianthe said. "I personally have never witnessed it performed. But the punished must collar himself for a month to a year, and when he takes it off, he has to start the degree all over again. It's a deep shame to have your degree stripped."

Beatrice's heart sank as a possibility, bright with promise, dimmed and went out. "So the device women have to wear for the safety of their children is an instrument of punishment to men in the chapterhouse. I could spend a very long time getting angry while thinking about that."

"I don't blame you at all, and I won't quibble about the intent of each. It's bothered me before too."

"So a woman would lose her right to claim the rose if she bore children. What if binding the spirit was enough? If all I had to do was prove that I could?"

Ianthe shook his head. "You need the bound spirit for the ritual."

"Why?"

"That's a secret. I mean that I don't know the answer, because I haven't done that ritual yet," Ianthe explained.

Beatrice slumped. "There's no way a woman could answer both the demands of family and magic."

"Few mages would take a woman as a student, regardless." Ianthe said. "The study of High Magic is a legacy. Once I become a mage, I will take on novices whose progress and success in the mysteries reflect on my standing and reputation in the chapterhouse. Taking on a novice who doesn't complete the Ordeal of the Rose soon enough—or even at all—"

"Would make the mentor lose respect."

"Correct." Ianthe clucked to his horses, nudging them into a trot. "So if a woman who studies High Magic changes her mind about what she wants once she's old enough to put away childish desires and accept the path of womanhood—"

"Childish desires," Beatrice repeated.

Ianthe went on, nodding to a cart driver who made way for him. "No mentor wants to see their initiate fail to live up to their true potential. They don't want to wonder what caliber of mage their charge could have been, if she hadn't given it up for a family—and it would be a rare girl who never grew up enough to become a woman."

"You're equating child-bearing to maturity," Beatrice said. "That a woman who doesn't want children isn't actually an adult."

"Adults, men and women alike, continue the legacy of their families. A man who never marries and has children hasn't grown up either."

The breeze shifted, carrying the scent of cherry blossoms on its back. "But we don't call unmarried men thornbacks. We don't mutter about how unhappy he must be to have never caught a spouse—"

"But an unmarried man can't take on the ordeal of the order," Ianthe said.

"Why not?"

"The oath," Ianthe said. "I'm shaving very close to telling you what I should not."

"The oath says you have to be married? Is there a magical reason for that?"

"If there is, I don't know it." Ianthe nudged the curricle around a slow-moving wagon. "But it's in the oath. It doesn't matter how quickly you learned or how strong your potential is. Magi are married men. So there is a social penalty."

"Not much of one."

"Perhaps not," Ianthe said. "And as I said, no Llanandari husband would lock his wife into a warding collar day in and day out. Nor would he get so many children on his wife that she was buried under babies for most of her life. Llanandari wives have freedom. If you had met my mother, you would see how much."

"I don't wish to speak against your mother, but consider this," Beatrice said. "Llanandari husbands allow their wives to use their magic—but those wives are only casting rhyming charms and cantrips. They're not allowed to explore their potential as mages."

"Yes, they are," Ianthe said. "I just told you. Llanandari women don't wear binding collars unless they're pregnant, and we plan our children. Women go years without being warded long before their courses end. My mother took off the collar for good when I was ten."

"But she was past the age of twenty-five. Does your mother have the bond of even a lesser spirit? Could she train in the chapterhouse, now that she's done with bearing children?"

Ianthe went still. "That's not the point."

"I assure you that it is," Beatrice said. "And marriage and fatherhood as a restriction to entrance to the higher orders of the chapterhouse isn't much of a restriction for men."

"But you cannot become a mage without it."

"How many intentionally unmarried initiates with enough training to take the ordeal do you know? Ten?"

"Not so many as that."

"Five?"

Ianthe sighed. "Two."

"Do you expect they'll never marry?"

"No. They'll marry, earn their initiation, and ignore their wives as much as possible."

"I have never met a married woman who had the luxury of ignoring her husband."

"All right. It's unfair," Ianthe said. "But how can we change it? There is no way to protect a sorceress from bearing a spiritborn without the warding collar. That's something you can't deny."

"But no one is looking for another way," Beatrice said. "The current system lays all of the restriction, all the responsibility, and all of the burden on sorceresses. Men aren't inconvenienced in any way. They may do whatever they like. For them, the system isn't broken, so why look for a solution?"

Beatrice went silent, too late. She had gone too far; she

had said too much. Cherry trees nodded in the ocean breeze, heavy with buds still flushed pink and ignorant of what it meant to bloom lining the side of the street. The scent of the sea just behind the curving, pale stone fronts of the townhouses twined with the drowsy, nectar-sweet fragrance of the cherry boughs. There was no way to take it back. The silence in the curricle sat between them, crowding them to the edges of the bench. Ianthe busied himself with driving the horses up Triumph Street. When he wheeled the curricle around to stop in front of number seventeen, Beatrice's fingers were laced together so tightly her knuckles ached. She'd ruined it. One of the doors beckoning her closer now swung slowly shut. She touched the hollow notch at the base of her neck and felt her throat go tight.

"Miss Clayborn," Ianthe said, as she rose from the curricle's bench. "You've given me much to think about."

Beatrice tried for a smile. She'd said too much. Ianthe would never wish for her company again. She had pushed the boundaries and torn the threads that had wound between them. A movement at a third-floor window caught her eye, and Mother gazed down at her and Ianthe, her fingers resting at the collar on her throat.

Beatrice looked away. A better daughter would try to mend what she had torn. A better daughter wouldn't have rent their friendship in the first place. "I apologize for that. It was ill-said."

"Please don't. I plan on thinking about it. You have a real, valid point about planning children before taking the ordeal. Maybe there's a way to do it."

Ianthe had brightened up again, optimistic and confident. Beatrice tried to smile for him. The world gave way to Ianthe Lavan, but he would want a son. And if Beatrice had the Clayborn luck, she would have daughter after daughter. If her twenty-fifth birthday drew near without bearing a son, would he be content without one? Would his family?

It was still the same problem. It relied on her husband's permission, not her own freedom. But she had argued enough for one day. "Perhaps the next generation will benefit from it."

"Perhaps. I will see you at Foxbridge Manor. I hope you're as good at cards as you are at explaining injustice." He touched the tip of his tricornered hat and smiled. "Until then."

Beatrice stood on the promenade, a fresh wave of sickness washing over her. The card party. She'd forgotten all about it. She hurried inside, gathering up her skirts to dash up the stairs. She had a plan to enact, and there wasn't much time.

CHAPTER VI

:Pretty,: Nadi crowed.

Nadi was correct. The front of Lord Powles's manor boasted the symmetry that was so important in beautiful houses, and once inside, the oval-shaped entry hall rose to the second story where an enormous, dazzling chandelier gave warm light to the statue standing in the center of the room. Beatrice and Nadi gazed at a marble-carved maiden with one arm raised, her fingers folded elegantly in the sign that the initiated recognized as a welcome and promise of hospitality.

:She's beautiful,: Nadi sighed. :Who turned her to stone?:

:No one did,: Beatrice thought. :She's a sculpture.:

:Touch her.:

:I can't. That's rude.:

:Stupid rules,: Nadi pouted. :Touch her.:

:That wasn't our bargain.: Beatrice smiled at the footman who guided her into a drawing room, leaving the marble maiden behind. She swayed in a polite greeting to the company gathered there—elders, mostly.

Ysbeta Lavan lounged in deep blue and lace, her arms bare to the elbow according to the etiquette of card playing. She cradled a cup of soft pink punch in one hand, and her attention diverted from Lord Powles to focus on Beatrice. "Here she is."

"Miss Clayborn! What excellent timing. A table's about to open," Lord Powles said. "As I'm sure you've already gathered, Ianthe won the chase around the oblong, and therefore is your partner tonight."

Ianthe bowed. Beatrice steadied her breath. She was going to partner him at cards, and be expected to converse, and every time she looked at him, she would remember how she had sneered at his pride in his culture's permissiveness toward sorceresses and declared it insufficient.

This was going to be a terribly awkward evening. She smiled at him and died inside at the hot flush that raced up her cheeks. "Congratulations, Mr. Lavan."

"The honor is mine." Ianthe was by her side in a breath, smelling deliciously of sweetwood and spring blossoms. "Do you play cards often?"

"With family, on rainy days. For buttons."

Ianthe nodded as if he expected no less. "A button a point?"

"Yes."

"Excellent! It's the same thing here. Though we're not playing for buttons," Ianthe laughed. "The stake is ten crowns a point."

Beatrice tried not to choke. Father had given her fifty crowns. She could lose that in a single slate—she could lose that in a single hand. "Oh. I only brought—"

"Don't worry," Ianthe said. "We don't actually put cash on the table. That's for card hells. We use chits and pay the cost the next day. Would you like some punch?"

:Yes!: cried Nadi. :And two more.:

"Thank you. Punch would be lovely," Beatrice said.

She sipped, as a lady should, and the nectar blended with the scent of elderflower and clean-distilled herbal gin with a quinine tinge. It was cold and refreshing, and Beatrice caught a small pebble of ice between her teeth.

:You need to drink three,: Nadi said. :That's the bargain. You didn't say pretty Ianthe would be here. Kiss him again.:

Nadi would have forced the matter too, if Beatrice had

let it. :Three cups of punch,: she reminded Nadi. :The sight of the sunrise. The beach on bare feet. That is our bargain.:

Lord Powles offered his arm to Ysbeta and led the way into a spacious ballroom, nearly as large as the assembly hall. Elders gathered on one side of the room, and young people the other. The young men had shed their jackets and wore their sleeves rolled to the elbows, their hands scrupulously above the table, laying down cards to be collected as tricks. Conversation hummed as players kept up chatter that carefully skirted around the subjects forbidden at cards. One table stood empty, and Beatrice passed by players with stacks of paper chits beside their punch cups. Every one of those chits represented at least ten crowns.

Oh, Heaven. How was she going to escape the tables unscathed?

Ianthe helped her seat herself. Ysbeta, on her left hand, leaned over to murmur, "I am so sorry about this," as Ianthe and Lord Powles took their seats. "You're in for a drubbing."

Beatrice glanced at her, but Ysbeta was already shuffling the cards, the waxed cardboard riffling musically. She held out the pack to her brother.

"Cut."

Inside, Nadi shivered. Beatrice's skin went cool and shuddering as the spirit's magic washed over her.

"Eager, are we?" Ianthe cut the cards and soon Beatrice held her hand, astonished at the painted faces of court cards filling her hand. She counted a singleton rose. What was honors?

"Sheldon's West," Ianthe announced as Bard lit a scented cheroot. Beatrice reckoned. Honors suit was staves, and Beatrice held ace, queen, and four pips, with offsuit court cards. She could slaughter the table with this hand.

She arranged her hand and smiled at Ysbeta. "I adore that color. You are beautiful in it."

Powles led with the rose king. Oh, poor Sheldon. She discarded her seven and glanced at Ianthe, who ignored the card to smile at Beatrice.

"It's a secret formula," he said. "People have attempted to infiltrate our dyers to learn the secret of its vividness."

:It's magic,: Nadi said. :I can smell it.:

:Alchemy?:

:Yes.:

Ianthe wore that same deep, clear blue, hand-dotted with golden thread and lavished at the button-fronts with golden scrolls.

"I think the color would be lovely on you, Beatrice," Ysbeta said.

"Indeed," Ianthe agreed, as he aced the trick and laid the captured cards facedown at his elbow. "I would like to see you in it."

With that remarkable statement, Ianthe led with the king of staves.

:He likes you.:

He did. He still did, even after she'd unleashed her polemic. He ought to have been icily polite at best, but he watched her with a half-hidden smile and it widened every time their eyes met. They met now, and Ianthe's eyes sparkled like starlight on night-dark water. It made her skin glow with warmth.

Beatrice smiled and dropped her lowest honor on the trick. "I think it might be a difficult shade. Is the technique alchemical?"

Ysbeta smiled and laid a finger on her lips. "Secret."

"I enjoyed alchemy," Bard said. "It was the best course at school. It contains wonders that match any summoning. I shouldn't let Gadaran hear me say that."

Ysbeta glanced at the cards, and carefully bit her lip. Beatrice and Ianthe racked four points on their victory. Split between them, Beatrice had won twenty crowns on the first hand.

"Who is Gadaran?" Ysbeta asked.

"A lesser spirit of knowledge, befitting a minister's son," Bard said through a cloud of smoke. "I was the studious one. Unlike your brother, whose best marks are on the hazards field. But if they gave out evaluations for pranks, Ianthe would be a legend."

A bouquet of rose suit cards greeted Beatrice on her next hand. She arranged them and asked, "You were a prankster?"

"He'd set the whole class on their heels," Bard said. "Ianthe once made everyone's pens dance in the air at final examinations, and then he scrambled them up so no original owner had his pen."

"That sounds like a benign prank," Ysbeta said, frowning as Beatrice led with the ace of swords.

"It wasn't so benign for the people who had magically engraved their pens with answers to the test." Ianthe caught her intention, and led swords again, clearing honors cards out of play. "Someone I didn't like was cheating, and I enjoy justice."

Beatrice picked up her punch cup. "What happened to him?"

"He failed the test," Ianthe said. "A rightful fate for cheating. And just general unpleasantness."

Beatrice nodded, smiled, and played on, her jaw and throat tight.

They won another twenty crowns. And another fifteen, then ten, and finally a server brought a second cup of punch, which Nadi drank too quickly. They spoke of music, of the upcoming performance of *The Count of Always and Never*, of the Blossom Ride and basket auction—

"You'll join Ianthe and me for the luncheon, won't you, Miss Clayborn? We're claiming places next to each other," Lord Powles asked, and simple as that, she had gained admittance to the highest collection of Bendleton society.

"I would be honored," Beatrice replied, and finessed the trick with a nine. "But my basket would have to be fairly won."

"It would indeed," Ianthe said, "and I shall win it, if it pleases you."

She shouldn't encourage him. But she nodded, dropping her last card on the table. "It would be a pleasure to share luncheon with you."

She and Ianthe had won the game again, and she tried not to smile too widely as Lord Powles jotted down another chit.

Ysbeta glanced at her for an instant too long on the next hand, eyeing Beatrice's second cup of punch and the small pile of chits she'd gathered. She and Ianthe had only lost twice, and Beatrice had lost tally of how many crowns she had won in this game at two hundred and ninety. :Nadi, that's enough for now. Ysbeta suspects.:

:But it's fun,: Nadi said, shimmering inside her head. :Isn't it fun?:

Oh, gambling was wonderful. She had never won like this, not even when the prize was a box full of buttons. Wait until she showed Father. He'd be so surprised to learn that she had won so much. Why, she could recoup every coin Father had spent on her bargaining season! She and Nadi could take it right out of their pockets.

:Yes,: Nadi said, wiggling in bliss. :You need Nadi. We can win and win and win.:

Her hand shot out and plucked up the cup of punch— :Nadi!:

:You said three.:

Her head tilted back, draining it to the dregs. It was lovely. Sweet, and complicated, and it made her soft and laughing inside. Elderflower punch was marvelous. She scooped up her cards and set the cup down in its saucer, faceup, signaling a refill.

:Not so fast,: Beatrice said. :There's only one left for the whole night.:

"Miss Clayborn," Ysbeta said. "Would you step out into the gardens with me? I suddenly feel unwell, and the air would be restorative."

"But we just dealt—" Beatrice set her suite of kings down. "I mean, of course I will, Miss Lavan. The air, absolutely. You need air. As do I. Yes!" she giggled. "The air, indeed! Most necessary, is it not?"

"Most necessary," Ysbeta repeated.

Beatrice scooped up her chits and thrust them into her pocket. Ysbeta offered her arm and led the way to the outdoors. But Ysbeta said she wasn't feeling well—shouldn't Beatrice be the one guiding her? It was absurd!

She laughed, a giddy, bubbling laugh that caught the attention of other card players. Ysbeta's pace quickened, and soon they were in the cool caress of the ocean air, scented by sea wrack and primrose. Beatrice heaved in a great breath, and Nadi laughed in delight.

Ysbeta kept moving—down the wide stone stairs of the terrace to the shell-paved garden path, glowing white under the moonlight, the fractured shards crunching under their satin shoes. She hauled Beatrice along exactly the way Harriet would, to rush her to this sight or that, and Beatrice halted, stopping Ysbeta's progress with a lurch.

"Don't tug me about," Beatrice said. "I don't like it."

"Don't speak to me of what you do and do not like," Ysbeta's harsh whisper rose above the susurration of the boughs overhead. "Do you have any idea what could happen to you if you're caught cheating?"

Beatrice gasped. "Miss Lavan! How could you—"

"You're hosting right now," Ysbeta said, shaking Beatrice's arm. "Don't pretend you're not. I am good at Honors Taken. No one is as good as you have been at the table unless they're cheating by sleight-of-hand dealing or magic. You did, didn't you? What did you bargain for luck at the cards?"

"I—" Beatrice began, but Ysbeta shook her again, and it made her head spin. "Don't!"

"Why did you do it?" Ysbeta let go of Beatrice's wrist, choosing instead to stroke her arm. "You know what could happen—why did you risk it?"

This sudden tenderness was too much. Beatrice quivered. A ball of thorns caught in her throat. Tears welled in her eyes and Ysbeta made soothing, shushing noises, stroking her arm from elbow to shoulder.

Beatrice shook, trying to hold it all in—for if she didn't, she would scream at the sky. She would kick the primroses until they were dead. She would want something to break, to tear, to strike.

"You can tell me," Ysbeta whispered. "You have my secret. Let me have yours."

It burst, a great dam broken by a sob.

"Father has spent everything on this bargaining season," Beatrice confessed. "Everything! He mortgaged our home. He dipped into his principal! If I came home with even more debts—"

"Debts?" Ysbeta asked. "How much debt?"

She shouldn't say. But Ysbeta wouldn't tell, would she? "I don't know exactly how much. But it's gotten worse these past few months."

Ysbeta's eyes went sharp. "Did he invest in the orchid expedition a few months ago?"

Beatrice's eyes watered. She clenched her fists. "He told us not to worry. He said there was no need to worry. He said—"

"He lost everything trying to profit on fashion." Ysbeta caught her up in her arms, laying Beatrice's head on her shoulder. "And now it's up to you, isn't it. You need a husband who will make up for the blow to the Clayborn fortunes."

No she didn't. No she didn't! She needed to ally with a greater spirit. She needed to pass the ordeal, become a mage, and then everything would be all right, in the end—

But Beatrice couldn't stop crying, and Ysbeta wouldn't stop stroking her hair.

Footsteps crunched on the shell-paved path. "Ysbeta? Ysbeta, it's all right. I know what happened," Ianthe said. "Miss Clayborn, I am so, so sorry. Hold still."

Beatrice gulped down a sob and gazed at Ianthe, who wore a look of deep worry on his face. Oh, she must look awful. Red and blotchy and—

She gasped as he laid his hand directly on the swell of her breasts, thrust half out of her bodice thanks to Clara's tight hand on her stays. But his touch bored inside her somehow, sinking underneath skin and flesh to wrap around Nadi.

:No! No! Beatrice, help! Help Nadi! Help!:

Her whole body shook as Nadi tried to flee from Ianthe's touch, still screaming. "What are you—"

"Quiet," Ianthe said, and he clenched his hand in a fist, flinging it backward.

Nadi's scream echoed inside her as Ianthe tore it away.

"There," he said. "Are you all right?"

Was she all right? He'd just caught her cheating. He had proof she had been practicing advanced summoning, but Ianthe gripped her shoulders and gazed at her with deep worry and concern. He should be dragging her before the host, and then to her father—why wasn't her world ending?

Ianthe peered into her eyes. "Miss Clayborn, listen to me. That strange feeling that came over you, as if your skin was over-full and you weren't quite in control of what you did—that was a spirit. You were possessed. I am so sorry—but it's all right. No one else caught on; you're safe."

She was what? "What did you do?"

"I banished it. I am so sorry, Miss Clayborn. That should never have happened to you."

Heaven, her wits had completely deserted her. She turned her gaze to Ysbeta, who gave her a look that showed the whites all around her midnight eyes.

"So that's what it was," Ysbeta said, composing her features. "I thought you had been behaving strangely, drinking all that punch . . . but is it true, Ianthe? Someone cast a spirit into her?"

That wasn't true at all, but Ysbeta leapt onto Ianthe's explanation without a murmur.

"That's exactly what happened." Ianthe's mouth was a grim line. "Someone wanted to disgrace Miss Clayborn to get the competition out of the way."

"What?"

Beatrice and Ysbeta said the word in the same instant, and Ianthe winced.

"I shouldn't tell tales," Ianthe said. "But I am the subject of a rather aggressive competition."

"Oh no," Ysbeta said, perfectly guileless.

"Indeed," Ianthe replied. "Eliza Robicheaux and Danielle Maisonette have each declared that they would be the one to attract my interest."

"How irritating it must be," Ysbeta murmured, "to have people decide that you are a prize for the taking, without even bothering to ask your opinion."

"What is that—oh," Ianthe said. "I owe you an apology, Miss Clayborn. We didn't ask you if you cared to have your company wagered over. I had no idea how infuriating it was. I am sorry."

Beatrice blinked. "I—thank you for your apology. I accept it. But what does this have to do with my possession?"

"I promise you I will explain, if my sister decides not to interrupt with her remarks," Ianthe said.

"Oh, please don't let me distract you, dear brother." Ysbeta was grinning now, and Beatrice looked away. Was this funny? Was she a joke?

"I will attempt to keep it brief," Ianthe said. "I have encountered each of the ladies a number of times this week—by chance, they claimed."

"Wait," Ysbeta said. "That woman with the overdone hat? The one from the café? That's Danielle Maisonette?"

Ianthe sighed. "Ysy."

"Sorry. Go on."

He slid his gaze off to the side, his shoulders rising as the tale unfolded. "Miss Maisonette's brother is here. I believe he waited until you had lowered your protection from the spirits by imbibing. The sensation of the spirit taking residence would have felt like a symptom of the drink. Then he could simply watch while the spirit gained control and disgraced you before the entire party. You would have been the talk of Bendleton."

It was a dastardly plan, if it had been true. Beatrice would have been completely shamed, her prospects vanished entirely. Her family would have gone home to the mortgaged Riverstone in defeat, and Father would find that his contacts and opportunities had vanished in the face of scandal. Ianthe was angry on her behalf—and Beatrice's neck flushed as Ianthe explained it all as if she were an innocent victim.

Perhaps he thought her too honorable to summon a luck spirit and cheat at cards. Perhaps he thought her too ignorant. Beatrice trembled. Why couldn't she be cunning? Why couldn't she be underhanded?

She was cunning. She was underhanded. And she was going

to save her own skin, and let Ianthe believe what he would.

Beatrice widened her eyes. "Someone would do that? How awful."

"But it couldn't have been Robicheaux, of course," Ysbeta put in. "He's mundane."

"I can't accuse either of them, for Beatrice's sake," Ianthe said, "but I have no reason to welcome Maisonette's company, and I will not."

"I won't either," Ysbeta said. "That hat was dreadful."

"I'm afraid our evening is over," Ianthe said. "But I would be honored to walk you home, if you don't mind the distance?"

"The distance is not so great," Beatrice said. "Ysbeta, you don't mind a walk?"

"It isn't even a mile," Ysbeta said. "And I would love to escape this place. Let us withdraw."

They skirted the house and Ysbeta marched past them at a swift pace. Beatrice hurried her steps to keep up, but Ianthe caught her arm and gently slowed her to the sedate stroll that invited conversation.

"But—"

"She's giving us a little privacy," Ianthe said. "Sometimes my sister is considerate. But now we shall lay our cards on the table."

Beatrice's heart kicked in her chest. "What do you mean?"

"That story about Danton putting a spirit in you is rubbish. He did no such thing. You are dabbling with High Magic."

A chill broke out over Beatrice's skin. "And you're going to report it."

"Properly speaking, I should," Ianthe said. "If it were not for you explaining your position earlier this afternoon, I probably would have without speaking to you. But now—"

"You don't know what you're going to do."

"I don't know whether to ask you how you accomplished it or tell your father, for your own good. What you are doing is dangerous," Ianthe said. "Even in the safety and supervision of the chapterhouse, the act of conjuration is terribly risky. And you're doing it alone. You must not pursue the mysteries without a guide."

"Very well," Beatrice said. "What chapterhouse will call me brother, Mr. Lavan? Which one? I will present myself immediately."

"You know very well that none of them will," Ianthe said. "But if Bard had caught you instead of me, you'd be in deep trouble."

"I'd be headed home in disgrace," Beatrice said. "Father would have to put a warding collar on me before I was married. The scandal would seriously diminish my prospects. I know."

"Then why did you do it?"

"What else could I have done? The stakes were ten crowns a point! I had fifty in my pocket. My family cannot bear the expense of such amusements."

"You could have told me," Ianthe said. "I would have assumed your debt."

"How was I to know that I could divulge the secret of my family's financial straits to you?"

Ianthe waggled his head, conceding the point. "After our conversation this afternoon, I want you to be able to tell me any secret you like. If you need help, I will help you. We're friends, after all. Aren't we?"

"Will you help me learn more High Magic?" Beatrice asked.

Ianthe winced. "Even if it wasn't utterly reckless and ill-advised, I could not. I don't have enough experience to protect you. And I don't think I have the nerve to do what must be done, if you faced a catastrophic failure."

Beatrice shivered. "What would be considered catastrophic?"

"When you bargain, you have to set clear terms. What did you bargain for luck at the cards?"

"Three cups of punch. The sight of the sunrise. The beach on bare feet."

Ianthe looked surprised. "That's a good bargain. A very good bargain."

"And since you exorcised me, I don't even have to pay it."

"I had to do it," Ianthe said. "Every second brought you closer to being caught."

"I know you were focused on my safety," Beatrice said.

"And I know you aren't going to stop using magic just because I said it was dangerous," Ianthe said. "You conjured a minor spirit of luck?"

"Lesser."

"And you successfully bargained something that simple," Ianthe said. "I wish there was some way to keep you safe. I know you're going to do this, no matter what I say."

"You could report me," Beatrice said. "You didn't have to discuss this with me at all."

"I have no wish to disgrace your family. I don't want you collared until you die. I would be a hypocrite if I doomed you to those things while claiming a wish to protect you."

"You're going to let me go."

"I must," Ianthe said. "But please. Don't step any further on the path of the mysteries. When an initiate of the rose trains further, his sponsor isn't only there to instruct and advise."

"What else is he there for?"

"If the worst happens," Ianthe says, "your mentor has to contain the damage whatever the cost—even if that cost is your own life."

Beatrice shivered. "Does that happen often?"

"The training is in place to protect against it," Ianthe

says. "Novices and initiates are protected and supervised. You are not."

Beatrice could lose herself to Nadi, he meant. A spirit would be happy to don a mage's body, if it meant it could run loose and do what it pleased. "Will you tell me how to protect myself?"

Ianthe's brow wrinkled. "I should not. But if I don't, won't I be responsible for your misfortune?"

"A troublesome dilemma. I would prefer that you help me, of course."

"Let me go to the chapterhouse and do some research. Then I can explain more if you'll consent to an outing with me. I was going to take Ysbeta to Pigment Street, so she could invest in some art. She's bound to give us a private moment, and we can talk then."

"I have never seen Pigment Street."

"Then come with us. I was planning to take her the day after tomorrow. I understand you two will practice at hazards tomorrow?"

"Yes. We're going to be partners at the tournament."

"If I make it back from Meryton in time, I would be honored to take you home," Ianthe said. "I believe I will need the benefit of your insight."

"What will you do in Meryton that leads you to want my insight? It's not that poor girl with the spiritborn child, is it?"

"It's Ysbeta." Ianthe nodded at the figure of his sister, walking just out of earshot. "I need a solicitor. I must see if there is a way to protect Ysbeta's wealth from her future husband, and we need a Church-trained lawyer for this, not just a business solicitor. Bard is my friend, but he's a Chaslander through and through. If we don't protect Ysbeta's fortune, he'll think nothing of taking it for himself."

"Ysbeta is to marry Lord Powles, then?"

"That's what Mother wants," Ianthe said. "I tried to

appeal to her. She didn't budge."

Beatrice nodded and held her tongue. Ianthe had been terribly understanding of her pursuit of magic, but she didn't trust that he would take the news of his sister's goals as easily. "I would be happy to offer whatever insight I can."

"Then you will allow me to take you home tomorrow?"

"I look forward to it."

"And you'll come with us to Pigment Street the day after?"

Beatrice's heart was beating hard enough that it battered against her stays. He knew. He knew she was practicing magic and was courting her anyway. She had waded in the waters of low tide, only to find that the waves had closed in around her, and the shore was so very far away.

Would it be so bad if she married Ianthe Lavan? He had a way of making her breathless when he wasn't striving so hard to understand her. He would let her explore magic, and wasn't that better than nothing?

Ianthe's expression faded into dismay, and Beatrice's breath clenched in her chest. It hurt. It hurt to hurt him. He glanced down at the promenade under their feet. "If you already have an engagement, I—"

"No, I don't," Beatrice said, the words rushing out of her. "I also enjoy art."

The sun rose on his renewed smile. "Thank you," Ianthe said. "I am honored by your acceptance."

They walked to the stone steps leading to Beatrice's front door, and Ianthe bent over her hand, pressing her palm to his lips.

"Sleep well, Miss Clayborn," Ianthe said. "I'll see you tomorrow."

"Thank you. Good night, Mr. Lavan. Good night, Ysbeta. Have a safe journey."

They waited until the footman let her inside and closed the door.

CHAPTER VII

Clara bounded to her feet as Beatrice slipped into her bedchamber, clasping her hands over the waistline of her apron. "You're home earlier than I expected."

"I had played enough cards for one night." Beatrice stuffed her hand in her pocket and chits slid out from between her fingers, fluttering to the heartwood floor and landing at her feet.

"Oh," Beatrice said. "I won quite a lot, I think."

"Miss Beatrice! Your maquillage is ruined—were you crying?"

"I— How bad is it?"

"You have kohl all around your eyes, it's streaked down your face—"

"Ianthe Lavan walked me home." Beatrice raised her hands to her cheeks, and chits slid out of her grasp.

"He didn't say a word about it. I'm a fright."

"Here, give them to me." Clara set the chits down on Beatrice's writing desk. Beatrice dug into her pockets and produced another dozen or so, and Clara plucked those from her hands before bending down to pick up the rest.

"I won hundreds of crowns, Clara. Father only gave me fifty. Fifty! What percentage of a return do you think he's reaped from his investment?"

"Quite a healthy one, Miss Beatrice."

Beatrice giggled. "Valdanas Island has gambling houses. I could go there and grow rich. Solve all of our problems."

"I think you may have difficulties with that, Miss Beatrice."

"Perhaps so. Ah!" Beatrice heaved a great sigh as the stomacher came free, and Clara stripped the mantua off her shoulders. "Freedom is at hand!"

Clara unlaced Beatrice's stays and rubbed arnica cream on the angry red lines etched into Beatrice's skin, soothing the ache of stiff steel flats that forced her form into a fashionable shape. "No bruises this time. And you left early after winning a fortune at cards," Clara said. "You walked home with Ianthe?"

"Yes," Beatrice said. "Ianthe and Ysbeta Lavan were my escort."

"Harriet's quite excited about your acquaintance with the Lavans."

"She'll be beside herself in the morning," Beatrice said.

Clara took her hair down, massaged rosehip oil over Beatrice's face to lift her maquillage, then dressed her in a nightgown. "I'll wake you at ten," Clara said. "Do you have plans for the day?"

"Hazards practice with Ysbeta. But Ianthe and Ysbeta have invited me to Pigment Street for the next day," Beatrice said.

"Excellent news, Miss Beatrice. I'll leave you to your rest. Good night."

Clara left, and Beatrice listened to her footsteps cross the short distance from Beatrice's bedroom to the narrow, windowless space where Clara slept. She would get a decent night's sleep. No one had expected Beatrice to come in until the sky was turning blue with the coming dawn, or even with the sunrise.

She should have been out there.

Beatrice waited, listening with every ounce of her attention until she heard Clara's snores, and then tiptoed out of her room on bare, silent feet. Down the stairs, down to the first floor, where she held her breath as she pushed open the terrace door and stepped onto the cool slate tiles of the townhome's rear garden.

She scurried along the path, wincing at the poke of the pebbles on her bare soles. She hurried to the gap in the hedge and more stairs. Beatrice's feet sank into cool, dry sand. A silvery stick lay in the path. Beatrice picked it up and made a dash for the shore, stopping at the place where the damp sand lay even and flat.

Beatrice's spine tingled, as if she were being watched. She turned a slow circle, searching for prying eyes, but there was no one out on the shore. The windows were closed to the sight of her in the moonlight. No one was looking.

She planted the stick in the sand and dragged it along as she turned in a circle. She marked each sigil with the stick, vibrating the correct tone just so. The tide crawled closer. She had to hurry. She must not make an error. The sea air thickened, and the suggestion of silver and match-flame blue glowed in the marks she had drawn.

"Nadi, spirit of chance, I know you," Beatrice whispered. "We struck a bargain together. I owe you the sand under your feet, the play of surf around your ankles, the sunrise. Come and take what is owed to you, Nadi. Come collect what you bargained for."

The spirit hovered just outside the circle, vibrating and tense. :Why should Nadi trust you?:

"Because I'm sorry. Ianthe thought he was helping me."

:And now you dare to bargain with Nadi again?:

"No," Beatrice said. "I'm keeping my promise to you. I owe you the sight of the sunrise. I don't want anything but to deal with you fairly."

The spirit sprang upward, stiff as a bolt. :You ask for Nadi, and you want nothing?:

"Nothing," Beatrice said. "I want to give this to you."

The spirit wavered, swaying with indecision.

Beatrice stretched out her hand. "I owe you this."

:No,: Nadi said. :You're giving it.:

Nadi drew closer, touching Beatrice's fingertips. The spirit slipped under her skin, filling her senses, and sighed.

:I want to run,: Nadi said. :Let's run, Beatrice.:

Beatrice gathered up her hem and kicked sand over the summoning circle. The tide crawled up the shore as she sprinted down the flat, damp beach and washed her circle away.

It was too bright. Daylight poured through the windows, and Beatrice groaned, rolled over, and buried her head under a pillow. Her legs were stiff as sundried leather. Nadi had delighted in running, and dancing, and wading into the cold water. They watched the sky change color from blue to rose and spikes of gold, sending sparks of dawn across the waves.

:So beautiful,: Nadi had sighed, and then slipped out of her body as the sun rose. Beatrice had snuck back inside without anyone noticing, but now she was paying the price of magic, and drink, and staying up too late.

"Beatrice, I let you sleep until mid-morning. Breakfast is already served," Clara said. "Come now, sit up."

Beatrice groaned. "I have a headache."

"Again?" Clara asked. "Did you drink too much?"

"Yes. Can't I just have a few more minutes?"

"I'm afraid not. Up you get."

"Beatrice!" Harriet burst into the room with the force of a tornado. "You're not up yet? I've already eaten breakfast, slugabed!"

"She's having a little trouble moving this morning." Clara peeled the bedlinens away. "Sit on the edge of the bed."

Beatrice slid her legs over the edge and sat. "Better."

Harriet pointed at her toes. "Beatrice! Your feet, they're filthy!"

Specks of sand spattered over her insteps and grimed the gap between her toes. She looked back at the streaks of sand staining her bedsheets. But she had scraped the sand away when she returned to the house, hadn't she?

Clara stood straight up. "Those feet aren't getting anywhere near your bath. Don't move."

She bustled out to fetch a basin, leaving Beatrice to her sister's beady stare.

"I couldn't sleep," Beatrice said. "I went down to the beach."

"In the middle of the night?" Harriet's face was pale with shock. "In your nightgown? What if someone saw you?"

"I needed fresh air." It was the worst excuse. Ladies did not run about on the beach in the moonlight. But she had owed Nadi. She would have had to do it regardless. "There was smoking permitted at the card party, and my lungs felt horrid."

"Did your card partner smoke?"

"No, thank Heaven. But Lord Powles does."

"Ugh," Harriet rubbed at her nose, as if her own senses had been offended. "You should have stayed on the terrace, though. Wait. You played cards with Lord Powles?"

"My table was the Lavans and Lord Powles himself."

Harriet's face shone. "Ianthe won the right to partner you? Was he good? Did you lose terribly?"

"I did not lose," Beatrice said.

"How much did you win?" Harriet stepped aside for Clara, who set a basin at Beatrice's feet. The water was barely warm but scented with roses.

Beatrice sighed and let her feet soak. "I don't know."

"What do you mean, you don't know?"

"I didn't count. It's rude to count your winnings at the table."

"You didn't keep a tally? Where are your chits?"

"On the writing desk," Clara said.

Harriet's eyes popped when she saw the pile. She scooped up a handful, sorting them by Lord Powles's mark and Ysbeta Lavan's, her expression completely aghast. "Beatrice! How did you—"

She backed away from the neat, orderly piles of chits, completely silent. She spun on one foot and stormed out of the room, slamming the door behind her.

"Harriet?" Beatrice lifted her feet from the water, but Clara grabbed both ankles and forced them back into the basin.

"You'll track mud everywhere."

"But Harriet—"

"You weren't as excitable as your younger sister, but you had your moods. Harriet's due in the next few days. She's bound to be touchy. Let her pout."

"But—" Clara didn't understand. Harriet had guessed how Beatrice had come into her winnings, and she could be racing to Father's side right now, telling him everything! She had to intercept Harriet. She had to convince her sister to keep silent, and Clara was worried about her feet?

"She's jealous, Miss Beatrice," Clara said, massaging the sand out from between Beatrice's toes. "You have everything she wants right now. She'll get her turn, but this isn't easy for her. She has dreams and fancies of what bargaining season is like—and here you are, being invited to private parties, just like the books. But sneaking down to the beach and getting sand all over your feet doesn't fit her image. She's fretting about you making a mistake, is all."

That was not all. But Clara had a point. "I should still talk to her."

"Naturally," Clara said. "After your bath."

Clara dried Beatrice's feet and herded her to the bathing room, where Beatrice floated in the square, tiled bath and tried to relax. When cool air from the hallway billowed over her face, she pushed herself to the edge and faced Harriet's ferocious, stormy expression.

"How could you?" Harriet's whisper echoed off the tile. "What if you were caught?"

"What was I supposed to do?" Beatrice hissed back. "Father gave me fifty crowns for the night. All he could spare, and the stakes were ten crowns a point. If I hadn't done it, do you know how much debt I would have brought home?"

"You won four hundred crowns, Beatrice! Four hundred!"

"It wasn't that impressive a sum. They're rich, Harriet. So rich I can't really understand the scope of it."

"And no one noticed?"

Beatrice studied the tiled edge of the bath. "Not exactly."

Harriet's voice rose. "What?"

"Keep your voice down," Beatrice said. "Ianthe thought someone had imposed a spirit on me to destroy my reputation. I didn't correct him."

"He caught you," Harriet breathed. "Only Heaven's grace saved you, don't you see? You can't do this again. If anyone finds out—"

"I can't promise that," Beatrice said. "Bargaining season's nowhere near over. I might—"

"You must," Harriet said. "It's always going to seem like a necessity. It's always going to seem like the right idea, but if I thought Father wouldn't overreact, I'd—"

Beatrice raised herself out of the water with a great splash. "Don't tell him."

"I won't," Harriet said. "But this is dangerous. Do you know why I never learned?"

She didn't. Harriet had never wanted to speak of higher magic, and Beatrice had never thought Harriet would keep quiet about any ambition she might have. "No one offered to teach you the secret?"

"Do you remember the Charleses?"

Beatrice nodded. They were cousins of Father's, and they had come to Riverstone to take the country air last summer. There had been two boys, who monopolized their riding horses, and a girl, too young for Beatrice's company but only a little younger than Harriet. They had run together for the whole visit, whispering to each other where Beatrice had to pretend not to see.

"Dorothy Charles taught me how to conjure a minor spirit," Harriet said. "Just a little one, to ask if it would rain on race day. We smuggled fruit for an offering, and she let me say the words to make the spirit come."

Beatrice stayed still and quiet. Harriet shivered. "I'll never do it again."

"Did it turn out badly?"

"No. It worked perfectly. And the feeling of that magic, of the way you can hear the tiniest sound and every smell is a fascinating perfume and your vision sharpens and your skin tingles with the slightest breath of wind—it was wonderful," Harriet whispered. "I want to do it again. And again. Until I would be exactly where you are right now, Beatrice. Trying to take a bite of what you cannot eat."

Harriet was right. It was wonderful. Sprinting down the beach with Nadi, she'd run faster than she ever had in her life. She'd leapt high in the air, spun and danced with pure abandon. Freed from having to restrain Nadi's impulses so she could keep up the appearance of a lady, she'd felt the grace and invincible will of the spirit, and for that hour before the sun rose and completed their bargain, all of it had been hers. It ought to be hers regardless. But no one else understood. No one else thought that magic belonged to women.

Ysbeta did. Ysbeta understood. They had a bargain, and Beatrice needed to make good on her end. She would teach

Ysbeta all the magic she knew. She would gain the use of Ysbeta's grimoires. Together, they would find their freedom from the warding collar and the gray future they were expected to accept as their only choice.

"I won't use magic unless I have to," Beatrice said. "I promise."

Harriet watched her, shaking her head slowly. "I know you believe what you're saying."

The door swung open, and Clara entered. "Miss Harriet."

"I'm going," Harriet said. She slid off the stool and headed for the bathing room door. "You have to do something about those chits, Beatrice."

Beatrice opened her mouth to answer, but Harriet had already left.

Beatrice couldn't look away from that pile of chits while Clara dressed her. Today's choice for hazards practice was a block-printed peach cotton walking suit, and Clara pinned the matching cartwheel hat atop Beatrice's carefully dressed hair so it shaded her eyes. She had to give those chits to Father. Father would use them to collect Lord Powles's and Ysbeta Lavan's debts, and Father would find a way to turn the meeting into a connection. Wouldn't he? Oh, why did she allow Nadi to win so much? Why didn't she think?

"Don't bite your lip like that, Beatrice. You'll mar your rouge," Clara said.

Beatrice released her lower lip from worrying teeth. "Sorry. Am I ready?"

"You are a picture," Clara said.

"Beatrice!" Harriet's shout carried up the stairs. "There's a message for you! I think it's an invitation!"

"I'm coming," Beatrice said. "One moment."

Beatrice grabbed the chits and hurried out before she could change her mind, descending one flight of stairs to the foyer, where Harriet clutched a square, hand-folded envelope in one hand, her teeth bared in a face-splitting grin.

"It's from Ellis Robicheaux! Open it, oh, open it! It has to be for tonight's party, it has to be!"

"How do you know there's a party tonight?" Beatrice asked. She slid her thumb under the monogrammed seal and broke it, catching the crumbled chunks of wax in her hand.

"Mother and I heard about it when we took lunch at the Swan. Hurry," Harriet urged.

Beatrice looked heavenward before she could stop herself, but she unfolded the paper to find an embossed invitation addressed to her family, inviting them to a dance honoring the fifteenth birthday of Miss Julia Robicheaux at ten in the evening.

"We must go!" Harriet said. "It's late notice but you have to attend this ball."

"And we have to match," Beatrice said. "What do you think, the lilac?"

"That's our best matching set. Should we wear it so early? Mother!" Harriet shouted. "Mother, please come out!"

A door upstairs clicked open, and Mother stopped at the top of the stairs. "What is it?"

Harriet gazed up the stairs, her face shining with joy. "We're invited to the Robicheaux ball tonight! Beatrice and I are wearing the lilac. What gown will you wear, Mother?"

"Gown? But your father—"

"What in Heaven are you ladies chattering about so loudly?" Father stood in the doorway of his library, where he spent his days poring over correspondence, half a dozen broadsheets, and his favorite pipe. Sweetly flavored smoke wafted into the foyer, and Beatrice suppressed a cough as it tickled her throat.

"Father, the most wonderful thing! Beatrice so impressed at the card party that she has an invitation to Julia Robicheaux's birthday ball tonight, and the whole family is invited! Julia's just my age, and befriending her would make an excellent connection—"

"Tonight!" Father said. "Impossible. We have a guest."

"A guest?" Beatrice replied.

"The inventor Udo Maasten has consented to have dinner with us tonight."

Tonight! What dreadful timing! Beatrice cast a look at her younger sister, who caught her eye before turning a pretty smile on Father. "But to turn down an invitation from Sir Gregory Robicheaux would be seen as a snub! Beatrice must attend this party."

"I invited Ser Maasten already," Father said. "Beatrice must attend this dinner. He's a little older than the fickle young men of your circle, my dear. He could be a grounding influence."

A little older, Father said. What did that mean? Was he thirty? Forty? One of the older gentlemen of wealth who brought their purses to Chasland for bargaining season, certainly. Beatrice tried to imagine marriage to a man around Father's age, and she swallowed before reaching for careful words. "The party doesn't begin until ten, so I can make time for both."

"Beatrice would have been invited earlier if she'd made a proper showing at the Assembly Dance," Harriet argued. "But she can't turn down her first invitation to a private ball! She'll be seen as too glum and shy to be a proper hostess for her husband if she doesn't go."

"She couldn't turn down the invitation to the card party, either," Father said.

"Speaking of that," Beatrice said, "here are my winnings from last night."

Father cocked his head, a frown creased deeply between his eyes. "Winnings?"

She produced the pouch with her original fifty-crown

stake, and a net bag containing the chits that tallied up her profit.

"What is this?" he asked, and outside the door, carriage bells rang. "Who is that?"

"That's my carriage. I'm on my way to visit Ysbeta Lavan, Father," Beatrice said. "And Ianthe will join us to play hazards when he returns from his business in Meryton."

"I have not yet met Ianthe Lavan," Father said, eyeing the bag of chits. "And thus far, he has not called on you, or extended any kind of invitation to you that would indicate his interest."

"He has asked me to join him and Ysbeta on a trip to Pigment Street tomorrow," Beatrice said. She stepped backward, once, twice. "I have to rush. They're waiting for me, I should—"

Father's gaze froze her in place. "How much did you win?"

She sighed and got it over with. "Three hundred and eighty crowns."

Father's reading lenses fell from his nose. "How?"

"The stakes were ten crowns a point."

"But you must have won almost every hand you played," Father said. "How did that happen?"

"Luck." A jagged little giggle spilled out of her mouth. It was true, after all.

"The Lavans and the Sheldons owe me half the money to finance our lease on the townhouse, due to luck? Beatrice."

"Chance put those cards in my hands, Father, nothing more." Beatrice said. "I really have to go, they're waiting—"

Father rubbed his face, smearing ink along his cheek. "And you're on a visit with Ianthe Lavan's sister."

"Yes. And I have to go—"

"But what about the party?" Harriet asked. "You haven't said if we may attend, and there will be a number of girls my age in attendance. I should take the opportunity to expand on my connections."

Father stood unmoved by this reasoning. "I can't uninvite Ser Maasten."

"I will go with the girls," Mother said. "And then you can stay with Ser Maasten. Her popularity should be understandable, in a season with only fourteen ingenues."

"That's right," Harriet agreed. "Why, if you tell him she couldn't refuse this other engagement, it will only help increase her appeal."

"And she is standing right here," Beatrice said.

"You may go to the ball tonight, after dinner with Ser Maasten," Father said with a sigh. He shook the bag of chits at her, still frowning. "We'll speak of this later."

Which could mean he would call her to the carpet, or that they would manage never to speak of it again. Beatrice bobbed her knees and fled across the foyer, scarcely pausing to allow the footman to open the door for her.

Ysbeta waited in a shade-filled nook with her self-waving fan and another wide shallow bowl heaped with colorful chilled fruit. She was dressed in a bright pink gown, her hair captured in a crystal-beaded net that glinted in the sunshine. The book lay on the table for anyone to see, but it was not the volume Beatrice wanted most. The maid who brought Beatrice out to join her left them alone before she could serve Beatrice some punch.

Beatrice could pour her own punch. But Ysbeta spoke as soon as she touched the handle.

"Why is summoning a greater spirit so important to you?"

Beatrice poured before she answered. "Because it's such a waste. You said it yourself. My strength in the power is notable. Why should I have that power locked away? Why can't I use it?"

"One may argue that you're acting out of a selfish pursuit of pleasure," Ysbera commented. "I seek to bring the knowledge of magic outside the chapterhouse's methods to the world, so that valuable techniques are not lost—a cause outside myself. But you have made no mention of similar aims."

"I enjoy using the power. I won't deny that. But it's a tool I can use to repair the fortunes of my family. I can give Harriet the opportunities I didn't have. Father can enjoy the comfort and the prominence he yearns for."

"And you will be the tragic thornback daughter," Ysbeta said. "You will never be recognized for your efforts."

Beatrice set down her glass of punch. "But I will be compensated by the freedom to make those efforts."

"Use of the power is reward enough for you. Are the higher magics really so exhilarating?"

"That and more," Beatrice said. "You'll see, when you're able to hold the four states of casting simultaneously."

"I want to do it now," Ysbeta declared. "Teach me something real. Not baby rhymes. A conjuration."

"Magic circle first. And we need somewhere to hide," Beatrice said.

"I know exactly where," Ysbeta said. "What do I need, besides the book?"

"Light," Beatrice said. "Chalk. Food from the kitchens. Spirits like sweet things, but anything will do."

"For the offering," Ysbeta said. She nudged a small valise with her toe. "I supposed we'd need a few things. This will do for the offering." She twisted a mound of fruit into a fine cotton napkin and stood up. "We're supposedly playing up to the house. That will give us an hour. Quintanis!"

Her voice carried across the lawn. A man looked up

from instructing a younger man on trimming a perfectly spherical hedge. “Yes, miss?”

“Miss Clayborn and I are playing hazards this afternoon and we do not wish to be disturbed. Please keep the staff from the back half of the grounds.”

The man, wearing the green neckerchief of a head gardener, nodded. “As you wish, miss.”

“That’s our privacy assured.” Ysbeta pushed her chair back with a loud metallic scrape. “Come on.”

Beatrice followed Ysbeta as she strode past the perfectly trimmed hedges and blooming spring tulips. She passed a freshly mowed ball court, the net between the sides swaying on its line, and the excellent hazards course where they had played just yesterday.

Beatrice sped her pace, finally coming abreast of Ysbeta. “Where are we going?”

“There was an older home here,” Ysbeta said. “Father had Trenton Waterstone design the new house but left the outbuildings alone. This is the old path to the sanctum.”

The path sloped gently downward, but Beatrice could see part of a domed roof nestled among the trees. Ysbeta picked up her feet and ran the last part of the path, and Beatrice panted, trying to get a good breath in her stays.

They looked upon the sanctum. The private little tower, probably five hundred years old, was formed of hand-cut stone laid by master stoneworkers. Moss and lichen flourished in the seams; creeping trumpeter vine snaked up the round walls. Ysbeta led them inside the space, with moss growing between the stone tiles on the floor, lit by shafts of light from the empty spaces that once held window glass. Beatrice caught her breath as Ysbeta set her packing case on the flagstones.

“We have no priest, and we walk the twisting path when seeking spiritual guidance rather than silent meditation in the darkness." Ysbeta said. "Our reverence for the Skyborn is different in Llanandras than it is here."

"But you kept the sanctum in place."

Ysbeta shrugged. "All praise to the Skyborn is valid. Everyone does it differently. Women are priests in Sanchi. Did you know that?"

"No."

Ysbeta picked up the case with a grunt. "They retreat to the mountains to live a life of spiritual contemplation from the age of twelve. When they descend from the mountain some decades later, they are fully trained mages, respected spiritual leaders, and childless."

"It sounds unreal. Why haven't I heard of them?"

Ysbeta shrugged. "What if Chaslander women decided they wanted to do that too? Haring up your mountains to cloister themselves. Do you think society would allow it?"

"You have a point."

"I wish I could go back and talk to them. It's a year's sailing, including the usual stops. If I could take my ship—"

"I hadn't thought of that," Beatrice said. "You have a ship. You own it. You're the captain of record. Doesn't that mean that you command it?"

"Yes. But it's only mine on paper," Ysbeta said. "I've never set foot on the *Pelican.*"

"Why?"

Ysbeta tilted her head, her lips stretched in a bitter smile. "Because I own it. Because I am the captain of record. By maritime law, if I'm standing on the deck of a ship I own and captain, my rule of the *Pelican* is absolute—but it's not really supposed to give me any power."

"But you could," Beatrice said. "Your ship is in harbor in Meryton right now. Why not just collect your crew and go?"

"I'd never see my family again," Ysbeta said. "Mother would never forgive me. Father would abide by Mother."

"He would abide by her?"

"She's the oldest child of three," Ysbeta said. "She rules her siblings absolutely. No one ever tried to stop her from taking charge. She had already made huge profits from the wealth she was allowed to control at sixteen. She used her money to buy her own treasure ship for the company. Mother is the heart of Lavan International Ventures, and everyone in Llanandras knows it."

Beatrice stared at Ysbeta. "I can't imagine that."

"Running a business?"

"Getting the recognition for it," Beatrice said. "I could probably help Father, if he'd let me. He has taught me enough that I can account for a business. That's not Father's problem, though."

"What is?"

"Father sees other people's success and it makes him jealous," Beatrice said. "He's knows it's because they already had more to stand on—but Riverstone, the farm where we live, that's Mother's bride-gift. Father was an account clerk, the son of the farmer who lived next door. They were in love, and Mother could have married a wealthy mage, but she had her heart set on him."

"Did her family object?"

"A little," Beatrice confessed. "They would probably help us now, but Father would die before he admitted he failed to grow a fortune. Mother won't tell her family—she's too loyal."

Ysbeta pressed her lips together, but she nodded, her eyes soft with sympathy. "Father would give Mother the moon, if he could build a tall enough ladder to take it out of the sky. Mother is used to ruling, and she's reaped incredible fortunes with Father's wealth. She's been in every fashionable home in Bendleton with Father, talking with the wives, and then talking to Father about what he should do or who they should visit with next. She's building a tapestry of connections, of opportunities, of future markets, all of it intended for Ianthe . . . and it all depends on me."

"On you marrying Bard Sheldon."

Ysbeta nodded, her arms clasped around her middle. "Yes. And with that thread couched into place, the rest will stitch itself."

"But if your family forces you into marrying someone you don't want—and worse, a man from a country who will lock you in a warding collar until you've exhausted yourself with birth after birth—"

Ysbeta held up one hand, quelling Beatrice's words. "Stop. I can't even think about it. The idea makes me ill."

"But if they do that to you," Beatrice persisted, "how could you forgive them? How can you forgive Ianthe, who will reap all the benefits of your sacrifice?"

"I know Ianthe doesn't want me to marry his friend. But he's only trying to smooth it over. He doesn't really understand why it's so awful." Ysbeta looked out the doorway, her jaw tight. "This is the only way. I must command a greater spirit. You must teach me how to win its service."

And then what? She didn't need a spirit's help to aid her family's fortunes the way Beatrice did. Would her mother forgive her for defying her plans? That skated too close to Beatrice's own worry. But Father wouldn't be able to resist a spirit's assistance in his ventures. He would allow Beatrice to quietly retire from social life and pursue the magic that would help the Clayborns grow rich. Wandinatilus, greater spirit of Fortune. She remembered the name. All she needed was to help Ysbeta gain her own independence. "What will you do with a spirit's service? What do you want?"

"I want to write books," Ysbeta said. "Books detailing all the common magic that women and working men use outside of the chapterhouse. Every country has its own traditions and techniques. They could be shared—I think they must be shared. So much has already been lost because it doesn't serve the men of the chapterhouse."

"So you want to travel the world and collect knowledge for the common magician."

"And share it with them. Vocational magicians do the real work. They make the discoveries. They drive the innovations. If they have more knowledge, we will make a better world for them—and that prosperity will raise us all," Ysbeta added.

"Who knew you were a radical?"

Ysbeta shrugged. "I've spent plenty of time in factories and laboratories. I know where our latest inventions have come from. We pay our inventors bonuses to keep them happy and encourage them to settle for the security of working for us rather than the risk of starting business for themselves."

"That sounds like a fair trade to me."

Ysbeta shrugged. "You'd change your tune if you saw the books."

"But think how many more inventions there could be, if we freed women from the marriage collar," Beatrice said. "Imagine how many great minds, how many creative spirits are lost to us because we found a cruel solution to the problem of possession and settled for it."

"You don't have to tell me," Ysbeta said. "I intend to be free. And when I have a greater spirit to aid me, I will find libraries lost to legend. Imagine hunting down the most ancient wisdom, lost secrets . . . Couldn't you spend your life doing that?"

It was something out of a penny story. Dangerous, and exciting, featuring Ysbeta as a true treasure hunter and scholar of the past? Beatrice nearly wanted to cast her own ambitions aside and join her. "I can see it. What an adventure it would be."

"If I don't do this, who will?" Ysbeta asked. "Every day, someone who knows a spell or a charm no one else knows passes on to Heaven, and their knowledge is lost. I can't save everything, but someone has to try. If I had a greater spirit—I must make the great bargain, Beatrice. You have to help me."

Beatrice heard Ianthe's warnings from last night: if catastrophe strikes, a mentor must contain the damage, whatever the cost. If this went wrong . . . if Ysbeta lost command of her body, she would kill Beatrice. She would go on a rampage that would only end in her death. And when the Lavans pieced together what she and Ysbeta had been doing, nothing would stop them from suing Father into oblivion.

"We don't have time to stand around thinking," Ysbeta complained. "Teach me how to cast the circle."

"We are going to cast a circle, and then we will take it down. You must master this casting before we can move on to the next step. You may practice casting and banishing circles on your own, but I will not teach you conjuration until you have mastered it."

"Beatrice," Ysbeta said, her voice careful and even. "I am not a child. This is dangerous. I understand the risks. Please begin."

"Right." Beatrice made a cradle of her hands, gathered just at her abdomen. "This is the sign of gathering."

Ysbeta copied her gesture exactly.

"You begin like this. Use your breath to fill your belly and hands with light."

She breathed, but the stays laced firmly around her waist stopped the breath from its fullest bloom. Ysbeta tried it and grimaced as fashion resisted her effort.

"We'll have to unlace," Ysbeta muttered.

More minutes wasted as they unpinned mantuas and unlaced stays—Ysbeta's were exquisite, the stay bones hand-embroidered in place, and she grumbled the whole time. "Even our fashion stands in the way of our potential."

"I've always done magic in my shift," Beatrice confessed. "I never thought of this."

Once freed, Ysbeta delighted in taking deep belly breaths. "I can feel the power."

"Perfect. That's the energy you shape with intent and hand sign to cast."

"Teach me how."

"There's something more important first." Beatrice folded the fingers of her right hand, so the index and smallest finger pointed outward, the middle and ring finger captured against her palm by her thumb.

"This is the sign of banishment," Beatrice said. She raised her left hand, fingers together and palm facing out. "This is the sign of the wall of light. Do it."

Ysbeta folded her fingers with expert dexterity.

"Good," Beatrice said. "Now take all that power you gathered and cast it out through your hands. Make this one reflex. This is how you banish a spirit back to the aether. Never forget it. It could mean your life."

"What does it do?"

"It hurts them," Beatrice said. "Now you're ready to start."

Beatrice taught her the sign of welcome, the sign of protection, and the sign of summoning before Ysbeta made a cradle of her hands and breathed, her rib cage swelling.

"In the belly," Beatrice said. "Imagine the air as light filling your body when you inhale, and then expelling as a cord through your navel as you exhale. Breathe slowly. Calmly. You can't hurry this part."

Properly, one couldn't hurry any of it, and Ysbeta kept trying. She hadn't raised a shred of power. She was simply too overcome to balance her mind to the necessary state. Now half-unclothed, the neck of her gossamer-fine shift unlaced so the garment fell off one shoulder, she looked like the old woodcuts of blood witches, those who made bargains with spirits to do evil.

Ysbeta had to calm down. "Here."

Beatrice stood behind Ysbeta, reaching around her to lay her hand over Ysbeta's belly. "When you breathe, make my hand move." She lifted Ysbeta's right hand by the wrist. "Left hand is the sign of what?"

Ysbeta curled her little finger down to meet the tip of her thumb, the other three fingers upraised. "Protection."

"Good." Beatrice kept her voice low, murmuring in Ysbeta's ear. "And the right?"

Ysbeta swiveled her hand so the palm faced upward. She crooked her little finger and its neighbor, her middle and index finger pointed. "Invitation."

"Don't hold down the ring finger with your thumb," Beatrice said. "That's a different sign."

Ysbeta adjusted. "It strains my arm."

"You'll get used to it," Beatrice said. "Now, the sigil is one unbroken motion. You draw the hexagram, thus—" She moved Ysbeta's hand in the gestures that traced the six-pointed sorcerer's star, and then relaxed her hold.

"Like this?" Ysbeta traced it perfectly, to Beatrice's relief.

"Precisely. Now we vibrate. You must direct the sound to the aetherial plane—not through your mouth, but through your navel. The first vibration is always Anam, lord of magic."

"Mages really do summon a starborn to oversee their works?"

"Yes. Where magic is done, Anam is there. Use your entire breath. Push the vibration out of your navel, through my hand."

Ysbeta's breath pushed Beatrice's hand away as her abdomen properly swelled. She caught the knack of voicing the syllables in her throat, bathing Beatrice's palm in tingling warmth.

"Perfect," Beatrice praised. Ysbeta was focusing, forgetting the fear that drove her to learn magic, learn it right now. "The vibration is Anam, Kefaa, Welan, Hado. Vibrate one in each quarter while you draw the hexagram."

She let Ysbeta go, and watched as her student tried to breathe, sign, scribe, and vibrate—and the first thing Ysbeta did was heave a great, rib-expanding breath.

Beatrice put her hand back on Ysbeta's belly. "Again. With me."

Together, they breathed. Two right hands curled in the sign of invitation rose to trace the hexagram. Two voices vibrated the name of the lord of magic, drawing out the sound through their navels. Two aetherial bodies expanded, inflated with breath, sign, sigil, and vibration. They wove the circle, filled it with their will, and the air took on the thick, stone-smelling pressure that hinted at lightning across a cloudless sky. Beatrice's hair stood on end as she inhaled the smell of magic, saw the shimmering, twinned sigils floating in the air. She had done the bulk of the work, but Ysbeta's efforts were unmistakable.

"That's it," Beatrice said. "You've cast a circle."

"Now conjure a spirit," Ysbeta said. "I know you won't let me do it, so conjure one for yourself. I want to see."

"We don't have much time left—"

"So you should get started. Call its name."

She could call the spirit without making a bargain.

"Nadi, spirit of chance, I know you—" Beatrice began, and the spirit hovered before them.

:Beatrice,: Nadi said. :You need me, and I am here.:

"Thank you," Beatrice said. "I have no need of your effort today, but I have cold fruit. Do you wish to dwell with me until sundown?"

"I can't hear the spirit," Ysbeta said. "What's it saying?"

"Shh," Beatrice said.

In front of her, Nadi vibrated with excitement. :Can we eat?:

"Yes. We can eat."

:I want to see things.:

"You will see the whole journey from Lavan House to Triumph Street," Beatrice said. "Do we have a bargain?"

:Who is the girl with you?:

"My companion is Ysbeta Lavan."

"It's talking about me?" Ysbeta asked.

:She is unlucky,: Nadi said. :We have a bargain. Let me in.:

Beatrice reached past the bounds of their circle, and Nadi seized her hand. It felt natural to have a spirit inside her now, and Beatrice turned back to Ysbeta.

"There's no more time if we're going to get dressed. Watch me take the circle down. I'll teach you at our next lesson."

CHAPTER VIII

"Curse you and Nadi both," Ysbeta muttered as she hiked into the meadow grass after her ball. "You can't cheat at the tournament. Promise me. You're a very good player, but this is flagrant."

Birdsong spilled through the air, and Beatrice grinned at the sky. She spun her mallet, tossed it in the air, and caught it, nimble as a juggler.

:This is fun,: Nadi said. :I love winning.:

:It is fun,: Beatrice agreed, :but people will notice you helping me when my luck is this strong.:

:So?:

:So cheating with magic is wrong, and I would be punished for it.:

:What would they do?:

:They would put a warding collar on me. They would make it so I could never call you again. You have to be a secret.:

:Move—: Nadi seized control of her limbs and she leapt aside just in time for the ball to come flying through the space where she stood.

"Oh, I'm sorry!" Ysbeta cried. "Wait. How did you know? You weren't looking at me."

"Nadi saw," Beatrice said. "Nadi jumped. Not me."

Ysbeta's face went wide-eyed with surprise. "It can control your body?"

"You get used to it. It's awkward at first, and then you learn to work together."

"Oh, I don't know—"

Beatrice didn't argue. She leapt high in the air, landing on one foot, and then did it again, twirling in the air before landing safely. "I could show you my tumbling, if I wasn't in stays."

"Is it fun?"

"It's wonderful."

"Not a lot of reason to run and jump," Ysbeta mused.

"It's freeing," Beatrice said. "Now that I am accustomed to it, I quite enjoy the enhancement."

Ysbeta stretched her arms and practiced her mallet swing. "I should call the spirit next time."

Beatrice considered it. "A minor one, perhaps. Think of what you want to bargain. Can you practice casting and dismantling the circle on your own?"

"That was an excellent shot," Ysbeta said, pitching her voice to carry. "We shall be the terror of the hazards course."

Beatrice stared at her until it finally made sense. She turned, and Ianthe strode up to the two of them, splendid in a saffron-golden coat decorated with scrimshawed ivory buttons.

"What a day," Ianthe said. "Good afternoon, Miss Clayborn."

Beatrice dipped her knees and nodded. "Your day has not been so fair as this weather?"

Ianthe glanced up at the cloudless, vivid blue that belonged on a summer sky and his expression went sober. "I'm just back from Meryton."

"Did you find a lawyer?" Ysbeta asked.

"I wish I had been able to," Ianthe said. "Instead, I stand before you chilled to my bones at the horror committed on a young woman and the child she bore."

Beatrice shivered as if a cloud had passed over the sun. "I'm sorry. It must have been awful."

"They took all the initiates to Meryton," Ianthe said. "They wanted us to see what came of indiscretions."

"How awful," Ysbeta said. "It was horrible, wasn't it?"

"I don't want to give you ladies nightmares, so I won't go into detail. We left the scene quite sobered. Well, some of us did."

Ysbeta gave Ianthe a sharp look. "Some of your party were unaffected?"

"Some of my party opined that they would never lie in the mud with peasant stock, and so it didn't matter. Not Bard," Ianthe said, nodding to Ysbeta. "But I don't feel like I can play hazards right now."

"Beatrice is trouncing me anyway," Ysbeta said. "Are you still up to driving her back?"

"I can ride with the coachman, if you'd rather not," Beatrice offered.

"I would rather take you with me. I have to return to the chapterhouse before the family attends dinner with Lord Gordon and his family, and then we're attending a party at the Robicheaux house."

Ysbeta groaned. "That's too much revelry. I shall be exhausted by the time we come home. And Lord Gordon is so pompous."

Beatrice paged through her memory of names. "You mean Bard Sheldon's father?"

"Yes." Ianthe flicked a glance at Ysbeta. "Bard asked me if I knew how to identify your basket for the Blossom Ride auction."

Ysbeta's expression went cordially blank. "Did you tell him?"

"I told him that I wasn't certain you had decided on an ensemble," Ianthe said.

Ysbeta's tension uncoiled just a fraction. "It will seem strange if you don't tell him."

Ianthe winced. "Ysbeta. If there was a way to stop this—"

"I know," Ysbeta said. "I know you would."

"Stall him," Beatrice said.

Ianthe and Ysbeta turned to her. "What do you mean?"

"How many suitors do you have on your string?" Beatrice asked, scraping her memory. What would Harriet say if she and all her knowledge of bargaining season were here? "If you don't have at least five—"

"I haven't encouraged anyone," Ysbeta said. "Cards come every day, and the maids take the flowers to their rooms, but I didn't do anything to make any of them think that I had an interest—"

"I know," Beatrice said. "But if you don't have a parade of young men trying for your hand, Bard's father is going to tell your father that bargaining season is a waste of time and negotiate the match now. Welcome some attention. Break some hearts, Ysbeta. Get those men between you and Bard Sheldon, fast."

Ianthe tilted toward Ysbeta. "Still going to stay home instead of coming to the Robicheaux party tonight?"

"I believe I have the energy to go out after all," Ysbeta said. "Are you invited, Beatrice?"

:A party!: Nadi exclaimed. :Dancing? Punch? Cake? I want to stay. Let me stay for the party, Beatrice.:

:Very well.:

Inside her, Nadi wriggled in glee.

"I am, but it is not my only engagement this evening," Beatrice said. "Father is entertaining Udo Maasten from the Eastern Protectorate of Vicny. He's an inventor."

"Udo Maasten is not a name I recognize," Ianthe said. "Is he a brother of the chapterhouse?"

"He is not," Beatrice said. "Nor is he titled."

Ianthe shrugged. "Titles aren't everything."

"But he is also unmarried."

Ianthe stood up straight. "He's unmarried, and dealing with your father? How old is he?"

"I don't know. Older, my father said."

Ianthe's face was carefully neutral. "Your father wants you at dinner."

Beatrice let her gaze drop to the thick, close-trimmed grass at their feet. "Yes."

"To meet an unmarried, wealthy man."

"Yes."

Ianthe smiled, as if he were about to enjoy a favorite game. "You may have heard of the party we give on the *Shining Hand.* A feast and a dance on deck, guesting our attendees overnight on the jewel of the Lavan family fleet. It is a special occasion."

Ysbeta smirked. "Can't take the competition, dear brother?"

"I like to compete," Ianthe said. "The only thing better than competing is winning."

"Now you've done it, Beatrice. If you thought he was solicitous before, you should brace yourself."

Ianthe ignored his sister. "I would like to invite your family to attend our gathering, Miss Clayborn. And I would like to meet your father. I hope we may be introduced this afternoon."

Oh. He did enjoy competition, and it made her heart ring like a bell—and the determined, level look he gave her smoldered like a barely contained fire.

"I'm sure he would be pleased to enjoy your acquaintance." Her voice had too much air in it, too small to be hers.

"I will do my best to be charming," Ianthe said.

Ysbeta passed her hand between the two of them, and Beatrice abruptly turned her attention to her friend's barely suppressed smile.

"Perhaps you two should moon over each other on the ride home," Ysbeta said. "I shall tell my maid to haul out a gown for this evening. I have to net some gentlemen."

She led the way through the house, her skirts swaying around her ankles. "Let's see how many gentlemen have sent invitations today, hmm? What do you wager? Nine?"

So many? But Ysbeta was easily the most eligible sorceress Bendleton had seen in years. Llanandari didn't trouble themselves to visit Chasland in the search for a husband. She was the height of beauty, wealthy beyond measure, and her aura shone with the bright prismatic flares of a powerful sorceress. Maybe nine wouldn't be that many.

"I say ten," Beatrice said. "And I will lose, because there are actually more than that."

"We shall see," Ysbeta said. "Will the two of you come along with me? I won't answer any invitations that are not public meetings, so you may come, Beatrice. We shall work out hand signals. Touch your face if you don't like him. Play with your lace trim if you do. But step wary, gentlemen, for I am coming!"

Laughter rang down the hall as Ysbeta hurried her steps, drawing closer to the grand foyer where the bubbling song of a fountain echoed against the high, vaulted ceiling—and halted so suddenly Beatrice had to swerve to keep from colliding with her.

Ysbeta's spine lengthened, her head high. Her shoulders shifted down, making her neck long. Beatrice copied the shift in posture immediately, then suppressed a gasp as she spied a woman at the greeting table, regarding the cut stems of fragrant, pale flowers.

Not a servant, though she wore a canvas apron around her waist. Her brilliant green cotton gown was vented all over with embroidered eyelets and layered in tiered ruffles. Hand-hooked lace dripped from her elbows. She wore a matching green cotton headwrap that added inches to her height, folded and pleated to a queenly elegance.

She looked so much like Ysbeta and Ianthe it was uncanny—or, properly, Ysbeta and Ianthe looked like her, sharing the same balanced, elegant features as the woman who had to be their mother.

She looked sharply at Ysbeta's unseemly haste, but it melted into an indulgent smile that deepened the merry lines next to her eyes. "Ysbeta, my dear. All done with your game?"

"Mother," Ysbeta said. "Beatrice has trounced me again, but this time I gained the benefit of her instruction. We shall be the terror of the hazards tournament."

"So this is your friend," Mrs. Lavan said, tilting her head. She set down a gorgeous stalk of breath-pink peony in too-early bloom and beckoned. "Let me see you, child."

Ysbeta stepped aside. Ianthe's hand landed gently on her shoulder, patted twice, and slid off. Mrs. Lavan's bright gaze shifted to Ianthe for a moment, but then that smile was back on her face as Beatrice came within three paces and then sank into a knee-bending bow that put her skirt hems on the floor.

"Mrs. Lavan," Beatrice said. "I am honored to meet you at last."

Nadi shrank inside the confines of her body. :She's unbound.:

Sure enough, no collar gripped her throat. Mrs. Lavan used her magic now that she was using Llanandari methods to prevent bearing children, years before her change of life. She had power of her own, the respect of her family, a voice that touched the ears of a vast business empire. Couldn't Beatrice bend a little? Couldn't she be happy, if her later years were like this?

Mrs. Lavan took in everything about her, from the stray curls that escaped Beatrice's coiffure to the wrinkles in her gown. "And I am happy to meet you, child. You have gained the friendship of both my children, I observe."

"Mother," Ianthe said. "This is Beatrice Clayborn. We met her in a bookshop, and she has been charming us with her company since."

"I note your curricle is waiting outside the door by itself, my boy. You were going to share the drive home?"

"Yes, Mrs. Lavan," Beatrice said. "Mr. Lavan is returning to Bendleton now, and it saves the harnessing of another carriage."

"Don't ever worry about that, child. We have a full staff in the stables available."

"I prefer to see Miss Clayborn safely home myself," Ianthe said. "It's a pleasant drive, full of conversation."

"So it must be." That gaze swept between Beatrice and Ianthe. "I do wonder what you talk about."

"Our conversations are great wandering things," Ianthe said. "Very diverting."

"Indeed. Well! I should get to know Miss Clayborn, then, since the two of you have befriended her." Mrs. Lavan picked up a pair of sturdy shears and turned to Beatrice, smiling. "Are you in a great hurry? I have looked over the flowers my greensman collected for today's arrangement, but I believe I need more color than this for such a pretty day. If you would come with me and select something bright, I would be grateful."

"Mother," Ysbeta said. "Ianthe needs to get back to Bendleton quickly—"

"Ianthe can wait for us."

Something final rang in her voice, and Ysbeta glanced at Beatrice before bowing her head. "Yes, Mother."

"I have time for Beatrice's selection," Ianthe said. "Perhaps you will meet later to make arrangements together."

"What a lovely idea," Mrs. Lavan said. "It's a pity you

don't have time to compose an arrangement now, Miss Clayborn, but I am most curious to see what choices you make."

Floral arrangement was an art in Llanandras, and therefore all the fashion here in Chasland. It was part of the womanly skills that made a good wife, based on principles like imbalance, profusion, contrast, harmony, and beauty. For Mrs. Lavan to invite her to give input—Beatrice must make a good impression. Her choice of flowers had to be tasteful, artistic, harmonious. It was an invitation, but it was also a test.

Mrs. Lavan knew Ianthe was interested in her. She was curious to see what kind of wife Beatrice would make. Her choices would reveal what sort of home she kept for her husband, and Mrs. Lavan would consider that carefully.

Beatrice ran smoothing hands down her skirts. She surveyed the peonies, white lilies, cream roses, and sprigs of greenery. A profusion arrangement, then. A celebration of all the most beautiful, indulgent and excessive. If there was some pink, some lilac, a bright flash of yellow . . . Oh, she could pass this test easily.

Beatrice dipped her knees again. "I would be delighted to choose flowers with you, Mrs. Lavan."

"Excellent," Mrs. Lavan said. "Come with me, then."

The jewel-box greenhouse on the east side of Lavan House was heady with perfumed flowers, and Beatrice's gown went heavy under the close-pressing, moist air. The sweet chatter of birds filled the space, and colorful flowers Beatrice had only seen in paintings thrived in raised beds on either side of a purple slate path.

Was this what Jy was like? Did people dwell in such abundant, lush beauty, breathing in the intoxicating fragrance of pink jasmine and perfume tree? How did people keep from just stopping in their tracks to marvel at it all?

"Oh, Mrs. Lavan, this is so lovely."

"My greensman designed the garden," Mrs. Lavan said. "It's a tiny slice of Llanandras, here in Chasland."

"I adore it." Beatrice clasped her hands together and turned in a slow circle, counting the gently swaying perches where jewel-bright birds gathered and preened, singing in clicks and trills. "Thank you for showing it to me. I would love to visit it again when there's more time to see all your astonishing specimens—"

"These are the flowers you may choose from," Mrs. Lavan said.

These? She was to choose among these blooms, each of them as precious as jewels? She was supposed to cut the life of this flower with sun-yellow petals framing a corona of curly pink fronds? Or this ruffle-petaled teaflower, its waxy, lush lavender color smelling softly of citrus? How could she choose—

"What are you thinking?" Mrs. Lavan asked.

"That they're all so rare. I have never seen these flowers anywhere but in paintings."

"Those still lifes that are so popular here?"

"The same. Some are better than others. They're an accessible subject for painting."

"Your command of Llanandari is very good," Mrs. Lavan said. "Did your mother teach you?"

"She did. She went to Coxton's, and they instructed in Llanandari."

"But you did not attend Coxton's," Mrs. Lavan said. She moved along the flagstone path, her wide skirts brushing against the retaining walls on either side of the walk. She reached out to stroke a pink-rayed sunshine, tickling its corona with long, lacquered nails. "Your family's fortunes didn't allow it."

How did she know? Was it Beatrice's accent? "My parents and the local priest oversaw my education. My father taught me business mathematics, including probability theory."

Mrs. Lavan moved past a wide, shallow bird bath before a raised bed in the southeast corner. Beatrice stopped dead on the path, her stomach swooping to the flagstones.

Orchids. Hundreds of orchids stood and climbed in that corner, in every color and variety Beatrice had ever seen in purchase catalogs. She had pored over those pages, memorizing the names, learning the prices the traders asked and what the most fashionable families had once been willing to pay for a single specimen.

"The pride of my collection," Mrs. Lavan said, and moved aside so Beatrice could see them all. "It's a pity they fell out of fashion, isn't it? They're my favorites. Such variety! Which do you like best?"

"They're all so marvelous." Beatrice coughed to clear her throat. "I couldn't possibly choose."

"Allow me to make a few suggestions, then." Mrs. Lavan pinched the woody stem of a long-petaled pinstripe star orchid and took her shears from the pocket of her canvas apron.

"This one, I think."

Mrs. Lavan squeezed the handles shut. The shears shushed together and cut the blossom free, coming together with a click.

Beatrice flinched.

:Beatrice?:

:It's all right,: Beatrice soothed.

Mrs. Lavan handed the white-striped maroon blossom to Beatrice. "I heard your name from my daughter a few days ago, Miss Clayborn. I understand this is your first bargaining season, and you have a younger sister who will follow your success here."

"Yes, ma'am," Beatrice replied. The orchid wafted its gentle, subtle scent through the air. Beatrice cradled it in one hand. Her stomach trembled as she watched Mrs. Lavan select another.

"It's an important time, bargaining season. An occasion unlike any other holiday or festival in the world. Chasland's custom is filled with pageantry, celebration, gaiety—all of it draped over the sober truth of marriage, dressing it in finery and ignoring everything important."

Mrs. Lavan chose a button orchid this time, a charming, vivid pink. One shush of the shears, a snip, and the flower came free. "So much depends on these six weeks while you young people mix and get to know one another. And as an ingenue, you are sought after, are you not?"

Beatrice's tongue felt thick. "Yes, ma'am."

"You are dressed in fine gowns and sent out to be merry, to meet the friends who will be with you for years. What friends have you made, other than my daughter?"

Harriet would know exactly what to say. Harriet would have made some friends by now, if it had been her. Beatrice thought of Danielle Maisonette laughing at her, and the tremble in her middle doubled. "I haven't had the opportunity to meet any of the other ladies yet."

"And you have no existing invitations from the friends you made at Coxton's, as you did not attend. What do you believe is the foundation of a good marriage, Miss Clayborn?"

It was so hot in here, and the damp spread itself all over her skin. Beatrice laid the button orchid in her hand. "Respect," she said. "Love is a fire set with paper. Respect is the log that holds the heat and the light."

Ianthe's mother glanced over her shoulder. "I prefer to think of love as a flower. Even as beautiful and intoxicating as flowers are, they inevitably wither. What do you think of this one?"

She held a spiderleg orchid with pale green petals, the top lobe spotted yellow.

:I will hex her,: Nadi said.

:Don't you dare.:

:She's hurting you. Nadi can feel it just under your skin.:

:She doesn't know,: Beatrice replied. :She doesn't know what she's doing.:

Her attention centered on the orchid pinched between Mrs. Lavan's fingers. She cleared her throat. "Isn't that flower terribly rare?"

"Oh, I suppose it is." Mrs. Lavan considered the spiderleg orchid. "I had heard they fetched a handsome price in Chasland last year, had they not?"

The question poured cold water down Beatrice's spine. She felt as if her third-best day gown had been torn from her, leaving the truth of her exposed and naked. She had been brought here, away from Ysbeta and Ianthe's protection, to be chased away like a garden pest.

"They did." Beatrice's voice was small, so small among the birdsong.

"Crazes are like flowers too. They blossom, they promise so much . . . but they inevitably die."

She cut the spider orchid, and what once had been a flower worth hundreds of crowns came free. "Marriage needs respect, it's true. It needs that more than it needs the quickly exhausted flame of infatuation. But what a marriage needs most of all is to understand that it's not about love, or even respect."

Mrs. Lavan cut another button orchid, and another, laying the blushing pink flowers in Beatrice's hands. "Hmm? What do you say to that, Miss Clayborn?"

They were heavy. Her arms were lead. But she would not bend. She raised her head, gathering the strength to answer. "Only a question, ma'am—what quality is of greater importance than respect?"

"Responsibility. When you are married, you are responsible to your marriage," Mrs. Lavan said. "You put away selfish joys to be part of a partnership. It's about pursuing what is best for your family, not yourself—each contributes to make a greater whole, to become better together than you were apart."

"Mr. Lavan and I have not spoken of marriage. We are only friends—"

"I know how my son looks at you, Miss Clayborn. You may have not spoken of marriage, but he can't help smiling when he sees you. It is better to speak of this now, before it goes any further."

Mrs. Lavan moved a little to her right, selecting another vivid pink orchid. "My son is not just in need of a wife. He needs the right wife. He needs someone who would be an asset to his family, through strength of the power, and an asset to his business, through connections and skills. She must bring advantage to Lavan International."

"Advantage," Beatrice said, and accepted the flower. "You mean wealth."

"Do not mistake me. If you came from a family newly raised to wealth through well-timed investments—"

A green and yellow bird landed on Mrs. Lavan's shoulder. She stroked its head with one finger. "If you had gone to women's college and made friends there, if you had the acquaintance of the resource owners in the north, if you had so much as organized a single party in your north country village—"

How did she know all this? How did she have the picture of their existence as lesser gentry in Meryton, only occasionally invited to the larger parties, rarely asked to dinner? How did she know of her family's disgrace?

"I could learn those things." The words tumbled out before she had a chance to wipe the desperation off them.

"Not quickly enough, for all your potential." Mrs. Lavan shook her head slowly, her sympathetic smile as cloying as the perfume tree's fragrance. "I love my son. I know he's currently imagining how happy he will be with you. But he is making a mistake that will make both of you miserable. Love wilts, Miss Clayborn. What remains is your commitment to your family, and to your business."

"And I'm not good enough."

"Never say that," Mrs. Lavan said. "You are every bit as good as you need to be. You are kind. You are intelligent. You are pretty, and your depth of power is impressive. But you are not skilled enough to step into my shoes and succeed me."

A vivid orange bird fluttered from its perch and landed on the lip of an iron bath, warbling as it played in the water. A mate joined it, preening the feathers on its neck. Beatrice flicked her gaze away to watch Mrs. Lavan, swallowing the lump in her throat.

"Ah. Now this . . . this is my favorite among my favorites."

Mrs. Lavan gestured with her shears toward an Imperial Lady, a ruffled deep violet specimen that made Beatrice stop breathing. Father had promised Mother an Imperial Lady when the ship came back. One branch supported only a single spectacular blossom. They were the most coveted, the most prized.

Mrs. Lavan parted the leaves at the base of the plant and cut. She lifted the bloom and breathed in its scent, her eyes slipping shut. "These smell the best. Round, with orchid's sweetness, but with a hint of smoky spices that makes it the most valuable perfume flower in the world."

She handed the cut stalk to Beatrice. "Ianthe needs a particular kind of woman, Miss Clayborn. I must make a careful, thoughtful choice of a proper wife for my son, who does not yet understand that love is not enough."

The orchids trembled in Beatrice's hands. "And will he accept your choice? Will he let you decide who his wife shall be?"

"Not if I tell him outright," Mrs. Lavan said. "He'd rebel, like any boy his age. You can understand the gravity of the choice before you. You understand the responsibility. Set your aim lower than the sun itself. Go home, Miss Clayborn, and wait for the invitations from gentlemen. Trust in your charms to attract a suitable husband. Perhaps a man who is not a sorcerer himself? You're so strong in the power that honestly that's all you need."

Beatrice's hands clenched around the stems.

:I'll hex her. I'll—:

:No.: But just one hex. One day of ill luck. Mrs. Lavan stumbling, falling, landing—no, no. Beatrice caught Nadi in webs of power, compressing the spirit inside her. :You must not. Stay still, Nadi:

:Why?:

:Because you will make bad luck for me, too.:

She raised her head and met Mrs. Lavan's eyes. "Thank you for your advice."

Mrs. Lavan nodded to the dying fortune in her arms. "I've ordered a carriage to take you home. You may take those orchids with you. Put them in sweetened water with a little vinegar, and they should last for days."

Beatrice cradled the dying flowers. Mrs. Lavan had to have ordered the carriage before she had even met Beatrice. She swallowed the lump in her throat. There was no flower arrangement she could have made to impress Mrs. Lavan. She hadn't stood a chance, and now she wouldn't even be able to say good-bye. "I will reflect on what you say, Mrs. Lavan."

"Wise girl. Good afternoon."

Dismissed, Beatrice turned and left the greenhouse, stifling Nadi's rage.

The smell of the orchids wouldn't fade. Beatrice had nearly torn out the underarms of her gown struggling to open the coach's windows, but it did no good. They lay in a loose heap on the padded bench next to hers, their delicate, expensive perfume impossible to ignore. It stung her eyes. It crawled into her throat. But she swallowed, and blinked, and breathed through her mouth.

She kept her gaze on the fields and lawns just outside the window, counting cattle through the lump in her throat. She mustn't cry. It would not do, to exit the gilded carriage whose turquoise color shouted that it was the property of the Lavans with kohl streaking down her carefully rouged and powdered cheeks. Tongues would wag if anyone saw her fleeing into the townhouse with her maquillage in a wreck. It was one thing to be a failure, but to look like one was unthinkable.

But she wanted to cry. She wanted to curl up in a tight little ball, tucked away in some nook where no one could see her, and weep until her eyes ached. Mrs. Lavan had stripped every fancy, every illusion, every cloud-sugar dream and left her naked, and then held her in front of a mirror and forced her to look at what she was: nothing of any significance. She had no skills. She had no connections. She didn't even have the solidity of a family reputation for business.

All she had to give was her strength in the power. All she was worth was the children she could give a man. A man with riches but no power of his own would be eager for such a bride. Udo Maasten was eager for such a bride. She couldn't expect to aim any higher.

But the thought of giving in to the demands of society—of submitting to their expectations and marrying someone who hadn't a shred of the indulgence Ianthe would have given her— She could not. Not when the solution was so close to her. Not when she could help Ysbeta— How could she help Ysbeta? Mrs. Lavan had not withdrawn Beatrice's welcome to Lavan house, but she wouldn't be pleased to find her there, after she had sent her packing. How could she teach Ysbeta and fill her end of the bargain?

She and Ysbeta had to make a plan. They both needed this knowledge, and Ysbeta couldn't gain it without her help. Beatrice had to attend the Robicheaux ball and speak to her. Ysbeta would be there, trying to attract suitors . . .

And Beatrice needed her own string of gentlemen vying for her attention, to keep her family assuming that she was doing her duty until it was time to reveal the truth. She had to go to the ball, and she had to shine.

She straightened from her curled, despairing posture and leaned against the seat back as a breeze carrying the scent of cherry blossoms overpowered the orchids' mocking perfume. She watched the gray stone fronts of the homes on Triumph Street, the house numbers counting down to number seventeen. She tucked the orchids into the crook of her arm and let the footman hand her out of the carriage, head held high as she walked inside.

"Put these in sweetened water with a little vinegar," she said to a maid, who took the bundle of blooms in an astonished hand. "I'd like them taken to my room and set where I can see them from bed."

She would look at them and remember that the only thing she had was strength in the power. But it was also the only thing she needed, if she had the will to use it.

"Clara!" Beatrice took up a handful of her skirts and climbed the stairs to her room. "I'm sorry I was so delayed. Is the bath ready? We don't have much time."

CHAPTER IX

Udo Maasten was so tall he towered over everyone even when he was sitting down. It was as if someone had taken a man made of rubber sap and stretched him. He swiveled his long head this way and that to regard anyone who spoke at the table, and when he swallowed a bite of braised lamb, his throat bobbed up and down above the napkin tucked into the neck of his shirt.

:He's old.:

:Maybe not so old as you think.: But Udo was a pink-faced, fair-haired son of the Protectorate of Vicny, and rather than don a wig, as most men would, he allowed his baldness to show, his thin hair gathered in a queue at the back of his neck.

"I am most fortunate to be in the presence of so many lovely young ladies, most fortunate indeed," he declared in his surprisingly deep voice, smiling at Mother. "You must be very proud of your daughters. They look so much like you."

He stole another glance at Beatrice.

:I don't like how he looks at you when you can't see,: Nadi said. :You can't marry him.:

:I won't have to,: Beatrice reassured. :We're going to the ball tonight. Ysbeta will let me copy the book soon, I'm sure of it. I won't have to marry Udo Maasten.:

Father set down his meat fork and drank ale. "Beatrice is a lovely young woman," he agreed. "Any man would be lucky to have her as a wife."

"Overeducated, you said?" Udo licked grease off his lips

and glanced at her again. Beatrice did her best to smile.

"I taught her how to analyze finances," Father said. "She knows how to spot the usual deceptions people attempt when swindling money from the household. She understands inventory ledgers and can detect thefts and embezzling from reviewing the books. She could probably manage a farm's finances or a small business without help."

Mr. Maasten raised his eyebrows. "Really."

"She has learned a great deal about geography and the politics of trade. You could talk to her about your difficulties with getting a fair bargain for your inventions."

Now he looked at her with curiosity, as if she were a long-tailed monkey someone had taught to count to ten. Ianthe had never looked at her like that. Ianthe would slap any man who would. "Miss Clayborn. I have made a modest fortune on my inventions, while my investors have made great ones. How would you suggest I maximize the sale of my next innovation?"

:I don't like him,: Nadi said. :Don't marry him.:

:I don't want to, believe me. But it's not that easy.:

"I'm afraid I don't know what your next innovation is," Beatrice said.

He smiled at her as if she were dissembling. "Does it matter?"

"Yes. What did you invent?"

He leaned back, weighing his words. "I have told no one about it."

Ser Maasten sold his inventions, and those who purchased them made the money—just as Lavan International profited the most off the innovations of their employees. Beatrice understood—he was loosening his grip on his inventions too soon. It didn't matter what he had built, not really. Beatrice set down her fork and dabbed at her mouth before speaking.

"Then I cannot ask you to confide in me," Beatrice said. "But generally, you want to improve your relations with legislators and justices when you have invented something new, rather than sell it to someone with the money to maximize it."

Maasten blinked. "I cannot sell my inventions to a legislator."

"True," Beatrice said. "But a legislator can introduce specific protections allowing you—or I should say, your corporation—to hold the right to duplicate and distribute your inventions."

"By what means?"

She furrowed her brow trying to find the right way to explain what she meant. "Don't sell your inventions, Mr. Maasten. Sell a license granting permission to produce replicas of your invention. Someone will inevitably improve on your original design, reducing the sales on your licenses, but you will invent something else, and then sell licenses to that."

He gazed at her with wonder. "If I had done that earlier, I'd be a very wealthy man today."

He couldn't have that modest a fortune, if Father had invited him to dinner. But she had just bungled it with her showing off. She had impressed him with her knowledge, instead of repelling him with her unwomanly demeanor. She reached for her claret, and Nadi forced her hand forward too fast. The glass fell over, spilling red all over the linen tablecloth and splashing onto Mr. Maasten's shirt.

"Oh, I'm terribly sorry!" Beatrice cried. :Nadi! What—:

:Trust Nadi,: Nadi said, and her hand groped for another napkin and closed on a fork, which clattered to the floor.

"I don't know what—" Beatrice stood up too fast and knocked her chair into a server, who fumbled the platter of tarts in his hands. Delicate pastries slid off the tray and cascaded onto Harriet, who shrieked and jumped to her feet.

"Harriet!" Beatrice moved to assist her, but her fallen chair was in the way. She shoved it aside, only to learn that the tablecloth had tangled itself in the legs. The whole dinner slid precipitously sideways. Her plate landed on the floor in a clatter of silverware, and her mother's glass of wine teetered and fell the opposite way, the contents splashing over Mr. Maasten's jacket.

"Stand still!" Mr. Maasten cried. "Don't move. Every time you move—just stay there."

Carefully, cautiously, Mr. Maasten rose from the table, wine-stained and terrified. "I must go."

Father wiped his mouth on his napkin, looking alarmed. "But Mr. Maasten, we still must speak of the corporation we touched on earlier—"

"I really must go," Maasten said. His final glance at Beatrice was etched deep with anxiety. Beatrice could see him imagining what havoc a clumsy wife could wreak on delicate inventions, precious notebooks, and valuables in general. "Good evening, Miss Clayborn."

"Good evening—"

She tried to bend her knee, but she stepped on a tart. Her foot shot out from under her, and she grabbed the table to break her fall, dragging Harriet's plate to the floor.

Udo Maasten all but ran from the room.

Beatrice clapped her hands on her cheeks, surveying the ruin of dinner, her food-stained dress, her shocked, gasping sister, and her father's horrified disbelief. Mother studied the place where Mr. Maasten had sat, her lips pressed tight and her cheeks pinched. She glanced at Beatrice and quickly looked away, covering her mouth as her shoulders shook. She shut her eyes and great gasping breaths hissed through her hands.

"Oh, my dear," Father said. "Don't cry."

Beatrice looked away hastily. If she kept looking at Mother, Beatrice was going to laugh until her sides hurt. She had ruined two dresses, a shirt, a tablecloth, and perhaps even the rug on the floor. It was the worst luck she'd ever had.

:Thank you, Nadi.:

Nadi giggled. :That was fun.:

She had to get out of here. She turned and nodded to her white-faced, appalled father.

"I think I should rest before the party," Beatrice said. "May I please be excused?"

CHAPTER X

Merwood Hall spread intimidating wings before the Clayborn women, who stood in the courtyard at the foot of two curving ramps that flanked the stairs leading to the front door. Their carriage had to wait out on the street with dozens more, the number of them promising a crowded party inside. Beatrice gazed at the statues holding up the carved face fronting a peaked roof, at the lights glowing from the glass dome in the center, at the image of wealth on full display, and gulped.

Her feet wouldn't move just yet. So she stood and counted the windows and doors, calculated the property tax fees on each one, and plumped each bow rising up the front of her stomacher. Cascades of hand-hooked lace shivered from her elbows. Her head ached from the weight of all the pins holding up her coiffure. She was as richly dressed as anyone could ask for outside of a royal court.

"Beatrice," Harriet said. "Have you taken a fright?"

"No," Beatrice said. "But look how lovely the house is."

"It will be beautiful inside," Harriet said. "What are you worried about?"

"Nothing," Beatrice said, and still her feet wouldn't move.

The house stood before her and she felt it again, the sensation that it knew that she was a debt-ridden banker's daughter. That those doors would not open to admit her. That she dared too much by coming here.

"Beatrice," Harriet said.

"I know."

:Go ahead, Beatrice,: Nadi said. :I'll help.:

:What will you do?:

:I'll see when we get there. Walk up to the door, now. You were invited.:

Beatrice's left foot lifted as Nadi took the reins. Together they strode up the stairs, her head high, the invitation in her hand. Nadi nodded to the man who opened the door for her. It tugged on the fingers of her embroidered kid gloves the moment her invitation left her grasp.

A servant carried trays of the soft pink punch she knew from the Assembly Dance and Bard Sheldon's card party, and Nadi plucked up a cup.

:Sip!:

:I know,: Nadi said, amused. :Look, more sculptures.:

:No,: Beatrice replied. :They can move.:

And so they did, turning their heads to track someone walking past. A young man waved at one of the figures, and it waved back.

:Are they alive?:

:No,: Beatrice answered. :They're automata from the Eastern Protectorate. They can move, and do complex things, like write whatever they're told.:

:Are they magic?:

:They are machines.:

She and Nadi watched their uncanny movements a little longer, surveying the octagonal hall where people paused in conversation and passed through from every room. Music fought to be heard above the conversation that echoed off the glass dome. Beatrice looked up, but all the light made the dome a faceted reflection of the scene below, and she couldn't see the stars.

"Oh," Harriet said. "That's Julia Robicheaux."

Beatrice found her surrounded by a phalanx of girls in richly decorated gowns, their hair dressed high, maquillage on their faces. They watched Harriet like a pack of sleek hunting cats, and the one in the middle, the one who had the same angled gull-wing eyebrows as her brother, beckoned to Harriet.

Harriet strode forward without a shred of hesitation. Beatrice watched as they formally greeted each other with bows, and Harriet laughed at something Julia said. Then the girls all gathered around, questioning Harriet. Her answers made them laugh, and as a pack, they stalked away into one of the side rooms out of Beatrice's sight.

Harriet hadn't even looked back. Beatrice cast about for her mother, but she was already drawn into a conversation with a woman and her husband. Beatrice was alone.

She could find Ysbeta. She had to be in one of these rooms. Perhaps she was dancing? Beatrice moved toward the music, crossing the octagon to a ballroom. A long line of dancers flourished small squares of silk as they traced out complicated footwork. That was the breakwater, named because the movement of the couples dancing was like the breath of the sea.

"Miss Clayborn?"

Beatrice smiled at a pink-cheeked man without the flickering crown of sorcery in his aura. "I am."

"Sir Charles Cross," the young man said, and his smile was pleased. "Have you only just arrived?"

"We were late," Beatrice said, and Charles shook his head.

"Only three dances. Nothing unforgivable. Do you dance the basketweave chase? It's next on the list."

"I know the steps," Beatrice said. "I'm looking for my friend. Ysbeta Lavan?"

"She's probably with Bard," Charles said, and offered his

hand. "I'll help you find her after we dance."

"Miss Clayborn!"

Beatrice smiled at another man, trailed by Danton Maisonette. Danton curled his lips in a passable effort, but his companion turned a dazzling smile on Beatrice, shiny and dimpled. "I've been waiting to meet you. You disappeared at the Assembly Ball, where I meant to ask you to partner me. Please accept my invitation to dance."

What was happening? "I've accepted Mr. Cross's invitation already, Mr.—"

"Poli," the gentleman said, and Beatrice did her best not to stare. "Elon Poli."

"The actor?"

"Indeed," Mr. Poli said. "I saw your painting in the ingenue's gallery and knew I must meet you. You will tire after too much dancing. May I walk you around the garden?"

"You are too bold," Danton said, "to ask such a thing of a woman alone. I would like to talk to you, Miss Clayborn, in the company of my sister—"

"Miss Clayborn."

Another gentleman pushed his way into the arc of men trying for her attention. Beatrice wanted to pretend to faint and remain in the ladies' lounge for the rest of the evening. She smiled at the newcomer, who had a ruby pinning down his cravat that would pay Father's mortgage.

"I am Peter Fowles, Lord Tiercy. Is your father in attendance?"

Lord Tiercy's father was the minister of finance. He was an initiate of the rose, from the ring on his hand and the dagger at his hip. He wished to speak to her father? "He remained at home," Beatrice said.

"I should like to invite both of you to luncheon at the tearoom in the Bendleton chapterhouse—"

"The dance is about to begin, gentlemen," Charles said.

"Don't crowd the lady so."

They all stepped back, and Charles led her out of the scrimmage and onto the dance floor, joining the end of a very long line. "I am sorry. You must feel positively hunted, after all that."

What in Heaven was happening? They parted, and Beatrice turned to greet the woman on her right with a courteously bended knee, then she rose on her toes and kicked one foot forward, stepping to the center to circle her partner.

"I admit I have never been the focus of so much attention."

"Bargaining season is said to be the grandest time of a woman's life," Charles said as they linked arms and smiled at one another. "That nothing matches these weeks of gaiety and friendship."

"I have heard that as well," Beatrice said, and skipped across the line to greet the lady on her other side. She smiled, but it was Danielle Maisonette, pretty, blond, and in an overdone dress. Well! So much for friendship from that corner. Beatrice let her arms float from her shoulders as she met Charles Cross again.

"I wonder what it's like after," her partner continued, "for the poor woman who marries a country lord, or a man who prefers his wife snugged up away from society. I have need of a wife who can manage my many social affairs."

As if a wife were a position like one's man of business. "Do you host many social occasions, Mr. Cross?"

He looked at her with an amused twinkle. "You don't know who I am."

"I confess I recognize your name, but I don't know if you're a musical Cross or a political one."

"My uncle is Philip Cross, the minister of foreign affairs," he said, and Beatrice spun away to dance a figure eight with the friendlier woman on her right. The nephew of the minister—who meant to become minister himself. An established, connected, influential man, who needed an astute and clever wife as a partner in pushing forward this agenda or that.

"I am embarrassed," Beatrice said, as they joined in the center once more. "I am pleased to make your acquaintance, Mr. Cross. Are you enjoying the party?"

Father would be overjoyed at the possibility of international connections. Mr. Cross would make someone a wonderful match.

"I have met some very promising ladies," Mr. Cross said. "Have you ever hosted a party before?"

The Clayborns weren't popular enough for that. Father preferred climbing the ladder in Gravesford when he traveled there twice a year, disdaining at-home country company. Did he even know how important it was that a young woman demonstrate her skill at organizing social events? Harriet had to become a hostess, and swiftly.

But for Mr. Cross, all she had was a smile. "Not outside of birthdays for my sister."

Stalwartly, he tried again. "Do you speak many languages?"

"Only Llanandari, I'm afraid. Enough Valserran to read."

He picked his smile up off the floor. "Do you know what has Eliza Robicheaux looking so amused?"

"I'm afraid I haven't met Miss Robicheaux, and I haven't had much opportunity to hear the gossip."

The quality of his smile diminished. "Well, are you interested in these things?"

Mrs. Lavan had been correct. She didn't have what a powerful husband needed in a wife. Her lack of education, connections, and skill in social organization would be a disappointment to every connected man she met. Mr. Cross would finish this dance and never speak to her again. She had to try harder. "I think it would be a very great undertaking to manage a busy social life," Beatrice said, "but an interesting one."

"Given the correct assistance, I think you'd do wonderfully. Is it true that you only have one sister?"

Beatrice skipped to her left, but the blond woman beside her refused to smile, her thin mouth pursed up tight. They danced apart and Beatrice took Mr. Cross's hands as they wove back and forth.

"It's true. I have one sister. She's three years younger than me." And no brothers, which was what he really wanted to know.

"That's a very small family. Do you have a great many cousins to make up for it?"

"I have six aunts and three uncles," Beatrice said. "One of my uncles is not much older than I."

"And are they mostly on your mother's side?"

Beatrice tilted her head. "Three of the aunts and one of the uncles," she said. "Do you also have an abundance of cousins?"

"Too many," Mr. Cross replied. "What quality do you most want your children to have?"

Beatrice sucked in a breath. It didn't matter if she had none of the skills he wished for in a politician's wife. Udo Maasten at least was interested in her skill at business. For Mr. Cross, only her ability to give him magical offspring mattered. If she told him about her father's debts, he'd probably pay for them without a murmur.

But she couldn't stand his company, not for another minute. She wrinkled her nose at the question, and let a small laugh escape her.

"I haven't devoted any time to thinking of it," Beatrice said. "What an interesting question."

They stepped back as the music drew to a close and applauded for the musicians. "It was wonderful to meet you, Miss Clayborn. I hope to meet your father soon. May I have your card?"

He escorted her off the dance floor, bowing over her hand before he took an invitation card from her and left. She'd failed to measure up to Charles Cross's criteria for a political wife, but she was still valuable. Did any of the gentlemen who had crowded around her see her? Did they care who she was? Did anything about her matter at all?

The grandest time of a woman's life. Mr. Cross probably didn't realize how true or how horrible that was. She searched the crowd for Ysbeta, but she startled as Elon Poli appeared before her, bowing.

"May I have this dance, Miss Clayborn?"

Behind him, other gentlemen were headed her way. If she said no, it wouldn't stop any of them. Danton Maisonette shouldered his way past the others, gaining the lead.

Beatrice smiled at the most famous actor in Chasland and took his arm. "It would be my pleasure."

The ballroom smelled more like sweat than perfume, and Beatrice couldn't find Ysbeta anywhere. She had danced with one partner after another for more than an hour. At least Danton never managed to become one of her partners, though she had to pretend to mis-hear him to accept someone else. But no more. Her feet ached. Her throat was dry. It was time to escape these sorceress hunters and find Ysbeta.

She had seen her friend once all night. Ysbeta had danced a pivot with Bard Sheldon, but when Beatrice tried to join her, she had been overtaken by the pack. She couldn't even remember half their names. And all of them announced their intention to meet with her father, rather than asking her to join them for any games or outings as she had a right to expect. Why the hurry to close the bargain? They were only in the season's second week—what was happening?

She fluttered her fan, moving a little of the too-warm air

across her face, holding it before her mouth as a shield signaling that she was disinclined to socialize. She roamed through the fringes of the ballroom, ducking into the conservatory where Harriet played a sparkling bit of piano to accompany Julia Robicheaux's command of the violon, her bow dancing over the half-dozen strings in sharp, precise movements.

Her pride of young ladies gathered around to listen and applaud. So did an astonishing automaton, which moved gracefully to its feet to lead the praise. Beatrice watched the masterwork raise its hands, nod its head, and then sit in a padded chair, lifting one hand to cup around its ear. Harriet laughed and surrendered her seat at the pianochord to another young lady, who began a brilliant solo. Julia took Harriet's arm and led the way past this amusement to find another out in the torch-lit garden.

Harriet was in her element. Now experiencing the pages of one of her silk ruffle novels, she had found her place and reveled in it. Harriet deserved a bargaining season of her own, one where she would probably dance her suitors into the floor and dash about all day, attending this social or that tearoom visit, and keeping up with dozens of friends. Harriet would make an excellent partner for a man like Charles Cross or a trade baron who needed a lively, connected spouse to take on a whirling social calendar.

Beatrice couldn't rob her sister of that. She would not. Somehow, she had to sail through this bargaining season without a single error, and then find a way to save Riverstone. She needed an opportunity. She needed impeccable timing.

She needed luck.

:Nadi,: Beatrice reached for the spirit inside her. :How do I win?:

:We do it together,: Nadi said. :Are we done dancing?:

:Yes. We need to find Ysbeta.:

:I see Ianthe,: Nadi said. :He's hunted too.:

:What?:

But then she saw Ianthe, splendid and vibrant in a primrose pink dancing suit that matched his sister's, doing his best to smile at half a dozen young women crowded all around him. They giggled. They heaved their bosoms. They touched his arm and tried to hold his gaze—and whoever held it smiled as she ignored the others glaring murder at her.

Beatrice watched a little longer. It shouldn't matter to her one bit. Her heart shouldn't ache. She shouldn't feel her breath fighting its way out of her chest as she waited for him to look up, to see her, and—

Beatrice's hands trembled. That dream was done. She had one path now.

:Do they bother you? I can hex them.:

:No. They're just talking,: Beatrice assured. :And it doesn't matter anymore.:

:You still like him. It still thrills you to see him.:

:That isn't important.:

:Isn't it?:

It wasn't. There was only one thing for her now. Ianthe was a beautiful dream, but she had to wake up. :Not anymore. Where's Ysbeta?:

:There.:

The only woman in a group of men. Beatrice should have figured that. But standing at her side was Bard Sheldon, smiling and leading the gentlemen in conversation in Chasand, while Ysbeta, beautiful even when sulky, remained silent.

Beatrice had grown so used to speaking Llanandari that she forgot that Ysbeta hadn't as much facility with Chasand. Imagine, leaving her out of the conversation like that!

"When do you suppose the automation and manufacturing scheme will be approved by the ministers?" a cheroot-smoking gentleman asked Bard.

"Once all those ministers have their own pursuits ready to sail," another said. "A dozen new corporations will form before the ink's even dry on the writ."

Bard laughed and conjured a flame to relight his pipe. "I can't say, fellows. You know that we can't speak on what the Ministry is going to do. But there are multiple opportunities afoot. Father gave me an interesting book on mine safety and management. It's all in Makilan, but it's worth the slog."

All the gentlemen nodded, avid for more hints from Bard.

"Pardon me, gentlemen." Beatrice took Ysbeta's hand and pulled her out of the ring of conversation. "Come on. If you're going to meet gentlemen, you can't do it stuck to Bard's side."

"I tried. He would— Good evening! Mr. Beecham, is it not?" Ysbeta smiled brilliantly at the gentleman who closed in on the two of them.

"Miss Lavan, Miss Clayborne." Mr. Beecham bowed. "I hope you are both enjoying the dance."

"Beatrice has been danced right off her feet," Ysbeta said, "but I haven't had much of a chance to take a turn around the floor. Mr. Harlow, how do you do? Thank you so much for the primroses last week. I enjoyed them so."

Mr. Harlow's smile faltered before he stretched it over his mouth. "I'm pleased to hear they brightened your day, Miss Lavan." He flashed another smile and turned to Beatrice. "Miss Clayborn. I would be enchanted if you would consent to dance with me."

It was all Beatrice could do to keep her expression from falling into shock. He'd nearly snubbed Ysbeta, trampling over her invitation to converse to get closer to Beatrice. "I couldn't possibly dance while Ysbeta is unpartnered."

Ysbeta snapped her fan shut and let it dangle from her

wrist. "I would adore a dance."

Mr. Beecham nodded. "Please allow me to escort you to Lord Powles's side."

Ysbeta laughed. "There's no need for that, Mr. Beecham. I know Sheldon believes that his work is done, but I am not that easily won, and I would like to dance."

A competitive light sparked in Mr. Beecham's eyes. "Then may I have the honor?"

Ysbeta lifted her hand and Mr. Beecham took it, leading her to the parquet. Mr. Harlow gave Beatrice a deep nod and guided her out to dance beside her friend.

CHAPTER XI

They danced another basketweave chase, a dash-in-square, and a triple-step. The hem of Ysbeta's pink gown belled out with every spin, her laugh like the chiming of bells as she danced with Mr. Beecham, then Lord Overston, and Ellis Robicheaux himself, and whatever Ellis said to her as they wove their teasing steps around each other had Ysbeta glowing with good humor.

Beatrice did her best to keep up, accepting another cup of punch and the partnership of Fitch Amesbury, the son of Amesbury Steel and Smithworks, Gilbert Arquelon, a much kinder citizen of Valserre than Danton Maisonette, and Neville Ordin, a wealthy landowner with the best Arshkatan horses in Chasland. They charmed. They flattered. They hinted at wanting a card from Beatrice's pocket, and then, invitation in hand, they bowed and brought her back to the corner she and Ysbeta ruled, back to the waiting gentlemen who jostled for a chance to partner them.

But when they returned from the triple-step, Bard Sheldon stood in their midst, an indulgent smile on his face. "Miss Lavan," he said. "If you wished to dance, you only needed to say so."

"You were quite busy, Mr. Sheldon," Ysbeta said, showing her teeth as her cheeks plumped in a smile. "But now I must retreat for the moment to the ladies' lounge."

Her fan unfurled with a snap of her wrist, blocking the sight of her mouth so they could retreat to the ladies' lounge in peace.

Once inside the lounge, Ysbeta's shoulders slumped. "Well, that was fun while it lasted."

"Have you been shackled with him all night?"

"He won't leave my side, even though I understand half of what his friends say," Ysbeta groaned. "I tried to say that I should see the dancing. He came with me. I waited until he was deep in a talk about spinning automatons with Ellis and mumbled about wanting some air. He stopped mid-sentence and came with me. I haven't had a moment to breathe until you came. You are my knight in shining aspect. My rescuer and hero, St. Ijanel herself come to save me."

Beatrice laughed. "I don't know where you heard of St. Ijanel."

"Do you joke with me? She's famous here. The maiden who repelled invaders with the blessing of the wind-lord, who sent a vicious storm to sink the fleet of conquerors before they could make shore?"

Beatrice smirked and leaned closer, as if confessing a secret bit of gossip. "Do you know what I think? St. Ijanel was a sorceress. But no one wants to admit that, so they made her blessed of a god and gave him the credit for her magic."

"It's as good a story as any, and in all honesty, I wouldn't be surprised," Ysbeta said, chattering until the last young lady left the comfort room. Once alone, she stepped so close to Beatrice their skirts pressed together, almost whispering. "Listen. Ianthe wants to talk to you, but he's buried in young ladies and is too polite to walk away from them. He tried to catch up with your carriage, but you were in the bath when he made it to your house."

He had? And Father hadn't said anything of it? "I'm sorry I didn't ride with him. Mrs. Lavan provided a carriage for me after she gave me some flowers from her greenhouse."

"They've already fought over that." Ysbeta led her to the vanity stands, where they could retouch their maquillage.

"She treated you like some common fortune hunter."

Ysbeta stood before a gilt-edged mirror and inspected her countenance. She didn't wear a mask of paint and powder over her face, as Chaslander ladies did, preferring a whisper of powdered pearl left to shimmer on her cheeks, which only emphasized the flawless, glowing skin she was blessed with.

"As far as she knows, I am a common fortune hunter," Beatrice said. "But I don't know how we will continue our studies if I'm no longer welcome in her house—"

"My house," Ysbeta said. "Remember? I own it. I direct the staff. I say who is welcome and who is not."

How like Ysbeta, to plant her feet and demand her mother give way to her. Beatrice would have attempted something gentler, more winsome and persuasive, but Ysbeta charged in, ready for a fight. "She'll be unhappy."

"I will take the brunt of her displeasure," Ysbeta said. "There is nothing she can do to stop me from entertaining my friends. But you need to talk to Ianthe. Tonight."

"Should I really be speaking to him?"

"Listen. You must let him know that you're willing to fight. We dined at Bard Sheldon's tonight. Lord Gordon spent most of the meal talking with Mother."

What did that have to do with Beatrice battling to stay at Ianthe's side? Beatrice tilted her head and watched Ysbeta's reflection. "Did they have a pleasant conversation?"

Ysbeta watched her for a moment, a corner of her lower lip caught in her teeth. "Lord Gordon toasted us with mouth-blown Makilan goblets, the finest glass in the world—and he wants a partnership that will bring Makilan glass genius to Chasland."

"Instead of rubber?"

"In addition to it," Ysbeta said. "He also mentioned that he hadn't visited Makila in years, but that he remembered the governor of trade had the most adorable daughter, who is probably near her eighteenth birthday now."

Beatrice's shoulders released and lowered. "He's interested in a different bride for Bard?"

The look Ysbeta traded her in the mirror was heavy with sadness. "He's interested in a bride for Ianthe. With me married to his son, and Ianthe married to a trade princess, he'd have exactly the fulcrum he needed to tip Makila's wealth into Chasland's coffers. Mother all but started planning her cargo for the trip."

A weight lodged in her chest. "And so she will trade another child's happiness for yet more wealth and power."

"Unless you act now. Father pointed out that we have to stay in Chasland to finish my bargaining season. Mother said that he and Ianthe could leave for Makila immediately. Father pointed out that he couldn't leave before they hosted the party on the *Shining Hand*—but the moment we're done in Chasland, she's taking Ianthe south to meet this family."

And then Ianthe would be gone. Forever. Ysbeta would be bundled off in a green gown and married as fast as they could make the arrangements. Everything was happening too quickly; everything was falling from their grasp.

They stood alone before the mirrors, the embroidered, lace-ruffled young women across the room out of range for any but the sharpest ears, but Ysbeta whispered into their reflections.

"Tell me how to read the books," Ysbeta said. "Ianthe's yours. I know you know it already, and I haven't a thing to bargain with you. But—"

But it wasn't that simple. "I need that book too," Beatrice said, "so you have plenty."

"You still want to—"

"Never mind what I want. You're not ready to undertake the ordeal of the greater summoning yet. We must find more time."

"There isn't any more."

"Then we must make some," Beatrice said. "If we are going to escape this—"

Ysbeta's eyebrows pushed together. "We? But Ianthe—"

"Would be the finest husband in the world," Beatrice said. "He'd give me everything it was in his power to provide. But I would have to give up my fight."

"Your fight? What do you mean?"

Beatrice leaned toward Ysbeta, her voice so low it only carried to her ears. "I want magic, Ysbeta. Not just to escape the marriage collar. I want the life of a thornback daughter, secretly aiding her father in his business affairs, but I will save my family and get Harriet into ladies' college. I will finance her bargaining season."

"Ianthe will gladly pay for all of that."

"I know he would. But I want magic aside from all that. I want it because it should be mine."

Ysbeta went still, her eyes huge. "You don't want him."

"I do," Beatrice said. "But I want magic, too. I can't have them both—Ysbeta, what would you choose, if it were you?"

Ysbeta's reflection pressed her lips together. "I'm not in your position. I can't imagine the choice you face. If a man turned my head the way Ianthe does yours, I'd be in agony."

She did need to speak to Ianthe. It was the least she could do. She owed him an explanation. "I will talk to him. Are you ready to brave the party?"

"What will you wager Bard is hovering outside?" Ysbeta asked.

"I'm not inclined to lose any coin to a fool's bet." Beatrice fished in her pocket for her handkerchief and wiped lip rouge off her teeth. "Ianthe is completely surrounded. What is our plan of attack?"

"What you did for me. Barge straight in and take him away," Ysbeta said. "It's simplest."

"Beatrice?"

A small figure in lilac silk brocade burst into the powder room and rushed to them in a flurry of skirts. "Beatrice," Harriet said. "Oh, Beatrice. It wasn't you. I was so worried—"

"What is it?"

"There's been an incident," Harriet whispered. "One of the ingenues is in disgrace. They're sending her home right now."

"Why?" Beatrice and Ysbeta chorused.

"Not so loud," Harriet scolded. "She used magic on a gentleman. He was troubling her, but it doesn't matter. She called a spirit's name and doused him in water that came from nowhere, so she's in trouble, and not him."

"That's not fair," Beatrice said. And society would extend her the same justice, if she were caught with Nadi. She'd be warded, marked as a disgrace. If anyone knew she regularly hosted a spirit, she'd be ruined.

:Nadi is lucky,: Nadi assured. :That won't happen.:

"What was she supposed to do?" Ysbeta demanded.

"I know, but it's done," Harriet said. "Wendera Heath has danced twice with Charles Cross. Genevra Martin introduced Stephen Hadfield to her father. You've been danced off your feet, Beatrice. The gentlemen are moving quickly to secure brides. There are only twelve unattached ingenues now, and that's not going to be for much longer."

"Twelve? What happened to the other one?" Ysbeta asked.

Harriet licked her lips. "No one wants to cross Lord Powles. Everyone knows your parents are talking to each other."

Beatrice's middle flipped over. Ysbeta did not suffer the same dilemma she did. Ysbeta did not want marriage—not to Bard, or to anyone. If she wound up a bride—no. She could not. She had to help Ysbeta, no matter what she chose for herself.

"I'm not off the market." Ysbeta went gray. "Not this early. I won't be."

Harriet looked sympathetic. "Was there someone else you wanted?"

"I think Miss Lavan is entitled to her privacy," Beatrice said. "She doesn't have to tell us who she's drawn to."

"I apologize, Miss Lavan. I didn't mean to pry."

"No offense taken," Ysbeta said. "But I slipped in here to rest and hopefully recover from this awful headache. I'm afraid it hasn't subsided. I think I should go home—I should fetch my brother right away."

"There are gentlemen hovering near the ladies' lounge," Harriet said. "I saw some of them dancing with Beatrice."

"Oh no," Beatrice groaned. "Maybe I should leave with you, Ysbeta—"

"You can't," Harriet said. "If you leave with Ianthe, it will be a perfect scandal. But you haven't danced with him yet. You have to dance with him. Everyone will notice if you don't."

Ysbeta regarded Harriet with a nod of respect. "You know more about this than me and Beatrice put together."

"You must tell Bard that you are unwell. Here." She slipped a hand into the fold of her skirt and produced a tin of fennel pastilles. "Eat some of these, so it seems like your stomach rebelled. It'll excuse why you've been in here for so long. I'll fetch Mother, and we will defend you against Bard's presumptuous attentions."

"Harriet." Beatrice looked on her sister—her knowledgeable, clever, socially adept sister. "You're a gift."

Ysbeta took another pastille. "I expect your bargaining season will bring you unprecedented success, Miss Harriet. I almost want to be there to watch you do it, so I can see how it's properly done."

"Thank you," Harriet said. Her smile deepened the dimples in her cheeks. "Stay here. I'll bring Mother."

Harriet had done more than bring Mother to the powder room where Beatrice and Ysbeta huddled in wait. Ianthe waited by the door, and clasped Ysbeta's hands. "You are unwell."

"I am, but I don't think I can manage the carriage just yet." Ysbeta's fennel-scented breath wafted from her smile. "Mrs. Clayborn has offered to sit with me until I feel steady enough to travel. Perhaps you could enjoy one more dance?"

Ianthe squared his shoulders and turned to Beatrice. "If I might have the pleasure?"

"I accept."

Ianthe carried her hand as if it were a delicate crystal, and just that was enough to feel as if she touched magic. It brimmed over in the valley of his palm as they took their place on the parquet, posed, waiting for the musicians to begin.

The first chord made her heart leap, as it was the Llanandari quanadar, one of their daringly intimate dances where the couples danced only in pairs. Beatrice turned to face Ianthe and raised her hands high, their hands and arms touching to the elbow, their faces close enough together to kiss. Perhaps they did kiss in Llanandras, but Beatrice hovered just a few inches away from Ianthe's mouth, drawn helplessly into the depths of his eyes.

"I have been wanting to dance with you all night," Ianthe said in Chasand, and Beatrice spun away from him, her arms floating at her waist, stretching toward the walls of the ballroom before Ianthe caught her arm and reeled her back, catching her up in his hold.

"Harriet said that we must, or it would seem that we had grown cold to each other." Her body bumped against his. She put her hands on his shoulders, ready for him to raise her in the air and spin.

Ianthe's hands gripped around her nipped-in waist, and her skirts flared as they spun. "I am not cold. Are you?" He set her down and they circled each other, palms touching. "I must know. Did Ysbeta tell you of our dinner with Lord Gordon?"

"Yes."

"And that my mother plans to sail for Makila once this bargaining season is done?"

"She told me."

Ianthe's brow furrowed, his eyes pained. "Is your heart cold at the thought of marriage? Do you—do we have a chance?"

Beatrice whirled away, but her steps spiraled inexorably back to Ianthe. "Your mother is not pleased at the idea of us marrying."

"I don't care what pleases her," Ianthe said. "I care what pleases you."

She had to choose. How could she? Now? In the space of a dance? "I thought magic was the clear choice. I thought I had nothing to lose."

Ianthe pressed his palms to hers. "But now?"

Their faces were so close that Beatrice could whisper. "No matter what I do, it will hurt. I am torn in two. But am I selfish? Shouldn't I be a good daughter and—"

"You know the mystery of the rose." Ianthe gripped her hands, stepping back, and then so close his personal heat radiated on her skin. "If you were a man, no one would dream of asking you to turn away from the starlit path. And yet I—"

He caught her up in his arms. "I am selfish. I know your anguish. But no one captivates me except you. And I tell myself that no one will understand what you sacrificed, that only I can ease the blow of coming so close. I am the selfish one, Beatrice."

Oh, he couldn't call her that. He couldn't just say her

name like it belonged to him. She wanted to hear it again.

He reached up to touch her face and slid his fingertips along her cheek. "I'm the selfish one. Because if you don't find what you seek, I must be there to be the one you turn to. And that's like hoping you fail—and I hate that."

He wanted her. He understood her need, and it tore him apart just as it did to her. The butterflies burst into delirious flight. Her heart cracked in two. "Ianthe."

They spun apart. Beatrice couldn't smile, couldn't weep. Her heart trembled with the knowledge of the sound of her name on his lips.

They met palms first, and Ianthe's gaze locked with hers. "Say it again."

"Ianthe. I understand."

Ianthe closed his eyes. He nodded, his face overbrimming with relief, and guilt—and when he opened his eyes, the longing wrote over it all.

"Beatrice," Ianthe said, and he drew closer, bringing with him the sweet fragrance of white flowers and sweetwood. They stood in the final chord in the same position they began—pressed together, their lips an inch apart. The sensation swept through her, sparkling like tiny lights.

The top of her head felt light as the rarest bubbled wine. She felt as if she were swinging high in the air, laughing at the swooping feeling in her middle just as she fell back to the world, falling and never crashing.

"Ianthe."

The final chord died from the air, and they stepped away from each other, staring. Beatrice still felt his touch. Her hands remembered the warm satin of his coat. Her heart beat as if she had run three miles, her breaths swelling against her stays.

Ianthe bent his head. He extended his hand, and Beatrice laid her fingers in his palm. He turned and led her back to the chairs lining the wall where Harriet and Ysbeta and Mother all sat, watching.

"Thank you for assisting my sister, Mrs. Clayborn, Miss Harriet," Ianthe bowed to them and then regarded his sister. "Are you well enough to travel?"

"I believe I can manage," Ysbeta said. "You dance the quanadar gracefully, Beatrice. It was a most absorbing sight."

Beatrice's face heated, and she glanced away, but everywhere she looked, young people watched her. In the corner, Danielle Maisonette clutched a handkerchief and turned her back on her brother's attempts to cheer her up.

Beatrice looked back at Ysbeta with dismay. "So it seems."

"We'll come get you after breakfast tomorrow." Ysbeta rose to her feet. "Until then."

Ianthe led her away, daring one backward glance before they left the ballroom.

CHAPTER XII

Father watched Beatrice with narrowed eyes as she deftly handled every dish at breakfast without incident. When she had finished eating and asked to be excused, he didn't answer immediately.

"I trust you have recovered from whatever ailed you last night?"

"I think so, Father."

"I hear you were popular at the dance," Father said, nodding to Mother. "And that you danced with Sir Charles Cross?"

"I did," Beatrice replied. "He's seeking a wife who can manage a demanding social calendar. I don't think I'm quite up to the job."

"Don't think you failed to impress him, my dear," Father said. "He's coming for lunch."

"I am sorry I won't be here," Beatrice said.

"He regrets that you already have an engagement. Another outing with Ysbeta and Ianthe Lavan," he said. "Do you have confidence in his regard for you?"

"Ianthe holds Beatrice in tender regard," Harriet said. "I saw how he is with her last night, and his interest is plain. Everyone sees it but you, Beatrice."

Father leaned back. "Mr. Kalman Lavan has invited us to the feast aboard the *Shining Hand.* It's a very exclusive party."

Beatrice reached for her cup of tea and gulped down a mouthful. "He did?" After Mrs. Lavan had all but run her off the property?

Father nodded, but his expression had doubt in it. "But Mr. Lavan cited your friendship with Ysbeta before he extended the invitation itself. He could have simply meant to include you for his daughter's sake."

"No, Father." Harriet shook her head. "Ianthe is courting her, believe me."

"Friendship with Miss Lavan is not courtship from Mr. Lavan. I understand that it's exciting to have his attention, but without knowing his intentions, you can't afford to drive suitors away. You must come away from this bargaining season as a bride. It is the only thing that matters."

Father had stuck with his usual habit. He had invested everything into a single enterprise—getting Beatrice married. If she failed, there would be nothing left to invest. The Clayborns would be ruined. She couldn't allow that to happen—she would not.

"As you say, Father."

"She did have the attention of many gentlemen," Mother said, and sipped her tea. "But you should attend me, Beatrice, before you leave on your outing."

"Yes, Mother," Beatrice said. "Father, Mother needs me for something."

"Go on," Father waved his hand in permission. "So Harriet. I hear you were also a success. Tell me about your new friends."

"They've asked me to come calling at Georgiana Sheldon's this afternoon for tea," Harriet began.

"Sheldon! A fine connection. Bard Sheldon's only brother is still a child, however. Who else will be there, my dear?"

The door to the breakfast room closed, and Beatrice could hear no more.

Mother moved swiftly up the stairs, leading Beatrice into the room that was for Mother's personal use, with a door joining on the private bedchamber she shared with Father. Beatrice adored the room's ribbon-and-rose wallpaper, and the delicate, shapely-legged furniture tufted in the same rose, a perfect companion to the gilded carvings that supported each seat.

"Sit here," Mother said, and patted the place next to her on the settee. "This came for you a few days ago. I wanted you to see it."

Beatrice watched as Mother picked up a low wooden box, carefully opening the lid. Silver glinted from a satin bed, and Beatrice's stomach wrenched as Mother picked it up and held it on her spread hands.

It was a round, silver collar, engraved all over with briar roses. Mother turned it over, showing the sigils worked into the underside—the symbols of warding that locked in the magic stored inside.

Father would give this collar to Beatrice's groom once they had drawn up the nuptial agreements. Her husband would lock it around her neck at the point of the ceremony when she became his instead of her father's. It made her sick just seeing it.

"Your father paid extra to have the sigils on the inside." Mother turned the collar back and forth, and it glinted in the sunlight. "He wanted it to be a pretty thing, I think."

It was hideous. Horrible! She couldn't bear the sight of it. "Put it away, Mother. I don't need to see it until I'm wed."

"I did not raise my daughters to hide from difficult truths," Mother said. "I didn't see my own warding collar until the ceremony. I swore I would not leave my daughters in the dark about the thing that would shape their futures."

"Mother . . ."

But she went on, using the same calm tone Beatrice knew from all the hours they spent in schooling. "This is an object of magic. It is made from an alloy of silver and antinarum.

The secrets of making it are forbidden to women, but you must be a magician to craft the metal. They have kept our bodies safe for children for thousands of years."

She would only wear it sometimes. When she was pregnant. Only then.

"I understand," Beatrice said.

"You do not understand," Mother said, and raised the collar. "Put it on."

Beatrice stared at the collar as if it would spring shut and choke her. "You're not supposed to," she said. "Not until the ceremony."

"I know," Mother said. "That is how I did it. That is how every woman does it—they don't know what the collar is like until they marry."

"It's bad luck."

"That is what they say," Mother said. "Raise your chin, Beatrice."

"But—"

The touch of cool silver and something hair-raising on her throat made her gag. She tried to pull away, but Mother was too fast for her. The collar clasp clicked shut.

Everything dulled. Colors washed out. Sounds dampened, and she heard a hiss, but it was inside her head, not her ears. The world was drab, as if a veil clouded her vision. She should have been sick. She should have cast up her breakfast all over her day gown and the hand-knotted carpet at her feet. But her stomach was just as she was—a little dull, something vital simply drained away.

"Take it off," Beatrice said. "Mother, please."

"Henry Clayborn was the handsomest man in the province. He memorized poems and recited them to me. I was entirely dazzled by his looks, his romantic gestures . . . I never stopped to wonder if he would respect me. I never considered that looks fade, and it takes effort to be charming."

Beatrice gazed at her mother. "Did you stop loving him?"

"It's not that I stopped loving him," Mother said. "It's that I started resenting him."

Mother took up the key nestled in the satin-lined box. She slipped her arms around Beatrice's neck and the catch popped open, the arms of the collar slithering loose to fall in her lap.

Color, light, sound all rushed back, and Beatrice covered her mouth with one hand. Mother plucked up the collar and key and put them back inside the box, snapping the lid shut.

"Now you know what I did not," Mother said.

"It's horrible," Beatrice said. "It's horrible. Oh, Mother—how do you stand it? How—"

"I remember what the world is like without it," Mother said. "I thought Henry was the light of my life. That I was simply going to be a safe haven for you and Harriet. I didn't know the price until it was too late."

Beatrice wrapped her hand around her throat. She couldn't get a decent breath.

"You grow accustomed to it," Mother said. "And I wouldn't trade you or Harriet for anything in the world. Not even magic. When you were born—that was when I could count the cost and be glad of it. But I couldn't let you go into marriage without the truth."

"I can't do it." She couldn't stand it. If she tried, she would lose her reason to despair.

"You are strong, Beatrice. Strong enough to know the truth. Strong enough to last through this. I saw you dance all through last night, and no one shone in your eyes like Ianthe Lavan. No one stirs you the way he does. And the way he looks at you—if you marry any man, my dear, it had better be him, for he will haunt you for the rest of your life."

"Then why show me this? Why, Mother?"

"So you will be able to fairly judge the price," Mother

said. "So you walk into that temple with clear eyes. So that first clasp of the warding collar will not betray you the way it did me."

So she could know the cost before she paid it. But Mother had said *if* you marry any man—did Mother know? Did she know what Beatrice planned?

"Mother." Beatrice reached out and took her mother's hand. "Do you want me to get married?"

"I want you to be happy," Mother said. "I want you to choose your happiness."

"I don't know what that is," Beatrice whispered. "Mother, I learned the grimoire code from the books you gave me. Magic is so wonderful. How can I give it up?"

"I didn't know what I was giving up," Mother said.

"The collar is horrible. Horrible. How do you stand it? How do you not take Father's key, and free yourself, and run far from here?"

"Then I would lose you and Harriet. I couldn't bear that."

"But how . . . how do you not hate it?"

Mother touched the silver collar at her throat. "I do hate it. I loathe the necessity of it. But it gave me my daughters. I hear the carriage," Mother said. "You'd better hurry."

Mother picked up the satin-finished wooden box and entered the next chamber, leaving Beatrice to rush downstairs, desperate to escape.

Ianthe Lavan waited on the step for her in a sunburst-orange coat and breeches, the weskit and coat embroidered in saffron-yellow silk. His smile lit his whole face as he guided her into an elegant ivory and gold lacquered landau. "My deepest apologies for our lateness."

"Were you delayed?" Beatrice asked.

Ianthe guided her to the landau, where Ysbeta lounged in the forward-facing seat, one elbow propped on the carriage's edge, her feet thrust straight out and ankles crossed under a froth of petticoats in the picture of complete leisure. Her orange gown, festooned with ruffles, centered attention on a row of plush saffron bows rising up her stomacher to her bosom, barely concealed under a filmy voile fichu.

And sitting beside her was a leather-bound book, its embossed cover monogrammed with CJE.

Beatrice averted her gaze from the volume and gasped. "Your gloves and hat! So clever."

Her ivory gloves and hat bore fantastical embroidery of vines and blossoms. "It's the fashion in Llanandras," Ysbeta said. "Shoes, too. See?"

She lifted one foot to display an ivory leather court shoe embroidered in the same motif. Beatrice took the other half of the seat, leaving Ianthe to take the backward-facing seat for himself.

"Ysbeta made us stop at a bookstore," Ianthe said. "She was most insistent. All for a tome on—what is it again, Ysy?"

"*A Scientific Garden,* by Conrad Jacob Edwards," Ysbeta said. "It's about planning your planting so you reap greater benefits by pairing some crops together, instead of row planting."

"I'm simply baffled," Ianthe said. "I could understand if it had been the latest Romance of the League of the Rose, as I am most impatient for the latest volume—"

"Scientific gardening sounds interesting," Beatrice said. "May I see?"

Ysbeta handed the book over. "I was curious to see what you made of it."

She opened the book to the first page, and breathed in the smell of it, as she always did.

Ysbeta gently kicked Ianthe's ankle. "What are you smiling at?"

"A prime day for sailing," Ianthe said. The sun shone on the curls standing out all over his head in an exuberant globe. "If only I could have convinced Ysy to change our plans. The two of us could take a single-mast rig just about anywhere."

Beatrice caught the first typographical error on the second paragraph and found another on the next line. She couldn't decode the book in front of Ianthe, but when she looked, Ysbeta was watching her reaction. Beatrice nodded, and Ysbeta smiled wider as she snapped open her fan and wafted cooler air at her face.

"I could sail a single-mast by myself." She lurched into Beatrice's side as if jogged by the swaying progress of the landau's movement. "What color will you wear to the party on the *Shining Hand*? Something pale, I expect."

"Mauve," Beatrice said. "But Father didn't actually tell me if he accepted."

"He did," Ianthe said. "Father told me."

"I am delighted he thought of our presence."

"I asked him to extend the invitation," Ianthe said, "after Mother thought you might not want to come."

"Will she—will she be surprised by our arrival?" Beatrice imagined standing on the ship's deck, head high, back proud, unfailingly polite as she looked Mrs. Lavan straight in the eye.

"You'll be our guests that evening. I don't know if you are prone to seasickness. You don't really feel it on the main vessel, but it's getting there that's the trick."

Seasickness! She never considered it. "In truth, I don't know if I get seasick," Beatrice said.

"We have our own physicians," Ysbeta said. "It will come out all right. Come on. I want to see if that woman painter is still here. Do you remember her?"

"The firebrand," Ianthe said. "Very well. We will see if Miss Storkley is still in residence."

He called the driver to halt, and Ysbeta sprang out of the carriage unassisted. Ianthe offered his hand to Beatrice as she climbed out of the landau, settling her skirts into place once she was on firm ground.

The ateliers of Pigment Street perched above the street-level shops and cafés that sold the artists' works and fed their bellies. Ysbeta strode ahead, sure of her destination, while Beatrice walked by Ianthe's side and tried to untie the knot in her tongue. Their landau clopped along behind, guided by the Lavans' driver, splendid in his eye-catching blue-green livery.

"Why do you call her the firebrand?" Beatrice asked.

"Miss Storkley? Because she's political." His profile revealed the elegant slope of his nose and the strength of his chin, and Beatrice glanced away before she could forget herself and stare. "We discovered her while she was in residence in Masillia and packing up to move here. She's a magnificent portraitist. Her work commands sums counted in the thousands of crowns. But she takes that money and uses it to make paintings that shine an unforgiving light on what she views as the ills of society."

"But she is still popular?"

"Immensely," Ianthe said. "You will have to see her work to understand. Not many women take up the palette and easel, but if this world is just, she will go down in history."

Pedestrians stood aside to let them pass. They touched their foreheads in respect, bidding them good wishes. It was Ianthe they were awed by—he was a figure of fashion, walking the streets in rich embroidery and hand-hooked lace. His expensive perfume cried wealth and power. And Beatrice, in her silvery green walking suit of good quality but little ostentation had passers-by noting the difference in their stations. Everyone who saw them knew exactly what they were.

"You sound as if you admire her."

"It's very brave," Ianthe said. "So few women painters

rise to such prominence. It would be a sad thing if she hadn't the opportunity to use her Skyborn-given talents in a way that honors them."

"But if she hadn't," Beatrice pointed out, "you wouldn't know if the world were diminished or not."

"You point out that we do not know how dark the world truly is," Ianthe said.

"Precisely," Beatrice said. "For every Miss Storkley who rises above the restrictions of her sex, there could be a hundred more, their talents and genius smothered by those who refuse to let women lift their gaze past society's expectations."

Ianthe turned his head to examine her. "You are a firebrand too, Miss Clayborn."

"I suppose I too am political," Beatrice said. "I forgot myself."

But Ianthe gazed at her, welling with admiration. "I hope that you will forget yourself again."

Oh, he couldn't do that. He couldn't look at her like that, as if the people swerving past them no longer existed and she was the only sight he wanted to gaze upon. How dare he be so openly besotted? It made warmth spread across her breast. It made her knees tremble. She couldn't look anywhere but at him. But her throat tightened, and she fought the urge to reach for a collar that wasn't there, for he was everything that stood in the way of her path—a man, a magician who sought to become a husband and father.

"You look so sad," Ianthe said. "What can I do?"

"I'm fine," Beatrice said. "Really. Thank you for asking. Ysbeta is probably a mile ahead of us; we should—"

"Ysbeta is just upstairs," Ianthe said. He nodded at a black-iron gate standing open to lead to a matching set of stairs running up the side of the building. "Shall we go up?"

The stairs rang under their feet, announcing their arrival

into a room that glowed with daylight. Tall windows filled the wall, angling to form part of the roof. The room smelled of linseed and freshly cut wood, and Ysbeta sat perched on a tall wooden stool, raptly watching the artist she had come to see stretch canvas over a large wooden frame.

Miss Storkley was a wide-shouldered woman with the golden-brown skin of a child born to parents of different cultures. Her hair was bound in a tall headwrap as expertly fastened as a Makilan craftswoman's, and she might have been part Makilan, from the narrow precision of her features. She glanced toward Beatrice and Ianthe but focused her attention back on her work with a brusque grunt.

Beatrice's chin came up at the rude greeting, but Ianthe paid it no mind. Ysbeta barely glanced over her shoulder before turning back to watch Miss Storkley clamp the canvas at the corners.

"Are you sure I can't help?" Ysbeta asked.

"You sit right there where you can't get paint on your dress," the artist said, and Beatrice startled at the tone the woman took with a wealthy potential patron. She glanced at Ianthe, who shared her look with a smile.

Ysbeta twisted on her perch. "Miss Storkley has finished her latest. It's right there. She wouldn't let me go near it and made me sit on this stool until you came—"

"It's very wet." Miss Storkley said. She gave up her task to come closer, her linen coat buttoned closed and splattered with paint. Her heavy black buckle shoes—a man's shoes, with a gentleman's hose—were a riot of splattered pigment. "Properly, no one should get near it for another week."

"Oh, please, Miss Storkley," Ysbeta said, leaning toward the woman. "I swear, I'll be careful. Who bought it?"

"No one," Miss Storkley said. "It's true art resting on that easel. No man's coin commissioned it."

Ysbeta bounced in her seat. "Oh, cruel! I want to see!"

Miss Storkley scowled, but it melted into a wink. "One hand on the wall. Don't get any closer."

"Thank you!" Ysbeta cried. She leapt off the stool. "Come, you two! One hand on the wall, as Miss Storkley said!"

Ianthe chuckled silently and moved to the wall. He planted his palm on the panels and followed Ysbeta, who was staring at the painting with—

Distress. Her eyes fixed on the sight of that canvas as if she beheld horror. Beatrice touched the wall and came up behind Ianthe, who could see the painting now, but his expression was thoughtful, his mouth a straight line. Beatrice lined up beside Ianthe and gasped, her dismay the loudest noise in the room.

The painting was of a couple emerging from the darkness of a temple, clad in wedding clothes. The woman's green gown glistened like silk; the man's coat, in the same shade, was embroidered in gold— Beatrice could make out the cleverly disguised phallic symbols in the thread, meant to bless him with virility. His attention was on the people congratulating him as a newly married man; his smiles were for his admirers and friends.

Beside him, his bride raised one hand to touch a richly engraved silver collar fastened around her throat as she stumbled into the sunshine. Her expression was a mirror of Ysbeta's, her eyes focused not on the witnesses but at the terrible sight of her own future. A tear glistened on her cheek, but no one in the painting paid attention to it.

Beatrice tried to take a decent breath, but the hollow in her middle, the tight band around her chest—oh, this painting was horrible, horrible! She couldn't bear to look at it, painted in colors too rich for a warded woman to see. It dragged her back into her mother's room, to that terrible five seconds when she learned exactly what a collar took from her.

Beside her, Ianthe stirred, released from his study of the scene. "How awful."

Beatrice turned her attention on him. "You think so?"

"Absolutely. It's utterly tragic," Ianthe said. "She had to marry for advantage, not love. Look how unhappy she is. Look at the groom, who cares nothing for her distress—I'm furious just looking at it."

Ysbeta choked down a sob. She spun away from the painting. She fled from it, right out of the studio and out the door, weeping.

"Ysbeta!" Beatrice cried. "I'll get her."

She ran along the wall, getting clear of the painting, grabbing a handful of her skirts as she ran down the stairs. Ysbeta stood just inside the iron gate, bent over as she cast up her last meal on the paving stones.

Beatrice reached inside her pocket for her vial of candied fennel seeds. Ysbeta stood up and gagged.

"Here," Beatrice said. "They'll settle your stomach, too."

"That is not happening to me," Ysbeta said, bile staining her breath. "By the Skyborn, it will not."

"It will not," Beatrice said. "We must push on with your lessons. The sooner you learn higher conjuration, the better."

Ysbeta groped for Beatrice's arm, her eyes round. "Yes. Teach me everything. Before it's too late."

"I will," Beatrice promised. "I swear on the Skyborn. Everything you need to know."

CHAPTER XIII

Ysbeta thrust the book into her hands the moment they boarded the landau. "Lavan House, Cornelius," she ordered. "Ianthe is seeking his own means later."

"But Miss—"

"Go."

The driver shrugged and guided the horses into the street, maneuvering through traffic to turn on Silk Row, aiming for the Meryton Highway.

Beatrice looked behind her one more time, but the landau was long past Pigment Street. "You left him."

"He can hire a cab." Ysbeta lounged in her seat in an unladylike slouch. "If I had to listen to him ask me what was wrong for the entire journey, I would have thrown him out of the carriage anyway. At speed." Her hand came up to trace a line across her neck. "What's the book about?"

Beatrice glanced at the driver, who kept to the business of driving the horses in a trot through the streets of Bendleton. She made the sign and cast the spell, blinking at the title:

Hazel and Chestnut: The Hidden Path of Women

"What is this?" Beatrice murmured, and kept reading.

"What is it?" Ysbeta asked.

"One moment," Beatrice said, and read on with rising excitement. "I was right. Of course, I was right. But here is proof."

"What were you right about?"

"There is a hidden network of women practitioners.

They're probably the ones who make the grimoires," Beatrice said. "They signal each other with hazel and chestnut—wisdom and warning—"

"I know," Ysbeta said. "But they're the sign of women who practice in secret?"

"Exactly," Beatrice said. "We can find other sorceresses. Maybe even a sorceress who knows the great bargain. Someone who can help us."

"And not a moment too soon," Ysbeta said. "How do we find them?"

"They mark themselves with the sign. Embroidered on a handkerchief, or the border of a fichu—we just have to keep our eyes open."

Beatrice glanced behind her again, and Ysbeta huffed. "You're looking for Ianthe. We're long gone."

"I know, but—" Beatrice sighed. "Will a cab go as far as Lavan House?"

"He'll be fine," Ysbeta said. "I will not."

"Has something happened?" Beatrice asked.

"Bard Sheldon called on my father this morning," Ysbeta said. "He stayed for twenty-five minutes. Mother was all smiles. The jaws of this trap are closing." Ysbeta swallowed. "I've made a terrible mistake not collecting other suitors sooner, Beatrice. You have to help me."

"I understand you don't want to marry Bard—"

"Or anyone," Ysbeta said. "I never want to marry, never."

"I don't blame you. But what if you meet someone who stirs your heart?"

"It won't happen," Ysbeta declared. "No man or woman has ever turned my head. I know beauty when I see it, but my heart has never ached for anyone."

"No one?"

"It's magic that stirs my senses," Ysbeta said. "Writing

my books, sailing to port after port, learning even the simplest charms brings me joy. That is what I must do to live a useful life. I must pursue knowledge of magic, preserve it, pass it on to the ones who thirst for it. My life will end the moment a warding collar wraps around my neck."

Beatrice shuddered. "You must never know what it's like."

"How do you know?"

"My mother took me aside and put mine around my neck this very morning."

Ysbeta lifted one hand to cover a soft gasp. "That's supposed to be bad luck for you Chaslanders, isn't it?"

"Bad luck," Beatrice grumbled. "I wonder how many brides made a run for it before that particular superstition took hold."

"Why did she do that?"

"Because she wanted me to know exactly what sorceresses sacrifice. She didn't know until it was too late."

"Does she not want you to marry?" Ysbeta asked. "Does she dislike Ianthe?"

"That's not why she did it." Beatrice turned her head and watched cattle graze. "She didn't want me to make a choice I will regret."

"Will you regret marrying my brother?"

Beatrice pressed her lips shut and breathed slowly. She smelled the dusty road and the green meadow and a ribbon of the southern sea. She studied the glowing aura of sorcery around Ysbeta's head. The same choice loomed before her, and she shook her head.

"I will regret something, regardless of what I choose. But if any man is worth warding for, it's your brother."

"But you don't know what to choose," Ysbeta said. "I do know, Beatrice. I choose magic. Show me how to save myself."

The journey to Lavan House took an age. Beatrice followed Ysbeta inside, and she dashed through the marble hall as if she couldn't see the beauty of it anymore. Beatrice hurried along behind Ysbeta, who deposited her in a soft green room with glass-paned doors leading to the garden.

"I'll be right back," she promised. "Wait here."

The room was filled with beautiful things. Beatrice circled the room at the slow pace of a museum visitor and gazed on the shapes and fabrics of the furniture, the intricate vines, leaves, and fruit on the enormous hand-knotted carpet, and the perfect, formal symmetry of the gardens outside. She drifted past a rosewood pianochord and stopped before a serpentine statue carved in the fluid, realistic style of Sanchi.

It depicted a Sanchan woman, tall and slim, dressed in elegantly draping robes and jewels. Pendant earrings hung from her lobes and her veil of hair was anchored by a jeweled diadem across her brow. A ring pierced the inner septum of her nose. But Beatrice stared at her corded, elegant, and completely bare throat.

Beatrice studied the woman's features. The youthful plumpness was gone from this woman's face; her cheekbones were high, her full lips curved in a half smile. Her body was a woman's territory—full-breasted, round-hipped, and robust. Her hands were half-raised, curled to signal protection and invitation.

Magicians' summoning signs. Beatrice used them while casting conjurations. This woman carved from serpentine was a magician, probably one of those who lived high in the mountains around Sanchi and mastered the art and science of magic.

If only she and Ysbeta could run away. But Beatrice couldn't abandon her family to the debtors. She had to remain in Chasland and save them. She thought of never seeing Father, or Harriet, or Mother, not even for a visit, and her eyes watered. They had to do the ordeal. Beatrice needed her grimoire back, and that meant getting Ysbeta to the point where she could attempt it first. It wasn't just she who needed this freedom. Ysbeta did too, and maybe more than Beatrice did.

Ysbeta carried a packing case heavy enough that she leaned the opposite way to compensate. Tucked under her other arm was a clothbound book.

Ysbeta nodded to one of the glass-paned doors leading out of the manor. "We're having an outdoor lunch in the wood," she said. "Let's hurry."

"Just cut them with a knife," Ysbeta said.

"Even if I had such a thing, you would have to explain why your staylaces were cut." Beatrice had managed to pull the knot a little more, and then the whole thing unraveled all at once. Ysbeta was nearly dancing with impatience, but Beatrice took care with this, as she had with Ysbeta's mantua and stomacher.

"The sun will be down before you're done," Ysbeta said, "and you said night conjurations were more dangerous."

It was hours to sundown, but they had no reason to dawdle. "Lift your arms."

Beatrice lifted the stays over Ysbeta's head, careful with her hair, and laid the boned garment on top of the case, now overflowing with ruffled orange silk.

"Cast the circle," Beatrice said. "I want to be sure your casting is strong enough."

"I practiced," Ysbeta said, a note of complaint in her voice.

"But you have to do this alone," Beatrice said. "This is what your brother did to gain the initiation of the rose."

"How do you know that?"

"He told me. Not in so many words, but he told me

enough that I could figure out the rest."

Ysbeta bit her lip. "Ianthe had been a novice for years before he earned the rose."

"I know," Beatrice said. "But there's no time to study everything he did, even if we did have the means to learn it. What we're doing is incredibly dangerous."

"You did it."

"And I had no idea what could have happened when I did. Ysbeta. You have to know who you are when you host a spirit. You have to be sure of yourself—not just your thoughts and reflections, but of your body."

"I know who I am," Ysbeta said. "I promise I'll be careful. Please let me do this."

Beatrice stood aside.

Ysbeta had practiced, just as she said. Her casting was stronger. She remembered sigil and sign and vibrated the names of the lords of magic perfectly. Soon a silver-violet chased dome of light protected her, and she called out to the aether to a particular spirit.

Beatrice held her breath. A shimmering shadow leaking black light flickered in front of Ysbeta.

"Elamin, spirit of joy. I have a suitor I do not want, but I bear him no ill will. I want you to stir his feelings for a different woman."

The spirit shimmered. Beatrice tensed. Could it do that? Was that a reasonable thing to ask?

"Let her be pretty enough. Let her have a sorceress's talent. But turn his attention away from me. Make him fall in love with someone who will make him happy."

No. It was too much. Ysbeta couldn't ask for this; it was wrong. "Banish it," Beatrice said. "I don't think a lesser spirit can do that."

Ysbeta didn't react. Could she hear Beatrice at all? "I will give you conefruit. Whiskey. A hot, perfumed bath," Ysbeta said. "An hour of music. The sight of the moon. I will carry you to midnight."

Beatrice shook her head. "It won't work."

Ysbeta ignored her, still speaking to the spirit. "Then I will carry you to the next noon. You will wear my most beautiful habit. You will ride a fine horse. You will dream my dreams while I sleep. You will have meat this evening and pastry in the morning. Everything I do from now until noon you will enjoy. Do we have a bargain?"

It was too much. "No," Beatrice said. "Don't agree to that. That's too much time, you could get caught—"

But Ysbeta thrust her hand through the barrier, sealing the bargain. The spirit engulfed her hand and slipped inside the circle. Sparks of black light streaked across Ysbeta's skin before sinking inside her, fading from vision and magical sight.

Beatrice's gut gave a sickening lurch. It was done. Ysbeta had bargained too much. And the expression on her face was wrong—it was too greedy. Too hungry.

Ysbeta snatched up the bottle of whiskey and drank till she coughed. Sweet, golden nectar ran down her arm to the elbow as she bit into the tender conefruit, chewing noisily.

"Delicious," Ysbeta said. "Where is more?"

Beatrice braced herself. That wasn't Ysbeta. Disaster stood in the sanctum with her, demanding more conefruit and whiskey.

"You have to control it," Beatrice said. "Spirits have no conscience. They don't understand restraint. You must control it."

Ysbeta's chin came up, her expression sulky. She took a step toward Beatrice, and Beatrice's heart tried to kick its way out of her ribs. "I want more."

"Please, Elamin. Withdraw yourself," Beatrice said. "Let me have my friend back."

"But it's fun."

The voice wasn't Ysbeta's either. Instead of her honeyed, throaty voice, accented in a way that rolled the words into shiny, smooth polished stones, the spirit spoke in high-pitched tones, piping like a child.

"You must let Ysbeta protect you." Beatrice raised her hands, putting a wall between them. "If you get caught, you will be caged. You will be hurt. My friend will die."

Ysbeta had to fight. She had to control the spirit. The longer she kept the spirit talking, the better chance she had.

But the spirit stared at her, Ysbeta's mouth spread in a petulant line. "You're spoiling my fun," the spirit inside Ysbeta said. "Get out of my way."

"Ysbeta!" Beatrice cried, but she already shaped the wall of light and the sign of banishment. Breath poured down her throat, and Beatrice intoned the name of Anam, ready to cast it out.

Her breath stopped as Ysbeta's hands slid around her neck, squeezing. No air! She grabbed at Ysbeta's wrists, trying to pull herself free, but her grip was too strong. Beatrice was going to die here. She couldn't!

She let go of Ysbeta's wrists and made the signs, pushing her will out of her palms. Ysbeta let go, and Beatrice sucked up a loud breath. She had one chance.

"Anam," she croaked. "Welaa, Har—"

Ysbeta squeaked and covered Beatrice's mouth with her hand. "Don't! Beatrice, it's me, it's Ysbeta, I have it. Don't banish it."

Beatrice tried to swallow, her throat coated with dust. She coughed. "Release it."

"I can't. I need this. Elamin, stop. You have to behave." Ysbeta scowled. "Don't talk back to me."

She looked so cross Beatrice would have laughed if she weren't trying to get her breath back. She touched her throat—was it bruised?

"You can't!" Ysbeta, fists clenched, scolded the spirit inside her. "If we get caught, you won't get to hear music. Do you want that? Oh Skyborn, Beatrice. I am so sorry."

"You can project your thoughts at it," Beatrice said. Her voice was hoarse. "So you don't attract attention. Elamin doesn't know any better. But you see how dangerous this is? Let me banish it."

"No. I need this," Ysbeta said. "I need Bard to change his mind. I need him to marry someone else. Anyone. I don't care who," Ysbeta said. "I need him to stop courting me. I'm not going to hurt him. This will help him. He'll find a good wife and forget all about me."

"But your mother and Lord Gordon want this," Beatrice said. "You could just wind up doubly miserable, with a husband who doesn't want you."

Ysbeta waved the argument away. "I'll buy more time once Elamin turns his head for someone else. Mother wants to shove me into a marriage with Bard, but Bard's opinion matters where mine does not."

"So Elamin makes Bard fall for someone else? Who?"

"Anyone," Ysbeta said. "I'm not the only bride who could make the Sheldons richer. The Maisonettes have money. Genevra Martin, that elegant girl with the rippling black hair—her father is a diplomat. Let him love that girl, heart-whole and happy."

"Can Elamin really make Bard fall in love with someone?"

"It says it can fill Bard's heart with joy at the sight of someone else."

Beatrice sighed. "You have to keep control of this spirit. If you had been doing this in the chapterhouse, I don't think you would be alive right now."

Ysbeta shook her head. "It was only for a minute."

"It tried to kill me. And then it would have wandered out,

and you would have paid the price for its actions. They kill the mage who is possessed, Ysbeta. They burn them alive."

Ysbeta blanched. "They what?"

"Sorcerers are cremated at death here," Beatrice said. "They can't leave the body where a spirit could get at it."

"We burn our bodies too. But alive?"

"It's cruel," Beatrice said. "I have never witnessed it. But that's what Ianthe witnessed in Meryton."

Ysbeta looked properly unsettled now. "Elamin. Did you hear that? They'll burn us if you don't behave."

"You can—"

"Project my thoughts at it," Ysbeta finished. She frowned, thinking loudly at the spirit inside her. "I think it understands. I am so sorry, Beatrice. I only lost control for a minute. I didn't know it moved so fast."

Ysbeta had teetered on the edge of disaster. But she snatched control back, and now she would be even more vigilant. The bargain would be fulfilled. She could escape this fate, and they could learn the magic in the next grimoire. And the next, until Beatrice held the spell for the great bargain in her hands.

"You need to get back into your stays," Beatrice said.

Ysbeta's shoulders slumped in relief. "And you need to get home. Will you play a little music while we wait for the carriage?"

"I'd be happy to," Beatrice said. "We have to banish the circle first. I'd like to watch you do that—"

"Miss Clayborn."

Ysbeta stared in horror at the sanctum doors, a shadow over her face. Beatrice spun, her heart in her aching throat.

Ianthe stood at the threshold of the sanctum, his form limned by the long rays of the sinking sun.

"What are you doing?" he asked, and the world flinched under Beatrice's feet.

CHAPTER XIV

All the words died on Beatrice's tongue. Caught. They were caught, and there was no hiding what they were doing when the circle they stood in glowed like starlight to the magical sight of an initiate. She stood frozen as Ianthe came nearer, his hands clasped behind his back as he walked around the candlelit circle. Every step made dust puff into the air around his ankles as he dismantled their circle, gathering it up with an efficiency that spoke to his training. Ysbeta moved, finally, a violent swing of her arms.

"Get out, Anthy! I'm not decent."

Beatrice moved to the basket and picked up Ysbeta's stays. "We'll be a moment."

But Ianthe ignored her, focused solely on the dome of magic he unraveled. His brow furrowed, and he paused. "A conjuration," he said. "You two summoned a spirit. Is that correct?"

Ysbeta crossed her arms over her chest. "If you say anything, I swear I'll—"

"Is that correct," Ianthe said, his voice flat.

"Yes," Beatrice said. Ysbeta twisted to give Beatrice an exasperated look, but Beatrice ignored it. "It's banished now; it's over."

A lie echoed on the sanctum's domed roof the same as any others, but Beatrice concentrated on juggling Ysbeta's stays and their laces. If Ianthe learned that Ysbeta hosted a lesser spirit even as they spoke, he would be furious. He would pull the spirit from Ysbeta's breast, and then Ysbeta's bargain would not hold. Bard wouldn't be lovestruck by someone else. But Ysbeta had to stay calm. She had to keep control over a spirit who had already gained the advantage, who had already asserted control over her body.

Ianthe must never know what they had done here.

"I warned you," Ianthe said. "This is dangerous. It has to end."

"You can't tell us what to do." Ysbeta lifted her arms and let Beatrice wrap the stays around her body. "You can tell Father, you can report us, but you can't—"

"Don't be a fool, Ysy," Ianthe said. "You've been lucky so far. But you must keep a tight rein on spirits. When we take the Ordeal of the Rose and make our first bargain, we're in danger. If we make a mistake, if we don't do it exactly right, then we're as good as dead."

Beatrice swallowed. They had come so close to disaster. Her throat still hurt—was it bruised?

"But you can wrest control back," Ysbeta said. "You might falter, but you can recover."

If she said anything, she would spill it all. Beatrice concentrated on threading Ysbeta's stays, studying the expert stitching around the lacing holes.

"If you're lucky," Ianthe said. "Whose idea was this, to come out here and toy with spirits?"

"Mine," Ysbeta said. "I wanted to consult a spirit about tomorrow's ride."

"You cast a circle and conjured a spirit to scry for you? In the face of all the dangers."

"Yes," Ysbeta lied. "There will be a commotion tomorrow. Everyone will be talking about it by sundown."

That wasn't much of a prediction. Any large gathering of the young burst with potential to cause a stir, and Ianthe looked properly skeptical. "You didn't need a spirit to predict that."

Ysbeta huffed. "I didn't say we were satisfied by the conjuration."

"Ysbeta—" Ianthe turned to regard Beatrice. "My sister talked you into this."

"That's hardly fair." Beatrice pulled on the cord. "I have a will of my own."

"But you wouldn't let her do something dangerous alone. That's not the kind of friend you are. I know that much. But tell me something. Why did you leave me stranded on Pigment Street?"

"That painting was horrifying," Ysbeta said. "I can't have a wedding like that. I can't."

Beatrice ducked her head. It didn't make sense that Ysbeta rushed off in a great upset and then whiled away the afternoon asking for gossip from a spirit. If Ianthe saw it on her face, they'd be sunk.

"I know," Ianthe said. "I am trying to help. Please believe that I will do everything I can to make this easier for you. But promise me you won't muck about with conjurations again. You are in far more danger than you realize."

"I will not promise," Ysbeta said. "I cannot promise. What will you do?"

They stared at each other, and Beatrice hardly dared breathe.

Ianthe clamped his mouth shut, then threw up his hands. "If you fail, no one will be here who can help you. If you fail, you will burn—and the spirit deserts you at the first flames, leaving you to die alone. Don't you understand that?"

"I can do this." Ysbeta took a half step toward her brother and nearly tugged the staylaces out of Beatrice's hands. "Help me. Don't just stand there and prattle of the danger to me. I'm already in danger."

"Enough. I am taking Miss Clayborn home, and this is the last you will see of her in privacy."

"Does that mean you'll help us?" Ysbeta asked.

"Ysy—"

"Perhaps I should go with a driver." Beatrice pulled the laces taut, and Ysbeta exhaled, allowing the stays to restrict her breaths. "If you wish to discuss this further, I mean."

"I am taking you home," Ianthe said. "And I mean it. No more meeting each other alone. This ends now."

"I can't marry Bard Sheldon. I won't. I will do everything in my power to escape it. Everything."

"You do not have the skill to make the great bargain," Ianthe said. "You don't know the ritual, you don't have time to learn it, and you won't have a chance. I'm telling the housekeeper to keep a maid with you when Miss Clayborn is here, and I am not."

"Ianthe." Ysbeta's voice broke. "Don't do this to me."

"I won't watch you die," Ianthe's voice cut through the air. "I will not."

Beatrice held up Ysbeta's mantua, and Ysbeta held the stomacher to her body as Beatrice pinned it into place. "Then don't watch me marry a man who will keep me warded day in and day out, forced to have child after child! Don't desert me in a country that strips me of my wealth and property, my very rights—simply because I am a woman! And for what? Don't we have enough money? Don't we have enough power? Do I have to die in childbed for Mother's rubber empire?"

Ianthe stood still. Understanding dawned on his face. "You will have the best doctors, the finest Llanandras has, I promise you. If your hesitation is about that—"

"It is about what I want, and what I do not," Ysbeta said. "I want my freedom. I don't want to marry—not Bard Sheldon, not anyone. I want to continue my study of magic. I never, never want to be pregnant. And no one cares what I want except Beatrice."

Beatrice's middle made an uneasy turn as Ianthe flicked a glance at her. "I care."

"Then do something! Help me."

"I will help you. I'm doing everything I can."

"But you're not doing anything to help me get what I want—"

"I can't allow you to dabble in High Magic again. It's too dangerous, and it's not the answer." Ianthe shook his head as Ysbeta voiced a wordless protest. "I am taking Miss Clayborn home. The subject is closed."

He held out his hand to Beatrice. With one last silent look at Ysbeta, she allowed Ianthe to lead her away.

Faced with no good options for conversation, Beatrice remained silent. A pair of glossy gait-matched black prancers settled into a brisk trot under Ianthe's guidance. She sat with her hands folded in her lap and watched the road, keeping her expression carefully neutral. The setting sun warmed their backs and cast long shadows on the road before them. Beatrice watched them stretch over the road, echoed by their own thoughts.

They had been caught. They had lied. Ianthe had forbidden his sister to pursue magic any further, but they had to find a way. If Ysbeta didn't give Beatrice the grimoire with the ritual to summon a greater spirit, their path went no further than the summoning of lesser spirits and their small favors—enough to get them locked into collars for the rest of their lives if they were caught, but not enough to free them, no matter how clever they were. They had to find a way around Ianthe's restriction. There was no time left for either of them.

Beatrice stole a glance at Ianthe. He knew she had successfully conjured a lesser spirit. He was permissive. He meant to allow her the liberty of her magic. He believed in planning his family. He was her best choice—even if it meant losing the chance to bond a greater spirit. It would save the Clayborns. Shouldn't she give this up? Wouldn't it be better if it were him—sophisticated, generous, and kind—where any other man would leave her trapped inside the dim, nothing world of the warding collar? He was the best man anyone could ask for, and all this secrecy, all this risk, would end.

But Ysbeta didn't have a man like Ianthe. Ysbeta faced nothing less than the obliteration of everything she wanted. Beatrice couldn't give up. She couldn't leave Ysbeta to her fate. They had to find a way.

Ianthe turned his head, showing her the devastating sight of his face in three-quarter profile. "I need to ask you something."

"Please ask."

"It's indelicate."

"I won't tell anyone," Beatrice promised.

He looked away, embarrassment rippling across his face. "Does my sister fear the marriage bed?"

Beatrice blinked. "You were right, it is indelicate. But in truth, I don't know."

Ianthe's shoulders came down. "Because if that's all it is —"

Beatrice huffed. "That is not all it is. She shouldn't be herded into marriage like this."

Ianthe waved one arm in a circle that encompassed the world. "But women do it all the time. They marry. They have children. That's the point of marriage."

"And we die in childbirth all the time," Beatrice said. "And what if she just didn't want to have children?"

Ianthe scoffed. "But it's—"

Beatrice pounced. "Natural?"

He went silent, frowning at something over Beatrice's

shoulder. "Are you saying that you don't want children? Is that why you'll risk your life to chase magic?"

"I am not saying that," Beatrice said. "But if I'm to do what I want to do with my life, then I can never have children. And what husband would accept that? Would you?"

Ianthe looked away.

Beatrice folded her arms. "You see, then."

"But you can't have what you want! You need the support of the chapterhouse to attempt it. You need a mentor. You need training—"

"I have no way to gain that support. No way to receive that training," Beatrice said. "The only way I can do this is alone."

"I can't stand by and watch you destroy yourself, Beatrice!" Ianthe shook his head and looked away. "I can't do it, not for you, or Ysbeta either. Face the facts. You cannot have what you want."

"What if I could?" Beatrice said. "What if I knew the mystery? What if I knew how to conjure the greater spirit of my choice, what if I could succeed?"

"This is no time for imagination and games. You need to stop this before it's too late," Ianthe said. "I'm not ready to know the mystery, and I have trained for years with every resource, with the best mentors, with the favor of the chapterhouse and the companionship of the lesser spirit Fandari. If you attempt this, you will die—but not before the spirit possesses you and destroys your family."

"Do you think me unafraid?" Beatrice asked. "Do you think I believe myself invincible? I don't know if I can do it. I don't know if I should try—"

"You should not try!" Ianthe shouted.

The horses sped up, and he soothed them back down to a jog. "Beatrice. Please. I know you have had impressive success with conjurations. If you were a man, you'd be an initiate of the rose—"

Beatrice didn't want to hear what she would have if she were a man. She didn't want to be a man. She wanted to be a magician! "But I am not a man."

"It's not that I believe you are incapable because of your sex. And in a different world—"

"I live in this one," Beatrice said. "There's no sense wishing I was the child of another star. I have to choose what to do here."

"How will you choose, Beatrice? And will you think of the people who love you when you do it?"

"I think of my family every day." Beatrice clenched her fists, sweaty inside her gloves. "Do you imagine that I do not? My family teeters on a precipice. If I fail them—"

"Then do not fail them," Ianthe said. "Do the right thing."

"Ianthe." Beatrice turned in her seat and had to tilt her head to shade her eyes from the sinking sun. "Please understand that while I have argued with you all the way down the highway, I am torn in two."

"Then choose," Ianthe said. "Use your wisdom and choose. Please."

"I could do as you say," Beatrice said, her voice low. "I could just give up. I could accept my fate—and maybe it wouldn't be so bad, in the end—isn't my mother happy? Isn't your mother? But Ysbeta cannot make the compromise that I face. She is resolute. Turn your thoughts to helping her."

"It's the question of what you will do that freezes me in place. I have the means to stop Ysbeta from pursuing higher magic. I can't stop you—and thinking of what could happen to you chills my blood."

"I understand."

"I don't think you do. Beatrice. If I could solve this for you—"

"You can't," Beatrice said. "There are only three things

you can do—tell my father what I'm doing, help me, or step back and let me decide. Which is it?"

Ianthe drove the curricle in silence, navigating street traffic as they trotted along Triumph Street.

"I won't tell your father," Ianthe said. "But you're in danger, and I don't know how to make you see it."

Beatrice raised one hand to her throat. "I understand the danger."

Ianthe shook his head. "If you did, you'd end this."

She understood the danger. But now they knew how to find the women of the hidden path. They had only been forbidden to be alone together in privacy. Nothing said about them riding through town, seeing the sights on Thornback Street.

They would get help, and just in time.

He halted the horses in front of Beatrice's townhouse. "I don't like arguing with you. But think about what you're doing. I'll see you at the Blossom Ride."

Beatrice nodded to him and let the footman help her down from the carriage. The front door swung open, and Harriet stood there, her face a picture of distress, her eyes leaking tears.

"Why didn't you come home?" Harriet demanded. "How could you—half the servants are out searching for you!"

"What? But I was with Ysbeta and Ianthe, as I said."

"You were only supposed to be gone until after lunch," Harriet said. "You were supposed to come back and help me pick a dress for tea."

"What has happened?" Beatrice asked, but her younger sister grabbed her arm and yanked her inside, sniffling and sobbing.

Harriet shook her arm. "You missed tea, you missed dinner—where did you go?"

"Lavan House," Beatrice said. "Ysbeta had to go home early, and I—"

"And you couldn't leave a note? Didn't you think we would— This is your fault," Harriet said, her voice furious and low. "Everything's ruined."

Beatrice stared at her sister. "What is ruined? It was only a few hours. I didn't realize I would be gone so long—"

"But you should have left a note! You should have let us know! And then I wouldn't have—"

The room went cold. "Wouldn't have what?"

Harriet's shoulders rose. "I didn't know what had happened to you. I feared the worst."

Beatrice grabbed Harriet's chin and forced her to face Beatrice's gaze. "What did you do?"

"I had to," Harriet said. "Sneaking off to the beach in your shift, cheating at cards—what if you'd lost all control and—"

She didn't. She couldn't have. But she knew already. She knew it from her sister's downturned mouth, from her refusal to look Beatrice in the face.

"Oh! You couldn't wait to hang me out to dry." Beatrice let go of Harriet and planted her fists on her hips. "You told! I can't believe you would do this to me!"

"You're so selfish! You never think of how we'd feel if you'd come to peril. You never think of what you're doing to the family!"

"I do! I wasn't in danger! You wanted to tell on me. You took the first chance you had!"

"You could have been possessed!" Harriet hissed. "You could have—oh, I can't even speak of it!"

"Good. I've heard enough from you. How could you do this to me? How?" Beatrice stalked past her sister, the rat, the chattering, backstabbing rat, and headed for the library door. How was she going to mend this with Father? Would he even speak to her? Would he even see her face?

"Please!"

That was Mother, shouting loudly enough to be heard through closed doors. Beatrice picked up her skirts and scurried across the tiled foyer floor. She pressed her ear to the wood and listened to Mother's sobs.

"She's our child! You must let me find her; we must know what's happened! Take it off, Henry, I beg you. I beg."

Beatrice's fingers flew to her throat. Mother meant to find her with magic. Mother knew enough magic to—what? Did she know how to conjure?

"What are you doing?" Harriet demanded.

"Shh." Beatrice held up a quelling hand and pressed harder.

"We can't take that chance," Father said. "What if my son slumbers inside you?"

Beatrice shivered. They were still trying for a son. A boy, who could take the helm of the Clayborns, attend the chapterhouse, and raise their fortunes with magic and political connections, better than merely bartering daughters. If Mother carried a son, Father would convince himself he didn't need Beatrice.

But listening to Mother beg twisted in her heart. Father was no magician; Mother had chosen the man she loved over the chance to raise her prospects. And now, because of choosing that love, she had to beg to use what the Skyborn had given her by right.

"It will be just like the last time, when you wouldn't consult the spirits about the orchid expedition. What if there was a son, you said, and plunged thousands into worthless plants."

Harriet came closer. "Beatrice—"

Beatrice waved her hand, as if a gesture could make tattling younger siblings vanish. Father had released Mother from the warding collar before? Mother knew the lesser conjuration. Beatrice's hands went cold. Father might love Mother. He might smile every time he laid eyes on her. But Mother should be on her feet. She should be casting by sigil and sign to search for her child. She was a sorceress, and she was begging on her knees before a powerless man.

"It's been six weeks since your courses," Father said. "I can't risk it."

"It won't hold. None of them have! Beatrice and Harriet are our only children. We can't risk a real daughter for a possible son."

Harriet scurried to the door, pressing her ear to the wood, but she misjudged the distance and thumped her head against it. Beatrice winced at the sound, and at the silence on the other side of the door.

"Harriet," Father called. "Open the door, if you please."

Caught. Beatrice shot a glare at her sister, twisted the doorknob, and stepped inside.

Mother was on her knees, her hands fisted into Father's weskit, tears soaking her face. Father's expression melted from relief to red-faced, brow-knit anger.

"Beatrice! Where have you been?"

Beatrice dropped a hasty curtsey. "Lavan House. Ysbeta took a mood, and I went with her to cheer her up. I should have sent a note, but she was most upset—"

"You're safe," Mother said. She picked herself up and threw her arms around Beatrice, squeezing tighter than her stays. "We didn't know what had become of you. We didn't know if you were hurt or lost or—"

If she'd run away, after learning the truth of the warding collar? "I'm here, Mother. I didn't mean to be gone for so long, it just happened—"

Harriet slipped into the room. "It's all right. Beatrice is

safe. Please don't punish her."

"Harriet," Father said. "Go out and shut the door."

"But Father, it's all right, I was wrong, please don't—"

"Shut the door," Father repeated.

Harriet retreated. The door swung shut. Father stood on the other side of his desk and regarded Beatrice, unspeaking.

Beatrice tried to find the right words, but what explanation could she give for her actions? "Father, I—"

"Lord Gordon called on me today to pay his and Ysbeta Lavan's debt. And when you didn't come home, Harriet told me something I can scarcely believe of my own daughter."

Beatrice's back went stiff. "I've been careful."

"Tell me exactly how you won so much money at cards. The truth."

Beatrice licked her lips. "I was lucky."

"The truth!" Father roared, and his fist thumping on the desk made Beatrice jump. "You conjured a spirit. You made a bargain with it. Say it!"

"Father, you only gave me fifty crowns," Beatrice said. "Only fifty, and the stakes were ten crowns a point. I could have come home hundreds of crowns in debt. It would have ruined the family."

"The finances of this family are my concern. If you had come to harm playing with conjuring . . . If you had been caught cheating! I am the one who decides what risks we take, Beatrice." Father buried his face in his hands, shaking. "But you are safe, even if you have come within a hair of ruining this family. With selfishness, with outrageous behavior —it ends now. You will leave playing with forces you don't understand immediately. Is that clear?"

Beatrice's throat ached. She had been caught. "I didn't want to drive us deeper into debt. That was all!"

Father went redder, his face pinched with ire. "That is not all. You have willfully abandoned proper womanly behavior. If it comes out that you are dabbling in higher magic . . ."

He huffed out a breath and began again. "But it will not. You will be married, as swiftly as possible."

There was still one chance. She was going to wait until the damage was done, but there was no time for that now. Perhaps she could bargain. "Father, I could help you," Beatrice said. "Like Mother does. I could keep learning. If I remain unmarried and become a mage, then you could always have the assistance of a greater spirit. Together we could—"

"Cease this nonsense immediately." Father cut off her words with a sharp sideways-chopping gesture. "Never speak to me of such a thing again. It's unnatural. It's unheard of. To think my daughter would even countenance something so outlandish! It ends now."

It couldn't. It couldn't! But if Father wouldn't be tempted by the service of a greater spirit, if he was resolute about her being married . . . the shards of her dream lay scattered before her. She had no choice.

Beatrice hung her head. "Yes, Father."

"I should confine you immediately. But there is another way. You have one chance to mend this." Father held up a square of soft blue paper. "We have been invited to attend a party on the *Shining Hand*. If you stand a chance of securing the likes of Ianthe Lavan, I must allow you to attend your daily life as if this hadn't happened."

Did she? Did she have a chance with Ianthe, after how they spoke to each other on the ride from Lavan House to Bendleton? It didn't matter. She and Ysbeta still had a way to continue their pursuits. "Yes, Father."

"However, after the Blossom Ride is over, this party will be the last invitation you will accept as an unattached woman. If you are not engaged by the time we disembark, I will choose someone for you. Do you understand?"

All her plans crumpled. The party at the *Shining Hand* was in two days. How could they be ready to become magi in two days?

It was over. Harriet had ruined everything. Beatrice would be married; magic would be taken from her. The only kindness Father had allowed was the chance to secure Ianthe's hand.

But maybe it wouldn't be so bad? Ianthe would let her out of the warding collar sometimes. Maybe she—no. That wasn't freedom. That was permission.

How could she open her hand and let magic fall from her grasp?

"Answer me."

"Father. Please. I can help—"

"That's enough."

Beatrice hung her head. "Yes, Father."

"Clara will sleep in your room at night."

So she would have no privacy, no chance to hide anything. "Yes, Father."

"You will go straight to bed after the search of your room is complete. Or you can tell me where you have hidden your ritual tools, and you may have dinner first."

Beatrice clenched her fists. She was caught. But she hadn't climbed the ladder to the attic in days. She knew the casting by heart; chalk and candles didn't matter anymore. "They're in the attic," she said.

Father nodded. "That's an honesty befitting my daughter. Sit here. I will return."

Beatrice sank into a chair, trembling. The game was up. Father's footfalls echoed on the stairs. Beatrice leaned into her mother's embrace as she buried her face in her hands.

It was over. Her choice had been taken. But she made the signs of summoning, breathed out her casting, and hoped.

:Nadi. I'm sorry.:

:Beatrice?:

Beatrice lifted her head, looking about the room. :Nadi?:

:You're sad.:

Beatrice sat up, sniffling. :You could come without a full summoning?:

:I see you,: said Nadi. :Ever since you called to me, I can see you. Our task is not done. I am near you until you have the book in your hands.:

Beatrice looked for a distortion in the air, something to show her where the spirit was. She saw nothing. :I don't have anything to ask you.:

:Nadi just wants to be here.:

:Can you stay? I don't need anything. Can you stay? I'm riding a horse tomorrow. And going on a basket lunch you can eat. Do you want to do that?:

:Yes,: Nadi said. :Let me in.:

There was no summoning circle to move her to the aetheric. There was only the air, and Beatrice stretched her hand out before her, fingers curled in the sign of welcome.

Mother stared, her eyebrows high. She looked at Beatrice, opened her mouth . . . and then shut it again. She remained silent as her daughter welcomed a spirit, offering to host. Beatrice could have wept.

"Thank you," she whispered. Her fingers prickled. Nadi slid under her skin, settling down next to her bones.

:Better,: Nadi sighed. :You're not so sad anymore.:

Beatrice folded her arms around her middle. :Thank you. This is—this is what a friend would do.:

Nadi hummed, content.

Father returned with four books tucked under his arm. "We found the candles, and the chalkstones, and these books. What were these books doing up there?"

Beatrice blinked away tears. "Books?"

Oh. *Tales of Ijanel and Other Heroes. The Philosophy of*

Persistence. A Study of Natural Pigments and Dyes. Gemstones and Their Qualities. To Father, they were just books—and if he read them, he would be irritated by the typographical errors in the text. He didn't have any way to know what they really were. She shrugged her shoulders and prepared to lie.

"They were up there when I found the attic," Beatrice said.

Father gave them a scowl and slid each volume onto the room's bookshelves. "Perfectly good books," he grumbled. "Go ask Cook for your supper. She's working hard on your luncheon basket for tomorrow."

It wasn't forgiveness, but the books hadn't been burned. And Father didn't know what they were—he had believed her when she claimed they had just been in the attic with the rest of the junk.

She knew the magic inside them. She could hide another grimoire in plain sight, then. She would find a way to find privacy. She still had a chance.

Beatrice climbed the stairs, thinking hard about how to escape.

CHAPTER XV

It should be raining right now—a cold, pounding rain that plastered all the fragile petals on the cherry trees to the muddy pathways of Lord Harsgrove Park. But cotton-fluff clouds sailed in a perfect blue sky without a drop of rain in sight. Marian frisked and dazzled on fresh horseshoes. Beatrice kept her spine straight, her head high, and breathed in the scent of cherry blossoms.

:More,: said Nadi. :Now make a jump.:

:The jump comes later. After the luncheon.: Beatrice hitched her reed basket containing the meal Cook had prepared for the orphans' auction, cursing the awkwardness of the burden. A fat violet silk ribbon matching her riding habit fluttered from the handle, and it was heavy with treats and hearty foods.

Beatrice hefted it again and glared at the basket. What if she simply dropped it and let it smash on the cobblestones? Then no one could buy it.

:No,: said Nadi. :You promised to let me eat it. You promised.:

:You will get your share.: Beatrice propped the basket on her thigh, but it interfered with Marian's reins. Confound the thing! She had to get rid of it.

"Please allow me," said a voice from her right, and she twisted in the saddle. Danton Maisonette rode beside her, one hand offering to take the basket for her. "I noticed your struggle."

:Oh, him.: Nadi would have rolled Beatrice's eyes, if she hadn't an iron grip on the spirit.

:You can't hex him again,: Beatrice thought, and put on a hasty smile. "I'm surprised at your efforts to speak to me."

"I was dreadful to you at the chapterhouse. I apologize, Miss Clayborn. It was quite churlish of me. Please allow me to lighten your burden."

He still had his hand out. Beatrice wished she had not taken breakfast in her room. If she had unbent from her anger and let her in, Harriet would have told her every detail of luncheon basket etiquette, and then she would have a chance of knowing what message accepting his help communicated. Stubborn anger had done her no favors.

Danton's smile faded as Beatrice rode on without handing him the basket—but what did it mean? Curses! She widened her smile and offered the heavy burden to him, and he cheered considerably.

"Thank you," Beatrice said. "It's an awkward thing to carry while sidesaddle."

"Exactly my thought," Danton said. "And if I may confess, I desired to speak to you before the bidding started."

What! Why? He had mocked her, and she him. She had witnessed the humiliating accident that surely had ruined a fine set of clothes. She had actively avoided him at the Robicheaux party, and now he was at her side, playing the gallant?

"This is a fine basket," Danton said, hefting it. "I'm curious to know its contents."

:I don't like him,: Nadi said. :His smile is too smooth. He wants something.:

:Of course he does.: Beatrice dipped her chin, as if it were a compliment to be the object of such attention. "I hope Cook packed her currant-fig tarts." She couldn't survey the chatty crowd that had gathered while she had the company of a gentleman. It would be rude. "Will you be racing in the competitions this afternoon?"

Danton smiled regretfully. "My finest horses laze about at home in Valserre," he said. " Have you ever been there?"

:Where's Valserre?:

:It's another country, far from here. Across the sea, to the west.:

:Can we go?:

:Not in a single morning.:

:Hmph.:

"Never, but Masillia is a city of legendary music," Beatrice replied, and turned to the source of hoofbeats to her left. "Ysbeta, good morning. What a lovely habit."

Ysbeta grimaced, but she was a picture—her golden silk embroidered weskit and cream jacket were the peak of fashion, and her warm brown complexion glowed in the presence of a color that would make Beatrice look bleached. "Good morning. Come with me."

Ysbeta rode off without waiting for Beatrice's response. She turned a helpless look at her companion. "I fear I am needed, Mr. Maisonette. My apologies."

She put her hand out for her basket, and Danton gave it over with some consternation. Beatrice hoisted it to rest on her knee as she wove through the riders to Ysbeta's side.

"What are you doing?" Beatrice asked.

:Why is she scared?: Nadi asked.

"Looking for somewhere to hide," Ysbeta said. "It's not noon yet. I don't want him distracted by me. Trying to keep Elamin under control on the way here was exhausting."

Perhaps ivory and gold riding habits were not the most discreet sartorial choice for one who wished to fade into a crowd, but Beatrice kept her silence. She followed Ysbeta as she found a place where the road featured a spot to pull away from the traffic of so many horses and young people trying their best to attract attention.

"I'd feel better under some cover, but—" She indicated the spotless drape of her skirts, the toe of a golden-yellow boot peeking from beneath. "I couldn't delay Ianthe's attendance any longer. He's scouting all around for you, wanting to know how to pick out your luncheon basket. You've thoroughly enchanted him. Who was that riding with you?"

"Danton Maisonette," Beatrice said. "You don't have a basket."

Ysbeta watched a group of young women laughing together. "Ianthe took it to the committee. You should do the same."

"In a moment," Beatrice said. "We can't meet at your house, but I know exactly where to begin our search for hazelnut ladies."

"Where?"

"Thornback Street."

Ysbeta grimaced. "That's so obvious I should have thought of it. I will call on you tomorrow to go to a café, and we will begin our search."

Beatrice winced, her shoulders rising. "I can't."

"What do you mean?"

"Father knows about my work with magic. He's put his foot down. While I am not confined to home, Father has only given permission for me to attend the party on the *Shining Hand,* and only if . . ."

"Only if what?"

Beatrice sighed. "He expects an offer of marriage from Ianthe."

Ysbeta tilted her head, amused. "And you think that won't happen? I will speak to your father after the ride and let him know that I wish to continue acquainting myself with my future sister-in-law. He'll let you go to a café with me."

"You seem awfully certain."

"There's no reason to refuse me, and every reason for

your father to maintain smooth relations between his family and mine. He won't do anything to jeopardize the engagement he hopes for. It will all come out fine. Now let's get your basket to the committee."

If they missed the deadline, they might not auction her basket at all, but she couldn't say that to Ysbeta. Clearly she hadn't thought of turning hers in late. "But we're hiding."

Ysbeta tilted her chin down, attempting to hide her face under the wide brim of her rakishly pinned hat. "Let's hand in your basket. Come on."

Beatrice sighed. "All right."

Ysbeta touched heels to a slender-necked, elegant mare and caught the flow of traffic on the path. "Are you entering the ladies' race?"

:Go fast.:

:No.: Beatrice caught her left boot going home in the stirrup, and slipped her foot back into the proper position. "I thought perhaps the hazards course. Marian's more of a jumper."

"She's a lovely bit of horseflesh. Bought or bred?"

"Are you horse-mad?" Beatrice asked. "Bred, but she was a gift for my twelfth birthday."

Ysbeta shrugged. "I can keep a horse by myself. I don't have to, but a woman who can't tend her own mount is a woman in a cage."

"I agree with that sentiment entirely," Beatrice said. "There is something I must ask you. I need the travelogue."

Ysbeta cast a sharp glance at Beatrice. "We have a deal."

"I know, but I may not be able to keep it unless I make use of Churchman's work," Beatrice said. "Circumstances have changed."

She couldn't go on with her plan. Father would disown her, and the Clayborns would sink. She had only one choice. But now that magic had been taken away, she grasped at it with desperate fingers.

"They have not changed that much," Ysbeta said. "Unless you are saying you won't help me."

"I must help you," Beatrice said. "I cannot abandon you to Bard."

"Then why do you need Churchman's book?"

"For myself."

:I will hex her.:

:You can't hex my friend.:

:But she won't give you the book. I promised to get the book for you.:

:Nadi. I promise you, when we meet someone you can hex, I'll let you do it.:

Nadi, satisfied, settled itself inside Beatrice's skin.

The greensward was dotted with bright squares of checkered linen waiting for the winners to unpack the luncheon they bought, accompanied by the lady who brought it. Beatrice and Ysbeta, already traveling at a walk, came to a halt as riders milled around while waiting for their grooms. Too many ears were in range of this conversation, but Ysbeta shrugged as if they were speaking of trivialities.

"You worry too much. Ianthe bears great regard for you. You have been cornered, but it won't be bad. A few years of the collar until you have two or three children, and then the freedom to pursue magic with a lesser spirit. Take the compromise."

A Lavan groom in a turquoise coat spotted them, and they turned their horses toward the man trying to navigate the crowd. Beatrice lowered her voice and leaned closer to Ysbeta. "But I do not wish to be engaged."

Ysbeta puffed out a curt laugh. "I see how you look at each other. Tell me you won't regret it if you walk away from him."

Heat flushed up Beatrice's cheeks. "My feelings do not

have weight in this instance."

Ysbeta's lips thinned. "I am sorry, Beatrice. I know it's hard. But you'll have Ianthe."

:Why won't she give it to you, if she's your friend?:

:Because she needs it too. As badly as I do.:

:But the book will teach you how to summon another spirit. You don't need the book,: Nadi said. :You have Nadi.:

:I am lucky to have you, Nadi.: Beatrice's eyes watered. :And I would miss you terribly.:

The spirit rumbled in pleasure. :Nadi is your friend. We can stay together.:

:But if I marry Ianthe, we will be separated. He'll have to put the collar on me for years.:

:Nadi doesn't want to leave you.:

:I know.:

The groom held Ysbeta's reins, and she dismounted in a flutter of skirts. Beatrice nodded thanks to the groom as he took Marian. Her scramble out of the saddle, burdened by the luncheon basket, resulted in a landing that jarred her knees. "I want freedom. Like you."

"You don't need it the way I do." Ysbeta stopped, whirling to face Beatrice. "I must have this, for the sake of the world and its knowledge."

She turned her back then, waving at one of the women who wore green ribbons identifying them as the committee in charge of the basket auction. Beatrice made polite murmurs as a number was affixed to her basket, accepting the card with the same number on it. She turned to Ysbeta again, whose charming smile dropped when she laid eyes on Beatrice.

Beatrice didn't want to beg. But she would, if she had to. "I need this just as much as you."

"But you cannot have it," Ysbeta said. "Your family has closed in. The only thing that will save you is accepting my brother's suit. And why not? He adores you."

"But my magic—"

"You want to know what I think? If you really wanted magic, you would not care. But you do care. You want him, and if it hadn't been for getting caught, you would have led him on until it was too late to have him," Ysbeta said. "How can I let you do that to my brother?"

"How can you do this to me?" Beatrice asked. "Do my wants mean nothing to you?"

"It would be different if you didn't want him, but you do. He will save your family's fortune. He will cherish you like a jewel. He will be good to you. He will certainly allow your explorations."

"I'm sure he will allow me," Beatrice said, her teeth gritted. "That is the sum of my objection. My skill and talents are mine. To have them controlled by someone else— It's abhorrent. I can't allow it. Even if it's him."

Nadi coiled up inside her, and a pulse of power moved through her body. :Hex.:

:Nadi, what did you do?:

:She's hurting you.:

What had the spirit done? What? Had it cursed Ysbeta with clumsiness, as it had done to save her from the attentions of Udo Maasten? :What did you do?:

:She is unlucky,: Nadi said. :So almost nothing.:

"It's the best arrangement you will get," Ysbeta said. "Think, Beatrice! What other man will be so generous, so lenient?"

Almost nothing? What did that mean? :Take it back, Nadi. Unhex her.:

:It's too late,: Nadi said. :Elamin is weak. My luck is strong. Here he comes.:

Beatrice stared over Ysbeta's shoulder. "Ysbeta."

But she folded her arms and went on. "Stop digging your heels in and think."

"Ysbeta—"

"If you must marry, and believe me, Beatrice, you must marry. You cannot save your family any other way." Ysbeta leaned closer to Beatrice, her expression set in stone. "You cannot do better than my brother, and you know it. I don't speak of money when I say that."

"Ysbeta, we have to leave," Beatrice said. "Lord Powles is standing right over there."

"What?"

Ysbeta turned around, and at that same moment, one of those billowing, pillowy clouds scudded away from the sun and bathed the cream and gold-clad beauty in sunlight. Lord Powles turned away from his companion and caught sight of Ysbeta standing in the sun.

His expression transformed as he recognized her. His mouth fell open as he stared at Ysbeta, and then his countenance sprang into a look of joy and adoration as he laid eyes on her.

Ysbeta covered her mouth with her hand. The whites showed all around her eyes. She backed up a step, another, and then her hand clamped around Beatrice's wrist like a vise.

"Run," Ysbeta breathed. "Run."

But it was too late. Lord Powles, a handsome figure in deep blue coat and breeches, had bent over Ysbeta's hand, his lips hovering just over her knuckles. When he stood, he saw no one in the world but her.

"Miss Lavan. You are astonishing. I will pay any price for your luncheon basket. I swear it."

Any other girl would be overcome by such a man making such a vow. Ysbeta stared at him with wide eyes, transfixed by horror.

Just at that moment, the chapterhouse bells rang the hour of noon.

As the bells tolled their last stroke, the first luncheon basket went on the auctioneer's podium. Gentlemen gathered near the stage, paddles in hand. Lord Powles lifted his own paddle in salute to Ysbeta and joined the throng.

"He was supposed to want someone else," Ysbeta said. "This wasn't supposed to happen. Elamin's gone."

:Nadi! How could you?:

:She was hurting you. No one hurts you when I'm there.:

:You can't hex people just because you don't like what they do,: Beatrice scolded. :Only when I say.:

:You should have said,: Nadi muttered. :You let people hurt you too much.:

Distress made Ysbeta's voice small. She groped for Beatrice's hand, turning wide dark eyes on her. "What do I do?"

"We can escape this." Beatrice took hold of Ysbeta's shoulders. "Hold him off for as long as you can. We keep working to get you skilled, and then you can make the great bargain too."

Ysbeta stopped nodding. "Too?"

"Don't you see? I must do the spell now. Father expects an answer the day after tomorrow."

"I do not see." Ysbeta shrugged out of Beatrice's grasp. "If you do this tomorrow, you will be the perfect scandal. Your father won't just let you skip out into the street to call on whomever you please. And even if he did, I couldn't be seen with you if you do this. If I give the book to you now, it destroys my chances."

Ysbeta was right. If she did this, Ysbeta couldn't be seen with her. Why, Beatrice would probably have to leave Bendleton immediately.

It was too late.

Ysbeta's expression turned sympathetic. "I'm sorry, Beatrice. But Ianthe will need you, after I'm finished. Why can't you—oh no, that one's mine."

Ysbeta stared at the podium, where a golden basket trimmed in turquoise ribbon rested. The auctioneer had barely listed the contents before Lord Powles raised his paddle.

"A thousand crowns," Bard Sheldon said.

The crowd murmured, but another paddle shot up.

"A thousand five hundred," Ellis Robicheaux said. "I adore berry-roasted songbird, you know that."

"Two thousand crowns," another bidder declared.

The crowd murmured as another gentleman raised his paddle and declared twenty-five hundred. Bard looked like a thunderstorm hovered on his brow.

"Five thousand crowns," Bard Sheldon said, and the crowd gasped. Ysbeta made a small noise of distress.

"Fine, if you're going to be that way," Ellis said, and bowed. One by one, each gentleman gave way to Bard's bid. The crowd applauded as Lord Powles marched up and accepted his basket. He returned to offer his arm to Ysbeta, and together they walked away to claim a patch of lawn.

:What are they doing?:

:Buying the right to eat with the lady who brought the basket.:

:But that's my lunch,: Nadi said.

:We'll get our share,: Beatrice soothed. :We share it.:

She put on an interested face to watch the rest of the auctions, but a figure stopped before her, and so Beatrice offered a smile to Danton Maisonette. "Hello again."

Danton bowed, his arms describing the graceful spiraling flourish of Valserran aristocracy. "Will you do me the pleasure of sharing your luncheon, Miss Clayborn?"

:I don't want to share with him. Make him go away.:

Beatrice donned her smiling, polite mask. "I would be happy to dine with you, Mr. Maisonette, should you prove victorious in today's auction."

"All I can ask for." He smiled. "Excellent. Ah. I see the moment is upon us."

Beatrice's reed basket was next on the podium, and Danton raised his paddle at the opening bid of a hundred crowns. Ianthe bid a hundred and fifty, but other paddles shot into the air, raising the asking bid swiftly.

"You have captured the fancy of many gentlemen, Miss Clayborn." Danton raised his paddle to accept a bid of four hundred crowns. Ianthe kept his arm raised for five hundred.

"Some of them have already dropped out."

"Convenient," Danton said. "But it will be a spirited battle. Lord Powles has made his choice clear. Other courtships are moving fast. Yours is a desirable basket among wealthy ungifted gentlemen, Miss Clayborn. I would expect to be extremely busy in the coming weeks. You have your pick."

Including Danton himself, and he said so with his smile. Beatrice slid the vanes of her fan open and wafted a breeze over her hot cheeks. "I never considered the circumstance."

:What do they want?:

:A wife,: Beatrice said. :And if I am made one, we may never speak again.:

:No. No!: Nadi clenched her fists. :Don't be a wife.:

:If I don't get the grimoire of the great bargain, I have no choice.:

:But if you make the great bargain, you don't need Nadi anymore.:

And she would miss the spirit, however difficult it was, however greedy and impulsive. Everything would be upset; nothing would be the same.

"One thousand, two hundred fifty crowns?"

Danton raised his paddle. Only two other bidders besides

Ianthe were still in the thick of it. Danton glanced at her, his face somehow inquisitive and secure in the bliss of knowing everything. "This is your first bargaining season, is it not?"

"You are correct," Beatrice said.

"It is my sister's third," Danton said.

"I thought she was a sorceress." Beatrice scanned the crowd for a woman in the same shade of pale green as her brother and beheld the woman from the Assembly Dance and the Robicheaux ball. She was pretty, with a tip-tilted nose and blond hair that shone in the sunlight, but her three-cornered hat had too many feathers in it, and the black ribbon ruffles trimming every seam of her jacket were just a bit too much. But over-trimmed clothing was no reason to pass over a sorceress. Three bargaining seasons? How?

"She is." Danton raised his paddle, a slight glow of sweat shining his forehead. "She has gone through two seasons without accepting a proposal, and our parents have determined that this will be the last. They will indulge her no more."

Beatrice glanced at Danielle again. Could she be resisting the yoke of the warding collar, as she and Ysbeta were?

"Is that unusual?"

"Most," Danton said. "But understandable."

Beatrice fought to maintain a serene expression. "I will not pry, but I admit curiosity."

"It's simple," Danton said. "Three years ago, we attended the premiere of the most fashionable opera in Masillia."

Beatrice's attention bloomed. "Masillian opera is the finest in the world. But how does it make Miss Danielle refuse matrimony?"

"True love." He swallowed and lifted his paddle to declare three thousand crowns. "The best of Masillia attended. As did the Lavans and their children: the beautiful Miss Ysbeta and her handsome brother, Ianthe."

Beatrice cocked her head. Ianthe raised his paddle to accept four thousand, five hundred. The crowd watched, entertained by the battle between two bidders. "You remember this."

"I shall never forget," Danton said. "It was the night my sister fell hopelessly in love. She gazed at him through the entire performance. He danced with her at a royal ball the next day. And then he sailed away from Valserre and returned home to Llanandras, taking Danielle's heart with him."

"Oh," Beatrice said.

"Five thousand crowns?" the auctioneer asked.

Danton bit his lip, then sighed and raised his paddle.

Ianthe had never lowered his. He stood amid the bidding crowd, hand raised like the statues of enlightenment earned, his bidding paddle the torch of knowledge.

"Five thousand, five hundred crowns," The auctioneer said. "Six thousand?"

All eyes turned to Danton. He clenched his jaw and lowered his hand in defeat.

The crowd cheered. Danton licked his lips and turned to Beatrice, his slightly sour breath billowing over her cheek. "You're pretty enough. And the power of your sorcery compensates for your low birth. You can have dozens of men in the palm of your hand if you reach out to take them, and your father will dance with joy to drive up the price. My sister has loved Ianthe Lavan hopelessly since she first saw him. I beg you—choose someone else. For love's sake."

Beatrice's mouth dropped open. "You ask this of me?"

"I will do anything to ensure my sister's happiness," Danton said. "I will beg. I will cheat. I will steal. And I will reveal that I saw you cast a circle on the seaside dressed in nothing but your shift and cavorted along the shore until dawn came, until the spirit you hosted left your body."

Beatrice's heart dropped like a stone. "You let a home on

Triumph Street? But your father had a house on Gravesford Road."

"My father does live on Gravesford Road. I let number twenty for the sake of my privacy."

Oh, Beatrice had known someone was watching! She had felt it, and dismissed it, while Danton hid away and watched her. This was blackmail! Danton was a knave!

:Let me hex him,: Nadi said.

:No.:

:But he's hurting you.:

"No one else saw you but me," he said. "Anyone else would have wagged their tongue the moment they stepped into a tearoom. I alone possess your secret, and I will use it. I must act on behalf of my sister."

:I hate him.:

"Mr. Maisonette," Beatrice said, but what could she tell him? What could she say? "I understand the sincerity of your feelings, but even if I agreed, that's no guarantee you can get what your sister wants."

"But you do not agree," Danton said. "You want him."

She didn't! She did. But the truth was crueler than that. "I fear I do not have the luxury of choice that you imagine, Mr. Maisonette. My heart aches for your sister, but you cannot buy another man's regard for her. You can't steal it. And you are welcome to report what you saw to my father, if you like. But I must do what I must do. I am sorry."

Danton grabbed for her hand. "Please."

"Excuse me."

Ianthe squinted at Danton, his newly won luncheon basket hanging in the crook of his arm. Danton Maisonette let go of Beatrice's hand, turned one pivoting foot, and left, headed for the horse pickets without a word of farewell.

"Was he bothering you?" Ianthe asked.

"He—was speaking to me of his sister. Danielle—"

"I'm acquainted." Ianthe offered his arm. "Slightly. Shall we see if Bard saved us the plot next to his?"

Bard had indeed saved a spot for Ianthe, and they rested under the spreading, fragrant canopy of a flowering cherry tree, far away from the open lawn that rang with laughter and the smell of a few hundred horses picketed at the lower end of the park. They shared the dishes tucked inside each lady's basket, and Beatrice did her best to hide her turmoil.

Ysbeta wouldn't budge. Ianthe had announced to all of society that he would spend a skilled professional's yearly wages to claim her for a lunch companion. Danton Maisonette had tried to blackmail her, and—what had possessed her to invite him to try? She didn't have a way to defend against his slander. If he did spread the story of her capering on the beach in her shift, her whole family would pay.

Lord Powles turned a pleased smile on Ysbeta. "Ellis heard a rumor that you had roasted songbirds in your basket, Miss Lavan."

"I do," Ysbeta said, and only someone looking closely would notice that her hands shook, and the cords of her neck stood out in distress. Her face, an enviable heart-shaped, flawless mask, smiled so prettily nearly anyone would be fooled.

Beatrice glanced away, reluctant to expose Ysbeta's facade, and caught sight of Danton and Danielle Maisonette, trailing a young man both siblings ignored. They wandered all around the greensward, dismissing empty picnic cloths as Danielle's overly feathered hat swiveled this way and that. Beatrice's stomach sank as she watched Danielle comb every foot of lawn, shaking off her brother's hand on her arm as she searched, but at last she came to the corner where smartly clad young couples shared an auctioned lunch under the cherry blossoms.

Danielle collapsed in a heap of skirts at an empty blanket, staring at Ianthe.

Ianthe didn't notice at all. "Bard and I were in the same chapterhouse for two years."

"Anthy all but dragged me through the dorms by the ear," Bard laughed. "I'm glad he made it here in time to stand for me at my Ordeal of the Rose."

"I'm glad I didn't miss it." Ianthe offered Bard a berry-roasted songbird from Ysbeta's dishes.

"Thank you." Bard ate the little creature whole, his teeth grinding the delicate flesh and fragile bones to morsels.

Ianthe looked away. "Chef outdid himself with your basket, Ysy."

"Indeed, it's a feast," Lord Powles agreed. "But it is the combination of rare morsels and well-made, solid fare that is the real success."

:Have one of those bird-things,: Nadi said.

:I can't bear them,: Beatrice replied. :They're cruelly made. They hurt the poor little bird terribly, and then they drown them in distilled spirits of wine.:

:You feel sad,: Nadi said. :Eat a strawberry. You like those.:

Lord Powles opened Beatrice's bottle, pouring out a white to accompany the small treats that began a basket luncheon. "This is a rare wine, Miss Clayborn."

"Thank you," Beatrice said. "You may have the other songbird, if you wish."

"Really? They're such a delightful taste," Powles said. Beatrice flinched as his teeth crunched together. He sipped some wine and smiled at Ysbeta. "I never complimented you on your habit, Miss Lavan."

"Thank you," Ysbeta said. "It's an old favorite."

"And you are enchanting in it," Lord Powles said. "I mean to turn over a new leaf with you. I know our parents desire this match, but Ianthe told me something important yesterday, and I mean to heed it."

"Oh?" Ysbeta offered up thick sliced white bread, spread with pale green herbed butter. "I have coffee-roasted beef. Beatrice, what do you have?"

"Duck breast in sweet mustard."

"One of each, please," Lord Powles said, and helped himself. "At any rate, he came out to Breakwater House, looking as if thunder was going to crash at any moment, and he said to me, 'If you don't feel love in your heart when you look at her, Sheldon, then find someone else.'"

Ysbeta shot a glance at her brother. "Did he."

Ianthe looked back, his expression apologetic.

"Oh, indeed. I could hardly sleep," Lord Powles laughed. "I knew he had promised me a mortal end if I'd done you wrong, Miss Lavan. I stayed up half the night wondering how I felt. But then I saw you standing in a ray of sunlight, and my heart knew such joy—it's unfashionable, I know."

Ysbeta gazed at Beatrice, and the hollow, horror-tinged set of her mouth was too much. Beatrice looked away, a weight on her shoulders.

Nadi shrugged. :She is unlucky.:

:But it's my fault.:

Nadi made a skeptical noise. :It isn't.:

Off at the Maisonette spread, Danielle watched Ianthe, who drank straw-colored wine from a round-bottomed glass. Her lips moved, and Beatrice guessed they were pleas for Ianthe to please turn, please notice she was there.

Oh, it hurt to watch, both Danielle's anguish and Ianthe's cheerful ignorance. He tilted his head and studied Beatrice, and then followed the direction of her gaze.

Danielle gasped and waved. Danton glowered. Ianthe turned back to Beatrice, his expression knitted in concern.

:Danton hates you. All those kind words earlier were lies.:

:I know.:

Nadi puffed up in aggression. :I won't let him hurt you.:

:Nadi, remember what we said about hexing people?:

:Only when you say,: Nadi said. :But you should say, Beatrice. Nadi can feel his hate from here.:

Ianthe cleared his throat, and Beatrice hastily gave him her attention. "Did you say something?"

"I know it's not my business, but I ask again. Is Danton Maisonette bothering you, Miss Clayborn?"

Beatrice looked down at her wine. "He wanted something from me, and I was disinclined to honor his request."

"—winter in Llanandras, and then return to Chasland for the summer. At least until I'm the minister," Bard Sheldon was saying.

Ysbeta ignored him to lean closer to Beatrice and Ianthe. "What request? Did he ask you to refuse Ianthe's victory? As if the likes of Danton Maisonette had anything to match my brother."

Beatrice sighed. "He did, but not necessarily so I would share my company with him."

Sheldon realized Ysbeta wasn't listening to him anymore. "Then what reason did he have?"

Beatrice bit her lip. "It's gossip."

"My favorite," Bard Sheldon said. "I am a most avid gossip. Now you have to tell us."

Beatrice glanced at the Maisonettes. "It's his sister, Danielle."

Ianthe groaned and dropped his forehead into his palm. "That cursed bet."

"Bet?" Lord Powles looked from Ianthe to Danielle. "What bet?"

"Eliza Robicheaux wagered Danielle that she would win Ianthe's attention before Danielle could," Ysbeta explained. "Embarrassing."

Lord Powles glanced at the Maisonettes. "Hm. She's not ugly. A little weak in sorcerous potency. But she dresses herself in the dark."

"That's unkind," Beatrice said. "Danielle is infatuated with Ianthe. She has been ever since they met in Masillia three years ago. She has resolutely refused all suitors, waiting for Ianthe to arrive in Bendleton so she could win his regard."

"Oh." Ianthe glanced at Danielle. Beatrice's heart wrenched as Danielle went pale under all the attention from Ianthe's party. She had to know they were talking about her. Ianthe slipped the napkin out of the collar of his shirt. "That poor girl. I have to explain to her."

"You will sit right there, Ianthe Antonidas Lavan, and you will do no such thing," Ysbeta said. "Stop staring at her, Lord Powles. Everyone stop and attend to our own business."

"But Ysy, I have to—"

"If you walk over there right now, she'll hope," Ysbeta said. "And then when you tell her, no matter how gently you tell her that her affections are not reciprocated, you'll break her heart."

"But—"

Ysbeta pointed an admonishing finger. "And you'll humiliate her even more than she is right now. You will pay her a proper call in the privacy of her home, and you will give her every dignity you can. Do you hear me?"

Ianthe sighed. "Yes. But it's so awkward. She's been 'accidentally' running into me all over town. I had no idea that she had tender feelings for me."

Beatrice blinked. "Why else would she pursue you so?"

Lord Powles coughed. "Because his family is even richer than mine."

"That can't be. For three years?" Beatrice asked.

"Oh, she's adorable, Lavan," Lord Powles said. "Keep her."

Ianthe smiled into his cup.

Beatrice studied the checkered surface of their luncheon cloth. "Cheese tarts?"

"I love those," Powles said. "And Miss Lavan? Don't think I didn't notice your concern for the girl. I am moved by your kindness. Crueler women would have kept silent in favor of a good show."

Ysbeta shrugged. "I just imagined how I would feel."

"Someone as beautiful as you could so easily be uncaring." Powles covered Ysbeta's hand with his. "The more I learn about you, the more impressed I become."

"Might I have one of those cheese tarts, Beatrice?" Ysbeta slipped her hand out from under Lord Powles's. "And also. I might have been a bit thoughtless when we were talking, earlier. I regret that now."

Beatrice gulped a swallow of wine. She had? Ysbeta had—ah. Lord Powles's spell-struck love had driven Ysbeta to this generosity, not the passion of Beatrice's arguments for the grimoire. "We can speak of it later, if you wish."

Ianthe eyed his sister. "What do you mean?"

"I was hasty and unfair to Beatrice this morning," Ysbeta said. "I wished to apologize for it."

Ianthe studied her a moment longer. "Is that all?"

"That's all," Ysbeta said.

A breeze set the branches overhead to shivering. Soft, pale petals drifted through the air, tumbling and swirling as the wind made them dance. Beatrice's heart fluttered. Ysbeta was going to let her have the book. Her own freedom depended on Beatrice's cooperation, and Ysbeta saw that. They would escape the customs meant to ensnare them both.

If everyone waiting for their mounts wouldn't crowd together so, the whole process would have gone so much faster.

Beatrice fought her way through the milling crowd to accept Marian from the Lavan grooms, who had Ysbeta's dainty mare and Ianthe's inevitable glossy black gelding, a gentleman's preferred ride. Marian shied away from Beatrice's hand, but soon came back to delicately lip a chunk of carrot from her palm.

"I've got to get her out of this crowd," Beatrice said. "She's touchy."

She headed for the least crowded area, murmuring nonsense praise to keep Marian listening to her. When she was away, she petted Marian, still soothing with her voice.

Ianthe and Ysbeta stopped a short distance away as Beatrice stroked every bit of Marian's hide, inspecting her tack.

"James did all that," Ianthe said. "He's an excellent groom."

Beatrice let go of Marian's white-socked hoof. "I know. I'm mostly just soothing her."

:Something's wrong,: Nadi said.

:There's something wrong with Marian?:

:Don't jump her. I know you promised, but don't.:

A chill shivered its way down Beatrice's back, but she didn't let Marian feel it. "No jump today, not for you. We're going to go home early, you and me. How's that sound?"

"You're not going to jump?" Ysbeta asked. "I was looking forward to watching you."

"You're a show-jumper?" Powles had finally caught up. "She has the lines for it. You could teach her to dance, like Robicheaux's fancy fillies."

Powles also rode a gentleman's black, and whatever white markings his mount had were disguised by dye. "And Miss Lavan, what a gorgeous specimen. Pure elegance. Did you bring her from Llanandras? She's the model of your Arshkatan breed."

"She's a champion," Ysbeta's mount sidled away from

Powles. "Five years old. I trained her from her birth. Beatrice, have you found anything?"

"Nothing," Beatrice called, "but I think I should take her home. She's not used to crowds."

"We'll accompany you," Ianthe said.

"Oh no, enjoy the day, please." Beatrice took hold of the horn and the cantle, and Nadi boosted her jump. She twisted into her seat, hooking her right leg over the top pommel, and planted the ball of her left foot in the stirrup. "Good girl, Marian! Walking."

Marian's skin shivered, but she walked. Beatrice circled her left and right, called a trot, and got Marian used to trusting her control.

"She seems better," Ysbeta said. "Perhaps we could just take an easy ride around the track."

"I don't—"

Ysbeta's eyes begged Beatrice to stay. Beatrice eyed the mounted traffic and nodded. "It might help her to overcome her unease."

She guided Marian to the track, the others nearby, and Marian stopped. Beatrice slid her weight back in the saddle as her horse's head came up, ears swiveling.

"Marian," Beatrice said. "It's all right, you're all right. Walking."

She didn't lower her head, but she put all four hooves on the track.

"Good girl!" Beatrice praised, stroking her neck. She turned to regard the rest of her company, twisting to look at them. "She's too nervy. I'm taking her home."

She guided Marian toward the southern gate, but something rushed through the crowd at speed. Beatrice turned her head and caught a distortion in the air, then it resolved into the shape of a mastiff. It barreled toward them, barking viciously.

Beatrice's heart leapt into her throat. Marian squealed.

Her front hooves shot up as she reared in terror. Beatrice pitched forward, her knees clamped around the pommel. She had to rein Marian in. She had one chance.

But Marian twisted in midair, landing on her front hooves as she kicked out at the translucent beast. Beatrice's seat drifted left—and as she tried to get back in the saddle, her foot slid too far home in the stirrup. She unbalanced completely.

She saw into the next few seconds that ended her life: a headfirst fall to the ground, dragged by the ankle as her terrified horse trampled her.

:No!:

She still had a tight grip on the pommel, but she dangled from it, the track and green grass a blur as Marian raced away from the terrible thing that tried to eat her. If she could grab the horn—

But her stays, her fashionable, tight-laced, rigid stays held her waist immobile. She couldn't bend against them. Only the pressure of her knees kept her from tumbling to her death. Beatrice tried to use her hips as a hinge. To raise her body and grab the horn.

Marian ran like hungry spirits nipped her haunches. Beneath her, the saddle slipped an inch. Beatrice couldn't stop the shriek that tore from her throat. She would go under. Dragged. Trampled. Dead.

:Stretch out your hand, Beatrice. Do it, do it now!:

What?

Beatrice turned her head, and half a length behind her was Ianthe, his mount's neck stretched out as they went all-out to catch up. Ianthe stretched out his hand, but the shimmering aura of his companion spirit extended past the limit of his fingers, and that sparkle was just in reach.

Beatrice grabbed it. The spirit slid around her, lifted her in midair, taking her unbalanced weight off Marian's back.

Ianthe rode harder, going neck and neck with the frightened horse, and he caught her rein. He pulled her head to one side, and Nadi, flowing through Beatrice's protection, flexed its control of chance.

Marian's pace faltered. Ianthe called out soothing words. Ianthe's spirit kept Beatrice cradled in midair, and they all came to a halt.

Marian's sides heaved with the effort. Ianthe jumped from the saddle and freed Beatrice's foot from the stirrup. A hot, sharp bolt shot through her knee, and she hissed in pain. His spirit let her down, gentle and easy, until she stood on solid ground.

"Where does it hurt?" Ianthe asked.

"My knee," Beatrice said. She tested her weight, and bolts of bright red pain shot along her leg. "Oh!"

"Fandari, help her. Try now."

With Fandari taking the weight, she could walk a little limping circle as her guts shivered and shook. She hobbled away to the bushes and cast up her luncheon, her limbs cold and shaking.

She spat out sour bile and gagged at the syrupy scent of cherry blossoms. She'd nearly died. She nearly died an awful, terrifying death. And she put a phantom mastiff next to Danton Maisonette conjuring an illusion of an archer taking aim at the moon at the Assembly Dance—

Heat seared through her. Every bone, every muscle, every hair on her body was aflame. She turned her head to regard the crowd who had chased her and Ianthe, hanging back just enough to get a look at the show, and saw one fear-pale face staring back at her.

Ianthe moved to her side, but she waved him off. "You."

The word dripped from her mouth with a slow, grinding menace. She walked straight for Danton Maisonette. Her knee flared with every step. She didn't care.

Nadi stretched to fill the bounds of her body, taking control. Nadi put her hands up just below her chin, her fists balled tight as rocks, thumbs on the outside. They stalked straight at Danton, who was trying to babble some excuse to Ianthe. He wasn't even looking at her.

"Danton Maisonette," she said. "I demand satisfaction."

He looked at her then. "What?"

:Hex,: Beatrice and Nadi chorused.

Power rippled through her. She never missed a beat. She and Nadi stepped into the swing, lending the full force of her weight and the spirit's potence behind the straight, fast blow that she aimed six inches past his jaw. Nadi flexed its power with hers.

Fist met face. His jaw shifted sideways. Something caved in under the battering ram of her knuckles. Blood arced out of Danton's mouth. His head swung with the force of Beatrice's right cross. He staggered and fell to the dirt, his eyes wide with shock and pain.

Beatrice stood over him, her hands raised to hit him again. Her knuckles ached. Her chest heaved in deep breaths, rage and triumph rushing through her body. Danton spit out a tooth and cradled his jaw in one hand. The crowd, set afire by amazement, watched avidly as she stepped back to give him room, her fists still raised.

"Get up," she said. "Get up and face me, Danton Maisonette. You just tried to kill me. I demand satisfaction. Will you fetch your pistols?"

CHAPTER XVI

Danton Maisonette apologized on the spot. He scrambled to get on his knees to beg her pardon, his punched-out tooth cradled in one hand. He pleaded overwhelming passion. He begged her forgiveness.

Beatrice wished the spineless little worm had the gumption to get on his feet and accept the thrashing he deserved. Her balled-up fists itched to swing again. She'd meet him on the greensward at dawn and shoot him right between the eyes. She'd—

She backed away from rage. She had to get herself under control. :Nadi. Stop.:

:I will kill him,: Nadi snarled, and its fury stoked a fire in her belly. :He tried to kill you. He hurt you. He deserves—:

:I know. But we don't kill, Nadi. Killing is wrong. We will use the law.:

She put her fists down. "You'll speak to my father," she said. "You will go to him and confess what you did, and you will accept his justice. In court, I expect."

"I saw the whole thing," Ysbeta declared. "I will be your witness, Miss Clayborn."

"And I," Ianthe said.

"And I," Lord Powles said. "You are finished, Maisonette. You have earned my ill regard forever. Get out of here."

Ianthe took Beatrice by the shoulders and looked her in the eye. "Are you all right?"

"My hand hurts," Beatrice said. She glanced at

Maisonette, skulking off. “I’d pay a hundred crowns for the chance to hit him again.”

“That blow was one for the ages,” Ianthe said. “You were magnificent. You—”

He folded her into his arms, holding her tight. “You could have died. I nearly lost you. I don’t know what I would have done if you had—”

He pressed his lips to her forehead. “Beatrice.”

Everyone heard him use her forename. Everyone saw the familiar embrace, the ardent kiss. Every soul in Bendleton would hear of Ianthe’s actions by teatime.

“Let’s get you home.” He swept her off her feet, carrying her in his arms.

Beatrice tried to wiggle out of his grip. “I can walk, if you’ll assist me.”

“I wouldn’t dream of it,” Ianthe said. “The landau isn’t far. I’ll speak to your father. You need a physician.”

Onlookers followed them to the landau and down the short ride to Triumph Street. “Send for Dr. Kirford,” Ianthe said to his driver. “No other. She’s a bonemend. I won’t accept anyone else in her stead. Bring her back here as soon as you can.”

The driver set off as soon as Beatrice had been lifted out of the carriage, and Ianthe carried her into the house, much to her mortification. He eyed the stairs, even moved toward them, but the footman stood in his way and he remembered himself. Beatrice watched over the footman’s shoulder as Ianthe knocked on Father’s office door, but lost sight of him as the footman carried her upstairs.

The doctor arrived less than an hour later, dressed in layers of sturdy gray linen that matched the sandy whiteness of her hair. Her face was wrinkled all over, but her knotty hands were gentle as she touched Beatrice’s swollen knee.

Beatrice winced as she moved to give the doctor room. "You're a bonemend? I've never met a woman bonemend."

She opened a satchel and took out a blank fabric doll and a packet of needles. "I was an herbalist all through my marriage," Dr. Kirford said. "Once my warded years were done, it made sense to follow medicine."

She sewed in light brown eyes and red silk yarn for hair, pausing to pluck a single strand from Beatrice's head, threading a fine silver needle with it and sewing it into the doll.

"Is that to make it linked to me?"

"That's the magic. It'll take the pain from you while Geret and I mend you." She lifted the blankets over Beatrice's propped-up knee, and even her touch felt like healing, warm and full of comfort, even through the pain.

"How did you learn magic?"

"Like any other working man, though later in life than they. I apprenticed myself to a master bonemend. I'm glad they sent for me," Dr. Kirford said. "You would have needed to use a cane the rest of your life."

"It hurts like fire."

"And it'll ache when the weather turns, but it'll be all right," Dr. Kirford said. "You'll need the poppet. Squeeze it tight, dear. That's it."

Beatrice clutched the soft rag doll and startled when the hot, throbbing pain in her knee faded to a cooler ache. The doctor smiled, showing off a set of well-made dentures. "It hurts for you, so don't let it go. Put all your pain into the poppet. That's right."

Harriet dashed into Beatrice's room, breathless. "Can you hear that?"

"Hear what? The sea?"

"They are calling you the Warrior Maid." Harriet paced across Beatrice's bedchamber, her agitation driving her feet faster and faster. "There's a group of men outside, shouting—"

Beatrice gripped the healing poppet tighter. "I can hear them. Ouch!"

:It hurts,: Nadi said.

:Do you want to go?:

:No.: Nadi curled up inside her, hissing at the physician's attention. Dr. Kirford looked at Beatrice, her white, wispy brows raised in surprise. Beatrice tensed, and the bonemend's gaze sharpened.

Oh, oh no. She knew about Nadi. She could tell. Beatrice squeezed the poppet, pleading silently for her to keep quiet.

At the front of the townhouse, the men outside sang battle-hymns of the hero Ijanel, a farm girl who became a vessel of the wind lord Gelder and successfully drove off the conquering forces of the Etruni from Chasland's shores with a gale that capsized ships.

"Hold still," the physician said. "I have been paid to heal your joint. It hurts. I told you that it would hurt."

"What are we going to do?" Harriet's brow pinched up as she whirled to face Beatrice. "What were you thinking? Punching a gentleman, knocking his teeth out, and then asking him to fetch his pistols? You can't fight!"

Beatrice shrugged. "I can shoot."

"You shouldn't know how to shoot," Harriet snapped.

"So Father should just let us be eaten by bears?"

Harriet ignored this. "He could have demanded swords. What if he'd chosen?"

"Then I would have fought him," Beatrice said. Nadi would have helped her. And made her lucky. "He tried to kill me, Harriet. What part of that is trivial to you? Would you have honestly preferred that the undertakers had to come for me?"

That shut her mouth, but only for a moment. "You

could have accused him."

"I won't wish the experience on you. But you really had to be in my shoes to understand. He chose a terrifying, painful way to die—and if I hadn't? I would have been so gravely hurt that I would have been out of the way anyway."

"Your father should take him to court, young miss," Dr. Kirford said. "Now hold still."

The doctor spread her wrinkled, age-spotted hands over Beatrice's knee. The joint soaked up the warmth radiating from the doctor's touch, and her spirit flared to life, seeping into Beatrice's joint. The heat became a throbbing, terrible ache. Beatrice hissed.

:It hurts,: Nadi said. :Hurts.:

:It's healing.:

The doctor glanced at her again. Beatrice froze. Had her spirit told her about Nadi's presence?

She patted Beatrice's hand and smiled kindly. "That's the way of a bonemend, my dear. We can't just touch you and you're good as new. You have to endure the pain of healing—hold the poppet, dear, nice and tight—yes. You feel it all at once, instead of spread out over long, long months."

"Thank you," Beatrice said, but it came out tinged by a whimper.

"You'll be in dancing shape by morning," the physician promised. She took her hands away and held out her hand for the poppet. "I'll go and report to Mr. Lavan, if he's still here."

"He's telling Father about the accident," Beatrice said.

The physician opened her packing case and produced a bottle. "You must stay off the leg. You are on bed rest until dawn. To aid that, I have a mixture here that will help you sleep, so you can't be tempted. It will make staying still easier."

"Thank you, Doctor."

The physician smiled, her eyes bright and pleased in her wrinkled face. "You're a good girl. Drink up."

The mixture was sweetened, but carried a dark, earthlike flavor alongside an insistent herbal taste. She swallowed it and a bit of water and rubbed her aching knuckles.

:What's that?:

:Medicine. I will sleep soon.:

:I feel funny,: Nadi said. :Can we dream?:

:Unless the drug stops me.:

:I want to dream.:

Beatrice smiled as the soft, cotton-packed feeling of the drug played over her senses.

"I see Ianthe. He's coming out," Harriet said, and dashed out of the room, returning with a worry-pinched face. "He's—oh no! He's joining the gentlemen! He's singing with them!"

"Harriet," Beatrice said, her tongue too thick to make her words crisp. "I'm very sleepy. Could you go out, please?"

"This is a disaster," Harriet said. "They'll call you nothing else. You are a figure of fun. No one will want to marry you now."

"That's a relief," Beatrice said. "Now please go. I want to sleep."

"Come along," the physician said. "Leave your sister to mend. She'll be ravenous in the morning—why don't you go plan her breakfast with Cook?"

Harriet allowed herself to be herded outside, and Beatrice listened to the chorus singing of Ijanel—concentrating on the bits of the story where she was the lord-general of Chasland, and not the part where she was painfully executed in order to break her power over the country and silence her alarming talk of deposing the king.

But that also meant leaving out the part where her spirit, robed in glory, rose out of her body to be embraced by the wind lord himself, earning her a permanent place among the emissaries of the Skyborn. And Chasland's ministers did depose the king, inspired by that nation's best-known saint.

Ijanel was a hero—but she had paid bitterly for standing outside of her place. It had come out rewarding in the end, but Beatrice didn't want Ijanel's suffering. She only wanted to be herself. She only wanted to live to her fullest potential, to make use of the Skyborn's gift, alive in her body.

Maybe she asked for too much. Maybe she couldn't have what she wanted. Ianthe would be kind. He would allow her as much freedom as he could. Maybe she should be grateful for that.

Ijanel didn't rise to power to satisfy herself. She selflessly gave everything to Chasland. Beatrice should be selfless too. For her family. For Ianthe.

:You're sad,: Nadi said.

:I am. It's all right, Nadi. Let's dream.:

She closed her eyes, and in her dream, she flew.

The bonemend had been correct. Beatrice slid gingerly out of bed, but swiftly proved with a chassé to the gowns Clara had chosen and a standing jeté that her knee was healed to a full recovery.

"The blue walking suit," Beatrice said, and after a bath and an hour of preparation, she ventured to the first-floor terrace to take breakfast, but faltered when Father was seated at the table with an empty plate and a full cup of coffee, reading the broadsheets.

Beatrice winced at an upside-down headline in the *Bendleton Tribune: Warrior Maid Vanquishes Knave with One Blow.* It wasn't at the top of the page—it was crammed on the second half, and the tiny print took up two inches. But she was in the papers, and Father would act like she wasn't even there.

He tipped a corner of the *Gravesford Times* down to look at her, and Beatrice smiled, hopeful. "Good morning."

"You look fetching," he said, and Beatrice vibrated with shock. He was speaking to her? "Are you on the search for anything you need for the Lavans' party?"

"Ysbeta Lavan wishes my company at a café today," Beatrice said. "We may browse the shops after."

"An excellent day. You have done well, to cultivate such a powerful friendship. All this fuss will blow over. None of it will matter in a year. Enjoy yourself today," Father said, and Beatrice had to sit down after he rose from the table and squeezed her shoulder.

He hadn't ignored her. He had praised her. After what she had done? It made no sense. But she hurried through her breakfast and her knee didn't trouble her at all as she climbed into the landau. Ysbeta, splendid in a pale blue that nearly matched Beatrice's walking suit in color even as it outstripped it in quality and ornament, rose to offer Beatrice her seat.

"An excellent choice of color," Ysbeta said. "Cornelius, take us by way of Thornback Street. We wish to see the gardens."

It was early in the season to admire gardens, but the first flush of flowers were in bloom by now. Cornelius slowed the carriage as they turned onto Thornback Street, and soon they saw what they wanted—before a modest little house with white painted sills and deep red bricks stood a hazel tree, as dense with catkins as its blooming chestnut neighbor.

Beatrice and Ysbeta smiled at each other. They had found one, exactly where Beatrice had predicted. "I must compliment the owner on her design," Ysbeta said. "Wait here, Cornelius. We're going to call on the lady of the house."

Cornelius touched his hat and pulled out a book to join him for the wait.

Ysbeta marched up the walk and knocked on the front

door, nodding to the maid who answered it. "I am Ysbeta Lavan," she said, and the maid's eyes widened a fraction and she bobbed her knees again. "I wish to compliment the lady of the house on her lovely garden. May we ask for her company?"

"I shall ask, miss," the maid said. "Did you wish to see Miss Tarden, or Miss Wallace?"

Beatrice spoke up. "We would enjoy the company of either. This dress is one of theirs."

They were shown into a parlor, a small room made smaller with the presence of a box-framed pianochord against one wall. They took spindle-legged seats and removed their gloves, and Ysbeta nodded as the maid asked if they would like tea. Beatrice opened her senses, but she could not detect the presence of grimoires nearby.

"You never told me your modistes were magicians."

"I had no reason to suspect they were."

"Do you think the trees were a mistake?"

"They're young trees," Beatrice said. "I don't think there's any harm in asking a few questions."

:Nadi,: she asked. :Can you tell a grimoire?:

:Yes.:

:Can you tell me if there are any inside this house?:

:Yes. I will come back,: Nadi said, and the spirit left her flesh and blinked out of view.

Ysbeta stared at the space where the spirit had been and frowned at Beatrice. "Did you just lose your spirit?"

"Temporarily," Beatrice said. "I sent it to look for grimoires. What if we could compare books and share knowledge? I think that's something the ladies are doing anyway. It could be our entrance to their society."

"We are sorceresses," Ysbeta said. "That should be enough."

The maid returned with tea, which they thanked her for, but the lady of the house didn't appear. The tea timer's last grains of sand fell to the bottom chamber. Properly, she should have been there to pour for her guests. What was the delay?

"She's making us wait," Ysbeta complained. "Did her maid tell her that I had called on her?"

"She may not have been dressed for callers," Beatrice said. "She could have been stained with ink from all the accounting and correspondence, and ink is stubborn."

"It may be as you say—"

The door opened, and Beatrice stood for the woman who owned the very shop where her walking suit had come from, and her newest ball gowns, and the green wedding gown she dreaded.

"Miss Tarden," Beatrice said. "Thank you for accepting our call." No crown of sorcery ringed this woman's head. Why the trees out front, then? They couldn't be a mistake.

Ysbeta cocked her head. "It seems we are an imposition, Miss Tarden. I had hoped to compliment you on your handsome shade trees, but clearly you are a busy woman."

"I thank you for the compliment," Miss Tarden said. "I don't wish to be rude—"

"But you're going to," Ysbeta interrupted. "I'm curious. Why did you plant those two trees in particular?"

Miss Tarden went white, her face pinched. "They seemed compatible," she said. "I apologize, but I must return to my shop. I have a busy schedule—"

Nadi returned then, settling back into Beatrice's body. :Eight. She has eight.:

Beatrice gazed at Miss Tarden, who had turned her head and tracked Nadi's presence, and her expression pinched up with fear.

"Please," Beatrice said. "I know you are a sorceress, even though you know a way to hide it from a knowing eye. You felt my spirit come in the room, and it has told me that you have eight grimoires in your possession—"

"You can't have them," Miss Tarden said. "I will defend my home and property."

"We don't want to take them from you. We're here because we want to learn more magic."

"We wish to make the great bargain," Ysbeta said. "As I believe you also wished, Miss Tarden. But anything you have to teach us would be useful."

"I don't—I would like you to leave."

Beatrice's jaw fell open. "What have we done to offend?"

"I saw that landau from the upstairs window. The whole street saw it. You are ingenues. You're here for bargaining season. I have sewn seams on your gowns, miss, and your bridal attire awaits the final fitting in my shop. I'm sorry. You stand too high for us. If we help you—"

Beatrice understood. "You're afraid you'll get caught."

"If anyone saw you here, I'm finished. The circle will ostracize me. We've worked too hard to stay hidden to risk having ingenues anywhere near us."

"It was the trees," Ysbeta said. "They pointed the way."

"I will have them cut down," Miss Tarden vowed. "I didn't put them there for you."

"But we know the code. We have grimoires." Ysbeta stood up, her voice pleading. "We want what you want, and you won't give it to us because we're—"

"You can never be one of us, Miss Lavan. I'm sorry, but I have no wish to leave you with flowery lies. If you don't marry, everyone will want to know why. You will attract too much attention—and your father is spending money like water, Miss Clayborn, trying to buy you an engagement. If you cry off, people will ask questions."

"But—"

"I must protect my colleagues," Miss Tarden said. "I am sorry. But we must not be discovered."

"I have five grimoires," Ysbeta said. "They include the names of greater spirits, and the ritual to make the great bargain itself."

"And I have four," Beatrice said. "Surely there is some worth in that. Will you admit us in exchange for that?"

Miss Tarden stared. She licked her lips. "I'll give you five thousand crowns for each."

"Miss Tarden. I am Ysbeta Lavan. I do not want your crowns. I want the alliance of a greater spirit. Put us in contact with someone who can guide us, and I will give you—"

"No," Miss Tarden's face shuttered closed, nothing on it but cold reproof. "I will not endanger my colleagues. I will not defy the code. There is nothing more to say. Good afternoon, ladies. I wish things could be different, but they are not."

She rang a bell and the maid came immediately. "Miss Lavan and Miss Clayborn are leaving. Wish them luck and see them off. Goodbye, ladies. I have work to attend."

Miss Tarden stood and walked out of the room, leaving Beatrice and Ysbeta to stare at each other.

"Well," Ysbeta said. "I suppose we should go."

They returned to the landau, and Beatrice finally spoke. "She wouldn't help us. I think none of them will. We're on our own, Ysbeta."

"We can do this," Ysbeta said. "I will think of something. We should go home. I'm going to need time to get ready for the party. I'll tell you what I come up with then."

The party. Beatrice would attend, and Ianthe would propose. But there was a society of women magicians, women who had hidden their talents, escaped the warding collar, and knew each other. Working women, business proprietors who knew higher magic, but didn't step out of hiding to help a sister sorceress. They were selfish, caring for nothing but their own power—

Just like Beatrice. She too had intended to work in secret, securing the fortune of her family, living a quiet life as a master magician no one would remember or even remark upon. She had thought herself alone in her desire to pursue magic. Meeting Ysbeta had crumpled that notion. But a whole network of women magicians should be in the light. They should be known, so other girls knew that they didn't have to lock themselves inside a warding collar with no other choices. If the hazel and chestnut ladies should be fighting for the freedom of other women, then shouldn't Beatrice make that effort herself? Shouldn't she and Ysbeta spread all the magic they had learned to everyone, so the knowledge would never die?

But how? She was only one woman, still. The ladies of hazel and chestnut chose the shadows. Someone had to step forward, but Beatrice couldn't be the one to do it. She had a family who needed her help—by magic or marriage, they needed her.

She brooded all the way back to Triumph Street. The hidden sisterhood couldn't help her. They couldn't meet at Ysbeta's house. But perhaps Ysbeta would have an idea tomorrow—something they could hold on to, knotting it into hope's hair.

CHAPTER XVII

Tomorrow came, and Beatrice was busy being slathered in beauty milk, her skin wrapped and plucked and waxed. The final day had come; her fate had been chosen for her. Today was her last day as an ingenue, and she stayed perfectly still as Clara painted lacquer on her fingernails, a poultice of clay drying on her face. She dressed and rode with her family to the modest dock just west of Bendleton to sail to the overnight party hosted by the Lavans.

Beatrice wore her best gown—a shining silk in the palest mauve, the stomacher the labor of a master needlewoman, glittering with faceted crystal beads and silver thread. Vividly embroidered songbirds of Chasland flew in a great murmuration along the full underskirt, their wings spread, their beaks open in song. Beatrice traced the outline of a plump blue-gray catbird resting over her once-injured knee and stared at the *Shining Hand*, anchored in the deep waters almost at the horizon.

They sailed on the deck of a light, rapid sloop, a richly appointed pleasure craft named the *Redjay*. The dip and roll of the sea bothered her not a bit, but Mother groaned with nausea.

"We're nearly there," Beatrice assured her. "Look how large the ship is now."

Father cleared his throat. "We may be sailing longer than you think. That's a Llanandari treasure vessel. They are of prodigious size."

"But it's already enormous," Beatrice said. "It's a hundred feet long, easily."

Father smiled. "It's three hundred and sixty-seven feet long, my dear."

Beatrice watched the *Shining Hand* grow until it blocked the horizon, so large she could scarcely fathom it. Their vessel was a dinghy compared to it, and Beatrice gazed on the rows of portholes—some were windows to sleeping quarters, but the rest bristled with guns. She craned her neck and gazed at the ship's tallest mast and tried to imagine the size of its sails.

The crew hailed the *Shining Hand* and secured permission to come aboard. How were they to board such an enormous vessel? But the crew of the *Hand* lowered sling hammocks on long lines.

She was to sit in that sling and be lifted on deck. Beatrice gulped.

:Can we make it swing?: Nadi asked.

:I think we shouldn't.:

:A little?:

:A little.:

Nadi wriggled in delight.

Beatrice kept a firm grip on the handles as she rose in the air. She kicked her legs to swing a little, to Nadi's pleasure. The sailors raised her high above the rails and swung the arm over the deck, lowering her as gently as Ianthe's spirit had set her on the ground after her escape from death. Ianthe stood with Ysbeta, Mrs. Lavan, and a stately, handsome man who must be their father. Beatrice found her feet and curtsied, raising her head to see the father smiling.

Mrs. Lavan did not.

"So this is the Warrior Maid!" Mr. Lavan said. He wrapped two warm hands around Beatrice's and shook. "I admire a woman of spirit. She's very pretty, Ianthe. Where are you from, Miss Clayborn?"

"Riverstone House, in Mayhurst," Beatrice said.

"The country, how splendid. And do you farm?" Mr. Lavan inquired.

Mrs. Lavan bumped her husband with an elbow. "There are still guests to be greeted, Mr. Lavan."

"Indeed there are, my starlight, but none of them so interesting to my son as this one." Mr. Lavan smiled at her, and Beatrice smiled back.

"It's lovely to meet you, Mr. Lavan."

"I've been so curious about you, my dear. Promise me you will join my table when we dine."

"I shall," Beatrice said. "Thank you for your kind invitation, Mr. Lavan, Mrs. Lavan."

Mr. Lavan chuckled and let her go.

She gave Ianthe a fleeting glance and then allowed the porter to guide her and the rest of her family to the rooms that would be theirs for the evening. She had a cabin to herself. She even received her own key, and Beatrice touched every polished, expertly joined, built-in piece of furniture. It was small, but so charmingly appointed it felt intimate rather than cramped.

On the bed lay a folded note. Beatrice opened it, and read—

> *I will meet you here before dawn.*
> *—Ys*

Ysbeta wanted to meet her. To say what? Couldn't she at least have given a hint?

Harriet stopped in the doorway. "It's so splendid."

Beatrice stuffed the paper into her pocket. "I can scarcely believe it."

"It's real," Harriet said. "They're going to serve dinner soon."

Beatrice and her family followed the porter again, up polished flights of stairs—ladders, they were properly called, even though they weren't, not remotely—and emerged in the fresh sea air of a deck far above the main one, where guests gathered at the railings to watch a pod of pale-bellied dolphins leaping out of the water and showing off for their audience. Ianthe broke off from the crowd to greet her, and she fluttered inside as he bowed low, one hand on his heart.

"I'm glad you're here."

"I'm grateful for your invitation."

"The evening is already sublime, now that you are here."

Ianthe took her around to meet the other young people who had been invited. "We're having the dance up here, and you can see we're setting up tables. Everyone's seat is by random chance, except the family table, where you and Bard are invited. They're nearly ready."

And so Ianthe led Beatrice down to a maritime feast—course after course of fish and seafood so fresh it astonished the palate, all prepared in the elaborate, delicately balanced sauce and spices favored by Llanandari. Wine flowed. Conversation sparkled like the dancing firefly lights overhead, brilliant against the ink blue of the darkening sky. Ianthe's father told stories that had his guests hushed in anticipation and laughing uproariously at the end. And every time Beatrice looked at Ianthe, he smiled.

This would be her life, this ease-filled, luxurious life, filled with the finest meals and the best of everything. Ianthe would cover her hand with his at the table while he listened to a guest, just as Mr. Lavan was doing with his wife, right now. He would find a name for her like "my starlight" and refer to her that way to others. Harriet would want for nothing when it came her turn to attend bargaining season. Her father would repay every cent he owed and rebuild the fortunes of the Clayborns.

Mrs. Lavan didn't like it. Beatrice would have to work very hard to meet the expectations Ianthe's mother had for her, but she was a quick learner, and she would win her over eventually.

It would be all right. And so when the music started, the flowery, inviting melody signaling that the meal was over and dancing had begun, Ianthe guided Beatrice up the stairs, enclosing her in the intimate, two-person dance called the damalsa in Llanandras, and taught her every step.

"Come with me," he said, after they had danced every set until the musicians took a break, and guided her to the highest deck of all, bringing her to the rail that faced the shore. Below them people scurried all over a smaller vessel, preparing fire-rockets.

"Not at that," he said. "Look up."

Beatrice gazed up at ten thousand points of light. The stars spread over the dusk-stained sky, twinkling and shining, every light a wish—or a world, if the stellarists were correct. Then a golden fire-flower bloomed in the sky, raising a gasp from the guests.

The musicians began an orchestral movement, played in a key of delight. Ianthe's arm settled around her shoulders as they watched blossoms of gold, green, orange, red, and even the rarest, most expensive violet-white light up the nighttime sky in a riot of booms and pops. Smoke tinged the sea air, and Beatrice watched, sometimes peering through the dazzle and smoke to the sky above.

Ten thousand wishes. Ten thousand worlds—more, as the sky darkened and more lights appeared. Worlds like this one. Worlds unlike anything she'd ever dreamed.

"I should have something clever to say to you," Ianthe said. "But for all my love of beauty, I have no gift that transmutes the depth of my heart into perfect words."

"That protestation had beauty in it," Beatrice said.

"But not enough," Ianthe said. "Not enough to explain what it feels like to be with you, or how deeply I long for a life with you in it. I wanted time to know, to understand, to be absolutely certain that this feeling was real. And then I nearly lost you—you came within a hair of death, and I knew I could trust it."

He moved, and Beatrice turned in time to see him slipping one hand inside his pocket. "I love you. I love you. I can't help it."

He held up a ring—emerald, she knew, from the bright green spark in the depths of its facets, the stone as dark as the sea. An emerald so flawless it had to have a name, like the very best of jewels. He held it out where Beatrice could see it, and fire-flowers faded, starlight dimmed, her gaze held only by this impossible, unreal jewel.

"I can't reason when I'm near you. Time flies like a thief when you're by my side, so much that I want a spell that slows the turning of the globe just for more time with you. Every time I see you, I am awed by you, delighted by you, comforted and moved by you. I am a greedy man, and I want every moment there is to have with you. I want to marry you, Beatrice Amara Clayborn. Please accept."

Beatrice Amara Clayborn. She hadn't told him her middle name. He had to have learned it from Father. When he spoke to Father after the Blossom Ride, it wasn't to report on what had happened to her.

It was to ask permission to marry his daughter.

It was done. She had secured the most eligible man in Bendleton for bargaining season, and more than that. He adored her. He loved her. He wanted her to be his wife, to live their lives together forever.

The sight of that ring blurred with her tears. Her heart swelled. She gasped at the feeling inside her like the rushing of a thousand wings, at the euphoria that crawled up her spine and burst from the crown of her head like a fire-flower. She loved him. She loved him so much it hurt, but she cherished the ache. She would always love him. She would make sure of it.

Slowly, she raised her hand. Gently, she curled his fingers around the ring, hiding it from her sight. She looked up into midnight-brown eyes so like his mother's and smiled as her heart broke into a thousand pieces.

"I love you, Ianthe Antonidas Lavan. But I cannot marry you. I am sorry."

The sky exploded with light. A dozen fire-flowers burst in the air and bloomed against the night, the sparks dying in Ianthe's eyes.

CHAPTER XVIII

"But you love me," Ianthe said. "Why would you refuse me?"

Beatrice's throat went tight. She fought for a calm breath; she blinked at the stars and made a wish. "Because I love you. You are so kind. You try so hard to understand. You love magic as much as I do, and that's the problem."

Ianthe licked his lips. "Go on."

The ship rose and fell with the ocean's breath, and Beatrice used it to breathe calm, to focus on getting the words out without breaking further. "I can't let magic go and still be happy. Not even for you."

"You can still do magic," Ianthe said. "If we know you're not pregnant, then we can—"

"You can take the collar off," Beatrice said. "If I can only use my magic when you deem it safe, does that magic belong to me, or you?"

"It would only be for safety," Ianthe said. "I don't presume to own your magic."

"But I would only be freed because you released me," Beatrice said. "This isn't a tightly laced set of stays or shoes that pinch my toes for the sake of turning up in fashion. It's my freedom! And even if that thing was not around my neck one day, it would be—as soon as you decided you wanted another child, or thought there might be one, or my courses were late by a day. If you marry me, you will own my magic, no matter how hard we pretend. And I will hate you if you do that to me. I will hate you, and it will tear me apart."

"I—" Ianthe's face crumpled. He squeezed his eyes shut, his face pulled into the taut lines of a man weeping without tears, without sobs. "I can't do it."

He couldn't. Beatrice knew that once he understood, he wouldn't be able to bear it. "You need to let me go. You need to let some other man become my enemy. If it's you, I'll—I'll want to die."

:It hurts,: Nadi said.

:It hurts,: Beatrice replied.

Nadi whimpered, but it remained in her skin.

Ianthe let his head fall back. He looked at the stars as he spoke. "I want you to be happy. My dearest wish is to fill your days with joy. My nightmare is you turning your face away from me."

She wouldn't make him live that nightmare any more than he would make her live hers. The knowledge slipped between her ribs and pushed deep. "Father gave me this chance to choose my husband, or else he would negotiate one for me. There is only one choice I can make. I am so sorry, Ianthe. But—"

"No," Ianthe said. "I understand."

"I have to marry someone else."

"You have to marry someone else," Ianthe said. "Someone you can despise."

"And I will hate him."

"We shall both hate him."

:I will hate him the most.:

Beatrice dropped her chin and blinked, but the tears still spilled. "I will teach Ysbeta how to read the grimoires. She still has a chance."

"Does any woman with the gift want marriage?"

Beatrice had believed that all of them did, once. That she was the unnatural one, the selfish one. But then there was

Ysbeta, and the other women on the hidden path. Even Harriet had whispered to her of how wonderful magic was, how she denied herself to keep her sights on marriage and family. "Ysbeta needs to escape. Will you help her?"

"Both of you." Ianthe cupped her face in his hands. "I'll help you both."

Beatrice shook her head. "I can't go. I'll teach her how to read the grimoires. One of us has to be free."

"I will bring you to her. I will help as much as I can," Ianthe said. "And I can take you away—"

Beatrice closed her eyes. Her eyelids were raw from tears. "My family needs this. If I run away, they will lose everything. Harriet will never have her own bargaining season. I can't do that to them," Beatrice said. "You must let me go. I must marry for their sake. I must—"

Ianthe nodded. Misery pushed his shoulders down. He lifted Beatrice's hand. "I love you."

"I love you," Beatrice said. "If this were a different world—"

"Yes. But we only have this one," Ianthe said.

"I should go to my cabin."

"I'll take you."

"I need to be alone," Beatrice said. "I need to—to—"

"Wait," Ianthe said. "One moment, please. Just—it's goodbye, and—"

"What?"

Ianthe stroked one knuckle down her cheek. He brushed a stray curl out of her eyes, and she couldn't look anywhere that wasn't him, at the soft look in his eyes that was remembering every moment, wrapping it in ribbon to cherish forever. Beatrice raised her fingers to Ianthe's cheek, skimming over his glass-smooth skin. His eyelids fluttered shut as she traced his lips, turning his head to chase the tips with a kiss.

It was goodbye. Beatrice slipped her hand down his jaw, curling her fingers on the back of his neck. She rose on her toes and met his mouth with hers, pulling herself closer.

They rocked with the waves under the *Shining Hand,* kissed to the distant melody of the musicians, clung to each other under the gaze of ten thousand stars. The hundred pieces of Beatrice's heart swelled against each other, quivering as the last cobweb strands of hope broke and drifted slowly ever downward, falling to dust—

This was goodbye, and when they stopped for breath, when they broke their hold, when they stepped away and drew in the parts of their souls that had touched and twined and tangled, it was over.

They gazed at each other. One last look; one final memory. Her Ianthe. She would love him forever. She squeezed her eyes shut. She clenched her fists and swallowed back tears. "I love you," she said. "Goodbye."

She turned away and hurried down the stairs. She didn't look at any of the dancers. She landed on the main deck, where Mr. and Mrs. Lavan, and Harriet, and Mother, and Father all stood in an expectant clump.

They stared at her, alone, her fingers bare and not an emerald in sight. Harriet looked like she would drag Beatrice back upstairs and make her change her mind. Mother touched her warding collar, her eyes full of sympathy, and Beatrice couldn't stand it.

Father, at last, was the one who spoke. "What have you done?"

She looked at the deck under her feet, and then lifted her head to look Father in the face. "Upon discussion, Ianthe and I agreed that it was best that we do not marry."

Mrs. Lavan's face shifted, the lines along her forehead smoothing out.

"He must be disappointed," Mr. Lavan said.

"That boy never had quite enough sense," Mrs. Lavan said.

"You agreed that it was best that you do not marry," Father echoed. He sealed his lips shut and stared at Beatrice as if he didn't quite recognize her. Then his features folded into a decision. "Very well. I need a vessel back to the mainland. Immediately."

"Child," Mr. Lavan said. "Is something wrong?"

"I am sorry, Mr. Lavan," Beatrice said. "It was such a nice party, and I—I'm sorry."

"There's a ship waiting for you," Mrs. Lavan said. "You may board when you wish."

Mother didn't utter a word.

"Our thanks for your hospitality," Father said. He stepped forward and caught Beatrice's arm in a squeezing, painful grip. "It's time to go home. Now."

But she had to tell Ysbeta! This was her only chance to—"Father, I don't feel well. I think I should rest before we go back in the morning."

"We will not spend another minute imposing on the Lavans," Father said. "We leave. Now."

They sent her to the sloop on the first swing.

She wrote a note to Ysbeta the next morning. She weighed every careful word, waited for the ink to dry, and carefully folded it into a small square, dripping wax on the corner to seal it with a simple monogram: BAC.

She set it on the tray where the mail gathered, ready to be sent out. She was halfway up the stairs when the footman plucked it out of the pile and took it to Father's office.

"Wait—"

"His orders, Miss Beatrice," the footman said, and Beatrice clutched the banister as she bent over it. Father didn't order the door closed. He broke the seal, read the contents—and took the letter to the hearth fire, watching the message curl up and burn.

He didn't look at her when he returned to his seat. She was

no longer present in her father's perception—he wouldn't look at her, speak to her, or react directly to her in any way.

The doorbell rang that afternoon. Beatrice moved to the windows, and the Lavans' enameled landau waited in the street. She wiped away grateful tears and waited. But the front doors opened, and Ysbeta Lavan stalked out. She didn't look back as she boarded the carriage and drove away.

She was the last caller to stop at her door. Beatrice roused every morning, allowed Clara to guide her to the bath and choose a day gown and dress her hair, but most days, Beatrice never even descended the stairs for supper. She drifted from her bedchamber to the retiring room, where she and her violon played the keys of sorrow, of anger, of bleak, empty futures. Days bled into the next; days when Beatrice huddled in her bed and looked at nothing.

No gentleman wanted the Warrior Maid. No one wanted a rebellious bride, a difficult woman, a willful, fickle girl from a line that produced daughters. She would be a spinster forever attached to her family, but not as a help to their fortunes. Not as a mage; just as a burden.

Father wouldn't look at her.

The scent of cherry blossoms faded from the air, the trees no longer cloudy with breath-pale petals but a haze of tender, spring green. Bargaining season was more than half over. Sanctum bells had begun ringing, announcing marriage after marriage as alliances were made and sealed.

No one called on Beatrice Clayborn.

Seven more days passed before hope kindled over a column in the copy of the *Bendleton Tribune* Father had left behind after breakfasting. She crept in a few minutes after he was gone to eat a cold slice of egg pie and tea gone bitter with tannins, picking up the paper to pass the time. The tip of her finger turned black as she ran it down the columns of advertisements offering everything from a charter sail to a subscription to a produce garden, when the tip of her finger sparked as it touched an advertisement.

She almost popped the digit in her mouth. :Nadi?:

:It's lucky. It's lucky,: Nadi said.

She lifted her finger and read the advertisement of an investor selling a share of a cargo expedition on a three-masted Chasand cargo ship called the *Cuttlefish.* Cacao, tea, spices. The asking price was two hundred crowns for a quarter share of the ship.

This was a low asking price for a quarter share. Beatrice flipped through the ink-scented pages to the shipping news. The *Cuttlefish* featured under a list of ships and their estimated due date. It was three weeks late—enough time for a nervous investor to presume the ship lost and want to recoup any amount from their investment, even at a deep loss.

If Father bought those shares . . . if the *Cuttlefish* came in . . .

:It will,: Nadi said. :It has strong luck.:

Beatrice read every word of the shipping news and pored over the advertisements, but the paper trembled in her hands. She had to tell Father. This was the key. No one would marry Beatrice now—her original plan, to be Father's secret partner in business, that was the only choice now. He had to see that. She had to show him.

She took the paper with her as she rushed to the door of his office. She knocked, imitating her mother's double rat-tat, and Father said, "What is it?"

His gaze slid past her once she stepped inside. It was worse than a slap. Beatrice laid the paper on the desk and folded her hands. "Father. There is a ship that is three weeks late. An investor is selling a quarter share of the cargo for two hundred crowns."

Father said nothing. He opened a drawer, and Beatrice caught a glimpse of scarred leather pouches that were exactly the right size to hold a hundred crowns. Father had not deposited the winnings from Beatrice's escapade with the card party. It made her mouth go dry.

She licked her lips. "It's lucky, Father. I know it is. It's a wild gamble to invest in a ship that is almost a month late from an expedition, but I know it will come in."

Father found a pen box and set it atop the newspaper, opening the lid.

Beatrice gathered up every last scrap of her nerve. "I know it will come in, because my luck spirit, the same spirit who helped me win at cards, knows the ship will come in. And it will be soon. If you bought that quarter share, Father, you would make thousands of crowns. The cargo is tea, cacao, and spices—all considered essential to the Chasland diet. You'd have a sale before you even had to warehouse the cargo."

:How soon?:

:Hurry,: Nadi said.

"I think you would have to buy the share quickly," Beatrice said. "Today. Nadi is certain."

Father flicked a glance at her, and her heart leapt. But he went back to tuning his pen nibs, as if she weren't there.

"This is how I can help you, Father. Please trust me. This ship will come in, and soon. And then I can keep looking, with Nadi to help me. I can find more ship shares to buy. You will have capital to invest. We will prosper . . . and it will begin with this quarter share of the *Cuttlefish.*"

He put one nib down and selected another, squinting at the tip.

"Father," Beatrice said, her voice breaking. "Please. I know no man is going to come and ask for my hand. But I can do this for you. Harriet will go to Coxton's. She will have her bargaining season in high style. We'll never want for anything, so long as Nadi helps us."

She begged Father to allow her to use her power, just as Mother had done. She clasped her hands together, choking on a sob, and whispered, "Father, please hear me."

The footman's knock sounded at the door—three gentle raps, and Father raised his head.

"Yes?"

The door opened, and James stood in front of Ianthe Lavan.

"Mr. Ianthe Lavan to see you, Mr. Clayborn."

"Ah yes. Come in. Miss Clayborn was just leaving."

Ianthe was here? Beatrice swiped at her cheeks, bare of maquillage. Ianthe had never seen her without it, and here she was, red-eyed and blotchy from crying, and Ianthe was here. Why?

He gazed at her for a long moment, and Beatrice kept herself from touching her hair, her coppery curls allowed to do as nature wanted, fought to keep from checking her apron for stains, and breathed around the tear in her heart. Ianthe. She thought she'd never see him again—

"Beatrice, go."

"I don't mind if Miss Clayborn stays," Ianthe said. "I've come with an offer."

Father sat back in his chair, his hands curled around the lip of his desk. "An offer?"

"I've come to offer you fifty thousand crowns, plus an additional ten thousand at the end of the year."

"An interesting sum," Father said. "What for?"

"To ensure that Miss Clayborn can remain single until next year's bargaining season, which she may attend again if she wishes. The ten thousand is to finance your return to Bendleton."

Fifty thousand crowns. That had to be enough to finance Father's losses. It had to be enough to save Riverstone. And then another bargaining season, if she wanted to attend one after a year of freedom. And Ianthe would be there. She knew that in her bones.

"Let me be clear," Father said. "You are offering this sum. Not your family, or Lavan International. You are."

"I am."

"I had no idea your personal fortune was already so vast."

"In truth, the sum is considerable," Ianthe said. "That is my income for the year, plus a portion of my personal principal."

"And you want me to take it so Beatrice can return for a second bargaining season," Father said. "Are you returning to Chasland, then?"

"I'm looking forward to attending another bargaining season."

"Does your family know you are doing this?" Father asked.

"They do not," Ianthe said. "I'm doing this on my own."

"That decides it," Father said. "No."

Beatrice's knees shook. She gasped. "Father—"

He held up a silencing hand. "If this offer had been a bride price . . ."

"Miss Clayborn has no desire to marry, and so I cannot make the offer, though it is my fondest wish."

That understanding crushed her. "Mr. Lavan—"

"Silence, Beatrice. This is not about my daughter's desires," Father said. "This is a generous, noble offer. I cannot take it, no matter what she's done to necessitate buying her off."

"Father!"

He ignored her. "If I take your income, your family will make me their enemy. I cannot operate in the business world with a severed relationship with Lavan International. And you do not have the power to guarantee that I will not," Father said. "Swear to me that you will keep your silence on this matter."

"It's not what you imagine," Ianthe said. "I'm not here to

bury a scandal in money."

"But you're not here to negotiate a marriage contract," Father said. "Not that I could enter such a bargain with you now."

What did that mean? But Ianthe pressed his lips together, gazing at Father for a long moment. "I understand. But Miss Clayborn is a woman of considerable worth. You would do well to keep her at your side."

"I will decide Beatrice's future, thank you. I have no need of your offer, though I appreciate the desire that spurred it."

He had no need for fifty thousand crowns? That made no sense, even for a man as proud and stubborn as Father. Why didn't he need it?

"You have an offer already," Ianthe said. "Someone has offered for Miss Clayborn."

No. No one would. Father's gaze dropped to the paper on the desk before him, open to the shipping news. The flame of hope leapt high, but it couldn't burn away the dread dripping down Beatrice's skin.

"I appreciate the offer, Mr. Lavan. It's generously done. But I cannot accept it. I hope you have a pleasant day."

Ianthe stood trembling for a long moment, before he dipped his head in courtesy. "A pleasant day to you, Mr. Clayborn."

He glanced at Beatrice before he turned and went out.

"Father," Beatrice said.

"No more," Father interrupted. "Take the rest of your meals in your room. I don't want to see you. Prepare for a caller tomorrow morning. Now go."

Beatrice left. She climbed the stairs to her bedroom, where she lay across her unmade bed and wept into a pillow.

This morning, like every morning, Clara had filled her bath, selected her gown—this one a soft, faded gray, the stomacher trimmed with peach satin bows—and Beatrice swung her legs out of bed, staring at her bare feet.

When the doorbell rang, announcing a visitor, Beatrice and Clara locked eyes.

"Hurry with your bath," Clara said.

Beatrice rested in the warm water, lifting a leg from the pool to scrub the skin soft, her hair slippery from the cream rinse that Clara swore made her curls tamer. Who had called? Father had told her to expect a caller. Who was it?

The door clicked open; Beatrice glanced at Harriet. "Go away. I know someone called."

"Beatrice."

"Go away, I said."

"Beatrice," Harriet said, and she sucked down a gulp of air. "Oh, Beatrice, it's—"

"A gentleman. I know."

Harriet shook her head. "You don't know. You couldn't just sit there if you knew—"

"What are you talking about?" Beatrice asked. "Who is it? Is it— Harriet! Who called for me?"

Harriet burst into loud, wailing tears and fled. Her feet pounded up the hall; her bedroom door slammed hard enough to make the house jump.

What— Beatrice stood up in a great cascade of water. She stepped from the bath and had a towel in her hands before Clara came, her lips a thin line.

"Clara? Who is my caller?"

"I don't know him, Miss Beatrice. But Harriet won't stop crying."

When she was dressed, her hair properly pinned, her stays laced firmly enough to cage her breath, she descended the stairs past the retiring room and down to the black and white marble tiled floor of the foyer. A footman led her across the floor to Father's office, and when he swung the door open, Beatrice wanted to run.

Danton Maisonette set down his delicate glass teacup and rose to his feet. "Miss Clayborn."

"Mr. Maisonette. Are you here to settle damages with my father?"

"Mr. Maisonette has come with an offer of marriage," Father said.

Beatrice took a step back. "No. Father, you can't."

"Powles's word has closed all doors in Bendleton," Danton said. "I am unwelcome at every party and event. The only choice left to go home with a bride is you."

Beatrice's knees went weak. Everything tilted to the right. She swayed, fought for balance, held. "No."

"We've agreed upon terms," Danton Maisonette said. "The ceremony will be in three days."

Nothing felt real. "Three days," Beatrice repeated. "Father, I can't marry this man."

"You do not get a choice in this agreement," Father said. "I have decided. You will marry Danton Maisonette. He has settled a generous sum on you, and his ship for Valserre departs at the end of the week. You will board that ship as his bride."

His bride! He had tried to kill her! "But Father—"

"I brought you here for instruction, not discussion," Father said. "Clara is gone to Silk Row right now, arranging a fitting for your bridal gown. You will be permitted to attend the appointment tomorrow. We are having dinner at the Maisonettes' on the eve of your wedding to celebrate."

Celebrate. Beatrice's stomach shuddered. "But I am to move to Valserre? Will I never—"

"If you have given me a son, we will return to Bendleton on the occasion of your sister's bargaining season." Danton's smile had a hole in it. Beatrice felt Nadi flutter in response.

This couldn't be happening. "Father, can't we simply do as I suggested before?"

Father sighed. "No. I never intended to spoil you, Beatrice, but to suggest such a thing, and in front of your future husband—"

"There is another way," Beatrice said. "If I make a bargain with a greater spirit—"

Danton cocked his head. "I worried about this. I'm afraid I have to insist, Mr. Clayborn."

Father's shoulders came up. "It's only three more days—"

"She must understand authority. Immediately."

Father sighed and pulled open a drawer. The flat wooden box came out, and Beatrice was going to be sick.

Danton opened the box and nodded. He lifted the collar from its satin bed. "This should prove to be a useful reminder of reality."

Beatrice swayed dizzily. "No."

Father sighed. "I had no idea she had this depth of defiance. Beatrice, come here."

"No."

Father held out his hand. "Danton Maisonette shall be your husband. You will obey him. You will obey me. Come here."

:Hate you hate you hate you hate you—:

Nadi screamed it at Danton, bubbling up so high that Beatrice was seized by it. "I hate you."

"I don't care," Danton said. "You ruined my family's name. I don't need your love. I need your sons."

:Curse,: Nadi said, and the power bolted through her body. Danton flinched.

"What did you do?"

"Father, please. You'll see. I was right about the *Cuttlefish.* Wait until proof comes if you have to, but I can do that again. And I will keep doing it. Only please don't give me to this man, Father, please—"

"What did she do to me?" Danton asked, his voice rising. "She did something."

"I laid my curse upon you," Beatrice said. "I will never give you a son, Danton Maisonette. I will never stop hating you. I will make your life a torment until death parts us. This I swear. If you force me to marry, I will—"

"I've had enough of your impertinence," Father said. "Cease this belligerence and come here."

"Father—"

Beatrice sobbed. She shook her head. But Father rounded the desk, crowding her. Danton held the warding collar open and aimed for her neck.

"Please," Beatrice said.

She turned and dashed for the door, but Danton was there before her. She raised a fist to strike him again. He ducked, and her knuckles met the hard wooden door with a red-hot crunch.

She snatched her hand back, and Danton pounced, seizing her in his arms.

"Enough," Danton said. "Your father has obviously spoiled you. No daughter of ours will dare a tenth of your outbursts."

Beatrice lifted one foot and stomped the heel of her slipper onto his instep. Danton howled, but he didn't let go.

"Beatrice, please," Father said. "Stop this violence at once. It's for your benefit, child."

"It is not!" Beatrice screamed. "Father! Stop!"

:No! No!: Nadi cried. :Beatrice! Beatrice!:

:Go, Nadi. Run!:

:Beatrice!:

The collar snaked around her throat. Nadi's scream of terror stopped. The sprit fled her body, leaving her alone.

Her skin shuddered. A high-pitched, ululating whine, so loud and awful it assaulted her ears. Her stomach lurched, as if she were falling from a very great height.

And then the collar clicked closed. She landed with a thump. The collar settled around her neck and all the color leeched out of the room. A soft whine sounded in her ears, dulling the sound of her own sobs. The world was drab, as if the light had dimmed—and inside, where Nadi used to be, there was nothing.

CHAPTER XIX

Filled with nothing, Beatrice left Father's library. The collar should have choked her, but it lay on the curving sweep of her collarbones, the metal already warming to her skin. Footsteps, a cough, both muffled by the soft, high-pitched whine troubling her ears, the marble table in the center of the entry hall dull and gray—everything had lessened after the robbery of her senses; everything diminished.

The parlor door clicked open. The soft tap of pillar-heeled slippers prompted Beatrice to lift her eyes.

"Mother," Beatrice whispered.

How alike they were now: the same rounded ears, simple pearl drops affixed to their lobes. The same autumn-red curls dressed for a day indoors. The same silver collars, denying them the talent they were born with.

Mother lifted her arms, and Beatrice rushed into them, pressing their tear-tracked cheeks together.

"My darling," Mother whispered. "I am so sorry."

"I can't do it," Beatrice whispered back. "I can't."

Mother held her. Beatrice clung to her.

"I wish I could make it easier," Mother said, and stepped back to look at Beatrice. "It weighs heavy on you."

"Help me. Please," Beatrice whispered. "Get a message to Ysbeta Lavan. Tell her I will teach her, but I need the grimoire."

A drawer in Father's office slid shut with a thump. Mother went tense. She flicked her gaze over Beatrice's shoulder, and stroked her daughter's arms. "You will grow used to it," she said.

Beatrice felt a dull, pale disbelief. "Mother?"

The door to Father's office opened. Mother went on in a tone that soothed without listening. "After a while, you forget it's there."

"How could I forget this? Everything is different. It's diminished. It's—"

"Beatrice," Father said. "Say goodbye to your fiancé."

Where was the heat that inflamed her senses? Where was the sensation of her body acting in concert with her feelings? She turned around. Danton Maisonette drew near, his hand offered palm up.

Beatrice stood where she was, her hands by her sides. She should be boiling with rage. She should make a fist and aim for his nose.

"Beatrice."

Father's disapproving look didn't send her heart fluttering. Father's expectation didn't ignite angry sparks over her scalp. She didn't even have the same body any longer.

She lifted her hand for Danton Maisonette. He captured it in his and bowed so deeply it was a mockery, his lips on her knuckles a muffled, half-dead sensation.

She pulled her hand away.

Danton's smile had not a drop of good humor in it. "I count the days, Beatrice."

Her name on his lips was appalling. It didn't belong to him, but he took it.

She turned back to Mother. "Please."

"You will forget," Mother said. "It will all fade away."

"You are overwrought," Father said. "You should take supper in your room. Take a novel and go to bed."

She had no wish to remain down here. She bowed in obedience and ascended the stairs, one flight and the next, and entered her bedchamber.

Harriet sat on the edge of Beatrice's bed, clutching a ruffled pillow. It fell to the floor as Harriet bounded to her feet. "Oh, Beatrice," she said, her voice quiet. "Oh, Beatrice, I'm sorry. It's my fault. It's all my fault, I shouldn't have told—"

She tottered forward and fell on her knees, hands clasped before Beatrice and begging. "I shouldn't have told," she said, and sobs wracked her. "I ruined your life."

"Get up," Beatrice said. "Come here."

Harriet scrambled to her feet and threw her arms around her older sister, and when had Harriet grown so tall? She came up to Beatrice's nose already. Harriet wept miserably, and Beatrice walked them to the bed, where Harriet had a great mess of a cry, and Beatrice held her.

"It's my fault," Harriet said eventually, sitting up. Her face was streaked with tears. Her maquillage was a ruin. When had Harriet's maid begun painting her face for the day? "I did this. If I had kept silent, you wouldn't be in that thing."

"Perhaps," Beatrice said. "I could have gotten caught some other way."

"Is it—you never wanted to wear it," Harriet said. "Is it bad?"

"It's the worst thing that has ever happened to me," Beatrice said. "Everything is dull. Nothing looks right. My ears ring. And Nadi—"

"Is that a spirit?" Harriet asked.

"Yes," Beatrice said. "A luck spirit. That's how I won so much at cards. That's why I was not trampled to death by my horse."

"Because the spirit served you," Harriet said in a small voice.

"Because Nadi was my friend," Beatrice said.

"I didn't know," Harriet said. "I only knew what I was supposed to. That it was dangerous. That it was wrong. That spirits are amoral, capricious, and wicked. That you had to have great strength to control them, to tame them to do good. I didn't know why you would trespass so. But—I took it from you. Your magic. Your friend. I'll never, never forgive myself."

Beatrice watched Harriet cry as if she were floating above it all, watching from the dispassionate view of a dream. She had to say something. Soothe her sister. Comfort her. "What if I forgive you instead?"

Harriet shook her head. "You can't."

"I can if I wish. After the wedding I will sail for Valserre; I won't return until your bargaining season. And then only if I manage to birth a son."

"He's taking you away."

"Yes."

"I don't want a bargaining season," Harriet said. "It's a lie. All of it. Lies in silk ruffles, lies in perfume—I hate it."

"You may hate it," Beatrice said. "But don't forget that you used to love it. You were going to be the star of the Assembly Dance. You were going to have a dozen suitors—"

"I won't do it."

"All right," Beatrice said. "Let's just lie here, then. You don't have to do anything you don't want to do right now."

Harriet settled next to Beatrice. She closed her eyes and slept, the kind of sleep that follows a soul-emptying cry. Beatrice looked at the cloud-painted ceiling and watched the light slowly fade into darkness.

She had given up love for this. For this. Beatrice touched the collar at her throat. Her future. Her prison.

She had given up love for this.

No. She would not give up. She couldn't just drift through this dull, washed-out shell of a life. There had to be a way to free herself, and she had only one chance—the fitting with Miss Tarden. She knew what the modiste wanted; she would gladly trade it for her freedom.

Clara was a snorer, and when she had snorted and growled for Beatrice's slow count to one hundred, she moved an inch away from her maid. Nothing. An inch more. Still she rasped and breathed, and Beatrice slipped out of the bed and stood for a frozen terrifying minute, waiting for her to wake.

Nothing. Her maid slept on, and Beatrice stole out of her bedroom, quiet as a spectre. :Nadi. If you're nearby, grant me luck.:

Not a single stair creaked under her weight. The foyer was empty, lit by the low flame of a single lantern. She scurried across the cold marble tile on bare cat feet and gripped the doorknob of Father's library, listening for the scratch of writing, the soft crackle of a turning page, the way he hrmphed and mused to himself as he read and worked.

Only silence, and she turned the knob all the way before pushing the door open a fraction, a foot, wide enough to pass into the dark and silent room, only a slice of light from the foyer's lamp drawing the shapes of Father's desk.

She had no candle. She couldn't sense the grimoires among three walls filled with shelves, her volumes resting within. She dared open the door a little wider, tiptoeing to the hearth, where the smell of ashes and seasoned wood reigned. She slid her fingers along the mantle, feeling for—ah! The octagonal base of a silver candlestick. Another foot of groping found a striker-box. The rasp of the striker, the flare of its flame—she touched the light to the candle's wick and tossed the spent stick in the hearth. She sighed and turned to survey the bookshelf.

She had seen where Father had paused to shelve them.

She lifted the flame to survey each title. None were what she sought. No. Not that one. Where is it? Where were her books?

She tried another shelf, reading over the titles. Nothing. They were gone. Gone.

A whisper of sound from outside.

Beatrice gasped and blew out the candle, hiding her light —and conjuring the smell of beeswax smoke curling into the air to betray her. Caught. She was caught, there was nothing she could do but watch the library door swing wider.

Mother stepped through the doorway, her hair bound up in rag curlers. She regarded Beatrice in silence. The collar lay against her throat; the white linen sleeping shift glowed in the faint light of the foyer's lantern.

Tales of Ijanel and Other Heroes, by E. James Curtfield, rested in her hand.

Mother put her finger to her lips. She took the candlestick from Beatrice's hand, and pressed the faded blue volume into her daughter's grasp. She laid her hand on Beatrice's shoulder, and in the darkness, lifted her face to plant a kiss on her daughter's cheek. Then silently, she replaced the stick on the hearth and went out of the library, leading her daughter back to the chamber where Clara still snored.

The smell of breakfast made her sick. Beatrice turned her back on the tray and tucked her face under the covers until Clara took it away. She let Clara dress her in a gray cotton jacket and a printed cotton skirt, a riot of strange flowers and visiting butterflies. She slid her feet into pillar-heeled mules; her hands covered in gray kid gloves. When Clara left the room to take the tray down, Beatrice slipped the grimoire into her pocket, where it hid under the fulling cage and pulled on the waist tie fastened beneath her stays.

"Beatrice?"

"Coming," she called, and made a hasty job of following.

She waited on a bench in the foyer, her chin tucked in so the brim of her hat hid her face. She pretended to read a novel—a miniaturized volume that fit in a maid's reticule and waited for the fiacre to arrive.

They were to visit the dressmaker and fasten the token seams that would make the dress finished, having successfully warded off the bad luck that came with finishing a bridal gown before securing a proposal. Clara carried the buff-colored case that protected Beatrice's gown, but Beatrice kept her eyes on the page.

She set the book on the bench just as the footman by the door opened it. "Your carriage, Miss Clayborn."

"Thank you."

The carriage set to take her to the dressmaker's and back. Beatrice kept her head bowed even though it made her feel as if the collar strangled her. She took Clara's arm and glanced at her maid-companion, cast in the role as her jailer.

"I don't think I can do this," Beatrice said.

Clara offered her arm for support. "I'm right here beside you."

She and Clara descended the stairs to the promenade, where the driver bent to set a boarding block next to the dip in the carriage wall. Beatrice put out her hand, but the driver had turned away to inspect a bit of the harness. Beatrice sniffed and made the climb by herself.

Clara settled beside her, the set of her mouth small with annoyance. "This driver is so rude. I shall not tip him."

Beatrice shrugged. "If he saw something wrong with the tack—"

"Perhaps."

Then the driver hopped up to his bench and the carriage lurched forward, its single horse already at a trot. They would come to the dress shop too soon, with the driver in a hurry like that.

Beatrice dreaded standing on the hem-box in the dressing room, robed in the green satin gown dyed with the sixteen herbs of love and fertility. She would stare at her collared reflection as the needlewomen finished hems, fastened buttons, and secured the seventy-point lace on her sleeves. They would tell her she was beautiful. They would look away from the collar on her throat, but they would whisper about it—and speculate on her indiscretion—to the others when she left the shop. And then dinner with the Maisonettes, where, if the Skyborn had any mercy, Beatrice would choke to death on a bone. She was moving too fast to her future. It was rushing toward her, blades drawn.

No. She had a grimoire, and Miss Tarden wanted those more than anything she possessed. She could secure her help —let her slip out the back and run. She eyed Clara, the urge to tell her poised on her lips.

"What is it?" Clara asked. "Miss Beatrice, you look so peculiar."

"I don't want to do this," Beatrice said. "I can't do this."

Clara's expression furrowed into concern and sympathy. "But there's no way out."

"But what if there is?" Beatrice asked.

Clara stared at her, indecision writhing over her face. "What do you mean?"

"I could run," Beatrice said. "I want to run."

Clara's eyes widened. The fiacre lurched to a stop. They were at Tarden and Wallace. The driver jumped down from his seat. Beatrice paused to allow him to assist her, but he circled his horses, inspecting their necks.

Clara made a disbelieving noise. "Really!"

Beatrice stared at the driver now. His broad hat blocked his face, and the driver's neckerchief was raised over his nose and mouth. All she could see was the dark brown skin of his hands that could have meant Makilan, South Sanchan, any of a dozen countries. But something flared in her heart at the sight of him. Something about his shoulders, the tilt of his wrist as he held the cheek strap—

"Come, Miss Beatrice. Think nothing of it. We must—" Her words hitched on a sob. "Come, now. They're waiting."

Clara led her into the shop, but Beatrice looked back at the driver. If he would only turn around. If she could just see his face. But he moved behind one of his ponies, and what if she were wrong?

"Telling off a rude driver won't change anything." Clara held the door open, and Beatrice stepped over the threshold. A dozen heads swiveled to stare at her. They knew who she was, and their expressions ran from fascinated disgust to pity to the tight-lipped determination to never suffer as Beatrice had. Were any of them sorceresses?

Only Miss Tarden looked at her differently, and fear shivered in the cords of her throat.

"Please come with me," she said. "The fitting suite is ready."

Beatrice walked past all those staring faces, past all the doors of the fitting rooms until they reached one in the back of the shop. Miss Tarden stopped Clara with one hand raised.

"Under the circumstances, it's best if Miss Clayborn has time alone," Miss Tarden said. "If you'll sit in the reception room—"

"I would never dream of leaving Miss Beatrice's side," Clara said. "If she cries, who'll wipe her tears? It's a terrible thing. They won't even allow me to stay with her after it's done—no. I won't leave her at a time like this."

"I must insist," Miss Tarden said. "It will only be a few minutes."

"Miss Beatrice?"

He wasn't even going to let her keep Clara with her? Oh, that awful, awful man. "I would like Clara with me."

Miss Tarden's eyebrows knitted together in worry. "She really should—"

"I must insist," Beatrice said. "Or I could leave."

Yes. She could leave. Clara held money in her reticule to pay for things Beatrice needed. They could give the whole purse to a cab driver. They could go to Lavan House. Once she found Ysbeta and taught her how to decipher the grimoires by hand, and the spell to reveal their contents by magic, she would find a way to help Beatrice, and—

Clara firmed her stance. "Yes. We'll leave. Immediately."

Miss Tarden's expression was pale. "You can't."

"We insist," Clara said. "We won't stand for this—"

Beatrice wrestled the grimoire from her pocket, holding it out to Miss Tarden. "Please."

Miss Tarden stared at it. Her nostrils flared as she breathed in its scent. Then she sighed, her shoulders slumped. "I can't accept it."

"But—"

Miss Tarden turned the knob on the fitting room door. "Please go inside."

No! Beatrice backed up a step. "No. I won't go in there, I won't."

She turned and two women in caps and aprons stood at the end of the hall. They looked to Miss Tarden for direction, and Beatrice's heart sank.

"I won't go in. Let me go. Please. By hazel and chestnut, please, I must—"

"Beatrice."

The fitting room door opened, and Ysbeta stood in the doorway.

"Ysbeta," Beatrice said. "You—how did you know to come?"

It had been Ianthe driving the fiacre! Her friend and her

beloved had come to rescue her. "How did you know?"

"Your mother sent word," Ysbeta said. "What on earth possessed you to refuse Ianthe?"

"The reasons seem so stupid now," Beatrice said.

Ysbeta shrugged, and Beatrice wanted to throw her arms around her friend. Her friend, who had come to rescue her from Danton and the collar. "Well, I'm here to save you from your mistakes. Will you consent to be abducted?"

"Yes. Yes. Please spirit me away," Beatrice said. "How will we leave the shop?"

"This way," Miss Tarden said. She opened another door and they moved past rows of dress forms, each one holding a gown in a different phase of construction. The room could have held twenty needlewomen, but they shuffled past empty stools and abandoned needle kits and wound up in the alley, where the same fiacre that brought them to the dress shop now stood.

"Welcome, ladies." Ianthe had removed his hat and neckerchief and smiled. "Beatrice."

Beatrice fell into his arms. "You came."

"Nothing would have stopped me," Ianthe said. "Nothing."

"We still have to make our escape," Ysbeta said. "Enough canoodling."

"Miss Beatrice," Clara said. "What will you do now?"

"Whatever she wishes," Ysbeta said. "You have two choices, Miss Clara. You can raise the alarm and betray Beatrice. Or you can wake up drugged in the fitting room alongside Miss Tarden."

"Or you can get in this carriage and continue to be my maid-companion." Beatrice clasped Clara's hand. "Come with me, Clara. Even if it's just to get a good reference from me—Father won't give you one, but I will."

"I will come, and I will stay." Clara picked up her skirts

and clambered into the carriage. She raised her chin, challenge in her eyes. "Just try and stop me."

"Hurry," Miss Tarden said. "This is no time to delay."

"Very well, Clara. I commend your loyalty. Everyone on board, now."

Clara picked up her skirts and climbed into the carriage. Beatrice took one step in Miss Tarden's direction, offering the book. "Take it."

"I couldn't." Miss Tarden shook her head. "They're priceless."

"I insist," Beatrice said. "I have learned all I can from this one. You must have it. Only promise me this. If another ingenue comes to your doorstep in distress, help her."

"I will," Miss Tarden said. "Now hurry."

Beatrice climbed into the fiacre at last and took a seat on the bench. Ysbeta turned to her, scolding. "I told you to meet me at your cabin before dawn."

"I wanted to, but Father insisted on leaving immediately."

"Because you were stupid enough to—"

"We should get moving," Ianthe said. "You have your draught?"

Miss Tarden nodded. "It's in the tea."

"Remember—you had tea with Beatrice, you must have fallen unconscious, and when you came to, Beatrice was gone."

"I should have helped you earlier," Miss Tarden said. "Now hurry. The girls will be back from lunch soon."

Ianthe hopped into the driver's box. The carriage lurched into motion, and Beatrice smiled for the first time in days.

"Thank you."

Ysbeta huffed. "You idiot. Why did you say no?"

Ianthe looked behind him. "She had her reasons."

"Stupid reasons," Ysbeta insisted. "I told you to meet me.

I was going to tell you my idea that night. All you had to do was be sensible, but that was too much to ask."

"What were you going to tell me?"

"That I think I know how to solve your problem."

"You should have said that in the note."

"I expected you to keep your brains in your head. I expected you to have a shred of sense," Ysbeta said.

"We'll speak of it afterward," Ianthe said. "Under your seat is a small box. Inside that box is a key that will release the collar from around Miss Clayborn's neck. May I ask you to use it?"

"How did you get my collar key?"

"Your mother sent it by messenger last night," Ianthe said.

Beatrice could have wept. "I wish she were here. I wish I could tell her how much she's done for me."

"I know she knows," Ysbeta said. "Come on. Mother and Father are in Bendleton, but they're supposed to be home for dinner. We need to be gone by then."

"Where are we going?" Beatrice asked.

"The sanctum. It's time to do the ordeal," Ysbeta said. "Ianthe, drive faster."

CHAPTER XX

The sun shone warm on Beatrice's face. She touched her bare neck and a delighted frisson shivered her skin, cooled by the breeze playing all around them. The rich smell of cattle and sheep wafted toward the sea, and Beatrice twisted her fingers and spoke the fleet-foot rhyme to the fiacre's sturdy-looking pony. The carriage sped immediately.

Beatrice laughed and hugged herself. Free! She picked up the hateful collar, wincing at the sharp whine that she could hear whenever she touched it, and flung it down the cliffside. "Never will I permit anyone to put me in such a thing again," Beatrice said. "Never. I will fight to the death for my freedom."

:Beatrice!: Nadi cried. :Beatrice, you're back! I couldn't talk to you. I could only watch.:

:Oh, Nadi,: Beatrice said, and burst into tears. Everything was back to normal. She was a runaway, she was free of the warding collar, she was a magician once more . . . and there was Nadi, her spirit, her friend, returned to dwell inside her.

:You're sad.:

:I'm mixed up,: Beatrice said. :I am so happy you're safe.:

:I'm glad you're free. You have to fight them now. You have to fight.:

:I will.:

:Nadi will help. Nadi will hex your enemies. Nadi will bring you luck.: The spirit trembled inside her, and then stretched out its boundaries to fill her body. :A hug.:

A tear rolled down her cheek. :Thank you, my friend.:

They hugged that way—Nadi, pressing the envelope of its body to the boundaries of her skin; Beatrice, with her arms wrapped around her middle.

"Now for my plan," Ysbeta said. "It's simple. First, I will summon a greater spirit of knowledge."

"You're not ready yet," Ianthe said. "Beatrice, tell her."

"You have to gain the companionship of a lesser spirit before you can attempt the ordeal," Beatrice said. "Ianthe has had the company of Fandari for years. I have Nadi, but it's only been a few weeks. You have to wait until you—"

"There is no time," Ysbeta said. "Ianthe, tell her what you told me."

"Bard Sheldon's father, our parents, and their lawyers are in a meeting today," Ianthe said. "They're negotiating the marriage agreement for Ysbeta. Right now. But Ysy, you can't do this. I know you want to help us. I do. But we have to follow my plan."

"Let you do it first," Ysbeta said. "But I should go first, because—"

"I have the most experience," Ianthe said. "I know the most. But Beatrice has to do this immediately after, once I have been through the risks. Then we will evaluate the difficulty and determine how much more preparation you need."

"But I need this the most."

"Your marriage is in negotiations. Beatrice's is tomorrow. She needs this more."

Ysbeta let out a gusty sigh. "If you'd just listen—fine. Very well. We shall abide by your plan."

They pulled into Lavan House's round driveway. A swarm of grooms took charge of the pony cab, taking Ianthe's battered hat and jacket used in his disguise.

"George. Take Clara inside, and have Chef prepare her a

meal. Is the staff still eating?"

"I think they've begun, sir."

"Good. Tell them she's Miss Beatrice's lady's maid, and that she needs a meal and refreshment."

"Oh, sir," Clara said. "Thank you."

"Now you will go where Beatrice does." He strode inside the house, calling for the butler. "Charles! I need a lawyer who isn't beholden to my parents. I'm about to destroy a marriage contract. Go to the cathedral in Meryton and get me a man who enjoys delivering justice."

Charles bowed and moved to obey Ianthe. Ianthe led the way to the back of the house.

"Have you eaten?" Ianthe asked. "It's important to eat before the ordeal. In the chapterhouse, the initiate is honored with a feast before they enter the ritual chamber."

"What happens in the ritual?" Beatrice took a seat in a painted iron chair and served herself. Toast points. Duck eggs. Goose sausage. Fresh tomatoes—that was their greensman's work, when he wasn't cultivating orchids.

Beatrice ate the goose sausage, which Nadi noisily enjoyed.

Ianthe sat between Ysbeta and Beatrice and took a toast point. "You aren't instructed until you enter the ritual chamber, and you can't tell anyone what happened if you succeeded."

"But if Beatrice doesn't succeed—"

Beatrice laid a hand over the anxious rumbling in her middle. "What will you do if the greater spirit possesses me?"

"It's very rare," Ianthe said. "But you will die."

"But the spirit will kill you to get you out of its way," Beatrice said. "Maybe you shouldn't be there when I do it."

"I must be there," Ianthe said.

"But I don't want you to—if I fail, and the spirit hurts you, that's more than I can bear."

Ianthe bit his lip. "I have a spirit blade. Everyone makes a fuss over the rose sword, but it's a shiny stick. The real power rests in the dagger."

"How?"

"It's crafted with the same material and technique as the warding collars. The sheath shields its effects."

"So spirits loathe it," Beatrice said. "It hurts them."

"Yes. I sink it in your body to the hilt, and it disrupts the body so much the spirit flees—and then you die."

Ysbeta and Beatrice sat back in their chairs. Beatrice let out a shaky breath. "So if I fail, you have to kill me."

"Yes."

"And you're willing?"

"I must," Ianthe said. "No one faces this ordeal without someone who will do what's needed. It's my duty to the mysteries. It's my duty to you, as my beloved. Will you face death to gain this?"

"Yes."

He knew her. He knew her fate in a warding collar was worse than death. Worse than dying. He knew her enough and loved her enough to be by her side while she faced it.

"Skyborn. I never thought anyone declaring that they would plunge a knife into their beloved's heart was romantic, but you two seem capable of anything," Ysbeta said.

Beatrice smiled. "Perhaps it's time we looked at that grimoire."

"Right. One copy of *To Summon a Greater Spirit and Propose the Pact of the Great Bargain,* coming right away."

Ysbeta left the table and went inside the house. Beatrice picked up a tiny, vividly red tomato and bit into it. Delicious, full of the flavor of slowly ripening on a vine in the sunshine.

:Beatrice?:

:Yes, Nadi?:

:What happens to me?:

All of the grimoires had remained silent about this. They instructed a sorceress to command, to conjure, to charge a spirit with a task. But Ianthe had spoken of a companion spirit, of summoning the same spirit many times. That was what they did in the chapterhouse. Why? Didn't they—

"Ianthe," Beatrice said. "Nadi is returned."

"So it's there even though you don't call it," Ianthe said. "That's excellent. That's the sign that you are ready."

"Is that what it is?"

"Indeed. My own sponsor told me that I was ready to risk the mage ordeal and become an initiate of the great mystery—after I married."

"But why call the same spirit over and over? Why get to know it? Why nurture its loyalty to you just to—"

"To prove you are capable of such things before you attempt the greater spirit. It's a demonstration of your skill—Oh. Nadi is back, and you have to say goodbye to it."

:But Nadi is your friend. You need Nadi! Nadi needs you.:

Her eyes filled with tears. She loved the spirit, full of mischief and opinions. Would a greater spirit love her? Would they want to ride in her body just to see, to feel? Or did she have to become the commanding mage, locked in an adversarial bargain with a spirit fully capable of destroying her if it wished?

Magic bargained for the things you weren't ready to give. It wasn't fair. Nadi would return to the aetheric plane, the endless nothingness that spirits drifted through. Until another magician called Nadi. Another magician would call Nadi. Perhaps her friend would remember her.

:Nadi, who called you before I did?:

:It was so long ago,: Nadi said. :I was nothing. I knew a sorceress, long and long ago, until her light went out and I became a memory, alone in the dark. Then I heard my name, and I was. I became. And you were so bright, so alive . . . :

:And when you're back in the aetheric, will you—:

:I don't want to go back. It's full of nothing. It makes me nothing too. But I can see you. I will see you until the nothing takes it all away.:

Oh, that was horrible. Horrible. Beatrice pushed her plate away and shut her eyes.

"Beatrice?"

"I have to—I hate this," Beatrice said. "I have to abandon Nadi, but . . . what happens to them? The spirits, I mean," Beatrice asked. "What becomes of them?"

"I don't know," Ianthe said. "Perhaps the ritual in the grimoire describes it."

"I hope so." Beatrice gazed out onto the formal gardens, at the winding circuitous path at the center—the road of right action, the exact path Llanandari slowly walked at sunrise or noontime or sunset or deep in midnight's arms when they had a spiritual question or a dilemma of choice.

"I walked it the day we came back," Ianthe said. "I asked the path to show me what I should have done and tell me what I could do."

"And what did it answer?"

"That the only choice I had, the only responsibility I had, was to honor your pursuit of freedom. To stand next to you as you faced death. That you are your own person, and love needs to be free, or else it's just ownership."

He understood. He comprehended her need, and he honored it, and—

Beatrice shook her head. "I was a fool to say no to you."

"You had your reasons," Ianthe said. "But maybe they don't matter as much. What will you do after you've become a mage?"

Beatrice paused, thinking. "I don't know. I was going to help Father and be a thornback. But he wants no part of that. I don't know what I could do."

"You could come with me and Ysbeta."

"But we can't ever risk a child."

"I know. It doesn't matter."

"But you need a son," Beatrice said. "You can't run away with me. I will never be able to give you a family. If we run away together, you'll be throwing away everything. They'll expel you from the chapterhouse, you'll be estranged from your parents . . ."

"I know."

"Then why are you doing this? You'll be giving up your whole life."

"It's no more than what is asked of you, and all women with the power. I thought about it. Marriage is a sacrifice. But it's the sorceress who gives up everything."

Beatrice trembled. "You will give up everything for me."

"I love you. And if I have to choose between you, fully within your destiny, or a son to continue the traditions that depend on keeping you diminished, I choose you."

Ianthe gathered up her hands in his. "I want to be with you. More than that. I want to stand by your side as you claim what ought to be your right. This is what I didn't understand until it was almost too late. Can you marry me now? Will you?"

Warmth swelled inside her, rushing all through her limbs. She had never imagined this. The way was clear, and she squeezed Ianthe's hand as she stepped into the first moment of her new life. "Yes. Yes, I can. Yes, I will."

They remained like that, hands clasped and smiling at each other, the moment bigger than any words that would try to cage it.

"Rebels and radicals, together. And Ysbeta, too? She keeps talking about her plan, but she's tight-lipped about what it is."

"She wants to travel the world and record all the magic used outside the chapterhouse," Beatrice said. "We could go with her. It could be a good life."

"I can still invest a sum with your father and offer him a strong share of the profits. Your family need not crumble because of this. And when we're all magi—"

"Ysbeta means to use the spell today?"

"Not yet," Ianthe said. "She isn't ready yet, but between the two of us, I think we can get her ready for next year. The important part is to get her away from Chasland and out of Mother's reach. I know she wants the power, but distance is more important."

"Where is Ysbeta?" Beatrice asked. "Surely Lavan House is not so large that she has to travel a mile between her room and back."

"She should be here," Ianthe said. "Maybe she didn't know which book."

"No, she named it exactly. *To Summon a Greater Spirit*—hold on," Beatrice said, her blood gone cold. "I never told her the name of the spell. How did she know that? Oh, no."

"What is it?"

"Have you noticed if Ysbeta has taken up puzzle books?"

"She's been up to her eyes in them. Every spare minute, she's deciphering codes— What is it?"

Beatrice jumped to her feet. "She's figured out how to solve grimoire code."

"What is that?"

"It's how women learn higher magic," Beatrice said. "I'll explain later. We have to find her before she gets into trouble."

Ianthe shoved his chair back with a grinding scrape. "Do you think she took the book to—"

"Do the spell first? I do," Beatrice said. "She was trying to tell us why she needed to go first, and we didn't listen—"

Ianthe's mouth went round in dismay. "But I told her she wasn't ready."

"Does your sister thank you for your excellent advice and do exactly as you say when you tell her how she ought to do things?"

Ianthe's mouth was grim. "No. Skyborn! We've got to find her."

"I know where she went," Beatrice said.

"The sanctum," Ianthe agreed. "Let's go."

Beatrice hitched her skirts up past her knees, kicked off her delicate pillar-heeled shoes, and dashed over the pebbled path of the ornamental garden in stockinged feet. Ianthe's long stride outpaced hers, his heels kicking up pebbles as he sprinted toward the sanctum. Beatrice kept on, her feet stinging with every step. Her stockings punctured, fraying right off her toes, and still she ran, ignoring the pain and the light-headed gasping breaths that fought against her stays.

Nadi poured into her limbs, making her run faster than she could alone. A thread snapped, and the foot of her stocking flapped around her ankle. She passed Ianthe's three-cornered hat, fallen to the path. He was still ahead, but she was gaining, thanks to Nadi's help.

The sanctum came into view, and from it, the thin wavering sound of a scream ribboned from its depths. Beatrice found more strength, more speed, and took the mossy stairs to the round, domed building two at a time, catching herself on the doorway to stop from blundering into the scene before she even saw it.

But the sight was terrible. Ysbeta struggled on her knees, trying to make the signs for the wall of light and the sign of banishment. Ianthe, circling the soft glowing light of the circle Ysbeta had cast to bring the aetherial and the material worlds together, shouting in Mizunh—"Ka! Genmas In Ka!"

It did nothing. The spirit rose higher in the air, so much larger than Nadi, its black light deeper and more powerful.

Ianthe shouted again, as if Ysbeta couldn't hear him.

"Cast it out," he called. "Make a golden shield of your will and cast it out!"

Ysbeta's voice broke on a terrified sob. All around her, the sparkling anti-light of a spirit, the largest such manifestation Beatrice had ever seen, coiled itself around Ysbeta and tried to slip under her untrained, fear-weakened defenses.

"I command you, Hilviathras, Greater Spirit of Knowledge! I banish you, Hilviathras, Greater Spirit of Knowledge! I—"

Ysbeta's words were muffled as the spirit engulfed her mouth. Ianthe, tears clogging his voice, still called to his sister. "Hold the signs! Cast the shield with all your might! Cast it!"

But Ysbeta was sinking, and Ianthe's open mouth stretched wide with pain and despair. Sobbing, he fumbled at the sheath at his hip and pulled out his dagger. The silvery blade glowed to Beatrice's sight, and the taste of raw iron filled her mouth. He settled the handle in his right hand and stepped toward the circle.

:No!: Nadi cried. :Beatrice!:

But Beatrice was already moving. She ran full tilt, her skin shivering as she crossed the line separating mundane space and between, the circle wavering to her sight as her intrusion snapped its integrity. Nadi swelled all around her like a pair of enormous, light-made wings, filling her with might.

She extended her hands and struck Ysbeta in the chest, right where Ianthe had planted his hand on her the night of the card party. Her power flexed its fingers as it sank under Ysbeta's skin and curled around the squirming, enraged form of the spirit trying to take her flesh.

"Hilviathras, Greater Spirit of Knowledge," Beatrice said, and her voice had a chorus in it, as she and Nadi spoke as one. "I command you. Abandon this body and face me."

The spirit flinched. It slid over Ysbeta's body, making a pillar of itself, rising and rising until Beatrice nearly whimpered at the size of it. At its power, outstripping her own.

:I am Hilviathras,: it said. :You presume to command me—you, who are nothing? You are a speck.:

It loomed over Beatrice, huge and light-consuming. :But you are a better speck than this one. More refined. Better trained. You will be less frustrating to use.:

:No,: Nadi said. :You will not have my Beatrice. You will not!:

Nadi gathered itself, growing larger, but still small against the greater spirit. It coiled magic inside itself, and cast it at the spirit, who flinched—once, twice.

Once for Nadi, who bit off a chunk of Hilviathras's form. Twice for Ianthe, who planted his hand against Ysbeta's back, his own spirit rising out of its body to challenge the knowledge spirit.

It turned, its form facing Ianthe, who glared up at it and bared his teeth.

"Hilviathras, Greater Spirit of Knowledge," Ianthe said, and his own voice carried that same eerie harmony. "You may not have either of these women, so long as I draw breath."

:Have it your way,: Hilviathras said, and struck.

CHAPTER XXI

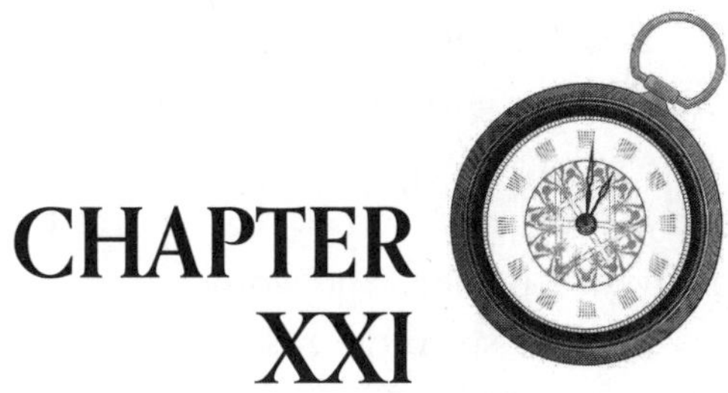

Ianthe gasped and clutched at his chest. The greater spirit struck once more, knocking Ianthe to the ground. The rose dagger clattered to the stone floor, sending up sparks as it landed on the line of the summoning circle, its power disrupting the casting.

The circle's light winked out, but it didn't matter. Hilviathras was tethered to the material, and it was too powerful. Too potent. It held Ysbeta in its grasp and extended a tendril of itself toward Nadi, siphoning the spirit's power away.

Nadi and Ianthe's spirit Fandari struck in unison, tearing pieces from the spirit's form, absorbing the power. Hilviathras ignored Fandari and countered with a gnashing bite of its own, and Nadi yelped. Beatrice screamed at the pain, and then the weak, hollow feeling of having something torn from her.

:You are weaker. You will diminish first, little luck spirit. And then the other. And then I will take the man's shell as my own,: Hilviathras said, its voice booming inside Beatrice's skull. :Or you can surrender to me, little witchling, and I will spare them both.:

"They will destroy you," Beatrice said. She twisted her fingers into sign after sign, battering her will against Hilviathras, but it barely left a dent. "They will never allow you to walk free in my flesh. Never."

:Beatrice,: Nadi said. :I don't have enough. I can't do it alone.:

The knowledge shook her down to her bones. Nadi didn't have enough. Fandari probably didn't either. They were going to lose. Hilviathras would don Ianthe's body like a suit and wreak havoc until it was captured. Destroyed. And she? She would already be dead.

Beatrice spied the rose dagger on the floor. She could do what was needed. She could be as strong for Ianthe as he was for her. She could do no less.

:Nadi. I'm getting the knife. When I say now, you run. Run, do you understand?:

:I don't mean that,: Nadi said. :We can still fight.:

:How? You don't have enough.:

:We have enough,: Nadi said. :All of us. Together.:

Hilviathras wound itself around Ianthe, who struggled to cast something, anything to drive it away. It was distracted. They could ambush it if they acted together.

:What do we do?:

:Let me in.:

:But you're already inside me.:

:I'm inside your body. Let me in your soul.:

How was she supposed to do that? She sought for something inside herself, something soul-shaped, but found only herself and Nadi under her skin. Closer to her than anyone or anything had ever been. How could they get closer still?

"Ianthe!" she shouted. "Trust Fandari! Let it in!"

:You have all the power I need,: Nadi said. It was smaller now, but it fought to distract Hilviathras from digging deeper in Ianthe's body. Ianthe had lost all his words to terrified screaming as the spirit shoved its way inside his flesh.

If she didn't find the way into her soul, Ianthe would be gone. She couldn't allow that. She had to let Nadi in. She had to!

Desperately, she tried to push Nadi inside her heart. That was where the soul dwelled, wasn't it?

:Not like that.:

"How?" she shouted.

:Let me. Let go. Let me.:

Ysbeta, whimpering, moved toward the knife. What was she going to do with it? She stretched out one hand, straining for a blade scarcely an inch away from her fingertips. What did she mean to do with it? What did she mean to do?

:Hurry,: Nadi said. :You have the key. You know the way. Let me in.:

Beatrice screamed in frustration. She didn't know how! She didn't know what to do! She stretched her hand up into the pillar of dark light that was Nadi's form, the way she would put her hand out for Nadi to slip inside her flesh. But she needed to go deeper. She had to let it in.

She had to let Nadi get in. All she had to do was open the way.

She breathed. Deep. Slow. Filling her stays with light, with power, deep into the core of herself. Imagined a flower opening to the sun, every petal unfolding. She focused, not on her center, but at the edges of herself.

Ysbeta batted the handle with her fingers and the dagger spun around, presenting itself point first.

Ianthe had stopped screaming. Stopped fighting. Surrendered—not to Hilviathras.

To Fandari.

Beatrice exhaled, blanked her mind, rose above the struggle. She twined with Nadi, her soul touching, opening to the spirit like an outstretched hand.

Nadi rushed in. :You must let go. Let go. Let me. I have enough. Trust.:

Beatrice's fingertips went cold. Her throbbing, bruised feet went chilly. Her power, her life poured from her and into Nadi, who swelled to great height, the violet-white starlight of Beatrice's power shining between the black sparkle of Nadi's might.

"Ianthe!" Beatrice cried. "We have to work together."

Ianthe lifted his hand. "Together," he shouted. "Ysbeta, get back."

"No." Ysbeta scrabbled forward and grabbed the blade. Blood dripped as she dragged it close. Her palm stained red as she found her grip on the handle. "Together."

Inside her, Nadi gathered up their strength so tightly her arms and legs trembled, weakening. They had one chance. Only one.

"On three!" Beatrice yelled. "One, two—"

Ysbeta bounced to her feet, thrusting the rose dagger high over her head. Golden light shot from the spirit blade's point, piercing Hilviathras. Ianthe rose on his knees, Fandari a shining dark column filled with his power. Together, Nadi and Fandari struck.

They leapt on Hilviathras. They tore at its form, biting, siphoning, feasting, their forms larger, darker, and more powerful with the bond. Beatrice watched through dizzy eyes as Nadi gorged itself on the screaming, struggling spirit, no longer enormous, no longer overpowering.

The spirit recoiled. It screamed, the sound like a bow drawn sharp and hard across the strings of a violon, a shriek like a human voice.

Nadi and Fandari fed and grew strong. Ianthe pitched forward, landing on his hands. Ysbeta lunged and stabbed the greater spirit's form, smaller now, tattered, weakened.

Beatrice's vision went gray. She fought to hold on, dizzy and nauseous as Nadi broke off from consuming Hilviathras.

Huge now, if not so large as Hilviathras had been. Powerful, filled with the energies of its foe and Beatrice's own, drained from her to lend her spirit strength.

:Nadi?: Beatrice asked. :It's getting dark.:

Dark, and distant. Beatrice was cold, cold and half out of

her body, watching as the light faded all around her. It felt like the final gray rush that came just before fainting, but she never quite fell. She kept her eyes open, fighting against the dark. :Nadi?:

:I am here.: Nadi touched her brow, and strength seeped back into her flesh. Its voice was different. More resonant, less childlike. :You have given me the best fruits, the sweetest wine, fine cheese aged in the darkest of caves. You have given me cake and dancing and starlight, and the first kiss of the man you love.:

Ysbeta dropped the knife and reached for the pathetic remains of Hilviathras. Ianthe lifted his head, reaching for Fandari. Beatrice stretched out her hand in echo. :You saved us.:

:When I thirsted, you gave me drink. When I craved, you fed my spirit. You gave me sunlight and sea-surf and sand between our toes. You gave me friendship and dreaming. You have kept faith with me, and made me grow strong, and now we are forever.:

Nadi's form twined around Beatrice's hand. The power filled her senses, filled her with an exhilaration that awed her. :What happened?:

:The great bargain is complete. You are my ally, and I am yours. I am Nadidamarus, Greater Spirit of Fortune, and I will always be by your side.:

"Nadidamarus," Beatrice said. "Are you still . . . are you still Nadi? Do you remember?"

:I remember, Beatrice Amara Clayborn. I am still your friend Nadi, though I am more. And we will win and win and win.:

Beatrice laughed. She bounded to her feet. Ianthe glowed with elation and joy and boundless power.

"We did it," Ianthe said. "We're magi."

Ysbeta made a cry of distress, and Beatrice was beside her in a heartbeat.

"Help me," Ysbeta said. "It's fading, I have to save it."

"That spirit nearly killed us," Ianthe said.

"It's begging me," Ysbeta cried. "It hurts. I feel it hurting. Help me save it."

"You have to let it in," Beatrice said.

Ianthe gasped. "Don't!"

"She needs that spirit," Beatrice said. "She needs to become a mage. Her life depends on it."

"Not just that," Ysbeta said. "I have to. I have to get the answer—"

"Let it inside your body, like you let Elamin in."

The ragged, black-lit thing seeped under Ysbeta's skin, lending its feeble dark starlight to her own aura.

"Good," Beatrice said. "Now you have to trust it."

"You can't," Ianthe said. "It tried to destroy you."

"I must," Ysbeta said. "You need this as much as I do. Now let me do it."

"Trust it," Beatrice said. "Open yourself to it. Let it have the center of yourself. You are a flower. It's the sun. Trust it."

They stayed silent. Ysbeta frowned in concentration.

"Don't try to force it," Beatrice said. "Just let it—"

"It misses Jonathan," Ysbeta said. "Jonathan was its mage until he died and left it alone. Then it was summoned, ordered around, commanded, forced to obey—"

"You will be its friend," Beatrice said. "You will be its mage. Promise it."

Ianthe kept quiet, his lips thin, and then spoke. "You can let it go—"

"No. Hilviathras is the key. If we don't have it, if it perishes because of what we did—Hilviathras. I have a mystery," Ysbeta said. "A puzzle that might never have been solved. Knowledge that might never have been found. You can help me find it. You can help me find them all. Bind with me, and we will travel the world."

Ysbeta closed her eyes. Beatrice went quiet. She couldn't bind Hilviathras for her. Ysbeta had to do this. She waited, and together, she and Nadidamarus nudged chance to favor Ysbeta's bargain.

Ysbeta let out a deep breath. "We will," she said. "We will find mysteries forever."

Peace stole over her face. "There. It's mine now."

"Is this the best idea?" Ianthe asked. "It tried to kill you."

"I made a mistake," Ysbeta said. "We will learn. Together. And now Lord Powles will never ask me to marry him. It's done. I'm free."

:She let it in,: Nadidamarus said. :She is a mage now, even if her bond spirit is weak. It is done.:

It was done. And as they picked themselves up and tried to dust off their clothes, Beatrice gazed at Ianthe, understanding at last what he had sacrificed.

"You gave everything for me," she said. "You brought me here so I could be free. Even though that meant I could never marry you."

"I love you," Ianthe said. "And that meant I couldn't leave you to a life of misery."

"Oh, Skyborn. Hold on, before you finish your farewells," Ysbeta said. "You certainly won't forget. You don't have to stay apart."

Beatrice blinked. "But we're magi. We can't ever be together."

"I'm a mage too. But unlike you, the inveterate gambler, and unlike Ianthe, who chose brute force over subtlety of wit, I bound a spirit of knowledge."

Ianthe cocked his head. "What do you mean?"

Ysbeta smiled, wide enough to show her crooked lower teeth. "I had the name of the spirit when I first called on Beatrice. She read it aloud from a grimoire in my possession, and it seemed most valuable to me. Later, I considered that such a spirit could help your predicament—but I had to go first. Just in case it mattered."

"You could have said that." Ianthe bent and retrieved his rose dagger. "You nearly died. You are so stubborn—"

"I tried to explain, but you wouldn't listen. I did what I had to do," Ysbeta said. "And when Hilviathras was an inch from dissolution, drained too far to reconstitute itself, I gave it what it needed to fight for life."

"And that was your soul-bond?" Ianthe asked.

"No. It was the mystery. I asked Hilviathras to help me solve the mystery."

"What mystery?" Beatrice tugged off her ruined, footless stocking, balling it up to stow in her pocket. "What is the mystery?"

"I asked it how a sorceress might protect her unborn child from possession," Ysbeta said.

"Did it know?" Ianthe asked. "Ysy. Does it know how to do this?"

"It remembers a nation of uncollared women, lost to legend and time. They knew how to protect their children. And I will get that answer." Ysbeta smiled and pointed at Ianthe. "It said your sacrifice was the key, but I don't know more. We have to find the details ourselves. Are you willing to sacrifice for your family?"

"Yes," Ianthe said. "Yes. Absolutely. As many times as you want. Let's have children, Beatrice. Let's have ten children."

"Let's start with one," Beatrice said, but she laughed, opening her arms for Ianthe. "We can get married."

He laughed and lifted her around the waist, spinning them both in delight. "We're going to get married."

"How?"

"We make all haste to Meryton," Ysbeta said. "We need to get on the *Pelican.* Now."

Meryton sped by in a blur. Ianthe drove the fiacre, demonstrating an ability to shout at traffic delays in Chasand, Llanandari, Sanchan, Valserran, and Makilan. Ysbeta fought laughter at some of the particularly ribald jokes in Sanchan. They lurched and paused and crawled through streets dense with wagons, carts, and people bearing loads on their backs, moving goods between seller and buyer. It was noisy and stank of cooking food, horses, and decaying scraps. When the wind shifted and swept away the odors with the salt and sea-wracked scent of the ocean, Beatrice breathed more freely.

Ianthe halted the ponies. "Ysy, you're Kalinda Damind. You're Ysbeta Lavan's new manager of affairs, and you've come to inspect the *Pelican* and report on his condition to your employer."

Ysbeta was dressed rather too well to pass as a working woman—the cut of her walking suit bore the standing collar and deep buttoned cuffs of high fashion, and her jabot ruffle was of fifty-thread lace rather than simply trim. But she stripped off her embroidered gloves and stuffed them in a pocket. "How do we explain Beatrice?"

Beatrice patted her hair, now released from its pins and smoothed into a simple braid. "I don't have stockings."

"No one will be looking at your feet."

"Another woman will notice in an instant," Beatrice said.

"We're not likely to run into another woman. You're Miss Damind's clerk. Paulina Fisher. There's a writing board under the seat. Scribble down anything, it's just a prop."

They moved through a town of warehouses and cargo guards, frowning and alert at the sight of a lady and her well-dressed attendant, driven through the streets by a hired fiacre and a gentleman driver. Some of them stepped into the street to challenge them. Ianthe handled it with swift, polite words and the flash of rings—one, the linked circles of a chapter-house magician, the other, the heavily carved signet used to legally seal documents on behalf of Lavan International Trade and Exploration. Sometimes it was hard to tell which mark left the most impact.

They crossed a street that felt like slipping into another country. Warehouses, shining clean and white, braced by sturdy timbers, lined grid-straight streets. Llanandari workers, clerks, and warehouse guards moved around with purpose, and many of them took one look at Ysbeta and bowed, doffing their hats.

"Nearly there," Ysbeta said, as the scent of seawater and a warehouse that wafted the rich scent of tanned leather overwhelmed the odors of horse and humanity.

"Which warehouse does your family lease?" Beatrice asked, and Ysbeta grinned, waving her arm to take in their surroundings.

"These are the warehouses for cleared goods. We keep it sharply organized."

Beatrice looked around again, taking in the sight. "You mean these buildings are all yours?"

"Beatrice, my dear, I'm going to have such fun watching you goggle at the scope of Lavan International," Ysbeta said. "Now wait . . ."

Ysbeta lifted one hand, waiting for Ianthe to cross yet another street and stop at a manned gate. The attendants raced to let them through, and Ysbeta dropped her hand.

"Welcome to Llanandras," she said. "Technically you are on foreign soil. Legally, your father has no right to extradite you from our country. You have asylum."

Beatrice knelt on the carriage floor to retrieve the wooden writing board that held a sheaf of paper, an expensive metal pen, and a portable inkwell. "What?"

"You're safe here," Ysbeta explained. "Even if they find you, so long as you're on this side of the gate, they can't touch you. If we take a ship and sail three miles out, you're in common waters, living under the rule of the sea. You can marry out there, and no one can do a thing."

Free. Safe. And after a very short voyage, married. But it wasn't quite enough. It was only her safety.

"But . . . it matters more if you're safe here," Beatrice said. "Your parents can touch you here—and when they do, they'll drag you back to Lord Powles."

Ysbeta pursed her lips and nodded. "That's why Ianthe was in such a hurry to get here. I have to pursue some legal safety of my own."

"How will you do that?"

"They can't haul me off my own ship," Ysbeta said. "I can even refuse them permission to board. The sooner I'm on the *Pelican,* the better."

Of course. Ysbeta and Ianthe had told her that Ysbeta owned a ship, and she knew that the captain of a ship was king on the water, enjoying absolute rule so long as he—she—stood on his decks.

"All we have to do is board, and that's us settled. Happy ever after." She sniffed the air. "Someone's steaming cockles."

They drove inside a warehouse whose windows boxed the long rays of sunset. A young man moved between support timbers, changing lanterns fueled with beeswax. A worker took charge of the fiacre, and Ianthe led the way to the dock. Beatrice winced at every step she took on bruised feet. Cats jumped down from their perches atop crates and followed them, spotting someone who might believe that they were starving to death and needed to be fed this instant. A silver tabby marched into the empty cargomaster's office as if she owned it.

:Why don't you have a cat?:

:Do you want a cat?:

:They are splendid,: Nadidamarus said. :Pet that one.:

A man standing at a writing desk glanced up, and when he smiled, it stuttered across his face. He watched Ysbeta and Beatrice, his mouth pursing shut. He put down his wooden pen and circled around it, standing in front of the door.

"My greetings to you, honored sir. How may I serve the Lavans today?"

Ianthe paused for a moment. "Nestor Patan. This is Ysbeta Lavan's manager of affairs, Miss Kalinda Damind. With her is her clerk, Paulina Fisher. Ysbeta wishes them to become acquainted with the warehouse operation in Meryton. You will see them conducting business here often from now on."

Beatrice bent her head, and then wrote "Nestor Patan" on the writing board.

Ysbeta stood tall. "What is your position here, sir?"

"Inventory control," he replied, still looking at Ysbeta and Beatrice. "A woman manager? Did your honored father approve of this?"

Ysbeta looked stormy, but she held her tongue.

"She was the only woman applicant. Ysbeta liked her," Ianthe said.

Nestor examined her again. "A thornback, with a face like that? It's a shame. The other's a pretty one too. Why aren't they settled?"

Ysbeta clenched her fists. Beatrice wrote "obnoxious character" on her writing board.

Ianthe tilted his head. "Both of them preferred making use of their educations."

"Ah, there's the problem," the controller said, nodding in agreement to his own statement. "Well, the damage is done. What did you want to tour?"

"Specifically, the *Pelican*," Ianthe said, as if he'd not

blinked an eye at anything Nestor had said. "Miss Damind is to tour the ship, inspect his records, and listen to the recommendations of the acting captain . . . ah . . ."

"Ranad Beleu," Ysbeta said. "Miss told me the names of the officers."

"Good memory!" Nestor complimented, and Ysbeta's smile stretched across her closed mouth. "The *Pelican* is in the second berth. He's taking a cargo—Mrs. Lavan put in the order to send him out immediately— Shit!" The inkwell on Nestor's desk toppled, spilling ink all over his papers. "My whole day's work!"

He turned away to mop up the mess, and Ianthe turned to wink at Beatrice. "Bad luck. We'll see ourselves to the *Pelican.* Thank you for your directions."

Ianthe stepped through the doorway first, turning to the left. From inside came a crash, and a string of curses billowed out the door with the smell of petty revenge. Beatrice smiled. It was sweet.

Ysbeta made a frustrated sound with her teeth. "Mother gave orders to load my ship? To send him out on a trading journey cargo I didn't plan? She did it just to make sure I couldn't—"

"Shh. You are Kalinda right now. And Kalinda has a right to be annoyed, but not furious. We arrived here just in time."

"We did," Ysbeta said. "That's what matters. We will board the *Pelican,* and we will sail to Rhaktuun, where the *Pelican* will take on art and gemstones while we journey to Otahaan—"

"What's in Otahaan?" Ianthe asked. "Other than one of the oldest libraries in the world—oh. It's in a book. Of course."

"What's in a book?" Beatrice asked.

"The means of keeping your unborn safe while they develop inside you," Ysbeta said. "Hilviathras said the information is very old. Naturally the ancient library of Queen Ishana is where it wants to go—it's only a week's sailing and two weeks overland to reach the capital. And then from there—"

"Shit," Ianthe said. "Look down. It's the cargomaster."

Ysbeta swiveled her head around, tracking Ianthe's gaze. Beatrice watched a steel-haired Llanandari in a deep maroon coat recognize Ysbeta, his face shifting from restrained impatience to dismay. He pointed at the three of them, and all the dockworkers and sailors looked up as he shouted, "Stop that woman! That's Ysbeta Lavan!"

CHAPTER XXII

They ran. Ianthe sprinted for the southwest end of the long wharf, and Ysbeta yelped as her pillar-heeled shoes rose in the air. Beatrice gripped Ianthe's shoulder, letting Nadi keep his feet sure and steady as he ran all-out to reach the second berth. Beatrice spied a long, three-masted ship bobbing in the water, and her heart sank, for instead of being lashed snugly to the dock, it was at anchor, out of reach without rowing to its side.

Sailors at a moored ship poured down the gangway and pursued them. Beatrice pointed and the first one tripped, tangling up the legs of a second, and the whole bunch had to stop and set themselves right. Ianthe swung one hand and a few feet away, a dockworker tumbled into the water with a yell.

"That's the *Pelican* out there," Ianthe said. "We're sunk."

Ysbeta screamed in frustration and tore open the front of her jacket. Embroidered buttons flew everywhere as she struggled her shoulders free of the sleeves. She flung the jacket away and it cartwheeled through the air, landing in black water. She fumbled for her skirt laces and let the printed cotton fall to the tarred wooden boards, fumbling with the cord that held up her fulling cage.

"You're going to swim for it?" Beatrice shouted.

"Ianthe has to protect you," Ysbeta said. "I'm getting my ship."

The cage floundered to the boards, and Ysbeta reached into the pockets still tied to her waist, producing a small knife. "Don't fret about the laces. Hurry."

Ianthe kept running, bearing the women behind him on a carriage of air. Beatrice popped laces, looking up as Ianthe stopped at the end of the berth. A knot of sailors advanced on them. Beatrice hissed as the blade nicked Ysbeta's back and a spot of red bloomed on her shift.

"She'll never make it aboard," the man in the lead called.

Other sailors appeared on the water in rowboats, sculling toward the *Pelican.*

"That ship is mine," Ysbeta said. "Mine. And I will stand on his decks or die trying."

She ripped the stays away from her body and whirled for the edge of the dock, diving into the water neat as a knife. A rowboat crew gave a shout and headed toward her.

Ianthe pointed. The nose of the boat rose high in the air, sending the crew tumbling into the water.

Ysbeta could swim like a fish. She cut through the water, one arm after the other in endless circles, her kicking feet splashing, her white cotton shift billowing around her—but on the deck of the *Pelican,* sailors gathered amidships to watch her progress. A dark man in a red-plumed hat stood front and center, still as a statue as Ysbeta swam for the *Pelican*'s hull.

A new rowboat sculled across the water. Beatrice and Nadidamarus beheld it, and the sailors dropped their oars to frantically bail the leaks sprung in the bottom.

Ianthe pointed at the only man on the dock in a coat. "Cargomaster. Help her."

"We have orders—"

"If you stand by and watch her drown trying to win her freedom, your orders won't mean a thing," Beatrice said.

"All you will be are the people who watched Kalman Lavan's daughter drown trying to get to her own ship," Ianthe added.

"Signal the acting captain to throw down a line," Beatrice said. "She will die out there before she'll allow herself to be captured. She will dive for the bottom and drown before she'll let you take her."

"Why?" the cargomaster asked. "What's going through her mind?"

"We don't have time to tell you that," Ianthe said. "Signal the captain to take her aboard."

"Please," Beatrice said.

The cargomaster watched as Ysbeta called up to the crew, treading water next to the hull. He watched, his jaw working as he weighed what to do.

"I will remember this," Ianthe said. He turned toward the water and pointed.

Ysbeta rose out of the water, her carefully styled hair now dripping wet, her cotton shift clinging to her skin. Someone behind them made an astonished yelp. Someone else rushed forward, reaching out to grab Ianthe. Beatrice pointed, and Nadi flexed its power. The dockworker rolled his ankle and went down with a cry.

Beatrice moved so she blocked Ianthe's body with her own. She bared her teeth at the crowd, and the cargomaster flinched as a seagull loosed its bowels, splattering his hat and coat.

"Leave before I hex every last one of you," Beatrice said.

A half-dozen workers cut and ran.

Ianthe grunted with the effort. Near the *Pelican*, Ysbeta rose high above the rail of the ship, over the heads of the astonished crew. Ianthe gasped with exertion as he floated her gently to land on the deck of the ship she owned, the ship she ruled outright the moment her toes touched the boards.

He bent over, trying to catch a breath. "It's done. No thanks to you, Mr. Caldet, and I'll be sure to inform my father of that. Give permission for the *Pelican* to dock. We're going aboard."

The *Pelican* was a fine ship, a sturdy vessel meant to ship cargo and hold its own in a fight. He was a sterling example of the naval might of Llanandras, of the cleverness of their shipwrights and engineers, and Ysbeta had every right to be proud.

Beatrice sat at the table bolted to the top deck, enjoying a meal from the galley. She waved as Ysbeta appeared from belowdecks. She had found breeches, a shirt, a fine weskit, and the former captain's deep red coat and red-plumed hat. She marched across the deck barefoot, just like many of the *Pelican*'s crew.

"I'll never wear a skirt again," she declared, raising a bottle of Kandish wine by the neck. A crew member brought them globe-blown goblets for their first toast.

"To freedom, happiness, and getting everything you want," declared Ysbeta, and they called hurrah and drank.

Beatrice breathed in, startled by a bouquet that made her think of summer-blooming roses among fresh, ripe plums—and the first mouthful flooded her tongue with delicate, shimmering flavors. Berries and a rounded, mellow tannin slowly unfolded, hinting at spices and minerals at the finish.

"Oh, it's marvelous," Ianthe said.

"Three weeks to the solution, and then I'll begin my travels," Ysbeta said. "Are you sure you don't want to come with me? You could manage the *Pelican* and expand the fleet."

"I go where Beatrice goes," Ianthe said. "Beatrice?"

Beatrice thought. "We'll go to Otahaan with you. We'll gain the secret of protecting sorceresses' unborn children. But we have to share it. Every sorceress has to know how to protect their children without the marriage collar."

"So you will return to the world. They won't thank you for it. I hope you realize that."

"Oh, I expect I'll turn the world upside down," Beatrice said. "But think how many women have hidden their resistance. I think I'll gain allies faster than you expect."

"You're going to go along with this, then?" Ysbeta pointed her wineglass at Ianthe, who nodded.

"I fight what she fights. Too many gentlemen believe that sorceresses are happy to deny their full potential. There must be other men who support freedom."

"But it would be so simple," Ysbeta said. "Beatrice, I dub thee Joseph Ezra Carrier. Write coded grimoires. We'll put them in bookshops."

"I don't think that will work," Ianthe said. "The men need to be told, not just the women."

Ysbeta poured more wine. "I have spoken with Hilviathras, and it confirms that we have to go to Otahaan for the details, but you don't know how the men will react. They have the power, and most of them won't accept anything that upsets that power. You'd have to convince the chapterhouse mages—"

Ysbeta stopped speaking as the beat of many footsteps echoed off the wooden dock. Men strode toward the ship, and Beatrice's pulse jumped. Father and Danton Maisonette walked behind Bard Sheldon and Ianthe and Ysbeta's parents, and together they halted before the ship.

Father moved to step on the gangplank, but Mr. Lavan stopped him with a hand on his arm. "Captain, I ask for permission to board the *Pelican.*"

"Permission denied," Ysbeta said.

"Ysbeta Mirelda Lavan." Her mother walked right to the plank, but Mr. Lavan caught her elbow to stop her from setting foot. "You will stop this childish nonsense immediately."

"Mother, I will not," Ysbeta said. "I told you. I told you a dozen times that I didn't want to marry—I begged you, and all you could see was profits instead of a daughter."

"How dare you! The impertinence! You will obey your mother—"

"And now I can't, Mother. My bond spirit is Hilviathras, greater spirit of knowledge."

Mrs. Lavan stared at Ysbeta in open-mouthed horror. "What have you done?"

"It's too late," Ysbeta said. "Mama, it's too late for that now. I told you I couldn't. I told you."

Mrs. Lavan stared at her daughter, speechless.

"You were happy to be married," Ysbeta said. "You love Father. You told me so many times when I was little that you knew it was love from the start. You had everything. You had Father. You had the trade you loved. And when we were old enough, you took on magic again. But you don't see me. I'm a person, not a trade agreement."

"This union will reap so much plenty—"

"Plenty for him!" Ysbeta pointed at Ianthe. "Plenty we don't need! Mother, look at me! I never wanted what you wanted for me. Ianthe is content with what we have. We don't need more."

"You are a child. You don't know what you want."

"I'm only a child when I want what you don't want, Mother. But please. This is what I want. I want to be a master magician. I want to be a scholar. I don't want anything else. Please—"

"No more," Mrs. Lavan said. "I have worked so hard. I have sacrificed so much. And you— Come down from there."

Ysbeta took a step back. "No."

Bard moved closer to the gangplank. "Ysbeta."

Ysbeta's voice was thickened by unshed tears. "Miss Lavan."

Bard bit his lip but nodded at the correction. "Miss Lavan. Is this because of Chasland law? I know there was a disagreement about your property . . . if we married in Llanandras, would that satisfy you?"

"No."

Bard stood up a little straighter. "Is it because of our customs? I know Llanandari women do not have as many babies as Chaslander women do—"

"No," Ysbeta said, her voice weary.

"I know I have been presumptuous. I didn't woo you as I should have. I know I have been inconsiderate. I didn't treat you with respect. I assumed you were mine when you never were any such thing. But I can change—"

"No, Mr. Sheldon," Ysbeta said. "You could have been the most handsome, the most romantic, the most considerate man on the globe. It wouldn't matter."

"Then what does?"

"My work," Ysbeta said. "I mean to record the magic the chapterhouse ignores. I mean to uncover lost traditions and find the truth of sorcery and spirits. I want to learn something new every day and teach another something that could have been lost. I will find cities lost to legend and preserve wisdom from dying traditions. But first I mean to learn the magic that will make my brother and my new sister safe from birthing a spiritborn child."

Bard watched Ysbeta, excitement stirring in his eyes. "I would go with you."

"No."

"But what an adventure it would be!" Bard swept his arms wide. "You and I, across the whole world, seeking knowledge and lost secrets, forever—it's the most romantic thing I've ever heard. Hang the Ministry. We'll have the sea—"

"No!" Ysbeta shouted. "Bard, you cannot come with me."

"But I love you!"

"But I don't love you," Ysbeta said. "And I'm sorry, Mr. Sheldon, but I don't think you love me either."

"I do," Bard said. "Don't you see that? I would give up everything for your happiness."

"And if that doesn't make me happy?" Ysbeta asked. "What then? I don't want you to give up everything, Mr. Sheldon. I don't want your sacrifice. I don't want to marry you."

Bard went silent and pale. He watched Ysbeta, his eyes wide, entreating, but the light in them dimmed as he heard her at last.

"I don't want to marry you," Ysbeta said. "Mr. Sheldon, I am so sorry. But it's the truth."

"I know." Bard bent his head. He sighed, and pain stole across his countenance as he looked at Mr. Lavan. "I withdraw my claim. The agreement is null."

He turned back to Ysbeta, swept off his hat, held it over his heart, and bowed. "Farewell, Ysbeta Lavan. May the Skyborn bless you."

He turned and walked down the dock, settling his hat back into place.

"What nonsense," Danton said. "Beatrice, come down from that boat immediately."

Ysbeta put her hand on Beatrice's shoulder. "Beatrice Clayborn has the right of hospitality on my ship. She cannot be compelled to leave it, under law."

"That law also requires that she be in service to the vessel," Mr. Lavan said, in the entirely reasonable tone one uses to mollify precocious daughters. "What position does she hold?"

"She's the ship's mage," Ysbeta said. "Her bond spirit is Nadidamarus, greater spirit of fortune—"

"Absurd," Danton Maisonette snorted in derision. "Women do not bind greater spirits."

"This woman has, Mr. Maisonette," Beatrice said. "I decline your offer of marriage, and I charge you with misuse of sorcery to inflict harm and attempted murder. Give up your claim to my hand and I won't put you in court."

Danton sniffed. "With whose money for the suit?"

"Mine," Ysbeta and Ianthe said in unison.

"Yours? But you can't marry her, not after what she's done—"

"You tried to kill her, Maisonette," Ianthe said. "I am happy to explain to the courts and the broadsheets exactly why you did. Will you do that to your sister?"

Danton took a step back. "You wouldn't dare."

"I have already contacted a lawyer," Ianthe said. "I invite you to try me."

"Think of your sister, Beatrice," Father said. "How could you do this to Harriet?"

It twisted in her chest. Harriet didn't deserve to suffer. She didn't. But neither did Beatrice. "I tried, Father. I tried to make my ambition small. I tried to honor my talent and my family. I would have been content to be your assistant."

"Then we'll do that now," Father said. "There's no other choice."

"It's too late, Father. I am a mage. I will conduct my life in the open instead of cringing in the shadows. As for Harriet, it may be best for her to travel abroad and board at a college."

"Any college she chooses," Ianthe Lavan said.

"She will have the best," Ysbeta said. "She may attend my college. She will go to Highpath Women's University. I will sponsor her myself."

"Then that's settled," Ianthe said. "I can include it in the marriage contract."

"If she's done what you claim, that's impossible." Mr. Lavan's mouth stretched into a sad line. "You can't marry, son. Not her. She can't be your wife."

"She can," Ysbeta said. "Hilviathras knows of a way for a sorceress to safely carry a child without a warding collar—and Hilviathras informs me that the knowledge is very old. There's nothing stopping them."

"No one in Chasland will marry them," Father said, his face going red.

Mr. Lavan raised his hand. "That's not a problem for them, Henry. My willful but clever daughter is the captain of record of the *Pelican.* All they need to do is sail three miles beyond Chasland's shore, and she has the power to legally bind them."

"But I hold the contract to Beatrice! I oppose it, and claim the rights of my contract," Danton declared. "Move that ship an inch and I will sue."

"I am not yours," Beatrice shouted. Nadidamarus rose silently out of her body, spreading itself to its fullest size. Danton's face went white. Mr. Lavan's mouth hung open. Father couldn't see what she was doing and continued to glower at her. "I will never be yours, Danton Maisonette. I am a master of fortune, and I can make your future a curse from which you will beg to be freed. You cannot own me, or any other woman. We are not objects to be locked up and used. Now get off this dock, and never bother me again."

The terror on Danton Maisonette's face deepened. "I withdraw my claim. She's your problem, Clayborn. I am done with her." The words were bold, but his voice quavered. Danton spun on the heel of his boot and hurried away without looking back.

Mr. Lavan gazed upward in thought. Father watched Danton leave, and then turned back to Beatrice. "It seems you three have an answer to everything. Mr. Maisonette has withdrawn. You will shield Harriet by removing her to an expensive school. What else do you demand?"

"I do not demand, Father. I ask—" Beatrice's breath hitched. "We're sailing out in the morning. Will you fetch Mother and Harriet, and bring them back here so they can see me married?"

"You—" Father stopped speaking. "You can't expect—"

"They've outfoxed us, Henry. My daughter will not leave that ship until she's miles from here. I know her too well."

"I'm sorry, Father. But this is what I want." Ysbeta joined Beatrice's side. "I'm going to travel the world. I'm going to write my books. I will never marry, Father. I don't want to. Mother, please understand."

"Don't you see what you're doing to this family's future, Ysbeta?" Mrs. Lavan asked. "I have done so much to make Lavan International the greatest firm in the world."

"But if I did what you wanted, I would be miserable. It would break me," Ysbeta said. "I know what I want, Mother. And it's this. I want to explore the world. I want to discover knowledge. I want to write books and preserve the magic that is disappearing under the chapterhouse system. I'm sorry it's not what you want for me, but I won't be a sacrifice to your ambitions."

"I don't accept this," Mrs. Lavan said. "What you've done—"

"You would applaud it if it were another woman," Ysbeta said. "You would call it ambitious, and bold, and brave. Why can't that woman be me?"

Mrs. Lavan went quiet. She gazed at her daughter and softly shook her head. "I can't deny that. But what you want is dangerous."

"I'll have my crew," Ysbeta said. "I'll hire assistants and guards. And I will come home every year, if you want me to."

Mrs. Lavan glanced at her husband. "You indulged her. Both of them."

"Did I? I think we did right by them," Mr. Lavan said. "We raised both our children to be independent, to know their own minds. I won't complain that I taught them too well. Permission to come aboard, Captain? I hear my son's getting married."

Ysbeta let out a relieved sigh. "Permission granted, Father. Mother?"

Mrs. Lavan eyed Beatrice. "Well, then. Are you ready to learn how to be the wife my son needs?"

Beatrice's heart beat fast. She tried to smile, but gave it up. "I'm afraid we have something we have to do first."

"And what is that?"

"We have to find the secret to protect our children," Beatrice said. "And then we have to tell the world about it."

Mrs. Lavan mulled that one over. "Why? I want to hear your reasons."

"Because sorceresses aren't free," Beatrice said. "All over the world, sorceresses face the same choice—they can pursue their magic, like the priestesses of Sanchi, or they can have children. How could I possibly learn this secret for myself and then hide it? The world has to know."

"Hold on," Mrs. Lavan said. "I grow weary of arguing with you by shouting up to the ship. Permission to come aboard, Ysbeta? I need to make sure your plans are going to work."

"Mother?"

"If this is what you want, it's my duty as your mother to help you."

Ysbeta's face glowed. Tears sprang from her eyes. "Really?"

"Really. Let me come aboard, little bird. We have a great deal of planning to do."

"Permission granted," Ysbeta gasped, and she ran to the deck to hug her mother, her captain's hat falling to the boards as they squeezed each other.

Father stood next to Mr. Lavan on the deck, his face tight with anxiety.

"Father?" Beatrice asked. "I understand if you can't, but . . ."

Father stood for a long moment, weighing his decision. Beatrice fought the urge to hold her breath. She kept her mouth shut and didn't argue, didn't wheedle, didn't beg. She was a mage now. Father had the right to decide whether he could accept it.

He raised his head and looked at her. "What will people say?"

"Whatever they please," Beatrice said. "Are their opinions more powerful than a father's love for his daughter?"

Father bowed his head. "I wanted you to have more, growing up. I tried to expand our fortunes, but then you were the only hope I had left. I wanted you to have so much more than I was able to give you."

Mr. Lavan put his hand on Father's shoulder. "We all want that for our children. But sometimes, what they need isn't what we imagined for them."

"You're going to upset everything, Beatrice. You aim to turn the world upside down."

"I mean to do exactly that, Father. If that means you can't accept me as your daughter anymore—"

"No. Don't say that. Don't think that." Father's shoulders rose—and then he sighed. "We'll be a perfect scandal, but you're my daughter. It doesn't change anything. If I may borrow your barouche, Kalman, I should like to bring my wife and younger daughter to a wedding."

EPILOGUE

Beatrice stood in the anteroom before the heart of the Great Chapterhouse in Gravesford and ticked off her mental list once more. She knew her speech. She had her pamphlet. Five miles away, the *Redjay* waited to take her family out onto the bay to meet the treasure ship *Triumph of Azjat* so they could leave Chasland behind.

Little Unknown Clayborn-Lavan had tired of dancing around inside her, for the moment. Fandariathras coiled protectively around Beatrice's child, always vigilant. A new passage of her book was floating in her mind, distracting her from listening to the lodgemaster general. She set the thought aside and listened.

"We have verified the child, based on every determination spell we have. The child is fully ensouled. We have the testimony of Master-Mage Ianthe Lavan, who dutifully logged every day of his wife's pregnancy. We have thoroughly questioned and verified all he told us. They have indeed succeeded in carrying a child from conception to birth inside an unwarded sorceress. The woman is here to speak on the—" He consulted his notes and scowled. "The Clayborn Method of Fetal Protection."

The lodgemaster general stepped away from the lectern poised at the end of the decagon, and Beatrice sighed. That, apparently, was all the introduction she was going to get.

A man in an olive coat stood up, and heads turned to regard him as he spoke. "That's ridiculous. We should be hearing from the mage, not his wife. Why isn't he here to answer our questions?"

"Because he's watching our daughter," Beatrice muttered, exasperated.

She bit back the uncharitable thing she was going to say when the room filled with the rustle of velvet coats and the slide of ceremonial swords. All heads turned to stare at her. Beatrice glanced at the ceiling, and quietly complimented the Hadfields on the acoustic skill that went into that dome. She hadn't known her voice would carry all the way across it.

Well, nothing to be done. She strode out of the shadows and watched her audience gawk at her. She sailed down the aisle, dressed in a deep gray velvet gown that gathered just under her bosom to drape gracefully over the rounded fullness of her belly.

"She's with child again," someone muttered. "Skyborn, I can't believe it."

She smiled and said, "We're very happy. I'm eight months along," just as if he'd meant to say it to her face. She walked the rest of the aisle in silence, chin high, and accepted the lodgemaster general's hand as she climbed the stairs. She settled herself at the lectern and pulled a pamphlet from the depths of her pocket.

She paused. Not a single one of these men looked at her with interest, curiosity, or respect. She had hoped to see a few people who wanted to know what she and Ianthe had done.

:I can make them spill ink on their clothes,: Nadidamarus said, and Beatrice smiled.

"I'm Beatrice Clayborn-Lavan, the woman who has challenged for the right to be admitted among the membership of the chapterhouse by right of equivalent degree. I have made the Great Bargain with Nadidamarus, Greater Spirit of Fortune."

She paused as Nadi stretched itself outside the bounds of her body, shaping itself into the approximation of an enormous pair of wings. Shouts went up from the onlookers. They stared in amazement as the dark shimmered form grew in size, displaying the power willingly bound to her soul.

Fandariathras stirred, and Nadidamarus slipped back inside her body, ever watchful.

"But today I am here to speak to you of the Clayborn Method," Beatrice said. "This simple ritual ensures the protection of the parents' greater spirits guarding the unborn child growing inside a sorceress without the need for a warding collar, which cruelly bars her from exercising her Skyborn-given, inborn talents. It takes the full attention of those greater spirits watching tirelessly to ensure the protection never falters."

"But you just displayed your bound spirit," a man said, rising to address the room. "Isn't your child now at risk?"

"Not at all," Beatrice replied. "The bound spirits keeping watch over Little Unknown Clayborn-Lavan must be mine and Ianthe's, as I said earlier. They protect the child and prevent the other from taking possession of the unborn fetus for themselves."

She kept silent on the problem that nagged her. There wasn't time to discover whether the spirits needed to be bound to the magicians involved in conception before this meeting. Ysbeta was still searching; perhaps she would know more when they met later in the year.

The man's face slackened with dismay. "But that means Mage Ianthe Lavan is unable to cast the higher magics. He's powerless."

A horrified gasp went up from the mages.

"Ianthe can still perform minor charms," Beatrice said, "but you are correct. My husband and I cannot use higher magic until our child is safely born, its soul developed and fully resident within its body. But once that's done, he's capable of working with Fandariathras once more."

Every man in the ten-sided chamber looked on, appalled.

"We can't do that," one of them declared. "Give up magic while my wife does her duty? It's unacceptable. It's outrageous."

"This information must be suppressed," another man spoke up. "We cannot be expected to make such sacrifices. And this woman must go into a warding collar immediately. To think that a master-mage has been reduced to children's rhymes for months? It's horrible."

So. They reacted just as Beatrice had known they would. Ianthe had believed that there were mages who would at least consider the idea. But she was never here to convince them. This was just a distraction to get them out of their houses.

:Sour their milk. Crack their carriage axles. An epidemic of stumbling,: Nadidamarus said. :I can do it right now, if you'd like.:

:As amusing as that would be, I think we should be circumspect.:

:Not even the stumbling?:

:Nadi.:

Beatrice waited for the lodgemaster to quiet the mages down. "I propose we vote, but first, let's allow Mrs. Lavan the chance to conclude her presentation. Mrs. Lavan?"

Beatrice gave him her best, most sparkling smile. "Thank you, Lodgemaster. I knew that no women with the talent would be in attendance today. It's a shame. Women should have a voice in their futures, and her decisions and her decisions alone matter when it comes to how she will use her own body."

Bored looks from the mages. Beatrice kept smiling and held up the paper she carried in her pocket.

"This is a pamphlet that outlines and describes the exact ritual and process of the Clayborn Method of Fetal Protection. Since the rolls of chapterhouse members are all a matter of public record, and census data is available with reasonable requests, I compiled a list of all of your addresses."

The room murmured. Some stared at her in puzzlement, but Beatrice watched the horrified faces of more astute members as they realized what she'd done. Her smile widened.

"A copy of this pamphlet addressed to your wives and any daughters over the age of sixteen has been mailed to them at home. They should all be delivered by now. Good night, gentlemen."

Every mage in the room bounded to his feet. They all shouted, their voices layering one over the other, shouting even more loudly, trying to be heard above the others.

Beatrice left the pamphlet on the lectern, nodded to the lodgemaster, and took the stairs by herself. She breezed down the center aisle and out of the decagon, retracing her steps to the small room where she had left her cloak, her husband, and—

"Mama!"

Her daughter Ysbeta stamped her little feet as she slid off Bard Sheldon's lap and barreled over to collide with Beatrice's leg.

Clara laughed. "She only has one speed, Mrs. Beatrice."

"She needs all of us to chase after her." Beatrice bent down to smile at her daughter's upturned, sunshine face. "Hello, little catkin."

"Yes, 'Beta, Mama's back," Ianthe said. "Mama caused an uproar at the chapterhouse."

"That I did," Beatrice said. "We'd better go, before they realize I'm gone."

Bard held one of the pamphlets in his hand. "They don't sound happy."

Behind her, the mages shouted at each other in outrage. Ianthe scooped the child up and smiled sadly at Beatrice.

"Well, my sunrise, you win the wager."

"I knew you had hoped."

"Not even one?" Clara asked. "I had hoped for at least one."

"I did too," Beatrice said.

"You did get one," Bard said, lifting the folded paper. "I count, don't I?"

"You do," Beatrice said, and Bard tucked the pamphlet inside his jacket. "But I did what I said I'd do. All of Chasland will know of this by the end of the week."

Ianthe bounced his daughter on his hip. "Chasland, done. Next stop, Llanandras. I'm sure you'll get a better reception there."

Clara swung Beatrice's cloak around her shoulders and fastened the collar. "We'll see soon enough, won't we? They can't all be like Chaslanders."

Ianthe set down little Ysbeta and donned his own cloak. Clara knelt to fasten Ysbeta into a velvet sleeved coat. Ianthe picked her up again, and together they walked out of the chapterhouse and into the night. A carriage driven by a man in turquoise livery waited for them at the side of the promenade.

Bard blew out a frosty breath. "I wish it had gone better for you in there."

"I never expected to convince them." Beatrice reached over and patted Bard's arm.

"It's brave, what you did. And it's smart of you to get on the next ship and flee the country before they figure out how to sue you."

Beatrice gripped Bard's elbow, and he saw her over an icy patch. "Cheerful."

"Then I will change the subject. Sabrina Weldon has invited me to an outing with her and her father."

Beatrice let out a laugh. "I knew she would! The way you two danced together at the Winter Ball—bring her to Jy after the wedding, will you? One good voyage before you settle down."

"I'd love to. And then I'll scandalize the country by adopting the Clayborn Method."

They arrived at the carriage, where a footman held the door open for them. "You'd better go. The tide waits for no one." Bard clapped a hand on Ianthe's shoulder. "And wherever Ysbeta the Elder is, I hope she's happy."

"She's probably digging up a lost city," Ianthe said, "and that means she is very happy indeed."

"We should go," Beatrice said. "Bard is right about the tide."

"Farewell," Bard said, and when he took Beatrice's hand he gripped her wrist the way he would greet a brother of the chapterhouse.

Ianthe let her board first, pretending to make little Ysbeta fly, and then tucked their child in the seat next to Clara. "So, it's done. Are you worried?"

"A bit," Beatrice admitted. "But we can't stop here."

"We won't stop until we get to Sanchi," Ianthe promised. "We'll bring the Clayborn Method to everyone. And Little Unknown will be born on the sea, just like her auntie."

Beatrice leaned against the back of the bench seat. "It could be a him."

Ianthe smiled. "Fandariathras told me."

"Oh! What should we name her, then?"

"I think . . . Harriet."

Beatrice laid her hand on her belly. "Hello, Harriet. Are you Harriet?"

Inside her, Harriet kicked.

ACKNOWLEDGMENTS

Thank you to Caitlin McDonald, my agent, who took a book I started writing for fun and turned it into a serious work, then found it a great publisher. Everything you do for me is amazing.

Thank you to Sarah Guan, who helped shape this book into the volume it is today with a dozen questions that deepened every aspect of this book.

Thank you to Liz Gorinsky, whose vision made Erewhon possible, and welcomed this book into the first year's schedule.

Thank you to Martin Cahill, who went big when it came time to promote this book and get it in front of the people who would enjoy it the most.

Thanks to everyone at Erewhon who dazzled me with their speed and attention to detail—my production team did amazing work to put this book together. Lauren Hougen, my production editor; my copy editor Liana Krissoff; my sales manager, Kayla Burson; and Jillian Feinberg, who did so many things known and unknown under the unassuming title of "assistant."

I want to thank Dr. A. J. Townsend, for reading and asking the questions that made me think harder about my world and what I was trying to say, and for the hilarious pitch of "Pokémon, but make it Jane Austen."

I had a number of readers who helped me smooth out the details after a revision. Thank you to Rachel Gutin, Virginia Wilson, Jen Coster, and Eva Papier for sharing your reactions and insights.

I also want to thank the Metropolitan Museum of Art for its online collection, which provided hundreds of visual examples of textiles and period fashions.

About the Author

© Mike Tan

C. L. Polk is the World Fantasy Award–winning author of the critically acclaimed debut novel *Witchmark*, which was also nominated for the Nebula, Locus, Aurora, and Lambda Literary Awards. It was named one of the best books of 2018 according to NPR, *Publishers Weekly*, *BuzzFeed*, the *Chicago Review*, *BookPage*, and the *B&N Sci-Fi and Fantasy Blog*. They live in Alberta, Canada.

CLPOLK.COM

@CLPOLK